THE GHOSTS OF DETROIT

ALSO BY DONALD LEVIN

THE MARTIN PREUSS SERIES

In the House of Night
Cold Dark Lies
An Uncertain Accomplice
The Forgotten Child
Guilt in Hiding
The Baker's Men
Crimes of Love

POETRY

Are You Listening? Selected Poetry
New Year's Tangerine
In Praise of Old Photographs

FICTION

The Arsenal of Deceit
Savage City
The House of Grins

DYSTOPIAN FICTION

The Exile
Postcards from the Future: A Triptych on Humanity's End
(with Andrew Lark and Wendy Thomson)

THE GHOSTS OF DETROIT

A NOVEL

DONALD LEVIN

Poison Toe Press

For Sue

I wasn't scared; I was just somebody else, some stranger, and my whole life was a haunted life, the life of a ghost."
— Jack Kerouac, **On the Road**

CONTENTS

THE GHOSTS OF DETROIT

February 26, 1952

Prologue

"State your name for the record."

"Jacob Lieberman."

"Where were you born?"

"I would first like to make a statement."

John Stephens Wood breaks in. "You may file your statement," he says. The chairman of the House Un-American Activities Committee hearing, Wood has a lazy drawl that shows his origins in northern Georgia.

"I would like to read it," Jake says.

"That will not be permitted." Wood regards Jake with a dismissive sneer. "You may file it with the Committee."

Fahl it wit' the Committeh.

At which point no one will ever see it, Jake knows. And Wood knows it, too. The statement will end up buried in the voluminous proceedings of this committee's poisonous activities. If it isn't "misplaced" first.

Counsel for the HUAC hearing Frank Tavenner moves things along. "Where were you born?" he asks Jake again.

"Detroit, Michigan."

"Who do you work for?"

Tavenner asks his questions in a calm, methodical voice, without looking up. From Virginia, he also has a marked southern drawl, but without Wood's deep-south twang.

"I've worked for the *Detroit News* for eight years."

"What is the nature of your work?"

"I'm a newspaper artist. I retouch photographs, create advertising layouts, and so on."

"Have you drawn cartoons?"

"Yes."

"For other papers besides the *News*?"

"Yes."

"What papers?"

Jake leans toward his attorney seated next to him at the witness table in room 740 of the Federal Building in Detroit. This is the third day of the HUAC Communist-hunting hearings being held in the city, Jake's first as a witness.

Heads together, they confer briefly. His attorney, Charles C. Cornish, whispers something and Jake straightens up and says, "I invoke my privilege under the Fifth Amendment and refuse to answer."

Now Tavenner looks up at Jake. "You are taking the position that to divulge the name of the papers would incriminate you?"

"Correct."

Tavenner signals his displeasure by holding Jake's eye for a second too long before returning to his notes. "Have you always used your own name in signing your cartoons?"

"I invoke my privilege under the Fifth Amendment and refuse to answer."

"Have you ever used the name of Gordon?"

"I invoke my privilege under the Fifth Amendment and refuse to answer."

Tavenner reaches across the gap separating them to hand Jake a sheet of paper. "I am handing you a photostatic copy of a page from the *Michigan Worker* from October 3, 1948. You will note the cartoon deals with the relative strength of the Progressive Party in Michigan, and it is signed with the name of Gordon. Would you examine it and state whether you drew it?"

"I invoke my privilege under the Fifth Amendment and refuse to answer."

"I am placing this cartoon in evidence as Exhibit 1," Tavenner says. "Are you acquainted with Richard F. O'Hair, the man who testified here yesterday?"

"I invoke my privilege under the Fifth Amendment and refuse to answer."

"In testimony yesterday," Tavenner continues, "Mr. O'Hair said you were the treasurer of the Communist Party of Michigan. Did you serve as the treasurer of the Communist Party in Michigan?"

Jake thinks this explains why, at one point several years before, O'Hair walked up to him and handed him two dollars with a wink. Jake thought O'Hair made a mistake thinking he owed Jake the dough, but now Jake knows O'Hair was trying to establish his bona fides as the Party treasurer.

"I invoke my privilege under the Fifth Amendment and refuse to answer."

Tavenner reaches across again and hands Jake a photograph. "I am handing you a picture and asking you to identify it."

Jake examines the photo. It shows a dark-complected woman with deep circles around her eyes, high cheekbones, and curly salt-and-pepper hair.

Of course Jake knows who she is: Bereneice Baldwin, the Detroit housewife who testified last week in Washington that she has been an undercover spy for the FBI. She has been giving them information about Communist activities in Detroit for years. In her testimony, she named names, one of which was Jake's.

"I invoke my privilege under the Fifth Amendment and refuse to answer."

Tavenner says, "Have you ever met Mrs. Bereneice Baldwin?"

"I invoke my privilege under the Fifth Amendment and refuse to answer."

Representative Wood breaks in again. "Under what provision of the Fifth Amendment are you referrin'?"

"To the provision relating to self-incrimination."

Wood sits back, shaking his head. He is a southern Democrat, a segregationist and former member of the Ku Klux Klan. This is who's passing judgment on me, Jake thinks.

Tavenner returns to his questions. "Did you attend the Michigan State Communist convention on January 23 and 24, 1941, at which

Carl Winter complained about the slowness of the drive to recruit new members?"

Winter was the head of the Michigan Communist Party in 1941.

"I invoke my privilege under the Fifth Amendment and refuse to answer."

"Are you now a member of the Communist Party?"

"I invoke my privilege under the Fifth Amendment and refuse to answer."

Tavenner sniffs, shuffles his papers together, glances at Wood. Nods.

Wood leans forward. "You are excused."

"I would like to read my statement now."

"No. You may file it on your way out."

Fahl it on yo way aht.

"I would like to read my statement."

"The witness is excused."

February 1955

1

MALONE COLEMAN

The nurse told him it was the last room on the left, but he already knows where it is from the smell.

Amid the usual odors of urine and shit wafting through the halls, the reek of vomit is particularly strong from one room.

The vet in the bed couldn't have been more embarrassed. "Sorry, man," he says when Malone Coleman comes in with his mop and bucket. The guy's almost crying, he's so upset.

Malone shakes his head. "I got you, partner."

The guy's nurse stands on the other side of the bed, near the window. She shifts the guy on the bed from left to right as she changes his hospital gown and sheets, which are covered in the same blood-and-caramel-colored lumps as the puddle on the floor.

Malone sets to work mopping it up. The mop smears the mess over the linoleum like a watercolor wash.

The only painting I've done lately, Malone thinks.

Appropriate.

"Sorry," the vet says again, his voice a weak murmur.

"That's okay, Mr. Lupovitch," the nurse says. "Malone's seen worse. Haven't you, Malone?"

"Just this morning."

A guy in a room in another wing went batshit crazy and pulled his IV out. Blood spurted everywhere. Malone had to clean it up.

"I'd hate to have your job," the guy in bed says. He raises the corner of his face that can smile.

Oh, don't worry, I do, Malone thinks.

Malone works as an orderly at the Allen Park Veterans Administration Medical Center, outside Detroit. He shuttles patients back and forth, sweeps and mops floors, empties bedpans, and does whatever else the nurses ask him to.

The vet's white. He might have been handsome once, but now one side of his face is a mass of corrugated scar tissue from the burns he suffered during the war. Somebody said he was a bombardier in a B-24, the plane churned out by the thousands at the nearby Willow Run plant. He went down over the English Channel. He made it out, but not before flames engulfed the plane and left him like this.

Malone continues mopping up the mess. He doesn't want to know what caused this. He's already learned more than he ever wanted to about what could go wrong in the fragile bundle of flesh that is the human body.

He gets the floor cleaned up and wrings out the mop. The vet in bed says, "Thanks, bud." He holds a hand up and Malone grabs it and gives it a gentle shake. Malone can't even imagine the hell this guy's been through. And it's not over yet for him. As if he doesn't have enough problems, the vet's in the cancer ward.

Malone rolls the mop and bucket down the hall to the utility room, where he empties and cleans it out and gets it ready for the next emergency clean-up.

Outside the utility room, Malone's immediate supervisor, a hatchet-faced white man, hands him a sheet of paper and walks away without a word.

It's a note. The Personnel Director wants to see Malone right away.

He leaves his bucket and mop in the utility room and goes through the halls to the Personnel office on the ground floor of the Administration wing.

The Personnel Director's secretary tells him to go right in. Tennessee Ernie Ford's "Sixteen Tons" plays on the radio behind her desk.

The Personnel Director is a tiny red-headed Irishman with a nose that glows an angry red. Mr. Clooney.

Clooney hands Malone a brown envelope with a receipt stapled to it. "Sign the receipt and open the letter."

"What's this all about?"

"Just sign it and read."

Malone signs the receipt and opens the envelope.

Dear Mr. Coleman,

It is reported that while you were an employee of the Ford Motor Rouge Assembly Plant in 1951, you joined an organization known as the National Negro Labor Council. It is reported that you attended one or more meetings of the National Negro Labor Council and that you had associations with one or more members of that organization. It is reported that at one time you attended several illegal activities sponsored by the National Negro Labor Council.

The United States Attorney General has branded the National Negro Labor Council a Communist front.

Therefore, you have been deemed a security risk and are hereby relieved of your position at the Allen Park Veterans Affairs Medical Center.

Malone looks at Clooney. "Is this a joke?"

"Not at all."

"I'm fired?"

"Yes."

"This is bullshit!"

"There's no call for that kind of language."

"Where does this come from?"

"The higher-ups."

"What higher-ups?"

"It's out of my hands, Malone."

"How's this out of your hands? You're the Personnel Director."

"You're dismissed, son. Don't make it harder than it has to be."

"How can I clear this up?"

"Like I said, it's out of my hands."

"There's nothing you can do?"

Clooney shakes his head. His hands tremble and he looks like he would kill for a drink right about now.

"Before you leave," Clooney says, "I'll need your employee badge."

I push wheelchairs and mop up puke, Malone fumes. How can I be a security risk?

He storms out of the hospital and across the parking lot toward the stop for the bus that will take him to his apartment in Detroit.

He's had this job for four years. He tried to volunteer for the army in 1943, but they rejected him as being "mentally unfit." The white doctor examining him for his physical asked him how he felt about segregation; he said he was against it. That must have been the wrong answer, because he was rejected from the army despite the urgent need for men as fodder for the battles the nation was fighting in the name of "freedom."

Later he heard many other colored men like himself were also rejected as being mentally or educationally unfit. Between half and almost three-quarters of colored applicants were categorized as 4-F, not qualified for military service.

Neighborhood men who served told him about the rampant racism in the military; even those judged to be fit for service were mostly confined to lowly positions in labor units.

Instead of the army, he found a job in the Ford Production Foundry at the Ford Rouge plant. It was hard, hot, dangerous work, manned mostly by Negroes, and it ended in 1951 when Ford eliminated Malone's job.

Standing at the bus stop, still fuming over losing his VA job, he doesn't notice a white man in a gray suit sidling up to him.

The guy says, "Hey, how are you." The words come out in puffs of breath in the cold February air. He extends his hand.

Malone tries to place him. The guy's wall-eyed. His right eye looks off into the distance, as though it doesn't want any part of what the other eye gets up to.

"Hey." Malone shakes the offered hand.

"Mind if I wait along with you?"

"Free country."

The guy says, "Beautiful day. Kind of cold, though."

Malone doesn't think this needs a reply, and he doesn't feel like making small talk. He keeps silent.

"Just getting off work?" the guy says.

Malone ignores him.

They stand in silence for a minute. The guy repeats, "Yeah, beautiful day."

Malone ignores him again.

"Hey, howzabout we get a cup of coffee," the guy says, "me and you?"

Malone's met a lot of people, and sometimes he blanks on a name. Maybe he's met this guy after all. "I know you?"

"You don't. But I know you."

Malone doesn't like how this is going. Says, "Piss off." Turns away.

"I'll tell you something, Malone, I've heard different things about you."

Malone turns back to him. "How do you know my name?"

"Some people say you're a subversive, card-carrying member of the Communist Party."

"Is that right?"

"I'm just telling you what I've heard. Other people are thinking you might be a dissenter from the Party line."

Malone stares at him.

"Me?" the guy continues, "I'm in the second camp. And I might be in a position to help you if you're interested in a mutually beneficial cooperative arrangement."

"What kind of cooperative arrangement?"

"You've got information the people I work with could find useful. If you help us, we can make it worth your while. I hear you just lost your job."

"How would you know that?"

The guy ignores the question. "I can get it back for you. And if you don't cooperate, well—we can make it hard for you and the two people you call your parents. I'm talking about Clarence losing his police pension."

Malone takes a step toward him. "Who are you?"

"Just calm down, now. There's no need—"

"No—I want to know who you are." Malone takes another step closer.

"Hey, we're just two guys talking."

Malone reaches out to grab him.

The guy backpedals and holds his hands up in surrender. "Okay, I get it. Not ready yet. Think about it, though? And don't say I didn't warn you."

He turns and fast-walks off.

Malone watches him disappear among the cars clogging the intersection of Southfield Road and Outer Drive.

2

ANNA MILLER

She lugs the small wobbling shopping cart over the sidewalk. Beside her, Chester Glowaki says, "Harvey Kuenn had a great year."

Anna Miller makes a sound she hopes Chester will take for interest.

"He hit .306, best on the team," Chester goes on. "Ray Boone was next, with .285. But Boone hit the most RBIs, eighty-five. Also the most home runs, twenty. Kuenn had the most hits, though. Eighty-one!"

He chatters on about last year's Detroit Tigers. He knows the players' names and statistics by heart—not only Harvey Kuenn at shortstop and Ray Boone at second base, but Al Kaline in right field, as well as Reno Bertoia, Frank Lary, and Bud Souchock, reciting their names like poetry and their stats like incantations.

And Chester's loud, too, because he's so excited to be talking about his heroes. He'll talk about them all the way up to the market on 7 Mile Road and all the way back to his home on Riopelle Street on the east side of Detroit. He loves the team, and in his eternal innocence he assumes everyone else does, too.

Three days a week Anna is his caretaker. He's a grown man, in his thirties. But he's mentally slow except for his remarkable facility with sports statistics. Anna has heard these names and numbers over and over again, but she doesn't mind—she enjoys the bearish

Chester, with his pop-bottle eyeglasses and sensitive, almost feminine lips.

Until his sister Dottie Kaczmarek gets home, Anna has Chester helping her with chores like shopping. That's where they're headed now, toward Tauber's Market to pick up a loaf of bread, a bag of potatoes, a can of green peas, and a half-pound of baloney.

They're the only customers in the store, so Mr. Tauber behind the register chats with them for a few minutes. He's known Chester for most of Chester's life; Anna's had this job for only a few months, so Mr. Tauber hasn't warmed up to her yet.

"How do your Tigers look this year?" Tauber asks Chester.

This sets Chester off again about the players at every position in the upcoming season.

While Chester goes on, Anna gathers the goods they came for.

Chester is still talking when she pays. The grocer gives Chester a free 3 Musketeers. Chester is in heaven.

All the way back home in between bites of the candy bar he talks about how nice Mr. Tauber is. When they get to the house where Chester lives with his sister and her husband, he has moved on to talking about the Red Wings.

Their names are even more musical than the Tigers': Alex Delvecchio, Marty Pavelitch, Marcel Pronovost, Terry Sawchuk, Ted Lindsay . . .

His favorite, of course, is Gordie Howe. Even Anna, who pays no attention to sports, has heard of the great Gordie Howe.

She's glad of Chester's good mood today. She hates it when he's annoyed about something. His sister Dottie told Anna he has medication that helps to keep him calm, and most of the time he takes it, but sometimes he doesn't, and his dark moods frighten her.

When the *Evening Times* comes, Chester grabs it and studies the sports pages. The Red Wings are headed toward the Stanley Cup playoffs, and he has a whole new set of statistics to memorize.

While he's quiet and occupied, Anna prepares dinner for the family. She roasts a chicken and boils the potatoes they just bought for mashed potatoes. She opens the can of peas and heats them in a saucepan on the stove.

At half past five, weary Dottie Kaczmarek drags herself in. She works in kitchenware at a Federal's Department Store. She started there when her husband Roger was let go from his job at the nearby Dodge Main automobile plant the year before and she was the only breadwinner.

Now he works three jobs—he's a gas jockey on different shifts at three different gas stations. But they still need the money, so Dottie stays on at Federal's.

Dottie kisses Chester's thinning hair on the top of his head and drops onto a chair at the dining room table.

Roger comes in after six-thirty, reeking of gasoline. He stops off from the stations and liquors up after every shift. So far he hasn't approached Anna, but she doesn't like the way he leers at her.

As always, Dottie invites Anna to stay for dinner. As always, Anna declines. She really does have someplace to be tonight—she wants to see an art exhibit by her former instructor at the Society of Arts and Crafts downtown.

As she gets ready to leave, a pounding comes on the back door. "I'll get it," Anna says.

A man in the doorway, tall and heavy, bandy-legged, brushes by her. "Where's Roger?" he demands.

Roger appears from the living room. "What's up?"

"You'll never guess who's selling to the coloreds," the man says.

"Who?"

"Rudzewicz."

"Are you serious?"

"As a heart attack."

"Better come in," Roger tells the man.

The man nods to Dottie, who returns the greeting coldly.

Roger leads him through the kitchen and down to the basement. When they are out of hearing, Dottie indicates the man with her head, says, "Al Swoboda. Lives up the street. He's the head of the community homeowners' association."

"What's his problem?"

"A guy down the block put his house up for sale. He must want to sell to a colored family. Al wants to keep the neighborhood white."

Dottie stands with a sigh and goes upstairs to change into her floral housecoat. When she returns, heavy footsteps tramp up the steps from the basement. Swoboda and Roger enter the kitchen.

"I'm going out," Roger says.

Dottie says, "We're just going to sit down to supper."

"There's an emergency meeting of the homeowners' association," Swoboda says. "We gotta nip this thing in the bud."

"What about your dinner?" Dottie says. "It's ready. You need to eat before you go to the station."

Tonight Roger pumps gas on the evening shift at the Standard station on 7 Mile.

"This is more important," Roger says. He follows Swoboda out the side door.

Dottie sets out the plates for their meal. "He'll go without eating and then he'll mouth off because he's hungry and he'll lose another job," she grumbles. "Sure you won't stay?" she asks Anna. "Going to be just me and Chester."

"Stay," Chester implores. "Please?"

"Well," Anna considers. She knows the food will be good; she cooked it.

She never makes this kind of meal for herself. And as long as Roger isn't going to be here, she thinks—and I'm not going to make it a habit—and I've got someplace else to be later so I have an excuse not to stay long—

Still, she says, "No. But thanks. Gotta get going."

Chester frowns.

"Cheer up," Anna tells him. "I'll see you again in two days!"

3

JAKE LIEBERMAN

The monkey sits on the highest branch, looking down on him. Jake Lieberman stares back.

It's a meeting of the minds.

The little creature's eyes are almost human, large and brown and filled with intelligence as he gazes down from his perch in the huge glass enclosure. He is the smallest of the eight jittery monkeys jumping around greenery and branches on the lower level of the Hughes & Hatcher department store in Northland Mall.

No one seems to know why this large glass monkey cage is here. The suburban shopping center, touted as the first one in the nation, has been open less than a year; who thought this would be a good spot for a monkey house?

Still, they're cute little buggers. Capuchin monkeys, Jake heard someone say they were. They have surprisingly human faces, like a club of little old men, *alte kakkers* playing gin rummy and gossiping about what the funny looking hairless monkeys do every day on the other side of their cage.

Jake hears the floorwalker behind him. Fussy clicks on the tile from his heels. "Nothing better to do?" Manning Willis demands.

"I love to watch these guys."

Willis looks at the monkey cage. He does not seem to appreciate them the way Jake does. He doesn't even seem to care they're here.

"Don't you wish you knew what they're thinking?" Jake says.

"That one up there's probably thinking, 'I wonder if that salesman doesn't have anything better to do than gawk at us monkeys all day?'"

"Sounds like he has a lot in common with you."

Willis gives him a look with daggers. He points toward the men's suits section.

"How about you get back to work? A shipment of new suits gets in tomorrow. The winter suits need to be inventoried and reorganized by the morning. Think you can manage that?"

Jake swallows his annoyance at the sarcasm. At least a decade younger than Jake, Willis bullies his underlings and toadies to his bosses.

"I'll give it my best shot," Jake says earnestly.

"Thank you," Willis says, missing the irony.

He continues on his way, heels clicking on the floor tiles.

Jake goes behind his counter and gets his clipboard with the details of the next day's shipment. Thirty lightweight H & H suits will be coming in as the store preps for spring and summer. His clipboard contains the list of winter-weight suits that will go on the sale rack to make room for the new merchandise.

He sets to work. He goes through the suits one by one, checking their tags against his clipboard, shifting the heavier suits onto a metal rack to be put on sale in the morning. The suits are all shades of gray, distinguishable by pinstripe threads that run through the fabric, some cerulean blue, some cadmium red, some gold ochre.

"Excuse me," a man's voice behind him says.

He turns. An older man beside a woman. The man is tall and ungainly, with very long legs. He stands as though embarrassed, as men are, to be buying something so trivial as clothing for himself.

"I'm looking for a suit," the man says.

"You came to the right place."

The woman is already on the job, picking through the suits Jake has just transferred to the sales rack. She says, "Are these on sale?"

"Not until tomorrow," Jake says.

"I'd have to come back tomorrow to get a sale price? Even though you're clearly marking them for the sale and I'm right here?"

"That's how it works, ma'am. Sorry. What kind of suit are you looking for?" he asks the man.

"Whatever happened to customer service?" the woman sniffs. "Let's try Hudson's," she tells the man.

The mall's big anchor department store.

She leads the man off. He follows dutifully.

From twenty yards away, Manning Willis watches this unfold.

Jake waits for him to click his fussy heels over to give him grief, but he only stands there shaking his head. He turns and clicks away to spy on someone else.

Jake sighs.

On the back of a sales slip, he sketches a cartoon. A tall man and his short wife in a clothing store. They are surrounded on all sides by racks and racks of suits. *"Excuse me,"* the man says, *"do you sell any suits here?"*

Jake crumples up the cartoon and tosses it in the trash bin under the counter.

He draws another cartoon on the back of another sales slip. The little monkey sits at the top of his branch in his cage, looking down on Jake. A dialog balloon from the monkey says, *"Yeah, who's the real monkey around here, chump?"*

He crumples that one up, too, and tosses it. He returns to the suit racks, to continue separating the heavy wool from the lighter weight.

Closing time.

Jake closes out his till and waits for Manning Willis to come around and collect the day's take.

After making his way from department to department, Willis comes over to Jake. "This everything?"

"That's it."

Willis counts the cash twice. He goes through the checks and verifies everything against the register tapes. He rubber-bands it all together and sticks it with the register receipt in a green canvas bag. It will all go up to Accounting.

"Jake, we have to talk."

No good conversation has ever begun this way, Jake thinks.

And the use of his first name?

Also not good.

"I've gotten some complaints about you," Willis begins.

"What kind of complaints?"

"From customers. They say you're rude and unhelpful. And from what I saw with that couple earlier today, I'd have to agree."

"The woman asked me a question and I answered it. I said no, I can't sell them to her now. The suits go on sale tomorrow."

"You should have gone looking for me."

"For what?"

"I would have given you permission to sell it to her."

I need to ask this pissant for permission to do my job? Jake thinks.

"If I'd sold one to her," he says, "you'd be over here bawling me out about breaking the rules."

"Without asking first, yes. It's not your decision. I'm just telling you where things stand. You're also our lowest-selling salesman. Unless things get better, we're going to have to let you go."

Manning Willis turns and walks away.

His fussy heels go *click click click* on the tile floor.

The Detroit Society of Arts and Crafts is an art school and exhibition gallery in a medieval-looking gray stucco structure with dozens of small windows on Watson Street off Woodward near the Brush Park area of the city. Tonight it's the site of an opening for an exhibition of artwork by Jake's former painting teacher, Sarkis Sarkisian, the director of the school.

Crowds of people fills the exhibition room. Jake spots Sarkis. He is a lean man with a wry smile in an expressive face. He talks with a group of older men who look to Jake like donors. Best let him alone; prying money out of the rich is hard work.

Jake walks around the huge room, admiring the artwork displayed on easels. It's a retrospective of Sarkis's work from the 1930s and 1940s. Oils, mostly portraits of men and women staring glumly at the viewer or else looking at something off to the side. The faces are rough-hewn and look ready to take on anything that comes their way. Like Sarkis himself.

Jake knows a few of the Negro artists standing with their heads together near an exit. He stops, shakes hands with them. These guys are the real deal, he thinks—LeRoy Foster, Charles McGee, Harold Neal, talented and dedicated artists who have taken classes here.

With them is a young Negro woman he doesn't know.

Sarkis now has only one donor with him, so Jake edges over. Sarkis brightens when he sees Jake and excuses himself.

"Jake, my friend." They shake and Sarkis enfolds him in a tight hug. "Good to see you. Thank you for coming."

"I wouldn't miss it. Terrific show."

"Ah." Sarkis waves the compliment away. "How are you? Are you still painting?"

"Of course. Still making your students go to the DIA?"

"Of course!"

They share a laugh. It's a favorite technique of Sarkis's. He makes his students stand in front of one particular painting at the Detroit Institute of Arts, a Ghirlandaio, the head of an old man with a tam, for an hour a week for a month, no analysis, just observation, and come back and talk with him about their insights.

And if you didn't come back with insights, Sarkis would pull them out of you with his questions. He would ask you about the emotional application of the paint, the artist's freedom, the content of the painting, everything down to the colors. It was one of the best exercises Jake had done. It taught him to really *see* and not just *look* at a work of art.

Jake took his classes with Sarkis before the war; the school was in bad shape then, on the verge of closing. The only other teacher was Jay Boorsma, who taught Jake commercial art and helped him get his job at the *Detroit News*.

Another donor-type comes up to Sarkis and pulls him away. Donors and the GI Bill have put the school in much better shape now.

Sarkis stops and leans back to Jake.

"Some of us are meeting for an after-party tonight at Cliff Bells—please come!"

He gives Jake an apologetic wave and lets himself be carried off.

It relieves Jake of the need to say: No, I won't be there.

He sees the two friends he came to meet tonight. Ronny Barit and Anthony Morris. Jake has known them for years; he met them at the Michigan State Communist Party convention in 1941—the very meeting he was asked about at the HUAC inquisition three years ago, which caused him to lose his job at the *News*.

After the war, all three fell away from the Party for various reasons. Ronny, a homosexual, because of the Communists' staunchly anti-homosexual stance; Anthony because of the slaughter of the Stalinist purges; and Jake not only because of the virulent antisemitism of Soviet Russia, but because he came home from the war in Europe convinced that every human institution like the Party was nothing more than a failed experiment designed by a species that was an evolutionary blunder, a murderous class of ape where cruelty came naturally and easily and was rewarded manyfold.

The thought of apes reminds him of his little friend in the monkey house at Hughes & Hatcher. Sorry to compare you to humans, Jake silently tells him; animals are much more civilized.

And this in turn reminds him of his job at the store.

A physical change must come over him, because Anthony asks, "You okay? You look like you just lost your best friend."

"It's my job. It's sucking the life out of me."

"So quit."

"Why didn't I think of that?"

"What's the problem?"

"I quit, I wind up sleeping in my car."

"You worry too much," Ronny says.

"Maybe if I was an heir to the Kelvinator fortune, I'd be more carefree, too," Jake says.

"An accident of birth. A fortuitous one, I admit. But an accident nonetheless."

Ronnie's uncle was in charge of the Hudson Motor Car Company until last year, when they merged with Nash-Kelvinator to form the American Motors Corporation.

Despite Ronny's pedigree and Anthony's breezy advice, all three have to work for a living. Anthony is a proofreader for a law firm who fancies himself a poet; Ronny teaches in Wayne University's Theatre Department and is a local actor. Anthony was drafted into the war; Ronny became a conscientious objector and spent time in prison.

In prison, he got religion and he now belongs to a Christian peace group, the Church Peace Mission, circulating petitions for peace and social equality. He keeps asking Jake to get involved; Jake keeps declining.

Ronny says, "Speaking of which, my uncle told me they're getting rid of the Hudson brand altogether. The plant on Jefferson's laying off people. They're looking for security men to keep an eye on the place until they shut it down. If you're interested, I'll get him to put in a word for you."

"What do I know about security?"

"You were in the army, weren't you?"

"I was a photographer, not a dogface."

"Doesn't matter. You're a vet, that's all they'll care about. Look, go down there and give them this."

He fishes a business card from his wallet and hands it to Jake.

```
               A.E. Barit
        Member, Board of Directors
        American Motors Corporation
```

"My uncle's card," Ronny says. "Flash it, they'll fall all over themselves taking care of you."

Great, Jake thinks. From radical rebel to protector of the commodities of the pernicious capitalist system in one fell swoop.

It was a long slide down, but I made it.

It wasn't so long ago when the United Auto Workers union was purging leftists from their ranks. Union members were physically ejecting known Communists from the factories. Now they're going to hire us to keep an eye on things?

He gives the card back to Ronny. "Thanks, man. Not interested."

Ronny says, "You're so down! We need to cheer you up."

"How about we go to the Flame?" Anthony says.

The Flame Show Bar, a black and tan music club downtown.

"Great idea," Ronny says. "Get our boy out of his own head."

Oh, but it's such a happy place to be, Jake thinks mordantly.

Still, he says no.

They keep after him until he agrees to go, just to shut them up.

4

BRIDGET MCMANUS

Flashlight beams play over the small body lying face down, partly covered by moldy rugs and bald tires and other debris in a dump site near the Kearsley Reservoir, ten miles from Flint.

A boy, clad in blue jeans and a tee shirt. His shoes are a hundred feet from his body.

He has been shot through the back of the head.

"Looks like a small caliber weapon," State Police Inspector Raymond Rausch says. He's a big red-headed man with a walrus mustache. "The coroner thinks he was killed the day he disappeared. He'll know more after the post-mortem. Also he'll say more about what else might have been done to him. Sexually, and so forth."

Sgt. Bridget McManus of the Detroit Police Department's Women's Division stands looking down on the boy's remains. "He's been missing for three weeks?"

"Right. We had fifteen hundred people out looking for him. Biggest search in the history of central Michigan. We looked all around here," Rausch says. "They either overlooked him, which would be easy to do if they were searching after dark, buried under all this shit. Or else his body was just recently put here."

The weather-beaten body has been nibbled by wild animals.

He's been here a while, Bridget thinks.

"Pretty isolated out here," Rausch says. "Then too, we've had some snow melt lately. Coulda been buried until the thaw."

We haven't had that much snow, Bridget thinks. It's been a cold but dry winter.

The ten-year-old boy is Joey Gallagher. He disappeared when his Boy Scout troop from Flint went on a winter hike the month before.

"We're doing a recanvas of local homes and businesses," Rausch says. "My captain wanted me to call you in because of what you did with the other child-killing."

Rausch emphasizes with his tone that his captain, not he himself, wanted her in on this.

He's referring to the murder of Kathleen Macready. A sixteen-year-old boy killed a nine-year-old girl, bashing her head in with a rock.

"Yeah," Bridget says, "we caught the kid who did it right away. He's off the board. This isn't his doing."

"The boss figured you worked that one so fast, you might have something to say about this one."

Again, his voice lets Bridget know he's not entirely happy with her participation, and doesn't believe she will have anything to offer.

Neither does she. She's way out of her jurisdiction.

Not to mention my league, she thinks.

"Whatever you can add," Rausch says. He seems to think it won't be much. "Family's been notified. They're devastated."

"Sure."

"The father's a personnel manager at the Chevy plant and he's been out searching the woods since the day the boy disappeared. Well. Seen enough?"

"Yeah."

Too much, Bridget thinks.

Rausch motions to the coroner's men to take the boy's body away and they move in.

Driving back to Detroit, Bridget remembers the case Rausch referred to.

It was chilling.

As a member of the Women's Division, Bridget can work only in her Division, investigating missing children and women, child abuse, sexual assaults, juvenile delinquency, and checking establishments for illegal minors. When nine-year-old Kathleen Macready went missing, Bridget was called in immediately. Policewomen in the Women's Division aren't allowed to investigate crimes without a male officer present, so she walked the neighborhood with a uniformed officer.

As part of the search in the little girl's neighborhood, witness statements led her to find a black and red jacket soaked in blood under the bed of sixteen-year-old Floyd Williams. He confessed immediately.

He was small for his age, a skinny kid with a buzz cut, a pimply face, and a large cold sore on his upper lip. The boy said he would only talk to Bridget, so that's why she was in on the interrogation. What Bridget noticed most about the kid was his lack of affect. He didn't seem scared, upset, or remorseful about what he'd done. Or even interested in what was happening to him.

The boy also said he didn't want to see his father or his stepmother. And they didn't want anything to do with him, either. Neither was present at the interview; beside him at the table was the public defender on call; beside Bridget was a male state police detective.

"Floyd," Bridget said, "we found this under your bed at your house." Out of a paper bag, she pulled the black and red jacket soaked with blood. "Recognize this?"

Floyd nodded.

"Is it yours?"

"Yes."

"Want to tell me how it got this way?"

Floyd shifted in his chair.

According to his stepmother, he was released three months ago from the Wayne County Training School for Boys, where he was sent for breaking into cars with a gang he ran with. Bridget wondered if he learned the silent routine at the Training School, or he just came by it naturally.

"Do you know why you're here, Floyd?" Bridget asked.

"I think so."

"Someone killed Kathleen Macready," Bridget said. "A nine-year-old girl. Do you know her?"

"Yes."

"Do you know what happened to her, Floyd? Somebody stabbed her and hit her over the head with a rock and threw her body in the pond where you kids play."

No response.

"Did you do that, Floyd?"

After a moment, Floyd said, "Yes."

Still no affect. No remorse. Bridget might have asked the boy if he liked vanilla ice cream.

"Want to tell me how it happened?"

He intertwined the fingers of his small hands and stared at them. "I went by her house," he said at last. "She was out front with her dog. I petted the dog for a little while, and Kathleen, she said she was going to the pond."

"What happened next?"

"I went with her. We started goofing around, tripping and pushing each other. But I started to get angry because she got rough and I pushed her down for real. She called me an asshole."

"Go on."

"I slapped her. She fell down. And then she got up and tried to run away. I caught her jacket and she started to punch me and kick me. I started touching her and stuff but she got loose and ran away again. I went after her and caught her and fell on top of her. Except my pocket knife was open and she got cut."

"Why were you chasing her with your open pocket knife?" Bridget asked.

"She got stabbed."

Got stabbed.

Like the knife had a mind of its own and Floyd was a bystander.

"And . . . I dunno . . ." Floyd continued. "All the blood . . . it, it made me feel funny. It did something to me. I dunno."

A chill traveled down Bridget's spine.

Floyd stared at a spot in space, as though remembering the feeling the sight of the blood brought on.

"I was stabbing her over and over until the blade broke. And I opened the little blade on my knife and kept stabbing her some more."

All the while, the boy deadpanned his tale.

"So then I grabbed her by the ankles and dragged her to the water. But when I got her into the water she started screaming. She started screaming really loud, so I grabbed a rock by the edge of the pond and I hit her on the head to make her shut up."

"You hit her just once?"

"No, I hit her maybe three times all together. Then I rolled her into the water and came home. That's when Mr. Reynolds"—the subdivision's security guard—"brought you to my house. You talked to me for a couple minutes and went up to look at my room. That's when you found my coat."

Floyd nodded toward the bag with his bloody jacket.

The boy was so expressionless Bridget didn't even know what to say to him.

Finally she said, "Floyd, aren't you worried about what's going to happen to you?"

"No."

Bridget kept staring at him. She had spoken with the kid's stepmother briefly when they picked him up. She said he's always been a problem child. After the fourth grade, he refused to go to school anymore. Before he went into the Training School, she said, he went after her with a knife.

"Floyd," Bridget said, "I'm going to take you downtown, so you can talk to the Wayne County prosecutor. He'll decide what to do with you. Do you understand what I'm saying?"

Bridget had already been on the phone with the prosecutor. He told Bridget he's going to seek a waiver of jurisdiction from Juvenile Court and file a charge of first-degree murder.

Bridget left the boy in the interview room with his public defender while she arranged for transport downtown.

Before she went back into the room with Floyd, she had to duck into the Ladies'. She leaned on the sink and looked into a stranger's eyes in the mirror.

She was shattered.

She'd never seen anything like this in the eight years she'd worked in the Women's Division. She'd never seen hardened criminals as unfeeling as that boy. She'd sat down with women who shot their husbands, with husbands who beat their wives, with girls who left their babies at hospitals and police stations, and none of them had as little affect as this sixteen-year-old boy.

What are we doing to our children, she wondered, to turn them into *this?*

The stricken face that stared back at her had no answer.

5

MALONE COLEMAN

"They *fired* you? Just like that?"

Malone shrugs.

"What happened?" LeRoy Foster asks.

"They told me I was a 'security risk,' Malone says. "You believe that? A security risk! I'm an orderly. I push wheelchairs and mop up puke. Sound like a high-security job to you?"

"Somebody must have called you out," LeRoy says.

Malone stands at a tall table at the Society of Arts and Crafts with the royalty of Negro artists in Detroit: LeRoy Foster, Ernest Hardman, Harold Neal, Charles McGee, and Harold Montgomery.

A young Negro woman stands with them, a pretty girl with a sweet heart-shaped face. Malone doesn't know her.

Charles McGee says, "Must have done."

Malone immediately thinks of the wall-eyed white man who buttonholed him at the bus stop. But who was he, and why would he bother doing that? Malone was nobody.

And anyway, Malone didn't run into him until after he got fired.

"But who?" Charles asks.

"Good question," Malone says.

Ernest Hardman says, "You're the third brother I heard of lost his job for 'security' reasons."

"Who else?" Malone asks.

"Air Force vet out at Willow Run, name of Jesse Rutherford.

Another one's Vincent Mitchell. Fucking war hero, got accused of being a Party member. Booted out, just like that. Rutherford, I know the dude. He got a lawyer. Dunno about Mitchell."

"That's what you need," LeRoy says. "A good lawyer."

"Who did Rutherford get?" Malone asks.

Ernest thinks for a few moments. "Cat named Cornish, I think. White guy, but he's helping the others get their jobs back, too."

A good-looking white woman wanders by. She pauses at their table. She gives a shy wave of greeting to LeRoy.

"Hey," LeRoy says, "look who it is!"

She says, "Hi."

She looks to be around thirty, with honey-blonde hair pulled back in a pony tail. She has a round face, with steel-rimmed eyeglasses that droop on her nose. She pushes them up with the knuckle of a slender index finger.

"This young lady is Wanda Mueller," LeRoy tells the others.

"Actually, I changed my name," the young woman says. "I go by Anna Miller now."

"Well, very happy to meet you, Anna Miller."

Her glasses droop down her nose and she pushes them up again with the back of her knuckle.

The gesture captivates Malone. He loves women's hands, and hers are particularly graceful.

"Haven't seen you in ages," LeRoy says.

"I haven't been around. I came to see Sarkis's show."

"I'm sure he'll be happy to see you." LeRoy points across the room. "He's right over there."

Anna Miller thanks him and tells the others it was nice to meet them. She heads off in Sarkis's direction.

"She used to be one of my painting students here," LeRoy tells them. "Haven't seen her in what, ten years? She was Sarkis's student, too. Malone, I know you need a drink after the day you had."

LeRoy pours wine from a bottle on the tall table into an empty glass and hands it to Malone. He fills up the rest of the glasses.

LeRoy raises his in a salute. The others raise their glasses. They drink, and the talk at the table turns to an artist they all know, Glanton Dowdell, another Negro SAC graduate. He went to prison for second degree murder, but he's continued to paint. Harold says,

"He did a painting called, 'Southwest Corner of My Cell.' Outstanding."

Malone notices the quiet young woman with the group is watching him. "Sorry about your bad day," she says. She holds out her hand. "Lucille Reid."

"Thanks. Malone Coleman." They shake.

Malone takes a good look at her. Dark brown eyes, high cheeks, broad nose, skin a beautiful shade of chocolate. "Sorry, not very sociable tonight."

"No need to apologize."

"Do you go to Arts and Crafts?"

"No, I'm still finishing up at Wayne. I work as Charles's assistant sometimes. You're a painter?"

"In theory."

"What's that mean?"

"I'm not painting much these days," Malone admits. "When I do get a chance, mostly I just stare at a blank canvas for an hour."

"That counts, too."

"Not to me."

LeRoy says, "Anybody feel like dinner?"

The Golden Bamboo, on Adams Street in Paradise Valley. The commercial and entertainment district, together with neighboring Black Bottom, are the sections of the city where the majority of the city's Negro population have been confined.

Lucille sits next to Malone. "What are you going to do now?" she asks. "About the job, I mean."

"First, I'm going to try and get it back. If that's not going to happen, I'll have to find something else."

"Good luck."

"Thanks."

"I thought of something you might be interested in. My father's on the board of the Urban League. They don't find people jobs anymore, but they have a Vocational Services Department. They try to convince white employers to hire qualified Negroes for positions that weren't open to us before."

"Good luck with that."

"Well, they get a lot of doors slammed in their faces. But they're making progress. If you want, I'll ask him if he has any leads."

"Thanks. Appreciate it."

"Sure."

She smiles, then leans away and tunes back in to the artists' talk.

LeRoy goes on about the need for a Negro aesthetic in contemporary art. As much as Clarence Brown was his unofficial foster father, LeRoy was his artistic father. When Malone moved in with Clarence and Bessie, Clarence noticed his artistic talent and signed Malone up for classes at the Pen and Palette Club, a training studio for Negro artists run by the Detroit Urban League. LeRoy was Malone's first teacher; he recognized Malone's gift immediately.

Clarence made Malone finish high school, and LeRoy helped the young man get a scholarship to study at the Society of Arts and Crafts with Sarkis Sarkisian, who had a reputation for accepting and encouraging Negro art students.

LeRoy wanted Malone to finish college at Wayne University. Malone started one semester, but never finished the year; he had had his fill of school. When the army turned him down, he started at the Ford Rouge Production Foundry, hired on because Ford desperately needed wartime workers.

The food comes. Silver serving platters heaped with beef chow mein, almond boneless chicken, General Tso's chicken, shrimp with lobster sauce, and mounds and mounds of white rice. Conversation stops.

The group lingers in front of the restaurant. They decide to continue on to Club 666, a nearby jazz club.

Lucille begs off: classes in the morning. Charles McGee begs off: he's going home to his family.

Before he goes, Charles pulls Malone aside. "I hear you say you're not painting?"

Malone nods.

"What's going on with that?"

"Don't have the fire for it anymore, I guess."

Charles shakes his head. "No good. You got too much talent to quit. Come see me. We'll talk. Got to get you back on track."

After Club 666, LeRoy says, "Still the shank of the evening." They decide to visit a blind pig—an after-hours club—in Black Bottom.

Now Malone begs off: he's already had too much to drink and this day is catching up to him.

He walks to the Barlow Apartments on Cass Avenue, where he stays in a tiny room in the basement. He doesn't pay rent because he's also the maintenance man for the building, carting out trash, changing broken light bulbs, shoveling snow in the winter.

Malone's apartment sits beside the massive boiler for the building and steam pipes run overhead across the room, so he's always sweltering in the winter. His head reeling from losing his job, his stomach roiling from overeating Chinese food on top of too much alcohol and now the intense heat of his apartment, he drops onto his cot.

When he feels his gorge rising, he sits up and tries, by force of will, to keep himself from throwing up.

He's not successful.

Fortunately, he has a toilet all to himself in his basement room.

It gets a workout for the rest of the night.

6

ANNA MILLER

It's one of those nights when Anna Miller's dark thoughts settle over her like a caul.

When she got home from the Arts and Crafts show, she couldn't wait to change her clothes and stretch out on her sofa.

Sleep never came, and she gave up.

Now she sits up drinking tea. She lives in a late Victorian house on West Canfield between Second Avenue and Third Street downtown. Once a stately home in a stately neighborhood, it was made over into a rooming house when the surrounding area began to deteriorate after the war. The street is as old as the house, one of the few streets left in the city with brick pavers.

Her little studio occupies the top floor of the three-story building, what was once part of the attic before being partitioned and marginally renovated with a tiny kitchenette and enough space for a bed, a card table and two chairs, and a sofa. Her clothes hang on a metal rack. She has set up the closet as a small darkroom for her photography. She also has an easel by the single window. It holds a barely begun canvas.

Along with her photography, she tries the occasional oil painting. This one will be an abstract of what she sees out the lone window. So far she's just split up the canvas into thirds, with just a suggestion of the diagonals of overhead wires and the alley behind the building visible in the direction she faces, and, fading off in the distance, the rectangles of Detroit's downtown office buildings.

This morning, she shot a roll of film on her way to the Kaczmarek home to take care of Chester. She has not had a chance to process it.

Now, unable to sleep, she goes into her tiny darkroom. Working solely by touch in complete darkness, she unspools the film from its roll and winds it around the spool in the developing tank. When she gets the lid on the tank and it's airtight, she turns the overhead red light on and goes about developing the negatives.

She hangs the prints on cords strung around her apartment.

This roll consists of houses, the modest brick bungalows and frame Cape Cods that make up the neighborhood where Dottie and Roger and Chester live. The houses are neat and tidy, and she knows they represent all the hopes and aspirations—as well as the life savings—of the people who live in them.

With all their planes and diagonals and shadows, they make interesting artistic studies.

She would like them to be more than "interesting," though. She would like them to be art.

While the prints are drying, she sorts through her piles of old *Life* and *Look* magazines for the photos by her favorites, Helen Levitt and Berenice Abbot. These women are artists with their cameras, capturing images of New York City that Anna yearns to replicate. Levitt concentrates on people, primarily children in Spanish Harlem, and Abbot focuses on the changing architecture of the city. Anna loves Abbot's photos of massive steel and stone structures, and the humanity in the faces Levitt captures.

Anna has studied the photographs from every aspect—as technical artifacts (angles, lighting, compositions, framing, gradations of blacks and whites), and as human records of a person's life, photographs as chemically-preserved glances into their souls.

She tries to do this in Detroit, but can't escape the notion that something's missing, some creative spark of street life, some energy, some pulsation . . . cities, like people, vibrate at certain frequencies, and for some reason she doesn't feel copacetic with Detroit. Unlike New York City, Detroit spreads out horizontally, in predominantly single-family homes. There are few towering apartment blocks as in New York City, and she thinks maybe it's the midwestern openness of Detroit as opposed to the compact east coast tension of New York that makes the difference.

Or maybe she's fooling herself; maybe she won't feel compatible anywhere. Maybe what she's been through in her life has ruined her for what else *might* happen.

Is she ruined? Already, at the age of thirty, spoiled goods, not even useful to herself, let alone anybody else?

If she is, what's the use of doing anything, she asks herself. It all comes to nothing anyway.

This is not the first time she has felt this way. It's just a free-floating sense of hopelessness hanging around her like a bad smell.

She gets up and pours herself a glass of chardonnay from an open bottle in the icebox. There's only just enough for half a glass. She stands at the kitchen sink and drinks it down.

Most nights Anna sleeps on the sofa. She would not be able to say why, but she seems to have disturbing dreams whenever she tries to sleep in bed.

She dreams of her adolescence.

They are nightmares.

Anna comes from money.

Money and trouble, two things that often go together.

Her father, Prentiss Mueller, runs the chemistry lab at the Ford Motor Rouge Plant—or did, anyway; she hasn't spoken to him for years, so she doesn't know or care what he's been up to. Her mother Frieda comes from old German aristocracy, though unlike many German aristocrats, she has a real fortune in her background. Anna doesn't want anything to do with either of them.

Likewise, she wants nothing to do with her brother Heinz, locked away in the Marquette Branch Prison in Michigan's Upper Peninsula. Anna hopes he will never get out.

She has not seen any of her family for over ten years.

She never wants to see them again.

She's tried to distance herself from them, even going so far as changing her name. She was born Wanda Anneliese Mueller; she dropped her first name and Americanized her middle and last and now goes by Anna Miller. She has not changed it officially, but all jobs are cash only so she has had no need for a formal name change.

Anna thinks back on her former self Wanda like a character in a folk tale, "Poor Wanda," a pitiful waif badly treated by others and forced to roam the world on her own, wraith-like.

Her family lived in Palmer Woods, a ritzy neighborhood in northwest Detroit. Her father and brother and mother were all fascist sympathizers before the Second World War.

When she was fourteen, Anna's brother Heinz started raping her. She told her mother the first time it happened, and her mother accused her of lying about it to get Heinz in trouble. Her father hired a doctor who kept her doped up as the treatment for what he called her "abnormal hysteria." Heinz's abuse continued as the drugs made her easier to manage, and when she was sixteen, she got pregnant with his baby.

Anna gave birth to a boy, whom she immediately named Franklin, after the president at the time—her way of sticking a finger in the eyes of her Nazi parents.

Except the baby died shortly after birth. The drugs the doctor plied her with before and during the pregnancy probably killed him.

The doctor and her father made her give birth in her bedroom at the house; maybe if she had been in a hospital, the child might have had a chance.

They swept him away from her right away; they never let her hold her son. Those fascist pigs used her dead baby to try to start a race war in the city, which was already deeply divided by racial animosity.

They didn't succeed.

But they never told her what happened to her baby. He was taken from her and then lost forever somewhere in the world (another reason she fantasizes about leaving Detroit and its painful memories).

She finally mustered the courage to leave her parents' home with the help of a Detroit police detective, Denny Rankin. He got her a job as a messenger at the detective agency run by his girlfriend, Elizabeth Waters. When Elizabeth joined the Women's Army Corps after the war started, Anna stayed on to help Elizabeth's partner at the firm, Eva Perlman; Anna helped Eva keep their business running until financial troubles forced Eva to let Anna go.

One of Eva's clients was a doctor's wife who was divorcing her husband; she needed someone to watch her children while she went back to work, so she hired Anna.

The doctor's wife was an amateur photographer who kept a variety of cameras around her house. She let Anna borrow one, and Anna was hooked; like a musician, she felt she had found her instrument.

Denny Rankin paid for a scholarship for Anna to study photography and painting at the Detroit Society of Arts and Crafts.

Now when she's not scrambling for money, Anna spends her off-hours taking photographs and developing them in her darkroom. Since leaving Arts and Crafts, she hasn't shown her photos to anyone; she would die of humiliation if anyone criticized them.

After the doctor's wife, she worked lots of catch-as-catch-can jobs, but mostly as a child minder, either live-in or on a daily basis. She wants to make sure no child anywhere would have to go through what she went through. She couldn't protect every child, but she could protect the ones she cares for.

Her last job as live-in nanny disappeared when the father lost his job at Ford's and they had to return home to Saginaw. She was looking for a job as a babysitter, but when she heard about Dottie and Chester, she interviewed with them and discovered how much she enjoyed talking with Chester despite his being older than the children she usually cared for, and he took to her immediately. He's a lot friendlier than most so-called "normal" people she knows; she keeps an eye on him during the day, makes his meals, keeps him out of trouble, keeps him company.

Lately, though, she's been getting restless. She wants to see more of the world than she's seen so far.

The problem is, her personal history pulls on her with a terrible, inescapable gravity.

Another hour passes.

Anna still sits on her sofa, hugging her knees.

Only now she weeps.

And wonders: When does this stop?

When does this ever stop?

7

JAKE LIEBERMAN

A single spotlight shines on a Negro man and woman sitting at the piano on stage at the Flame Show Bar. A few dozen others, Negro and white, sit at curved red leather banquettes around the room.

The man at the piano is Ivory Joe Hunter, heavy-set, bespectacled, with a round face and pencil-thin mustache. He's playing a slow, graceful tune and turning his broadly smiling moon face toward the listeners. He sings in a silken smooth voice:

Since I met you baby
My whole life has changed.
Oh since I met you baby
My whole life has changed.
And everybody tells me I am not the same.

Jake recognizes the woman sitting next to Ivory Joe. Della Reese, a local jazz and gospel singer whose career took off after she won a talent show and performed here at the Flame a few years ago. Now she's getting more and more well-known—she recorded a handful of albums and toured with trumpeter Erskine Hawkins and his band.

She picks up the next verse with her rich mezzo-soprano.

I don't need nobody
To tell my troubles to.
I don't need nobody
To tell my troubles to.
'Cause since I met you baby, all I need is you.

They get to the end of their song and the small crowd claps. Ivory Joe and Della Reese laugh and hug, and Della gives him a peck on the cheek and hops down from the stage. She disappears into the darkness at the edge of the club.

Ivory Joe jumps into the jaunty swing of "Perdido." It's a song about a woman who loses her heart to a man while dancing the bolero in Mexico.

When he finishes, Ivory Joe announces a short break. The stage spotlights go off. A woman comes to their table and takes drink orders.

The three friends put their orders in and Ronny tells them about a guy he met in prison when he was a conscientious objector. Meanwhile, Jake—still trapped inside his own head; this outing hasn't worked to extricate him so far—stews over the possibility of losing another job.

Well, he considers, if I do get fired, it's comforting to know I've been thrown out of better places.

He thinks back to the first place he was thrown out of, beginning the chain of events that led him here. The day three years ago when he was called before the House Un-American Activities Committee and immediately afterwards lost his job at the *News*.

After his interview with the committee, he stepped around picket lines protesting the HUAC hearings because HUAC had called several of the city's prominent Negro radicals as witnesses.

Jake nodded to the demonstrators and shook hands with Rev. Charles A. Hill, pastor of the Hartford Avenue Baptist Church. The previous March, Jake traveled with a few hundred others to Washington DC on a pilgrimage for peace; the Detroit contingent was headed up by Rev. Hill, who came back to Michigan and started the Michigan Peace Council.

Before he reached his desk at the *Detroit News* building nearby, his boss in the Art Department intercepted him and told Jake he was fired, effective immediately.

"I don't want to do this," his boss said, "but when the publisher heard you were subpoenaed by HUAC, he didn't give me any choice in the matter."

Jake had many periods of unemployment after that. No one in the local newspaper business would hire him with HUAC's taint on him. He had to pick up temporary work where he could, like toiling in the furniture store his late father started and his father's business partner now ran, or selling suits at Hughes & Hatcher.

Worse was when his wife Carol left, the year he lost his job. She said she needed a more stable life than was possible for them after HUAC, and she moved to Cleveland.

It took her, oh, maybe a month to get over Jake before she latched onto the squarejohn manager of a Jolly Roger donut shop down there.

He later discovered the manager had been transferred from Detroit to Cleveland, and Carol went to be with him. Jake figured she'd been seeing the guy before he was transferred, and used Jake's firing as the excuse to leave him.

He also heard they started a family, which she never wanted to do with Jake.

So it all worked out well in the end.

For everyone except him, of course.

On the bandstand, the spotlights pop on again and Ivory Joe returns to the piano. He starts right in with a down-and-dirty blues number.

> *The moon is rising*
> *And the sun is sinking low*
> *The moon is rising*
> *And the sun is sinking low.*
> *Lord, I can't find my woman*
> *I wonder where did she go.*

At least I know where my woman went, Jake thinks.

She's down in Cleveland, making whoopie with Jolly Roger.

On a napkin on the table, Jake doodles a cartoon: Carol and Jolly Roger sitting on a huge donut like an inner tube floating in a gigantic cup of coffee.

Ronny leans into him. "I'm serious, man," he whispers. "This security job I was telling you about? Go for it! *Carpe diem!*"

Maybe he's right, Jake thinks.

Maybe I need this kick in the ass.

Since he found out about Carol and her new family last year, and especially since he's been working at Hughes & Hatcher, he's been in a kind of trance, sleepwalking through his days.

He's been *perdido*, he thinks.

Lost.

The only people he sees on a regular basis are Anthony and Ronny. He's fallen away from his other friends from the progressive movement and from the movement itself. Where once he was so involved, so dedicated to tearing down this rotten society and building it back up, now he's stumbling through his days as if with his eyes closed in a nihilistic haze, battling nightmares when he does finally fall asleep.

A new job might shake things up enough to get him going. Maybe bring him back to the life he once knew before he became a recluse.

At the least, it would get him away from H & H.

And anyway, he tells himself, is a failed suit salesman really purer than a failed security guard?

There may in fact be something droll about an ex-Communist, ex-radical as a security officer.

At the most, it might give him some spark to start the art project he's long had in mind but has been too filled with ennui to begin.

He draws another cartoon: a man waves a hammer-and-sickle flag as he's borne along on an automobile factory assembly line.

"Hey," he says to Ronny, "let me have your uncle's card after all, will you?"

8

BRIDGET MCMANUS

Bridget pulls into the driveway of her home on Westmoreland Road, in a neighborhood of compact 1930s brick bungalows on the west side of Detroit near Milan Park. By the time she gets home, her two children have gone to bed.

Or so she thinks.

Looking up, she sees Timmy's face in the window of his bedroom. Her sweet twelve-year-old.

The same age as Joey Gallagher.

Timmy waves.

She waves back.

Her daughter Lydia, a precocious thirteen-year-old, left a plate of pot roast and mashed potatoes for Bridget in the refrigerator. But Bridget has no appetite even though she hasn't eaten since she grabbed a sandwich for lunch hours ago.

Bridget tiptoes down to the basement. Her brother Darren's bulky shape rises and falls in deep sleep on the cot. When Darren moved in, she set up a little apartment for him down here. He's supposed to watch the kids when she's working, but Bridget knows he spends most of his time alone in the basement. At least she knows someone's in the house with them.

Back on the first floor, she goes into Timmy's room. Whispers, "What are you doing up?"

"Can't sleep," he whispers back.

"Why?"

"I dunno."

I know why, Bridget thinks. You've got the family curse, insomnia handed down from generation to generation like a prized heirloom.

Bridget kisses the top of the boy's head. She thinks about the damage done to Joey Gallagher's head. She pulls Timmy into a hug.

"Mom," Timmy protests, and begins to squirm like a cat that refuses to be held.

She lets him go. "Go to sleep, panda," she whispers. "Try."

She helps him slip under the covers. Obedient, he at least closes his eyes in the pretense of doing what his mother asks. Bridget has no doubt once she goes into her room, Timmy will be up and at the window again, keeping an eye on the quiet neighborhood.

Bridget tiptoes into her daughter's room and kisses the sleeping girl's seal-sleek dark hair. She goes into the bathroom to shower. Back in her room, she gets her pajamas on.

And Bridget, too, like her son, settles in to spend most of the night awake.

Except she's not guarding the neighborhood. She's staring at the ceiling, seeing in her mind's eye Joey Gallagher's frail body lying lifeless among the trash.

At quarter to two in the morning, unable to sleep, she goes out to the dining room. She makes a cup of tea and sits reading *Three Men Out*, a Nero Wolfe anthology by Rex Stout.

The phone rings.

She grabs it before it wakes the others.

She knows who it is.

"Wake you?" the man's sleepy voice says.

"I wish. I was up."

"What are you doing?"

"Reading."

He yawns. "What happened in Flint?"

"It was the kid," she says, "no question. It was messy." She doesn't want to talk about it. "What are you up to?" she asks.

"Couldn't sleep either. Also wondering if you'd like a visitor in that big empty bed."

"Tonight?"

"Technically speaking, it's morning."

She bundles her robe around her as if he were in the room with her. "Not tonight. Or this morning, as the case may be. Okay?"

"In that case, I'll let you get back to your reading."

They hang up.

Sometimes they go through a you-hang-up-no-you-hang-up routine like a couple of teenagers. Thankfully, not tonight.

Her tea's cold. She takes the cup into the kitchen and dumps it down the sink.

The instant the phone rang, she knew it was Ed Hauser. He's the only one who calls at this time of night, and the only one who wants to get some midnight action in her bed and sneak out before the kids wake up.

As she's asked herself many times, why does she do this?

He isn't handsome, or smart, or sensitive.

Or particularly good at what he does. She's seen first-hand: he's a lazy detective with the Detroit Police Department. She has been teamed with him several times because policewomen are not allowed to make arrests or investigate crimes without a male detective.

It's how this started, him thinking he has an open invitation to her. He went with her late one night to arrest a man who was beating his wife, and Hauser asked her if she wanted to stop for a drink after they got the guy processed.

She said yes.

Big mistake.

She must have been putting out some strong signals because after one drink he talked about how beautiful she was. Which she knew was a load of bullshit, but who doesn't like to hear it?

And his wife didn't understand him, of course.

Bridget guesses his wife understands him perfectly well.

The thing was, she was terribly lonely for human, skin-to-skin contact. She hadn't been with a man since her husband went off to war and came back in a box. She hadn't met anybody worth her time since. And while Ed wasn't worth it, either, he was there, and he was insistent, and it was late, and she was tired of being alone . . .

Blah blah blah.

So she let him think he was seducing her with his charms (such as they were) when really she was giving herself up not to him but to her need for human warmth.

It was only supposed to happen once, but it happened six more times. Each time she swore it would be the last time because whatever need she had was sated.

Until the next time.

And the next.

She didn't feel like she was betraying the fading memory of her dead husband (she was sure he would understand) (though maybe not about somebody like Hauser), but rather her own increasingly wobbly idea of herself as someone in control of her own desires.

And of course Ed's wife, let's not forget that betrayal. Bridget hated the way she was helping him two-time his wife.

And she was doing it with Ed Hauser, of all the crass, arrogant boobs on the force.

This really must stop, she tells herself yet again.

She goes back to her book to spend what's left of this night with Nero Wolfe and his breezy legman Archie Goodwin.

9

MALONE COLEMAN

Clarence Brown says, "Bad night?"

Malone can only groan in reply.

His head is killing him, his stomach upset, and his mouth bone dry. He drank too much and stayed out too late the night before.

"Hope it was worth it," Clarence says.

Clarence used to be a heavy drinker, Malone knows. He's been off it for years, but like many who quit their vices, he has no tolerance for those who still overindulge.

Malone is no drinker, either; he saw what it did to people, his mother especially—turned her into the worst version of herself, unleashed all her anger onto him. But last night, he needed to blow off steam. This morning he's paying for it.

He didn't spend the whole time drinking and yukking it up with LeRoy Foster and the others. They started to talk seriously about the responsibility of Negro artists to celebrate the histories whites have tried so hard to erase. Malone believes this strongly; one of the things he most loved about painting (and most misses now) is how it allowed him to memorialize the daily lives of his people. The quiet heroes, who worked their jobs and raised their families under often terrible circumstances.

But he wasn't just thinking about art last night. He was also thinking about how the VA could have found out about his past.

The artists were right. Somebody probably did turn him in. But who?

This morning when he woke up in his basement apartment, he knew he didn't want to face the rest of the looming empty day alone. He wanted to come *home*, which meant here. Ever since Clarence and Bessie Brown took him in, their homes have been his, first their place in Black Bottom, and later when Clarence retired as a Detroit Police detective and he and Bessie moved to the 8 Mile-Wyoming area, where new housing had gone up for Negro Detroiters. Malone stayed in the basement in their new house.

Bessie and Clarence have been his surrogate parents since the night in 1941 when Malone snuck into Clarence's cellar. Malone's mother had given him another beating and he tried to find refuge with Clarence. He remembered Clarence as one of the few Negro Detroit policemen at the time, a man committed to helping the neighborhood children with the baseball leagues he used to organize and the parties he and Bessie used to put on for the kids.

Frightened, hurting, Malone was drawn to Clarence's house just to be around adults who cared about kids. Malone was seventeen, wanting to be out on his own but knowing in his heart he wasn't ready to be independent; he didn't have the skills or the confidence to make it on his own.

He wouldn't be ready until he had lived with Bessie and Clarence for a few years and they made him feel he was worth loving.

It took a while. He was a silent and morose teenager. He was always big for his age, more thoughtful than he was given credit for being; the other kids saw him taking his time to digest new situations and information and concluded he was slow; they called him Dummy. Adults heard this and assumed the same about him.

In the first years of his life with the Browns, he kept hearing his mother's voice in his head, telling him he was no good and never would be; telling him he deserved every beating she gave him; telling him he was stupid and would never come to anything. Mercifully, his brother and sister escaped their mother's drunken wrath; she saved it all for him. When the men who came in and out of her life saw how she treated the boy, they felt justified in treating him the same way.

Finally Bessie's soft, low tones and Clarence's baritone replaced his mother's voice. They told him often enough that he was worth something—Bessie because she was convinced Jesus loved him (all appearances to the contrary, Malone thinks), and Clarence because he wanted to make sure Malone had the self-regard a colored man needed to make his way in a hostile world—until at last Malone began to believe it.

Clarence, too, got him started on his creative journey by connecting him with LeRoy Foster at the Pen and Palette Club.

As much as they helped him, Malone filled a gap in their lives, too. Their son DeMarco had died in the Spanish flu epidemic back in Kentucky, and they had moved to Detroit to start a new life up north.

Now Clarence picks up the tray he prepared and says, "Come on, say hello."

Malone follows him into the back bedroom. Bessie lies in bed, recuperating from getting her leg amputated below the knee from diabetes.

She naps, snoring gently, mouth a purring O in her round face. Clarence doesn't want to wake her; he and Malone tiptoe back into the kitchen.

"She okay?" Malone asks.

Clarence shrugs. Malone knows this Clarence-speak for no, not really, and I don't want to talk about it. Clarence asks, "Want some lunch? Make you a sandwich?"

"No, thanks. Stomach's still a little queasy from last night."

"Go out drinking, that's what you get."

"I should have known better than to try and keep up with those guys. With all the stops we made, I guess I got overserved."

Clarence snorts. "One way to put it."

Clarence pours himself a cup of coffee from the battered aluminum percolator on the stove. He holds it up to offer a cup to Malone, who declines. They sit at the kitchen table in the sunny breakfast nook. Clarence sweeps invisible crumbs off the red checkered oilcloth. "No work today?" he asks, off-handedly.

Malone doesn't answer right away. He knows the question Clarence really wants the answer to: *why aren't you working?*

Have to tell him sooner or later, Malone thinks. "I lost my job."

Clarence takes the news calmly. He knows plenty of Negro men who get fired who don't deserve it. Clarence himself came close to being thrown off the Detroit Police force several times even though he was one of the best detectives in his precinct serving Black Bottom and Paradise Valley.

Clarence sighs. "What happened?"

Malone tells him the whole story—the tap on the shoulder in the hall, the interview with the Personnel Director, the discharge letter, the accusations, the guy at the bus stop afterwards.

Clarence listens, his face impassive. Finally he says, "You want, you can stay here till you find another job."

"Thanks. Might take you up on that. But I'm good for now."

"Like I always said, you ever need a place to lay your head, you got one here."

"Appreciate it. Ever heard of Jesse Rutherford?"

Clarence shakes his head.

"One of the guys I was with last night said the same thing happened to him, a colored man fired for being a security risk. He got a lawyer."

"Who?"

"Name's Cornish. White guy. Maybe I could get him to take my case, too."

Clarence heaves his bulk to his feet. It takes a couple of tries to get out of his chair. He's a big man, and his knees are starting to go. He balances himself against the kitchen table for a moment before going into the dining room. Malone follows.

The telephone sits in a wall niche on top of the phone book. Clarence hands the book to Malone.

Clarence's hands shake, Malone notices; he has developed a tremor in the past year.

Charles C. Cornish, Attorney-at-Law, is listed in the phone book at 922 Hammond Building in Detroit.

"I'm going to see him," Malone decides.

"Best call first," Clarence suggests. "These lawyers, they don't like people just showing up."

Malone is too anxious to call; he wants to go right down and talk to him. But he admits Clarence has a point so he dials the number.

A woman's voice answers. "Good morning, Kenyon and Cornish."

"Hello, I'm calling for Charles C. Cornish."

"I'm sorry, Mr. Cornish isn't in. Would you like to leave a message?"

"Can I make an appointment to see him?"

"Mr. Cornish is mostly retired these days. Can his partner help you?"

Malone doesn't reply. He wants to see Cornish.

"If you could tell me the problem, we could go from there."

"I was fired from my job. I think it was unfair. I was hoping Mr. Cornish would take my case on, like he took on the other cases of Negro men who lost their jobs."

"Just one minute. Let me speak with Mr. Kenyon. What's your name?"

"Malone Coleman."

"Hang on, Mr. Coleman."

In another minute a man's deep voice comes on the line. "Mr. Coleman?"

"Yes."

"Kenneth Kenyon. Why don't you tell me about your situation?"

Malone goes into it. Kenyon listens.

"So I wanted to talk with Mr. Cornish," Malone concludes, "because I heard he took on the other cases like this one."

"It's true, he has. Tell me about the group you were accused of belonging to."

"The National Negro Labor Council."

"What is that?"

"A labor organization for Negro workers. I was in it when I was in UAW Local 600 when I worked at Ford's. At the time—this was the early '50s—the NNLC and Local 600 were trying to put pressure on the company to stop relocating jobs down south and other places Negroes couldn't get a fair shake."

"Do I remember the Attorney General called the National Negro Labor Council a Communism front?"

"Yeah, but that's wrong, Mr. Kenyon. Nobody understood what we did. I don't understand how the VA found out about me and this Council. And why they care. That was years ago. So does it sound like you want to take on my case?"

"Honestly, Malone, I just don't have the time this will need."

"What about Mr. Cornish? Is he really retired?"

"Pretty much. Tell you what I'm going to do. He likes this kind of case. Do you have a phone number where I can reach you?"

Without a phone at the Barlow, Malone gives him Clarence and Bessie's number.

"Good deal," Kenyon says. "Give me a few days to get in touch with Charles and pass all this on to him. If he wants to get involved, he'll give you a call. If he doesn't, I'll give you a call, and let you know."

"I appreciate you for talking to me."

"Not at all. Good luck."

Malone goes back into the kitchen, where Bessie Brown now sits at the table. Gauze wraps her left leg's stump at the knee.

He hugs her. "Hey, mamma."

"Hey baby. What you doing here this time of day?"

Malone fills her in.

"Sorry, honey," she says. "Ain't right."

"No ma'am."

"What are you going to do?"

"Find another job, I guess."

"But you going to fight this, too, right?"

"I just talked to a lawyer about it, but he wasn't going to help."

"Only one man's opinion."

"I need to get in touch with another lawyer, the one who defended some other guys this same thing happened to."

"Meantime, you need you a job," Bessie says. Always practical, always thinking of how best to solve a problem.

"I know the director of the Maintenance Department at Harper Hospital," she says. "That's where I worked. Mr. Rheinhardt. You want, I'll call him for you."

"That would be great."

Malone helps her into the dining room with the aid of her crutch. It takes her a few minutes to connect with the director, and she tells him she's sending somebody down to talk with him about a job. The director promises to speak with Malone.

"Thanks, mamma."

"Anything for you, baby."

Clarence lends Malone his car to get downtown to the hospital.

Malone finds his way to the maintenance director's office among the overhead steam pipes and electrical conduits in the hospital basement.

The white secretary tells him the director, Mr. Rheinhardt, is out.

"Bessie Brown spoke to him today about my applying for a job."

"How is Bessie?"

"Hanging in."

"Tell her Harriet says hi."

"I will."

"So first, you have to go up to the Employment Office on the second floor and fill out an application. Let them know you want a custodian job and they'll send it down here."

"When will Mr. Rheinhardt be back? I was hoping to talk to him."

"He's in a budget meeting. I'm not sure when he'll be done. You could check back after you fill out the application."

Malone takes the elevator to the second floor. He has to wait in a corridor with two dozen other people who are also looking for work. The secretary on the desk gives him an application form and tells him to fill it out and drop it in the basket on her desk. Completed forms already fill the basket.

After he drops off the form, Harriet in the basement tells him Mr. Rheinhardt is still in his meeting, but Malone can wait if he likes.

He doesn't have to be anywhere, but he doesn't have the patience to spend any more time here. The hospital reminds him of what happened at the VA.

He goes outside and walks along Woodward Avenue. The day is mild, so being outside is pleasant. A steady flow of pedestrians passes by, hospital workers and patients and Detroiters on their way places. The people go by without a glance at him.

He might as well be invisible.

No, he thinks.

Not true.

The white men and women who bustle by deviate from their straight paths just enough to put a hair's breadth more space between him and them.

They sense something there . . . some entity that may represent a danger; they ever-so-gradually inscribe an arc away from him on the sidewalk without actually acknowledging him or meeting his gaze.

Funny, how an invisible entity can be such a dangerous presence.

He rouses himself. He can't be put off by these people. He really does need to start filling out more applications. This will not be an easy process.

He retrieves Clarence's Ford from its parking spot and drives north, away from downtown.

He goes another half-mile up Woodward Avenue and parks near the employment office for Wayne University. He goes inside and looks through the positions posted on the bulletin board in the office. There are several openings for custodians. He asks if he can fill out an application for the jobs, and the clerk behind the counter gives him one.

He fills it out and drops it off with little hope. When it comes to employment in Detroit right now, all bets are off for Negro men. It always takes longer for a Negro man to find a job than a white man.

Back in the car, he doesn't start out right away. He should return the car to Clarence—but instead he thinks about the previous night at the Society of Arts and Crafts.

He feels drawn to it again, away from the hubbub of the opening.

He turns the car around and drives south, toward downtown. Passing Mack Avenue, he sees the Arts and Crafts building on the left.

He slows, parks the car. He goes inside.

The familiar smells—the perfumes of paints and spirits and the dry smell of clay from the sculpture studios and the rich heated air from the kilns—welcome him.

He passes the ceramic studio. No classes are in session, but a half-dozen students bend over their throwing wheels. They look up when he appears in the doorway, and quickly turn back to the lumps of clay on their dampened bats.

Everything—the floor, the walls, the worktables, the racks holding flat slabs of drying unfired tiles—is covered in gray dust from the clay. In the center of the room are shelves with giant white tubs of glaze and blocks of wrapped clay. Along the walls, shelves hold all kinds and sizes of clay vessels: bisque-colored plates, bowls, cups, vases.

In the corner a door leads to a room where more clay vessels are drying, waiting to be fired in the kiln.

He peeks inside and sees a young white woman taking a large clay pot off one of the shelves. She wears a beige smock stiff with clay dust and wet clay, with a plain scarf wrapped around her head.

She brings the pot to a low, round kiln made from bricks surrounded by chicken wire. She bends over the kiln and carefully lowers the pot to the bottom.

When she gets it in, she straightens. Wipes her hands on her smock. She touches her hair above the kerchief; it leaves a dusty fingerprint.

She turns and spots Malone. Raises a hand in greeting.

He raises a hand in return, and continues on his way down the hall. Even though he doesn't know the woman, the sight of her working with such focus revives his spirits and reminds him of the time he spent here.

Because he loved his time at the Society of Arts and Crafts . . . when he comes back, it's to the place where he felt more comfortable than anywhere else except for Clarence and Bessie's. With the support and tutelage of the teachers here, he felt his brain grow and his talents flourish. He began to feel like he might be able to be a success at something he loved.

So how did that end? And why did he stop painting?

As high as his spirits were a few moments ago, now they plummet.

Rather than wrestle with the question of why he stopped painting, he turns away from it—again—and tells himself he has to get going; Clarence needs his car back.

He leaves, feeling himself expelled from the building by what he considers his greatest weakness—his inability to face up to himself with honesty and clarity.

10

ANNA MILLER

Perpetually short of money, Anna works two other jobs besides taking care of Chester: she waitresses at a diner near her apartment, and she cleans the offices of a savings and loan company, a tailor, and a dentist in a small office building on Woodward near West Canfield.

Each weekday, she's up at six a.m. to clean the three offices.

Afterwards, she trundles off either to Chester's house or to Nick's Grille.

Today she's at Nick's, a greasy spoon on Second Street. On Tuesdays, Thursdays, and Saturdays, her shift starts at eleven in the morning and ends at seven at night.

Back from cleaning the offices, Anna washes breakfast dishes in her apartment when she hears an odd sound coming from the stairway.

Step, slide, thud, repeating and growing louder as it draws near.

The sound stops and she hears a gasping outside her door, followed by a timid knock.

She wipes her hands and goes to the door. Selma Stenhagen stands on the stairs. She lives in the apartment beneath Anna's with her brother Fred. Fred chain smokes and Anna smells the smoke coming up through the floorboards from morning till night.

Selma couldn't even make it to the landing; she holds herself up on the stair railing as she catches her breath. She is a thin and ragged woman in a tattered mouse-brown cardigan. She's in her sixties with long limp gray hair and a mouth downturned in a perpetual frown.

She nods at Anna but still hasn't caught enough breath to start talking. She wheezes heavily, the breath hissing like a bag of sand shifting through her chest.

When she can, she says, still breathing hard, "I've always admired the Jewish people."

Anna doesn't know how to respond to this. She can only muster, "Okay."

"I knew many Jewish people. They were fine people."

"Good to know."

Selma takes a few more loud breaths. "I need to ask for a favor."

While Selma catches her breath, it dawns on Anna that the older woman thinks she's *Jewish*. That's why she's telling me she admires the Jewish people? She's trying to butter me up?

When she ordinarily won't say boo to me? All the times we've passed on the stairs, and all Selma could ever manage was an almost imperceptible nod.

That must be it. Why else would she say it? She wants something.

"You have a car," Selma says.

Aha. Now we get down to business.

"I do," Anna says.

And no, you may NOT borrow it, Anna thinks.

She hardly ever drives the pre-war Chevy her parents tried to bribe her with. They wanted her to come back and live in their house again after the first time she left. And it worked, too. She went back; she was not in good shape; they convinced her she couldn't live independently; all was forgotten.

After she had been back for a month, she realized she couldn't stay and left again, taking the car.

And now what does Selma want with it?

"My brother Fred has trouble breathing," Selma rasps.

Fred has trouble? Anna thinks.

"He needs to go to the hospital," Selma continues. "I need to ask if you would give me a ride with him. Please."

Anna hesitates for the briefest second as she wonders how this will affect her schedule this morning. She's not due in until eleven.

Selma picks up on the hesitation right away. "Oh, I can see I'm disturbing you. Never mind."

Selma turns to begin the arduous trip back down stairs.

Thud, slide, step.

"Wait, wait," Anna says. She reaches out to grab Selma's skeletal arm. "Of course, I'll take you. Just let me get my coat."

Selma heaves a noisy sigh of relief.

When Anna gets down to their apartment, she finds Fred sitting on the sofa in the living room. His basset-hound face is glum. His lips are lilac. Anna helps him to his feet. He feels soft, like a gelatinous mass, as if he has no bones.

She and Selma get him in her car, and she speeds off to Harper Hospital where Selma says Fred's doctor practices.

She parks at the Emergency entrance and runs in to find someone to help. She collars a nurse and brings her out to the car. The nurse immediately recognizes Fred's distress; she runs back into the building and comes out with an orderly pushing a wheelchair. The orderly lifts Fred out of the car and sets him in the wheelchair, and together the nurse and orderly rush inside with him.

Selma gets herself out of the car and takes off after them. She can't move as fast, so they are inside and out of sight by the time she gets through the Emergency doors.

Anna stands watching her go. There's nothing she can do now for either of them. If she didn't have to work, she would wait with Selma.

She goes inside and tracks down Selma inside the Emergency area. A nurse and doctor are already working on Fred; they have a tracheal tube down his throat. "I have to go," Anna tells Selma standing outside the cubicle. "I'll check back after work if you need me to take you home."

Selma stares at her blankly. Does she understand what Anna's saying? She looks like she's in shock.

"I can't stay," Anna says. Again, she doesn't know if this gets through.

Anna runs out to her car. She has only enough time to drop the car back at her building, throw her waitress's uniform on, and run the two blocks to Nick's.

Nick Papageorgiou stands at the cash register. She can't tell if he gives her a dirty look or not when she rushes in—his usual resting face bears a disgusted sneer—but she's not late so he can't quibble.

It's a small diner, with a long counter on one side and a line of tables on the other. She goes through to the Ladies' and pins her hair back and fits her snood over it. She doesn't wear makeup; she wants to make herself look as plain and uninviting as possible, but that still doesn't keep the creeps away.

Her work partner, Maisie, is already there when Anna comes out of the Ladies' and stows her purse in her locker in the back. She straightens her apron, and makes sure she has a pencil and enough checks in her pad. She will be here until close.

"How was the morning?" she asks Maisie. Maisie gives an order to George, the big Greek who works the grill, and helps Anna fold silverware into paper napkins to get ready for the lunch rush.

"Morning was slow. Not much business."

"I heard there's a new restaurant up on Cass, closer to Wayne. Probably taking customers away."

"Might explain why Nick's in an even worse mood than usual."

They sneak a look at Nick, still at the register, gazing out at the traffic on Second. A cigarette with a long ash droops from his lips; stubble peppers his lower face.

"How was your morning?" Maisie says.

"Yeah, good. Just that my neighbor's got some troubles."

"Ain't we all."

Maisie comes from Kentucky. She's a tough-looking bird with lines in her face that look like they've been etched by knives and she looks out at the world through hard, cynical eyes, but she's been nothing but sweet to Anna. Maisie and her husband came up from the south when her husband got a job at Ford's; he was killed in an explosion at the Rouge plant and now the union helps her out, but she still needs to work as many hours as she can. When she finishes here, she goes to another waitressing job at an all-night joint on Grand River.

Now two enormous white Detroit motorcycle cops stroll in with leather jackets and high boots. They sit at a table near the front of the restaurant. Anna knows them. She's waited on them before.

They act like they own the place. And her, too.

She takes a deep breath.

She takes menus over to them.

"Hey, gorgeous," one of the cops says. The other gives her the eye from head to toe.

Anna feels Nick's eyes on her from the register, so she has to be polite to these lugs.

"How you boys doing today?"

"Better now," the second cop says. He reaches out to give her thigh a pinch but she brushes his hand away and moves back before he can get to her. When she started here, Maisie clued her in to the drill: cops are used to waitresses and divorcees being cop-lovers, so they expect all of us to want to put out for them.

"What can I get you?" she asks with her check pad out.

"I wouldn't mind a little piece of you in a prone position," the first cop says. "You got that on the menu?"

"As luck would have it, we just ran out."

The goons laugh, and her day at the diner begins.

Later in the afternoon, after the lunch rush, she goes into the back storage room for a new stack of carry-out pop cups. Maisie said the lunch business was better than the morning, so the tips weren't bad.

Nick follows her.

"Hey." He stands in the doorway. Short and fat, built like a hairy fire plug, he blocks the doorway.

"Nick, I'm kinda busy right now—"

"No time for me?" He gives her a ghoulish smile that shows his green teeth.

He tries to box her in against a counter with his big belly.

He moves in with his arms up and here he comes with his disgusting slobbery lips puckering up for a kiss.

"Stop!" she cries.

She pushes his hands away and turns her head so he kisses her hair. The carry-out cups go flying.

He briefly wrestles with her. He's not particularly strong for a man his size, so she easily foils his advance.

Maisie comes to the door.

"Everything okay in here?"

Nick turns his head toward Maisie and Anna scoots by him. Maisie moves over so Anna can get past her, and stands there giving Nick the fisheye, daring him to chase after Anna.

Nick tried this once with Maisie right after she started, but he got a knee in the balls for his troubles so hasn't tried anything with her since. Anna hasn't ruled it out, but she can't stand the idea of harming anyone, so she simply puts up with his occasional awkward attempts. She knows he'll either get the message or fire her.

In the meantime, she needs the job.

The ultimate reason for putting up with any indignity: we need the job.

Even though his assumption that he could pull that shit with her any time he wants makes her furious.

She has long since convinced herself these men don't respond to any signals she throws off. She had to work through it after she left home and scrutinized her interactions with her brother to discover if she did anything he could possibly interpret as encouraging him. By now she knows she did nothing. And now she understands she does nothing to encourage Nick. He just assumes she's fair game, like the cops do, like they all assume it's their prerogative to do what they want with her.

The world would be a lot better off without men.

Her life certainly would.

She re-stacks the carry-out cups and brings them out to the counter.

When she finishes at Nick's and gets back to her building, Anna taps on Selma's door.

The door across the hall from Selma's opens. The spooky-looking man who lives there sticks his head out. "She's not home," he says. He has deep black circles under his eyes, as if he hasn't slept in a month, and he smells of urine. "I haven't heard her all day, not since this morning."

She gets in her car and drives to Harper Hospital. If Fred had to be admitted, she guesses Selma would still be there by his side.

She asks the clerk at the reception desk if Fred Stenhagen has been admitted. The clerk checks her records, shakes her head. "I don't see a Fred Stenhagen on the Admissions list," she says. "When did he come in? Sometimes it takes a while for the records to show up."

"He came into Emergency this morning. He would have been admitted sometime during the day."

"Let me just check again."

She goes through her papers one more time. "Nothing here. He might still be waiting for a bed." She holds a finger up to ask Anna to wait and picks up the phone.

"Ruthie, it's me. Did a Fred Stenhagen come in today?"

She listens. Throws Anna a worried look. "I'll send her back."

She hangs up. "If you could just go back through those swinging doors, they'll help you."

Now Anna is worried.

Her distress ramps up when she gets to the Emergency Room and she sees Selma sitting in the waiting area. She looks more haggard than ever, dozing in a chair with her head down.

Anna sits next to her. The movement makes Selma stir.

"Selma, what happened? Is Fred okay?"

"He's gone!"

"Oh Selma, I'm so sorry."

Selma leans into Anna and wails.

A nurse comes over and directs them into a side office away from the prying eyes of the others in the waiting room.

Selma cries and cries.

Selma runs out of breath. Before she can get herself revved up again, Anna says, "What happened?"

"Right after you left, he passed out. He never woke up. They said he had a heart attack."

"And you've been here all this time by yourself? Since this morning?"

"What am I going to do without him?"

Anna holds Selma until she stops sobbing. "I'll be right back," Anna says.

She goes up to the nurse's station. "One of your patients died earlier today? Fred Stenhagen?"

"Yes," the nurse says. "His wife's been here all day."

"Actually, she's his sister. Where is he now?"

"In the hospital morgue. We're waiting to hear about

arrangements. The hospital priest tried to talk to her"—she indicates Selma—"but she was too upset."

"I'll talk to her now."

Anna asks Selma if she knows of any funeral homes they might use. She doesn't. Anna asks if they ever go to church—she knows nothing about them at all—and is surprised to find they go to nearby St. Patrick's every Sunday for mass.

Anna calls St. Patrick's and explains the situation; the woman she talks to tells her she will make arrangements for the body and talk to Father about the funeral mass Fred would want.

Anna lets the nurses' station know about the arrangements. By now, Selma has stopped crying, but she's in a daze, staring straight ahead like a woman in a trance.

Anna eventually gets her up and moving out to her parked car.

Selma still seems bewildered when they get back to their building, and it's only when Anna gets her settled into her apartment that Selma seems to come out of it. She becomes ultra-practical, bustling around the cramped space that reeks of cigarette smoke, plumping the pillows on the sofa, washing the dishes in the sink, even sweeping the floor, all the while wheezing and chattering about how Fred wouldn't want things to be so messy.

Selma trembles with adrenaline, desperate for something to do to take her mind off today's terrible event.

As Anna suspected would happen, Selma collapses when she can no longer maintain the pace.

Anna helps her onto the sofa and makes them both a cup of tea. Selma wants a splash of schnapps in hers, and Anna accommodates her.

When she calms down, Selma gets a shoebox full of photographs down from the top shelf of her bedroom closet and goes through them with Anna. She narrates their lives through the photos.

It turns out Selma and Fred are Canadian, from Amherstburg, a farming community across the Detroit River, south of Detroit. Selma evidently kept a complete photographic record of their childhood and adolescence—or at least Fred's; with trembling hands, Selma shows Anna photo after photo of little tow-headed Fred on the family farm, at the beach in Grand Bend on Lake Huron, in high school, in his cap and gown, in parades, carnivals, working on the harvest on the family farm, and in general joining in the life of a small town. Some of the photos include Selma, but she explains she took most of them and that's why she's in only a few.

They are good-looking children and happy and hopeful teenagers, so unlike the glum older pair Anna would pass on the stairs in their apartment building after life closed in on them.

The whole time they were growing up, she and her brother were inseparable. No boyfriends or girlfriends, no husbands or wives, no friends of either sex, to judge by the photos, no apparent romantic life outside of the bond they shared.

The family lost the farm in the Depression. When their parents died, the brother and sister moved across the river to Detroit where they both worked at Packard's until Fred's emphysema caused him to retire. Selma found another job that wasn't as taxing as the auto plant. She worked in a movie theatre downtown.

But she didn't make as much money. As their finances declined, so did their living arrangements until they wound up in this apartment house, where Selma predicts she will end her days as Fred ended his—except she would be unmourned at the end; at least she's still here to remember him.

Anna listens to Selma tell their story and is immensely saddened at where their lives have taken them.

She helps Selma get ready for bed. The older woman sits up and grabs her arm with surprising strength and says, "Thank you. *Thank you.*"

Anna eases her back to bed and returns to her apartment.

After all the drama at the restaurant and the emotional strain of helping Selma, she lies down on her own sofa and discovers—surprise, surprise—even though she's exhausted, she's too keyed up to sleep.

She gets up and sits by her window. It looks out on the alley that runs behind the buildings that, like hers, are former single-family homes turned into boarding houses. She thinks about the life Selma will face now—broke, bereft of the soul she has been closest to throughout her life—and her heart breaks for the older woman.

And for the conditions of life that bring such heartache and pain.

And she thinks, of course, of her own life. After looking at Selma's photos, she considers that her own childhood was split in two parts:

Before what Heinz did to her, and After. She doesn't remember much of the Before; it's veiled by the pervasive sadness that set in as a result of the After.

Like Selma now, Anna is alone, with no one to turn to and nothing to look forward to, with the extra burden of a terrible past to try and outrun. She never even had the consolation of a devoted brother to accompany her throughout life, as Selma did. Anna's brother was the monster behind her troubles.

Also unlike Selma, Anna has more years ahead of her than behind her. She wonders again how she will face them—especially if the years ahead contain as much loneliness and pain as the years behind.

11

JAKE LIEBERMAN

Another few days at Hughes & Hatcher with his boss breathing down his neck convinces Jake to use Ed Barit's business card.

Men and women stand in a raggedy line outside the door of the Personnel Office of the Hudson Motor Car Company on Jefferson and Conner in Detroit.

They must still have the impression that Detroit is the place to find work, Jake thinks. Drawn by the dream of an autoworkers' paradise and memories of war-time employment, they don't know about the boom-and-bust cycle that leaves most autoworkers in a state of constant worry about a paycheck and scrambling for alternative work.

This year, things are looking up for auto production as a whole. The industry claims they're having the best year ever for automobile production, but for the auto worker things are as precarious as always. People think auto workers have it made in the shade because of their union contracts, but most auto workers Jake knows still need second or even third jobs; they are still prone to layoffs or plant closings or relocations.

And there are still thousands of people looking for work. More arrive daily even though the plants are not hiring; instead, they're starting to turn to overtime hours and automation to reduce the number of new hires.

And, not incidentally, reduce the power of the unions.

Jake waits his turn in the employment line. Most people are turned away. Standing there, Jake had determined not to use his connection with Ronny Barit's uncle, but by the time he gets to the front of the line he's ready to drop the uncle's name.

"Say," the clerk at the desk says, "what do I look like? A sap?"

The guy has a fringe of graying hair around his bald head and jiggling jowls. He sort of does look like a sap, Jake decides.

"You know how many people try to pull that crap on me?" the guy says. "Get lost."

He waves Jake away and looks past him to the next man in line.

"Wait." Jake shows the clerk the business card Ronny gave him: "A. E. Barit, Member, Board of Directors."

The clerk looks at the card as though insulted by it. "Where'd you get this?"

"I told you. I'm a friend of Ed Barit's. He sent me down here for a job."

It's not even stretching the truth much. Jake met the elder Barit once, when Ronny brought Jake around to the family mansion in Grosse Pointe. He was not a friendly man. Most of his energy was tied up in his failing efforts to save his company in the face of crippling competition from the Big Three: Ford, GM, and Chrysler.

The clerk takes a second look at the business card. "Wait here." He gets up and goes through a door into a back office.

The waiting crowd of job-seekers shout at him.

In a minute he returns with another man, this one younger, in a suit too big for him. The clerk points at Jake and the man motions him over.

Voices in the line start yelling now. "Hey—how's he rate?" "What about us?" "What the hell?"

The man in the suit leads Jake into the back office and through a warren of cubicles.

In one, the guy points to a chair across from his desk. Jake sits. The guy has slicked-back hair and razor burn on his jaw.

He holds up the business card. "This on the level?"

"Absolutely."

"How'd you get it?"

Jake considers stretching the truth again, decides not to. "I know

Ed Barit."

"You know we're closing down the plant, don't you? Most of the manufacturing already got sent to Kenosha. Far as anybody's concerned, Detroit can choke on a bone."

"I heard you were looking for security guards to keep an eye on things until you shut it all down for good."

The guy nods. Mulls it over. "Ever do any security work?"

"I was in the army." Not really an answer to the question, but close enough.

"In the big war? Or the police action?"

"The big one. Germany."

"How's your police record? Any convictions?"

"It's clean."

The guy gives Jake a sheath of papers from his drawer. "Find an empty desk and fill these out."

After Jake signs the paperwork, the guy walks him out across the yard to the security office. It's eerily quiet outside the buildings. Jake doesn't hear the constant juddering of machines he expected. Production has mostly ceased here.

Three uniformed men sit in the security office inside the main entrance to the plant. One of them talks on a radio transmitter with what sounds like two other guys.

The Personnel guy introduces Jake to the three men. Says to one, who seems like he's the head man, "You got a night opening, right?"

The guard, whose name badge reads Haskins, says, "Yeah. Eleven to seven."

"Work for you?" the Personnel guy asks Jake.

"Perfect."

"Good deal." To Haskins: "Here's your new officer. Show him the ropes, eh?"

"Can you start tomorrow?" Haskins asks.

"Sure."

The Personnel guy blesses them with a quick cross drawn in the air—he says, "Domini, Domini, Domini"—and leaves them to it.

"Let's get you fixed up," Haskins says. He leads Jake out from the security office and across the silent yard to a cinder block building nearby. Inside is a locker room and closet filled with uniforms. "Pick out your size," Haskins tells Jake.

The uniforms are all shabby and smell like they haven't seen a washing machine since Pearl Harbor.

Jake picks out one that looks like his size.

"No sense in showing you the job now," Haskins says. "Come back at ten tomorrow night. The officer on duty will show you what the job's about. Basically, we show our faces around the buildings, make sure nobody steals nothing."

"Got it."

"Ain't the hardest job in the world. Most nights the biggest problem is staying awake."

"Won't be a problem."

"Yeah, they all say that."

"It won't. Trust me on this one."

His car won't start in the visitors' parking lot.

He turns the key in the Ford and the lumpen piece of shit just sits there in dead silence, like it's thumbing its nose at him. Jake's brother Saul runs a used car lot and knows cars; he's been warning Jake the pre-war heap is on the way out. Jake hasn't had the spare cash to replace it.

He gets a jump from one of the security vehicles and drives out to Hughes & Hatcher at Northland, where he tells Manning Willis that he quits. Manning does not seem any more broken-hearted than Jake.

After getting yet another jump for his car, Jake drives home. He lives in downtown Detroit, in the upper flat of a two-family frame house in Corktown, the oldest section of the city. The area is starting to show its age; many of the houses are poorly maintained, with a slice of the neighborhood being torn up for a new highway system.

When he was married to Carol, they lived in a rented flat in northwest Detroit. After Carol left, he couldn't afford the rent anymore—and anyway he wanted to be away from the scene of his former happiness—or what he took for happiness—so he moved down here.

His landlady, Mrs. O'Neill, a widow, takes better care of her home than most in the neighborhood. He pays his $25 rent in cash each month, plus another $5 to use the large shed behind the house, one of the few in Corktown. Mrs. O'Neill's late husband earned extra money shoveling snow and mowing lawns for the neighbors, and he built the structure to keep his tools and machines in. She gave them all away when he died so she has no use for the space.

Jake's flat has a tiny refrigerator and a tinier stove, almost toy-sized, which are all he needs.

Since Carol left, he feels as if his world has shrunk. He's fallen away from all his groups—his cousins, aunts, and uncles, with the occasional exception of his brother's family, whom he still sees, but even with them he's mostly a ghostly presence; the radicals, who have all gone silent in the relentless pressure from the McCarthy anti-Communist crusades; the artists' circles he moved in; even the people he knew at Central High School who have cocooned with their families and now own shoe stores and women's fashion shops and jewelry stores, or became plumbers or teachers or accountants or, occasionally, doctors and lawyers . . . all those who have plunged into that tide in the affairs of men leading on to fortune, as the Shakespeare play he once read put it—leaving Jake behind, splashing in the shallows with his miseries.

When he gets home from Northland, he opens a can of spaghetti and dumps it in a pot on the stove. It starts to bubble and he gobbles it down right from the pan. Thank you, Chef Boyardee.

He changes his clothes, makes himself a cup of instant coffee (the end of the jar; have to remember to get some more), and bundles up with two coats. He takes the steaming cup out to the shed.

There he turns on the lights and a space heater. It's freezing out here now, but in a few minutes it'll be warm enough to take one of the jackets off.

He turns his radio on. It's tuned to WJLB, a strange mix of ethnic news and music (Greek, Polish) during the day, and rhythm and blues at night. Jake loves when Frantic Ernie Durham comes on at eight o'clock and the format switches to Frantic Ernie's favorite R&B music, which are Jake's favorites, too.

He has erected two work surfaces out here, a drafting table with a stool and a workbench against one wall. He sits on the stool and begins work on the next issue of *Correspondence.* He volunteers to do the layout for the radical newspaper that comes out every two weeks to spread the voices of revolution. It's a worker's newspaper, not a union organ, and it tries to give voice to women, youth, and Negroes whose perspectives are missing from the public arena. It's anti-Communist, written and circulated by people from all over the country. Jake also draws satirical cartoons for it.

The original idea was for readers to take over writing of the news articles, first-person accounts, and opinion pieces, but that hasn't worked out. A small group of writers does most of the work.

Jake plugs in the waxer on his workbench so it can heat up while he gets the strips of copy laid-out on the boards on his drawing table.

He scans the articles. He doesn't like to read them; they remind him of a different time in his life, a time when he was engaged in large social movements and he suffered for his engagement. Instead, he turns this into a visual exercise, a matter more of finding the most pleasing pattern instead of highlighting stories.

Besides, there's a basic template for the twelve-page newspaper: "Worker's Journal" on the front page, and sections for news on labor, youth, women, Negroes, and so on.

Working with his T-square and waxing the backs of the strips, he finishes the work in a few hours. He turns his attention to his other big project.

He has spread a three-foot-by-four-foot sheet of butcher's paper on the workbench. He's been mulling a plan for a work of art, a painting, the largest he's ever done. The finished canvas will take up the entire wall of the shed; he hasn't gotten around to thinking about what will happen to it once he's done.

Nailed up on smaller sheets around the shed are pencil sketches, scenes that burned themselves into his memory when he was in the army during the war. He plans to include these in the finished piece.

He wasn't a combat soldier. He was a reporter and photographer for the army newspaper *Stars and Stripes*, where they put him based on his work for the *Detroit News*. He was with Generals Dwight D. Eisenhower, George Patton, and Omar Bradley on April 12, 1945, when they toured Ohrdruf, the first Nazi concentration camp in Germany to be liberated by U.S. forces.

He will never forget the sights—and smells. Corpses were scattered around the camp grounds, lying where they were killed prior to the camp's hasty evacuation. A burned-out pyre contained the charred remains of prisoners, proof of the SS's hurried attempts to cover their crimes. The few surviving prisoners who were too sick to evacuate described for the generals the various torture methods the guards used for punishment or execution: dragging prisoners barefoot over sharp stones on the camp pavement; submerging ill prisoners in tubs or small barrels; exposing prisoners to cold showers until they died of exposure; hanging prisoners with their arms tied behind their backs; beating them— often to death—with axes, sticks, and shovels; injecting phenol into children's hearts . . .

In a shed, several dozen naked emaciated corpses were sprinkled with lime in an attempt to cover the smell of putrefaction. Patton, a man used to the violent scenes of war, refused to enter the shed as the sights and smells in the camp had previously caused him to vomit against the side of a building. Battle-hardened soldiers were walking around the camp with handkerchiefs to their faces, sobbing at what they'd seen.

The horrors have stayed with Jake ever since; the vicious, deliberate suffering and death inflicted on Jews and others continue to torment him.

So, he's going to try painting the visions out of his thoughts. He has no illusions they won't still haunt him, but he hopes transferring his despair out of his head and onto canvas will at least mitigate the pain.

He plans something large, something capturing all the horror he felt, the same way Picasso's "Guernica" captured the tragedy of the Fascist bombing of a Spanish town. Jake knows he's no Picasso, but he hopes he has the skills to complete this task.

Or at least empty his mind of the sights and sounds and smells of the camps.

So far, he's been having trouble coming to grips with the magnitude of it. He's made sketches of possible approaches, and he thinks he's getting close. It's become a collage of hands, flames, heads grimacing in unbearable torment, old faces, young faces, the emaciated corpses of men and women, children . . . all those whose lives were lost in the hatred that gripped Europe during the last decade, as if the Nazis were able to condense centuries of antisemitism into a concentrated seismic spasm of Jew-hatred.

The studio warms up as his coffee cools, and he works through the day and evening, trying different combinations of colors and shapes, filling in his sketches with the demons of his dreams.

12

BRIDGET MCMANUS

In the morning, Bridget's brother Darren already has the kids fed and their lunches made. Now he tries to get them out the door for school.

In between collecting their books and shoes and coats, the kids give Bridget a hug and greet her loudly; they are glad to see her because she gives them one more excuse to dawdle.

Darren hurries them along. "Coffee's ready," he tells her over his shoulder as he sweeps the kids out the door.

Bridget comes out onto the porch with her brother and watches her children scurry down Westmoreland Road and turn right on Curtis Street to their school.

Darren goes back inside and immediately begins washing up the bowls from the kids' breakfasts. He has nothing to say to her, as usual. His silence isn't angry, just habitual. Since he came back from the war in the Pacific, he has struggled with terrors he can't talk to her about. She trusts him completely with her kids, but as a former social worker she knows Darren suffers terribly. She wishes she could do something about it. But he refuses to talk about his wartime experiences.

A few days a week, he works at a collision shop painting cars while the kids are in school; the rest of the time he lives in Bridget's basement, inside his own head.

Once he finishes washing the breakfast dishes and setting them on the drying rack, he goes downstairs without a word to her.

He used to live with their mother and father, but the older woman couldn't stand his long periods of silence and the older man couldn't abide his inactivity. Bridget's not home during the day, so Darren doesn't have the stress of her presence to deal with, as he had to cope with their mother being around constantly.

The white and Negro policewomen of the Detroit Police Department Women's Division sit together at morning roll call in the duty room at police headquarters. Their lieutenant, Emily Richardson, goes through the litany of crimes against the city's most vulnerable citizens, the women and children the Women's Division is responsible for.

"McManus," Emily calls after the report. She waves Bridget up to the front of the room.

"How's the search going?"

"Slow."

"Here's one you might be interested in. Could be related."

Emily hands Bridget a file. Bridget quickly scans it. "Yikes."

"Tell me about it."

"He went missing yesterday and nobody's done anything until now?"

Emily shrugs.

The house is a small brick bungalow on a newly-developed dead-end street on the west side of Detroit. A rotund older woman in a floral housecoat answers the door. A cigarette droops from the side of her mouth.

"Mrs. Piscatelli?" Bridget says.

"Yeah?"

The woman has a deep voice, suspicious, raspy from years of smoking.

Bridget shows her badge and identifies herself as a police officer with the Women's Division.

"I'm here about a report of a missing juvenile."

"Oh," the woman says, "you want my daughter-in-law."

She opens the door for Bridget to enter. It's as small inside as it seems from the outside, with a tiny living room, dining room, and kitchen. In the back of the house, Bridget sees two tiny bedrooms off a short hallway. A typical bungalow from the thirties, similar to hers.

At the dining room table sits a young woman, obviously distraught, thin with blowsy, unfocused eyes and curly blonde hair. "This is Clara, Leon's mother," the older woman says.

The young woman looks up. Bridget identifies herself.

"Any news?"

"No ma'am. May I sit down?"

"Can I get you a cup of coffee?" the elder Mrs. Piscatelli asks.

"Great, thanks."

Bridget sits at the table and lays the file folder her boss gave her on the oilcloth.

"You're police?" Clara Piscatelli asks.

"Yes. In the Woman's Division, we don't wear uniforms. I'm here to follow up on a report of a missing child. I'll do the first interview, and I'll turn it over to the detectives."

The elder Mrs. Piscatelli returns with a cup of coffee and cream and sugar. "Didn't know how you take it."

"Thanks. Black is fine." She turns to Clara. "Could you tell me what happened?"

Clara says, "My son Leon. He's only six. I don't know where he is."

"When did you realize he was missing?"

"Late yesterday. He was playing in the street with the other kids on the block, and he didn't come home at dinner time when I called him. None of the other kids remembered seeing him go. One minute he was there, the next he wasn't."

"You talked to the other children?"

"I talked to them, and I went around and talked to their parents. When nobody knew where he was, I called the cops."

"Neither the kids nor the parents remember seeing him leave?"

"No."

"Did they see any strangers hanging around?"

"Nobody said nothing about it."

"When was the last time you saw your son?"

"Just after lunch yesterday, when he went out to play."

"Did you see where he went?"

"No. But he usually plays down at the end of the street."

"Where the field is?"

"Yeah."

"And you checked there?"

"I didn't see no sign of him."

Bridget tries not to seem disturbed in light of the recent spate of child killings.

"What's Leon's father's name?"

"Ricky."

"Last name Piscatelli?"

"Yeah."

"Does he still live here?"

"More or less."

"Sorry, what does that mean?"

"It means we're married, but he comes and goes. He likes to call himself a free spirit."

"Have you checked with him about where Leon might be?"

"Course. You think I'm stupid? That was the first thing I did."

"What did he say?"

"He said he don't know where Leon is."

"Do you believe him?"

"What are you saying?" the elder Mrs. Piscatelli puts in sharply. "You think my son would do anything to hurt his little boy?"

"Just covering all the bases, Mrs. Piscatelli." Bridget turns to Clara. "When was the last time you saw your husband?"

"A few days ago."

"Where does he go when he's not here?"

"He stays with his brother Charley."

"That where he is now?"

"Yeah. They go on benders together and he stays there till he sobers up."

"That's where you talked to him?"

"Yeah. I went down to see him, too, in case you're wondering. But Leon wasn't there."

"None of Leon's friends said they saw his father hanging around?"

"No."

The elder Mrs. Piscatelli gives Bridget the fisheye.

"I think I have what I need," Bridget says. "I'll turn this information over to the detectives. One last thing, Clara. What's Ricky's brother's address?"

Clara gives Bridget the address of a boarding house on the west side. It's a walkup. Number 5 is all the way at the top of the four-story building.

Bridget knocks on the door.

A heavy-set man flings it open. He looks at her in desperation.

He steps around her and peeks out at the hallway.

Asks, "Where's Desmond?"

"Are you Charley Piscatelli?"

The guy's all shaky and shivering. Pinpoints for eyes. "Who are you?"

She tells him and shows her badge. "Charley, right?"

"You got to get out of here!"

He turns her around and shoves her a step down the hall.

She pivots back and jams her foot in the door before he can slam it. She shoulders the door in.

He's really desperate now. "What do you want?"

"Where's your brother?"

He looks to the rear of the apartment, points in that direction.

She heads back to a tiny bedroom where a man lies stretched out on a bare mattress. The guy's dead to the world. She feels for his pulse on his neck; it's slow but strong.

She slaps his face but he doesn't rouse.

Charley comes back to the room. "Lookit, if Desmond finds you here, he'll take off. You gotta go—please!"

"Where's Leon? Your nephew?"

Charley turns and rushes to the front of the apartment. Bridget takes a quick look under the beds and in the closets in the three tiny bedrooms. No Leon.

She goes out to the dining room to find Charley rooting through a drawer in a large china cabinet.

"Where's Leon?" she demands.

"I'm looking!"

"You think Leo's in the drawer?"

He turns holding an envelope. "He's here."

The envelope is addressed to Angelica Fortuna.

"That's where he is," Charley says. "Now scram!"

The lower flat of a two-family on West Dakota, north of 6 Mile Road on the near east side of Detroit. Bridget knocks on the outside door.

After a few moments, a woman who could be Clara's twin opens the doors. Rail-thin, heavily made-up, except a brunette instead of a blonde. She looks Bridget up and down. "Yeah?"

Bridget flashes her badge, introduces herself. "I'm looking for Angelica Fortuna."

"What do you want with her?"

"Are you Angelica?"

"I might be."

"Do you know Ricky Piscatelli?"

She makes a sour face. "What's he done now?"

"Can I come in, Angelica?"

The woman sighs, steps back from the door.

The flat is sparsely—but neatly—furnished, with a sofa and an easy chair facing the blank square eye of a television set beside the fireplace.

"He's passed out at his brother's and his brother's climbing the walls for a fix," Bridget says.

"Is he back on the stuff?"

"I'm afraid so."

"The rat bastard told me he was done with all that."

"Angelica," Bridget says, "is Leon here? I have to take him back to his mother."

Angelica hesitates, says, "Wait here."

She goes into the back of the flat. She returns carrying a little boy with his arms around her neck like a little monkey. Another boy around the same age follows her, except brown-haired and the spitting image of Angelica, with a sharp nose and long chin.

"Hi Leon," Bridget says to the boy in Angelica's arms.

"Say hello to the lady," Angelica prompts.

"Hello."

Angelica transfers the boy to Bridget.

"What's he doing here?" Bridget asks.

"Ricky brought him over last night. He told me he was leaving Clara and moving in with me. He was going to take this little guy with him."

"He can't just decide that by himself, you know."

"Yeah. I was going to talk to him about it last night. But after dinner he told me he had to go see his brother and we'd talk when he got back. He never came back. I would have taken Leon back to Clara today, but . . . well . . ."

"She doesn't know about you."

"And I didn't want this to be how she finds out."

Angelica gives Leon a pat on the bottom. "And anyway," she says, "if Ricky's back on drugs, he's not coming back here. I told him the last time. So you may as well take the little guy home."

"Am I going home?" Leon asks in a little voice.

"You are, honey," Bridget says. "I'm taking you to your mommy."

To Angelica, Bridget says, "I might have to tell Clara about you after all."

Angelica nods, resigned to it. "I'm guessing Ricky won't be able to stay there, either, after this. Dumb shit. Excuse my French."

13

MALONE COLEMAN

"Hey Mamma."

Malone puts his arms around Bessie from behind at the kitchen table. "Hey, baby," she murmurs into his shoulder. "How you doing?"

"Hanging in."

She's not his birth mother, who drifted out of his life years before—but he calls Bessie "Mamma" because of all she's done to raise him.

He sits beside her at the table. Clarence is out grocery shopping.

"Talked to Mr. Rheinhardt?" she asks.

"I went down there but he was in a meeting. I filled out an application. Haven't heard anything."

"You won't for a few days. How's the other thing going?"

"I'm trying to get hold of the lawyer but I haven't heard anything from him either."

"Know who you might talk to?"

"Who?"

She purses her lips. "Coleman Young."

Coleman Young, a labor activist, currently executive secretary of the National Negro Labor Council, the group Malone was fired for belonging to. Young, too, has been fired from jobs and booted out of the labor movement because of his activism.

"We didn't get along all that well, me and him," Malone says.

"Don't have to tell me."

Back in 1928, when Clarence was new to the city and new to the Detroit Police Department, he had a dispute with Coleman Young's father. The elder Young was a federal security guard, so he was armed, as Clarence was. Clarence thought he himself should be the only colored man who could carry a gun in Detroit. One day they had a run-in that ended when Clarence punched the elder Young in the face and told him if he said anything he would beat his brains out with his club.

The elder Young filed a police report, and there was bad blood between him and Clarence ever since.

After Coleman Young learned Malone in the National Negro Labor Council was a sort of foster son of Clarence Brown, Young never spoke to him again.

Now, sitting with Bessie in her kitchen, Malone starts to wonder if Coleman Young himself was the source of the information that got Malone fired.

Would he turn on Malone because of a thirty-year-old beef? A beef he didn't even have with Malone himself, but with Clarence?

No, he decides. It's inconceivable Young would do such a thing.

"Always thought it was a bonehead thing to do," Bessie says, "beating on that man. Back then Clarence, he had him a temper. We was both still new to town, hearts still heavy from losing DeMarco. And Clarence drinking, too. Shouldn't have happened, shouldn't be a bone in their throats all this time."

"Still, you think I should go talk to him?"

"It's what *I'd* do. You do what you think is best. By the way," Bessie adds, "you got another phone call."

"From who?"

"Message under the phone."

Malone goes into the dining room. Under the telephone is a slip of paper. He reads the name and phone number in Clarence's scrawl. He goes back into the kitchen. Says, "What's *she* want?"

"Only one way to find out."

The National Negro Labor Council's Detroit chapter offices are on Grand River Avenue, one of the main arteries in Detroit. A pretty

Negro woman sits in the outer office.

She gives him a sweet smile. "How can I help you?"

"I'm Malone Coleman. I used to belong to this group a few years ago."

"Nadine Baker. Pleased to meet you."

"Likewise."

"What can I do for you, Mr. Coleman?"

"Is Mr. Young around?"

"Do you have an appointment?"

"No, sorry. I'm just hoping to catch him."

"Can I ask what this is in regards to?"

Before he can answer, he hears a murmur of men's voices behind a door. It swings open and Coleman Young stands there laughing and glad-handing another man. Malone recognizes the man as William Hood, reporting secretary of Local 600 of the UAW and president of the NNLC. The two look like they could be brothers, both handsome, light-skinned men with thin mustaches and full beaming faces.

Hood nods to Malone and steps around him. "Take care, Nadine," Hood says.

"Bye, Mr. Hood."

Coleman Young looks right through Malone without any recognition and asks Nadine, "Anything else on the schedule?"

"This young man asked to see you. His name is—"

"I know who he is," Young grumbles. Now he looks right at Malone. "What the hell you want?"

"Talk to you for a minute, Mr. Young?"

Young pauses in his doorway as if considering the question. He says, "Come in."

Young points to a chair on the other side of his desk. It's a functional office, with bare floors and a wall filled with photos of Young and other NNLC members at various protests—picketing at Sears, Roebuck, Big Bear Markets, Sam's Cut Rate, and Bank of the Commonwealth to get them to hire Negroes.

Young sits behind his desk. "Well?"

"First of all, Mr. Young, do you remember me from the Labor Council?"

"I sure as hell do."

"I know Clarence Brown and your father had problems back in the day, and I just want to say I'm sorry for it on behalf of Clarence."

"Would have been nice if the apology came from him."

"I can't do anything about that now, Mr. Young."

"Cut the 'Mr. Young' bullshit. Call me Coleman. How is the big motherfucker?"

"Getting on in years. Got some health issues, but otherwise he's good."

"What do you want with me?"

Malone tells him about getting fired at the VA because of his old connection with the National Negro Labor Council.

Young lights up a smoke. He offers the pack to Malone, who shakes his head no. "What do you want me to do about it?"

"I'm not asking you to do anything about it. But somebody must have passed my name on to the personnel office at the VA. I want to know who did it."

"You think *I* did it? What, because I'm still annoyed at Clarence Brown for busting up my old man?"

"No, sir. I don't think you'd do that to another working man. You didn't name names to HUAC, and you wouldn't now."

Coleman Young was legendary in the community for the way he stood up to the crackers who tried to make him feel small at the House Un-American Activities Committee hearing in 1952. He turned the tables on them and had them on the defensive the whole time he testified, even calling them on their disrespectful Southern pronunciation of "Negro" as "Niggra."

Young says, "Plenty of working men spit in my face along the way. Walter Reuther and his goddamn UAW, for one. There's a few I wouldn't mind getting back at. You're not one of them."

A few years ago, when Reuther was making a big deal about purging the labor movement of leftists, he kicked out Coleman Young along with hundreds of others. Now Reuther wanted nothing to do with the NNLC, and Coleman Young wanted nothing to do with Walter Reuther.

Malone says, "What I really want to know is, do you have any idea where that information about me came from? And who would want to do something to hurt me or the Labor Council?"

Young blows out a lungful of smoke. "Who the fuck *wouldn't* want to hurt the Council?"

"Anyway," Malone continues, "that's what I wanted to ask you. If you knew anything about who might have done this to me? Or to any of the other colored men getting fired because somebody called them out as security risks?"

"The guy who talked to you right after you got fired—he ever show you any ID?"

"No sir."

"I'm betting he was FBI. Same exact thing happened to me. They come up to you and threaten you unless you cooperate."

Young sits back. He takes another drag on his smoke. "But look. Let's assume he was FBI. You don't want to take them on unless you're ready to go balls to the wall against them. Even so, you got to be prepared to lose. Are you ready for that?"

"I'm ready to get some justice."

This makes Coleman Young throw back his head and roar with laughter. "Justice. Let me know when you find it."

Young's laughter fades to a chuckle. "Tell me something. You been keeping a low profile these last few years?"

"Yes sir."

"Well, you're right about one thing: *somebody* must have turned you in. There's one guy I know been causing trouble. He used to be in the Party, but he flipped. Now he's cooperating with the FBI, and whoever else'll listen to him. Naming people he knew in the movement. Name's Willy Hodges. You remember him?"

"I think I do. Big-time Communist back in the day, if he's the guy I'm remembering."

"That's him. Only the motherfucker's ratting out everybody and his mamma now."

Malone didn't know him well. He had seen him at meetings and maybe was introduced to him a couple times.

"Why would he rat me out?" Malone says.

"Ask him. Come on."

He stands up and Malone gets to his feet, too. He puts a hand on Malone's shoulder and guides him out to Nadine. "Sweetheart," Young says, "see if you can find Willy Hodges's address for Malone here."

"I appreciate this, Mr. Young."

"What I tell you about that 'Mr. Young' bullshit? Just remember this, Malone: whatever he did, whatever you want to do to him, it's not worth going to jail over. The sonsabitches find enough reasons to lock us up as it is."

Malone closes himself into the phone booth outside Coleman Young's building. He stands at the payphone and pulls a sheet of paper out of his wallet. Drops a dime and dials the number on it.

A woman's voice answers. "Good morning, Harper Hospital Maintenance. This is Harriet."

"Hi, this is Malone Coleman. I was in applying for a job?"

"Oh, yes, Malone. I remember. How are you?"

"Yeah, good. I'm just wondering if the Personnel office sent down my paperwork, and if Mr. Rheinhardt made any decisions about it."

"Hang on."

Malone hears the rubbing of her hand over the receiver as she mutes the phone. He can hear murmuring in the background. They seem to be having some kind of back-and-forth.

He hears the hand being removed and the squeal of chairs.

A man's voice comes on. "Larry Rheinhardt."

"Hello, Mr. Rheinhardt, I'm Malone Coleman."

"Hey, Malone. Sorry I couldn't get back to you. Yeah, listen, we have a job for you if you want it."

"I do."

"It's full-time, starting at the minimum wage."

A dollar an hour.

Malone expects this, but it's still disappointing. He made $1.30 an hour at the VA because he was there so long. Now at Harper he will have to start at the bottom again.

At least it's something until he gets his job back at the VA.

If he can get it back.

"What do you say, Malone?"

"Yes, sir. When can I start?"

"Our payroll period starts on Thursdays. How's next Thursday sound?"

Malone says it sounds great. He thanks Rheinhardt and hangs up. He stands in the phone booth for another few moments.

Now he has to do something even more unpleasant.

Duffield Elementary School in Black Bottom was built in the twenties as an "open-air" school, when it was thought tuberculosis could be cured by fresh air; the children with TB were isolated on the third floor, where the teachers could open all the windows year-round—which was good for kids with TB except for the children who died from pneumonia in the frigid winters.

The practice was stopped in the thirties, when they began to realize this was not the cure for TB.

Now Malone climbs the stairs into the building. He continues to the classroom at the end of the hall on the first floor. It's a second-grade classroom; all the low tables and chairs makes Malone feel like a giant in the land of little people. School is over for the day, so the classroom is empty except for the young Negro woman kneeling in front of a bulletin board on the back wall. She staples sheets of yellow construction paper onto the board, which has a green border of cut-out tulips.

From the back he can see she has filled out, as having children will do. He recognizes the set of her head, at an angle when she concentrates on something. He would bet her tongue sticks out the side of her mouth.

The old wooden floors creak, so she hears him come in. She says, "Hello," without turning her head away from the bulletin board.

Malone says, "Hey."

She stops, turns, gazes at him for a few moments.

She turns back to her work.

"Not even going to say hello to me?" Malone asks.

"I expected you to just call me back."

"I was surprised to get your call. Haven't seen you in a while. Thought it would be good to get back in touch."

"Oh yeah? You miss your sister, do you?"

"Yeah, I do."

She finishes stapling the yellow sheets to the bulletin board roughly, as though transferring her anger at Malone to the paper.

She stands, brushes her skirt off. Dusts her hands.

"Since when?" she asks. She glares at him.

That's what he remembers from their last meeting: the look sending daggers into his brain.

"Beverly, you gotta—"

"*I* gotta? You stop. Just stop."

She picks up her supplies and carries them up to the teacher's desk at the front of the room.

She and their brother Larry have never forgiven him for leaving the family when he went to live with Clarence and Bessie. He doesn't know if he's forgiven himself. He just knows if he hadn't left when he did, he would have started fighting back to his mother, and he was a big kid for his age. People thought he was mentally slow because he always seemed to be one step behind.

But when he left his mama's house—even though it meant leaving Beverly and Larry, and his aunt, who did her best to take care of them all in the frequent absences of his mother—and the beatings stopped, and the Browns started feeding him better, and he started thinking more clearly about things—he changed.

Besides, Beverly was being unfair; she knew he kept in touch with them as long as he could, until their mother forbade them from talking with him and then disappeared, moving with them across the state to Benton Harbor. Malone was out of touch with his brother and sister for years; it was them, not Malone, who decided they didn't want to stay in contact.

When Beverly moved back to Detroit to start teaching second grade at Duffield, where they had all gone to school, she got back in touch with Malone. Larry was away in the army, so Malone and Larry never saw each other.

Their reunion, Malone and Beverly's, was painful for them both. Though she was married with two children, Beverly still blamed Malone for moving out on them. She had grown mean, too—the sweet-tempered little girl he remembered developed a harsh, cutting tongue. He left their reunion without any desire to see her again.

Until now.

He had hoped she would have mellowed over time, with a family of her own. But no . . . here they are, picking it up right where they left off.

"Telling me what *I* gotta do," Beverly says.

"You know," he says, "you called me."

"I expected you to return my call. Not come out and see me."

"What did you want?"

"Tell you Mamma died."

"When?"

"Two weeks ago."

"You've been in touch with her?"

"I was."

"Where was she?"

"Here in town. She lived with me. She moved in when I moved back."

"So she's been here this whole time? And you're just telling me this now?"

"Why? Would you have come to see her? What would you say to her, after all this time?"

Malone doesn't know. He doesn't even know why this stirs him so now to find out. He hated his mother for years.

"How did she die?" he asks.

"Cancer."

"How long was she sick?"

She picks up more construction paper and returns to the bulletin board. "What difference does it make?"

Malone doesn't know the answer.

"When is her funeral?"

"It was last week."

Malone stands there, stunned. His sister starts cutting out flowers from different colors of construction paper.

Beverly turns around to glare at him. "If you got something to say to me, say it and go. Otherwise, just go."

He stands in her classroom, feeling stupid, feeling as though the rug has been pulled out from under him.

"I wish I'd known," he says.

She doesn't reply. He feels the waves of anger radiating from her even with her back turned to him.

He feels like crying. He leaves her to her bulletin board and goes outside. He wanders the remaining streets and empty lots where houses used to be in Black Bottom until finally he can't hold it in anymore.

He ducks inside an alley, where he leans his head against the brick back wall of a store that has yet to be leveled in the city's urban renewal program and sobs. A few men and women stop and ask if he's okay, and he nods. But he feels simultaneously bereft and rejected.

He knows he's not mourning for the loss of his mother in his life, since she's been no part of his life for over a decade. No, he's grieving, standing in Black Bottom surrounded by considerate people, for the death of the possibility that he and his mother would ever reconcile, that she would ever mean something more to him than a series of terrible, aching memories.

14

ANNA MILLER

Chester Glowaki always has breakfast before Anna arrives. He likes Rice Krispies, and he always cuts a banana into the bowl in careful, equal slices, then sits and enjoys a cigarette with his second cup of coffee. It's a daily ritual.

When she arrives from her morning cleaning jobs, Anna always keeps him company with a cup of coffee; she doesn't smoke, so he's on his own with that.

"Hey Chet," Anna says. "Dottie gone?"

"Yup. Long time ago."

Dottie has to walk up to 7 Mile to take the bus down to the Federal's store, so she's usually gone when Anna gets there.

"How about Roger?" Anna asks. "He still here?"

"He's still asleep. He had a late shift last night, and he's got another one tonight, so Dottie told me not to disturb him."

Exactly what Anna doesn't want to hear. It means Roger will be around at least until noon, when he goes into his first job of the day, at the Clark gas station on Conant. She hates the way he looks at her, like he knows something about her that she doesn't know. He gives her the creeps.

Anna tidies up the newspapers strewn around the living room and washes the breakfast dishes. Chester has another smoke and she pours herself a cup of coffee. She flips through the papers she has just collected.

She turns to the movie guide. "Hey, buddy," she says, "how about we take in a movie today?"

"Sure," Chester says. "What's playing?"

"Let's see . . . *One More Tomorrow's* at the Madison downtown."

"What's that about?"

Judging by the stars—Ann Sheridan and Dennis Morgan—and the ad in the paper, it's a romance. Definitely not for Chester.

"Here's one," she says. "*Bad Day at Black Rock.*"

"I saw an ad for it. That looks good!"

The display ad shows a man wearing a cowboy hat and holding a rifle. Good sign, Anna thinks. "It's at the Eastown." Van Dyke and Harper . . . not terribly far. They can walk to it.

Chester loves the movie. There's just enough violence to satisfy him without making him squeamish, and the theme of a stranger coming to town and unearthing a buried secret keeps him interested all the way through.

It's all he talks about on the way home. They stop at a Sander's lunch counter and she buys them lunches—two hot turkey sandwiches for sixty-five cents each plus two chocolate sodas for a quarter apiece.

When they head down Conant toward Nevada Street, they pass a hardware store. A half-dozen women, some pushing baby carriages, are walking back and forth on the sidewalk in front of the store.

They hold hand-lettered signs:

MY HOME IS MY CASTLE. I WILL DIE DEFENDING IT.
THE LORD SEPARATED THE RACES FOR A REASON.
KEEP OUR NEIGHBORHOOD SAFE FROM OUTSIDERS.

One woman passes out leaflets. Anna takes one. It identifies the owner of the store, Stanley Rudzewicz, and urges a boycott of his business until he corrects his moral error of selling to an invading Negro family. This is what Roger and Alois Swoboda were talking about, she realizes.

The leaflet goes on about the need to save their neighborhood from turning into a slum like Black Bottom, with Negro men hanging out on every streetcorner.

Chester stops and takes a leaflet, too. He reads it with his lips moving.

He looks at Anna with distress. "Somebody's invading our neighborhood?"

She takes the leaflet from him. "This is just a way for bad people to keep people they don't like from moving near them. It'll pass."

Anna tosses the leaflets into a wastebasket. "Come on. We have to get home."

They leave the demonstration behind and start walking down East Nevada toward Chester's home. Anna starts seeing hand-lettered signs tacked to light poles. One says, "Whites Only."

Another says, "KKK."

A third says, "Colored Stay Away."

She takes Chester by the arm and keeps him walking toward home.

"What are all these signs for?" Chester asks.

"What we were just talking about. Colored families want to move into your neighborhood. Your neighbors don't want them here."

"Roger says they're dirty. And mean."

"Roger doesn't even know any colored people, Chester. He doesn't know what he's talking about. They just want to live in places as nice as yours."

Chester tries to process this.

Anna can tell it's not going down easy. He idolizes Roger, who no doubt represents everything Chester wishes he had for himself: a wife, a family, his own home, a job, an independent life.

She guides him back to his sister's house, where she will start to make dinner.

"I don't understand," Chester says finally.

"Honestly, I'm not sure I do, either, bud."

"Where's that flyer?"

"I threw it away."

He frowns and looks like he's doing some serious thinking about it all. She wishes he would just let it go. But of course, that's not Chester.

15

JAKE LIEBERMAN

The Hudson plant on the corner of Jefferson Avenue and Conner Street in Detroit is a collection of twenty buildings.

The year before, Hudson Motors merged with Nash-Kelvinator to form the American Motors Corporation. As the clerk who hired him said, most of the auto manufacturing had been transferred to Kenosha, Wisconsin; a few of the other Hudson plants in Detroit had been converted to military contracting, but this particular plant was all but shut down. What activity there is here consists of trucks carrying supplies and equipment to the Kenosha and Milwaukee plants. The company also sells some of its equipment to other car makers, so that all goes out the door, too.

The night security detail is small, ten men who work out of the security office by the main entrance on Jefferson. Jake's shirt and pants are khaki; the pants have a dark blue piping down the side and the winter bomber jacket is almost threadbare, it has been reused so many times.

The Captain is in charge—"Call me Cap," he tells Jake—and the others are responsible for making the rounds of the plant. A heavy-set man with bleary, drink-besotted blue eyes, Cap smells like the cheap hooch he keeps in his drawer. He sits by the radio at the main desk; the guards have to report in every twenty minutes.

Of the other roving guards, only one is Negro. His name is Samuel Jones, an older man with a round, pleasant face and a soft voice.

One of the white men promises trouble, Jake can tell—a lean, ropey Southerner named Lee Dixon. As soon as roll call finishes on Jake's first night and the men disappear to their stations, Jake hears him say to one of the other white guards, "First they saddle us with the old nigger, and now they give us a kike. What the hell we sposed to do with them?"

Dixon says it loud enough for both Samuel and Jake to hear. Getting their goat is exactly what he wants.

Samuel and Jake exchange a glance. Neither one will give him the satisfaction of a response.

"Always like this?" Jake asks.

"Every damn night."

"How do you stand it?"

"Over my whole life in this city, somebody call me a nigger about ten times a day. Most days I can ignore it, just like the cold in winter and heat in summer. But it never go away, that anger, white man call you a nigger."

Jake has been called a kike before—the army was full of Jew-haters; if they didn't know he was a Jew by his looks, they did when they got a load of his name. He always saw red, a flash of anger clouding his vision, and only great self-control (and an awareness of always being outnumbered) kept him from lashing out.

He has the same feeling now with Dixon. Only Dixon turning away lets Jake keep his temper in check.

Jake shadows Samuel for the first week, until he learns the job. Jake keeps going with the thermos of coffee he makes before he gets to work. After a few hours it's cold, but the caffeine stays potent; it helps him to put one foot in front of the other. So does talking with Samuel.

All the guards carry a clipboard to record their rounds. They carry a little key they use to check in on recording devices at various points in their rounds to prove they were at certain locations at certain times.

Samuel is a good tutor; he's calm, thorough, and unflappable.

Jake finds out he's originally from Detroit, born in Black Bottom and educated through junior high, when he had to leave school to help his family after his father left. He's married with three kids. He knows he's had a good life in Detroit, but he also knows he would have had a better life if he had been white. It's a fact.

"Worked at the Rouge," he tells Jake, "before I came here."

"Local 600?"

"You got it."

Jake knows the local. Some of the members write for the *Correspondence* paper he lays out.

"Bunch of firebrands, for sure," Samuel says. "Still, we just wanted what's best for the working man. Nothing you can do about your life except live it the best you can," he tells Jake during one of their breaks when they're having coffee in the guard room. "Tomorrow is not promised us."

At the end of the week, sitting yawning in the locker room, changed back into his street clothes, Jake feels like he's walked for ten miles. He's going to have to get more comfortable work shoes for this job. He expects he'll get used to all the walking, but after his first week he's bushed.

Samuel has already gone home. He wants to see his kids before they head off to school.

Jake sits on the bench in front of his locker with his head in his hands, trying to muster the energy to go home, when Lee Dixon strolls into the locker room.

"Hey, Jewboy," he says.

Jake ignores him.

"Talking to you, kike."

Dixon's locker is on the other side of the bank of lockers from where Jake sits. Jake hears Dixon open his locker and change out of his uniform.

Dixon goes on about Jews, talking to himself so Jake can overhear.

"Myself," he says, "I don't like those people. Never did, never will. Never met a Jew I liked. Or trusted. Matter of fact, I hate those people worse than I hate niggers." Dixon steps around the locker bank so Jake can hear him.

"Oh, they're filthy, don't get me wrong. But a nigger won't try to screw you out of your last nickel. Least niggers know how to spend a buck. Not like those people. Hey, *Lieberman,* know why Jews get buried standing up? Because when they lay you down the change falls out of your pockets, and it pisses you off highly."

Dixon cackles at his own joke. He disappears around the lockers.

Jake hears the rustle of clothes. The locker door slams on the other side. Dixon laughs as he exits the locker room.

Jake can hear him squawking like a chicken as he walks down the hall.

His older brother hasn't left for work yet by the time Jake gets there. Saul Lieberman sits at the kitchen table, drinking his coffee. He raises a hand when Saul's wife Pauline leads Jake into the room.

"Yacob," Saul says, using Jake's Hebrew name.

Jake hugs his brother and sits across the table from him. Pauline pours Jake a cup of coffee.

"*Nu, boychik*?" Saul says. "You look beat."

"I'm just coming from work."

"Still on the graveyard shift for the *goyim*?"

"Yeah."

"How's that working out?"

"Meh."

"You should have stayed at the department store."

Typical of Saul, with his constant second-guessing. Jake turns to Pauline. "What's new?"

"Dicky got an audition for Auntie Dee," Pauline says.

"No kidding? That's great."

Auntie Dee hosts a kid's talent show on WXYZ television, Channel 7. Winners get either a six-pack of Faygo pop or a can of New Era potato chips.

"He's excited about it," Pauline says.

"I bet."

Dicky has a surprisingly mature baritone voice for a fifteen-year-old. When Jake hears him sing, he closes his eyes and imagines the kid's a middle-aged lounge lizard. Dicky wants to be a cantor. Saul's family lives on Santa Rosa Drive across Curtis Avenue from the Adas Shalom synagogue; they go to shul there every week, and occasionally the regular cantor lets Dicky lead the congregation.

Saul tries to get Jake to go, too, but Jake has no desire to attend services there.

Or anywhere. Whatever religious impulses he might have had, including belief in an all-powerful god, went up in smoke in the crematorium chimneys of Germany and Poland.

"Dicky and Alan are at school," Pauline says. "Shelley's home today. Not feeling good. Jake, did you have breakfast?"

"Of course he didn't have breakfast," Saul says. "You heard him say he just got off work."

"What can I make you? An egg? Some cereal? Farina?"

"I'm good, Pauline. I don't want to be any trouble."

"No trouble. I'll make a couple eggs. How do you want them?"

"Scrambled, if you insist."

"Scrambled eggs, coming up."

She gets to work at the counter, cracking eggs into a bowl and whisking them with a fork.

"Toast?" Pauline asks over her shoulder.

"I'd love some."

"Hey, don't treat him so good. He'll wanna come back," Saul says with his booming voice. Saul has their father's sense of humor: cruelty masquerading as wit.

"Sha," Pauline says. She melts butter in a frying pan and slices two thick pieces off the loaf of challah on the counter. She jams them into the toaster. She pours the egg mixture into the frying pan and starts to cook it, lifting the sides so the runny eggs flow underneath.

Even though he scorns the bourgeoise life, Jake yet envies the warm, comforting domesticity of his brother's home. Even when things were good with his ex-wife Carol, Jake never felt this sense of belonging to a particular place, in the company of particular people. When he got back from the war, Carol would complain because he was never "there" with her. And it was true, he wasn't; he was back in the camps the army liberated or on the European killing fields, wallowing in the inhumanity he was documenting.

"Ma?"

Shelley's voice from upstairs.

"Ma!"

"What?" Pauline shouts back. "I'm cooking."

"MA!"

Pauline mutters something under her breath. The house shakes as Pauline and Saul's fourteen-year-old daughter stomps down the stairs.

"Ma, I'm calling you." Shelley comes into the kitchen and sees Jake sitting at the table and squeals in glee. "Uncle Jake!"

She pads over to him in her slippers. She is a chubby young woman in a pair of boy's husky pajamas printed with cowboys. She wraps her arms around Jake from behind his chair.

"Hey sweetie," Jake says. "I hear you don't feel well?"

"I was sick to my stomach when I woke up but I'm feeling a lot better."

"She had a test at school today," Saul booms.

"I didn't have a test!"

"You want something to eat?" Pauline asks from the stove.

"Fried eggs."

"Sit at the table, you're feeling better."

The three members of Saul's family start talking at once. Whenever Jake's with them, it's always like this—loud and fast comments go from one to another like a supercharged game of telephone. The other two boys, Dicky and Alan, are just like this, too—fast talking, loud, everything *me-me-me*.

Pauline puts his plate of eggs in front of him. They are perfectly done, with steaming robust yellow curds and beside them on the plate the golden-brown challah toast gleaming with butter.

"All right," Saul says, "I gotta go to work. Make sure this *macher* pays for his breakfast."

He stands. Where Jake is tall and lean, Saul is shorter and bulkier, with large, thick hands. Again, like their father.

Maybe I'm not from this family after all, Jake thinks for the ten-thousandth time. Kidnapped from my original family and sold to George and Ruth so their real son Saul could have someone to torment.

Jake says, "Saulie—I'm going to need another car. You got anything on the lot I could afford?"

"That piece of shit finally give out on you?"

"Its days are numbered."

"Told you that a month ago."

Saul thinks for a minute. He owns a used car lot on Grand River. "Lemme see what we have in. I'll call you."

"No phone," Jake reminds him. "Leave a message with my landlady."

"No, you call me."

Saul gives Pauline (still cooking Shelley's breakfast at the stove) a kiss and a playful pat on the ass. He plants another kiss on the side of Shelley's face. "Be well," he tells his brother.

After breakfast, Jake heads toward James and Grace Boggs's building at Townsend and Agnes Streets in Detroit. He needs to drop the newest *Correspondence* mechanicals off.

On the way, he thinks about his family.

With their parents both dead, older brother Saul is the only family left. Saul has grown into their father in many ways; when he was young, Saul was handsome, almost pretty, like his boys Dickie and Alan, but as he's aged he's developed their father's thick, homely features and booming voice.

At least Saul doesn't share their father's shame over Jake.

Their father George ran Lieberman's Furniture downtown. When Jake took a left turn into radical politics, George advised against it; as a first-generation American Jew, and an independent capitalist, George felt their position in this Christian nation was too precarious to make the kind of noise Jake was making with his calls for refashioning society.

But when Jake's name appeared in the newspaper as a Communist on the HUAC list of witnesses, George was mortified. He said it was a blessing that Jake's mother Ruth died before she could be shamed by him. George refused to talk to or see Jake after that, and they never spoke again before his father keeled over with a heart attack in the store.

Jake's mother was more forgiving, though; Jake believes she would have understood. She thought more like Jake anyway, but never made a big deal about it in her own marriage to keep the peace.

It was through his mother, in fact, that Jake first started realizing the inequities in the world. As a young teenager, he worked in the stockroom at the furniture store. He saw how the Negro stockmen were insulted by the white warehouse manager, and when he mentioned it to his mother she schooled him about social injustice in

America, particularly in regards to Negroes; she was a Lithuanian immigrant and her own parents were socialists, having escaped the European pogroms before the First World War began. She never adjusted to the gap between this nation's stated ideals and its reality.

She passed that capacity for ideals—and disappointment—on to her younger son. Saul got their father's business acumen along with his booming voice.

Grace Boggs answers the door. A slender, gracious Asian-looking woman whose infectious smile hides a radical's steel spine, she asks if he wants to come in for coffee, but Jake tells her he must get home and hands her the mechanical boards.

"Have you heard the news about this?" she asks, holding up the boards.

He shakes his head. He isn't tied into any channels of communications anymore; he has turned his back on most of them.

"The different political factions have been having disputes," she says. "There's a rumor Raya will be leaving, along with half the members of the group."

Raya Dunayevskaya, a Marxist intellectual, one of the leaders of the *Correspondence* organization.

"If that happens," Grace continues, "the paper will probably stop for a while so the rest of us can figure out what its function should be."

"No, I haven't heard that."

"Well, I'm telling you now so it won't be a total surprise."

"Keep me posted?"

"Of course."

By the time he gets back to Corktown, Jake has no energy left for working on his art project.

He sleeps.

He doesn't call his brother until late afternoon.

"This is how bad you want a car?" Saul asks. "You forget to call?"

"I didn't forget. I was sleeping. I work nights, you know."

"I got one you might like. A Chevy. Not in the best shape, but it'll do. You want it, I'll save it for you."

"I'll be down there soon as I can."

His car surprises him by starting.

He gets it to his brother's used car lot and it promptly dies.

Saul tries to get it started. No luck.

"Not much I can do with this piece of shit for a trade-in," Saul mutters. He calls his mechanic Howard, under a car inside the garage.

Howard is a compact Negro in an oily jumpsuit. "Take a look at this, will you?" Saul says.

"She won't start?"

"Nope."

"See what I can do," Howard says. He brings out a portable charger and connects it to the battery. Nothing.

He opens the hood and sets to tinkering.

"If he can't get it started," Saul says, "nobody can."

They watch Howard fiddle with something deep inside the engine block. Satisfied, he slides behind the wheel and cranks the car. Still dead.

He shakes his head.

"I'll get it on the hoist, but I don't have much hope for it."

He puts the car in neutral and Saul and Jake help him push it into the garage.

"What do you have for me," Jake says.

Saul leads him out across the small apron of the lot crowded with used cars. Overhead, triangular pennants flap in the chill wind.

Saul points to an older model tan Chevrolet Bel Air.

"Does this even run?" Jake asks.

"Like a top, it runs. And the price is right."

"How much?"

Jake gets behind the wheel. The car stinks of cigarettes and stale automobile dirt. He turns the key and the car starts right up.

BLAT BLAT BLAT BLAT BLAT.

"I'd say it needs a muffler," Jake shouts above the din of the car.

Saul turns his wrist, miming turning the engine off. Jake silences the car.

"What?" Saul asks in the sudden quiet.

"How'm I going to take this on the road?" Jake asks. "It sounds like a cement mixer."

"I'm giving it to you," Saul says, as if that answers the question.

"I was going to pay for it."

Saul waves him away. "Pauline says I gotta give you a car on account I'm your brother. Here it is. Take it or leave it."

"Can you put a new muffler on it first?"

"Now it's starting to look like an investment. You want the car or not? I'm giving it to you, free for nothing, schmuck."

Jake stares at the vehicle. If he's stopped by the police for excessive noise, it won't be much of a bargain.

But it's better than nothing.

"I'll take it," Jake says. "Soon as I get some spare dough, I'll throw a new muffler on."

"That's the spirit, baby brother. Come on inside. Let's sign the papers, and get you back on the road."

16

BRIDGET MCMANUS

Three weeks after they found Joey Gallagher, Bridget McManus gets a call about another dead child.

This time it's a little girl in Chandler Park, a large green space on the east side of Detroit.

Bridget turns off Warren Avenue onto Connor Street and follows Chandler Park Drive around to where cars are already parked—Detroit police, Wayne County Sheriff, and state police. Police tape ropes off a site around a shallow drainage basin.

Ed Hauser stands beside the site.

Of all the detectives in all the world to be on this case, she thinks.

Hauser nods at her. "This is a rough one," he warns.

Bridget looks over the scene. A small body lies on a grimy army blanket at the bottom of the basin. A little girl, her face white in the flashlights shined on her. Her eyes are closed. A breeze ruffles her blonde hair. She wears a bloody torn undershirt, shoes, and socks. Scattered around the site are the rest of her clothes: pants, gloves, a snowsuit ripped into shreds, a bloody red-and-blue babushka.

Plus her school supplies. A notepad, a plastic pencil case, a box of crayons, the mundane articles obscene in their connection to what happened to their owner.

"It's her," Hauser says.

"No doubt," Bridget agrees. "Looks like she's been here a couple days."

She recognizes the girl's face from the photograph sent to all the area police agencies. Barbara Nicholson, seven-years-old. Missing since last week, when she disappeared walking home from her Catholic school near her house.

A second dead child. Unlike Joey Gallagher, there's no evidence of a head shot.

"Who found her?" Bridget asks.

Hauser nods toward a man sitting in a Detroit police squad car. "A bum. Claims he was looking for a place to sack out and saw her."

"You talk to him?"

"Yeah. We'll bring him in, but I don't think he's good for it."

The coroner's assistant standing nearby says, "Can we take her?"

Hauser asks Bridget, "Anything else you need to see?"

Bridget looks around. She sees a technician making a plaster cast of tire tracks ten or so yards from the body.

She shakes her head. She's seen enough. Too much. "You can take her. What's the coroner say?"

"They'll do the post-mortem as soon as they can. Meanwhile, she's got strangulation marks around her throat, a slew of stab wounds, and her head looks staved in by something round. Maybe a rock."

"Jesus," Bridget murmurs.

"I don't think Jesus had much to do with this one."

The uniformed Detroit cops canvas the area. Bridget ignores the rule against policewomen in the Women's Division investigating crimes without a male officer. She particularly doesn't want to be in Hauser's company.

She walks around the park, getting a feel for the location. She drives down Conner Street toward Jefferson. She goes slowly, looking for something—anything—helpful. At this time of night, stores are closed and few walkers are out.

She passes Mack Avenue and turns left on Charlevoix Street, and drives slowly up and down the residential streets, shining her car spotlight into the shadows and dark bushes.

She approaches the Hudson complex, mostly dark and quiet. No more working around the clock . . . She has heard the rumors: this plant will be the next one to close.

She sees a lone figure standing outside the guard's kiosk at the Jefferson entrance. A man, slender, smoking, leaning back against the small structure. He's in a security guard outfit, khaki jacket and pants with blue piping down the leg.

Bridget pulls up to the kiosk. The guy flips the smoke away in a sparking arc and ducks back inside the kiosk.

Bridget stops the car. Rolls down the window. "Evening."

The guy nods.

She shows him her badge, tells him her name. "There was some trouble in the park up the road earlier tonight. Young girl was attacked. Wondering if you saw or heard anything about it?"

The guy shakes his head.

Bridget gives him the eye, says, "How about you pull out some ID real quick and let me take a look at it."

It's not a request.

Slowly, as though he's doing her the biggest favor in the history of favors, the guy reaches into his pants pocket and extracts his wallet. Hands it over.

Bridget stares at his driver's license. Leeland Dixon. 5'10", 160 pounds. Address on the far west side.

She hands it back. "How long you been on the gate tonight?"

"I come on at eleven. Been here ever since."

It's quarter past one now.

"So what happened?" he asks.

"We found the body of a little girl, up the street in Chandler Park. Seen anybody suspicious hanging around the plant?"

Bridget sees something forming behind Dixon's eyes. He's a stupid guy who thinks he's smart; she can tell by the dull gleam in his eye.

"Now you mention it," he says, "one of the guys on the night shift came on duty tonight looking the worse for wear. Like he's in a fight or something. Blood everywhere and whatnot. Got himself cleaned up before he started his shift. Not saying he had nothing to do with this little girl, but . . . might be worth looking into."

"What's his name?"

"Jake Lieberman. A yid. You know how those people are. What they do with Christian children. Just saying, you know? I think he's working in the supply hanger tonight. You want, I'll get him for you."

"I'll find him. Just point me in the right direction."

Two guards are in the supply hanger. One is a tall Negro and the other a slightly shorter white man. Based on the name Dixon gave him, Bridget guesses the white guy is the one she's looking for.

She shows her DPD buzzer and identifies herself. "Mr. Lieberman?"

"Yeah?"

"Talk to you for a minute?"

"What about?"

"Would you come with me?"

Bridget finds an empty office where she can talk with Jake Lieberman alone.

"Walk me through what's happened on your shift tonight," she says.

"I clocked in at 10:58. I just got hired, so I'm shadowing Sam during the week. That's my partner, Sam Jones."

"You've been in the supply hanger all night?"

"Pretty much."

Bridget looks Lieberman over. He has dark good looks, thick black hair combed back, thick black mustache. Sad eyes, turned down at the outer edges.

His rumpled uniform shows no signs of a struggle. "You got another uniform in your locker?"

"Nope. This is the only one. I take it home on my day off to wash it."

"What were you doing before you clocked in tonight?"

"I was home."

"All day?"

"Yeah."

"Doing what?"

"Sleeping, mostly. Hanging around the flat the rest of the time."

"Anybody see you?"

"No. Well, maybe my landlady heard me puttering around."

"You live by yourself?"

"Yeah."

"How about the past few days. Can you account for your whereabouts?"

"At night I've been here. During the days . . .I was by myself for most of the time, too."

"You're a security guard," she says. "Do you carry a firearm?"

"No. There's a shotgun in the cupboard in the main office for emergencies, but nobody else is supposed to be armed."

"Do you own a weapon yourself?"

"No. I saw enough of guns during the war."

"You were in combat?"

"I was a photographer for *Stars and Stripes*. I saw the results of combat. That was enough for me."

"How about you show me your locker, okay, Jake?"

"What's this all about? Somebody say I did something?"

"Just routine."

"Doesn't sound routine to me."

"The faster you show me your locker, the faster I'm out of your hair."

Bridget follows Lieberman through the quiet halls to the guard's locker room. When Jake opens his locker, she steps in to rifle through his stuff.

The locker contains only Lieberman's street clothes, and they don't show any signs of the struggle somebody would have had with little Barbara Nicholson, or the description of the clothes the other worker mentioned. Considering how the girl's body looked, her killer's clothes would have been filled with blood, brain matter, rips.

Bridget closes the locker. "Okay. How about you write down your address and phone number for me and I'll leave you in peace."

"I still don't get what this is all about."

"Like I said, just routine elimination procedure. Nothing at all to worry about."

"Yeah, but elimination for what?"

"A little girl's body was found up in Chandler Park tonight. We're trying to eliminate suspects."

"I'm a suspect? You think I had something to do with it?"

"If you're telling me the truth, we're copacetic here, Jake. Nothing to worry about."

She gives him her notebook and he writes down his address. "No phone," he says.

"You're on Leverette. Corktown?"

He nods.

"My sister and brother-in-law live on Church."

"Street right behind me."

"Small world. All right, Jake." She gives him her business card with her division's phone number. "You hear anything might be useful, give me a call?"

"How'd she die, the little girl?"

"I can't really talk about it. Have a good night, okay?"

She finds her way back to where she left her car. She drives out past the guard shack. Lee Dixon watches her go without acknowledgement. He was just trying to get Lieberman in hot water.

"Asshole," she mutters as she pulls out onto Connor.

17

MALONE COLEMAN

As he suspected would happen, Malone gets assigned to the 11 pm – 7 am shift on the custodial staff at Harper Hospital. Most of the workers in the overnight shift of the department are new to the hospital. The old-timers, like Bessie Brown, have graduated by virtue of their seniority to the day or afternoon shifts.

He meets the other workers on the late shift when they stand in line at the timeclock in the basement to punch in and punch out. They're a pleasant, even cheerful group.

In general, he finds the work isn't hard. It's familiar from the VA—he mops floors, he runs floor polishers in hallways, he sterilizes operating rooms and rooms where patients have died or otherwise caused messes, and he empties waste baskets and the mayonnaise jars where the nurses dispose of used needles.

The advantage of working nights is that his days are free to search for who gave him up to the VA. Now that he's working, it doesn't have quite the same urgency. But he used to see how dogged Clarence Brown was when he was on a case, and some of that has rubbed off on Malone.

On one of his first mornings off from the Hospital, Malone knocks on the door of an apartment at 110 East Hancock, the address he got from Coleman Young's secretary. It's in a nondescript building around the corner from the soaring Gothic Cathedral Church of St. Paul on Woodward Avenue.

No response to his knock.

He knocks harder.

The door swings open. A man stares groggily back at him. He's tall but rail-thin, dark-skinned with deep parentheses at the sides of his mouth and a fringe of white hair sticking up crazily around his head. He looks to be in his 60s. He's in a soiled sleeveless tee that bulges over his belly and the zipper in his pants is down.

"Yeah?"

"Willy Hodges?"

"Who want him?"

"Are you Willy Hodges?"

"Fuck off."

The guy goes to close the door.

Malone puts his shoulder behind it and muscles the old man backwards. It doesn't take much; he can't weigh more than a hundred pounds.

"I want to talk to you," Jake says.

"Get out my house! Gloria!"

"Do you recognize me?"

Hodges peers at him through clouded eyes. He takes a long time, as though seriously trying to place him.

Finally he shakes his head. "Never seen you before."

"I'm wondering why you're talking about me."

"Talking about you? I don't even know you."

"I'm Malone Coleman. Ring a bell?"

"Don't know no Malone Coleman."

"Have you been talking about me to anybody? Maybe the FBI?"

"Boy, I don't know what you talking about. Get out my house." He shouts to the inside of the apartment: "Gloria!"

A Negro woman with long gray hair comes out from the rear.

Gloria, Malone presumes.

Pointing a pistol at him.

It's small caliber, maybe a .22, but at this range it could do some damage.

"Hold it right there," she says.

Malone puts his hands up and backs away. He does not want to be shot over this.

Or over anything, come to think of it.

The woman is short and round in a white terrycloth bathrobe. To Hodges, she says, "What's going on here?"

"This here boy push his way in and steady asking dumb-ass questions."

"Look," Malone says, "let's start again. I'm Malone Coleman. I'm looking for Willy Hodges. That you?"

"None your goddamn business."

"What if it is?" Gloria asks.

"I heard Willy Hodges might have given my name up to somebody for something that got me fired from my job."

"I ain't never heard your name until thirty seconds ago," the man says.

"All right," Gloria says. She drops her gun into her bathrobe pocket. "Let's all just go in the kitchen and sort this out. Come on."

Hodges drops into a chair by the stove. Malone sits across from him and the woman sits in between them.

To Malone, she says, "Spill it."

"Somebody told the VA I was in this group and I got fired because of it."

"What group?" Gloria asks.

"The National Negro Labor Council."

The man scoffs.

"Coleman Young said this guy might know something about it," Malone goes on. "I want to know if it's true."

"Coleman Young!" the guy says.

Gloria says, "You saw Coleman Young?"

"Yes ma'am."

"When?"

"A few days ago.

"And he told you Willy gave your name to somebody in the VA?"

"He said Willy used to be a Red, but he flipped and now he's naming names all over the place. Somebody told the VA about my past. I put two and two together."

"Okay," Gloria says, "Willy doesn't work for the FBI anymore. He only works with the Immigration Department on naturalization and deportation cases."

"But you're the Willy Hodges who used to be a Communist?" Malone asks.

"I am. I turned against the Party after what the Rosenbergs did."

Ethel and Julius Rosenberg, the husband and wife executed in 1953 for sharing atomic secrets with the Soviets.

"Saw the error of my ways. Been trying to make amends ever since."

"By turning people over to be deported?"

"By standing up for the American way."

"Defending a system that won't even grant you your basic rights as a citizen?"

"Things'll change one day," Hodges says. "You'll see. In the meantime, our system's the best thing that ever happened to mankind."

Malone has to laugh at this. Hearing a Negro—particularly this Negro—defend the system that keeps his race down is ludicrous.

"Well," Malone says, "I won't sit here and debate it with you."

"Son, I never heard of you before you came to my door. That's the truth. The National Negro Labor Council—that where you ran into Coleman Young? He used to run it or something, didn't he?"

"Still does."

"Old Coleman. What do you think of him?"

"Seems to be sincere about advancing the race."

"Old Coleman never been sincere about advancing nothing except his own self."

Malone doesn't want to argue with this turncoat. "Be that as it may, he put me onto you."

"Oh, I see. It's okay for him to name *my* name?"

Malone gets up to leave.

"I never trusted him," Hodges says. He follows Malone. "And if I was you, I wouldn't trust him either."

Malone gets to the door.

"But lookie here, when you see him again," Hodges says, "ask him about Frank Carmody."

Hodges pushes him out and shuts the door in his face before Malone can ask who that is.

Back at the Barlow Apartments, Lucille Reid is sitting on the front steps with a young man. She waves as Malone approaches.

"Hey," he says.

"I want to invite you somewhere."

Malone looks at the young man beside her.

"This is my friend. Melvin Kennedy, Malone Coleman."

Melvin stands to shake his hand. He's tall and rangy, athletic, light-skinned, hair cut short and natural, handsome. He wears khaki pants and a white button-down collared shirt. He reaches out and gives Malone's hand a bone-crushing shake.

"How'd you find me?" Malone asks.

"I asked the Registrar at Arts and Crafts."

"Resourceful."

"I have my ways."

"I live in the basement," he says. "It's not really in any shape for company, or I'd invite you in."

"That's okay. Remember I told you my father's on the board of the Urban League? I wondered if you wanted to meet him."

"Sure."

"He's going to be at a community meeting, and I thought you'd like to go. It's an interesting meeting, too. You might like it."

"What's it about?"

"Convincing whites in Detroit to reject segregated housing."

"Lord have mercy."

"I know. It's run by the Coordinating Council on Human Relations. They go around to different community groups and talk to the white homeowners. They tell them how racial change is inevitable, and it's to the whites' advantage to do whatever they can to work for safe and stable communities for everybody. What do you say?"

"Sure. Why not?"

The meeting is at the Mayflower Congregational Church on Curtis in northwest Detroit. Melvin drives Lucille and Malone in his Ford Fairlane. It's a new car, from the smell of it.

White men and women occupy several dozen folding chairs in the church assembly hall in the basement. At a table at the front of the hall are three Negro men and two white men. Lucille, Melvin, and Malone sit in the back of the room.

Lucille leans into Malone. He can smell the floral fragrance of her perfume. "That's my father, Harold Reid, on the left. Beside him, that's Sidney Walters, from the Coordinating Council on Human Relations. The skinny guy next to him is James Boggs. He's a community activist. The two white men are Arlie Porter, he's the pastor of the Mayflower, and Rabbi Segal, he's from Adas Shalom synagogue next door."

"How do you know these guys?"

"They're all active in the Urban League and interfaith projects. They've all been to our house."

Malone knows James Boggs—or has heard of him, at least. He works at the Chrysler Assembly plant on Jefferson Avenue in Detroit, a job he got—like Malone's job in the Ford Rouge plant—thanks to the war effort; like Malone, indeed like many Negro men in Detroit, finding steady work was hard until the war made it necessary to hire Negroes and women.

Rev. Porter gets up and calls the meeting to order. He welcomes everyone, and asks Rabbi Segal to give an opening benediction.

Lucille leans in again. "Some of the people here are Jewish," she whispers. "This is turning into a big Jewish area. The few colored people who moved in around here moved into streets where lots of Jews live."

"Have the Jews been resistant?"

"Not as much as the Catholics and Protestants. Daddy said it's because Jews run into a lot of prejudice themselves, so they know what it feels like to be hated. Plus they're used to moving around. The others are more tied to their parishes."

Rabbi Segal gets up and opens the meeting with a relatively nonsectarian prayer. He asks for God's blessing on what they are going to do today, but he doesn't mention Jesus.

Rev. Porter turns things over to Sidney Walters. "We have to get away from the idea that Negroes moving into a neighborhood will inevitably cause housing values to drop," Walters says. "It's not true. If we approach the inevitable changes with intelligence and courage, we can maintain safe, stable, and livable communities for everyone."

He also talks about all the instances of violence that are occurring around the city as white neighbors try to keep out Negroes who want to move in. "You won't read about them in the white papers," Walters says. "But they're happening more and more often."

When it's his turn, Lucille's father talks about how the Negroes moving into the houses in this area are either professionals or else stable members of the working class who can afford their homes. Like everybody else, they just want a safe neighborhood for their families.

James Boggs talks about how unions used to be the catalyst for change, but aren't anymore. "The unions used to be the prime mover for social change in this country. It was true in the thirties, but not anymore. Now the primary mover for social change is going to be the Negro's struggle for human rights in every area of society, but most especially for equality in the workplace and in housing."

Lucille leans in again. "Boggs is a Marxist. He's a factory worker and a really smart thinker about social issues."

There's more discussion between the five men at the front of the room as they try to convince the assembled group of the benefits—indeed, necessity—of open housing in the City of Detroit.

Finally, Rev. Porter gets up. "Before we open the floor for questions, I just want to say one thing."

He pauses and looks around the room. He is a portly, intense man. A pair of jug ears soften his stern look.

"And I say this to both my fellow Christians and our Jewish friends," he continues. "The Old Testament talks about the prophetic witness to do justice and love mercy. The witness of the New Testament is that of God entering into the world and not standing outside and preaching. The church has to do the same thing. I know I speak for my friend Rabbi Segal when I say we have a duty to do everything we can to promote fair housing through sessions like this one."

The question-and-answer period starts, and everyone in the audience talks at once. Rev. Porter quiets the crowd. "Please, raise your hands and be recognized. Just like in school. You'll all have a chance to talk."

The group settles down and the five men at the front of the room respond to all the questions.

They have no doubt heard many of them before: questions about safety ("I heard Negro men spend all day hanging around streetcorners"), crime ("I heard the numbers of robberies and assaults always go up when 'those people' move in"), housing values ("Why do you say housing values will remain steady when it's common knowledge they drop?").

After an hour and a half, the questions peter out and the meeting breaks up. Notably less tension fills the air than before the meeting started.

"Come on," Lucille says to Malone. "Meet my dad."

Malone follows her to the front of the room. They wait their turns; men and women from the audience are lined up to talk to the speakers.

When their turns come, Lucille says, "Daddy, I'd like you to meet my friend, Malone Coleman. Malone, my daddy, Harold Reid."

Harold is tall, distinguished in a charcoal suit. "Pleased to meet you, young man. Thank you for coming."

"I enjoyed it very much."

"Daddy," Lucille says, "Malone's the one I was telling you about. He got fired because of some bogus 'security' problem."

"Oh yes," Harold Reid says. "Do you have an attorney?"

"I'm trying to get in touch with Charles Cornish. I hear he's helping other colored men get their jobs back."

"He's good," the older man says. "If you have trouble reaching him, give me a call."

He hands Malone a business card.

```
Harold R. Reid, Esquire, Attorney-at-Law.
```

A line forms behind them to speak with Harold, so he says, "Lucy, you're coming with me after?"

"I am. I'll wait for you."

There's a line in front of James Boggs, too. Malone wants to say hello to him, but it looks like he's going to be tied up for a while.

James happens to look over the shoulder of the woman he speaks with and catches Malone's eye. He nods.

Malone nods back.

At least they've made contact.

In front of the church, Malone says, "Thanks for inviting me to this."

"I thought you'd like it. And I wanted you to meet my father. And my friend."

She reaches out a hand. "Goodbye for now."

Malone shakes it. "Goodbye."

Melvin says, "Nice to meet you, Malone." A wicked glint in Melvin's eye says, *Ha ha, Lucille's mine. Eat your heart out.*

She and Melvin go back inside the church and Malone starts toward Livernois to catch a bus downtown for his shift at the hospital.

18

ANNA MILLER

In the weeks following Fred Stenhagen's death, Anna checks in with Selma every day.

Sometimes Anna has dinner with Selma—usually canned spaghetti—and sometimes she just has a cup of tea with the older woman when Anna gets home from work. Selma spends their time together crying or else talking about how overwhelmed she feels by what she has to do by herself without Fred.

The siblings didn't have much money, but it was Fred who took care of the bills. Anna does what she can to help Selma get the few household accounts in order; Fred, it turns out, wasn't paying the bills for the last few months before he died.

Anna helps Selma with phone calls to the creditors, begging them not to turn off the electricity and gas, and Anna makes sure the refrigerator and cupboard have food. Anna even cooks meals for Selma, who was the beneficiary of Fred's cooking skills as well as his financial acumen. In her distress, Selma claims she can't eat anything more than eggs, so Anna makes her eggs all the ways she knows how: scrambled, fried, boiled, shirred, and poached.

As Anna spends more time with her, Selma's complaining eases and she starts opening up about her life—which, it turns out, is much more interesting than Anna would have expected.

Tonight, for example, over tea, Selma sits on the couch with Anna in their living room and hauls a cardboard box onto her knee. The box contains photos, not only snapshots but 8x10s, of her with movie stars and local celebrities. Here is Selma standing next to local television celebrity Bill Kennedy; there are Fess Parker and Buddy Ebsen dressed as Davy Crockett and his sidekick George Russell towering over Selma in the lobby of a movie theatre; here standing beside Selma are Jeff Morrow, Mamie Van Doren, a darkly handsome young man in a Marine uniform whom Anna doesn't recognize; and Larry, Moe, and Joe Besser of the 3 Stooges . . .

Selma's elegance in the photos surprises Anna. Years ago, dressed in ladies' suits that emphasized her long legs and trim shape, she was so unlike today's shabby, frumpy woman.

"You're probably wondering," Selma says in her ragged, wheezy voice, "what happened?"

Anna nods. Indeed.

Selma tells Anna she left her job as a seat cover finisher at Packard because she couldn't stand the stress or physical demands of factory work anymore. She became an assistant manager of the Broadway Capitol Theatre, one of the movie palaces downtown off Grand Circus Park and Woodward. She initially applied for a job as a secretary with the company that runs the show, but there were no secretarial openings. They did have a sudden opening for an assistant manager at the theatre because the young man who held the job quit. It was mostly paperwork, so the company asked Selma if she'd be interested and she accepted at once.

Her sole condition, she let them know, was that she could only work during the day, opening up at ten in the morning for the matinees and leaving at five, when the theatre manager, a tough-looking Greek who also appeared in some photos, came in and worked until after the last movie ended and the place closed.

She handled the paperwork and the books for the show—she learned how to do the staff scheduling, the payroll, the weekly profit/loss statements for the theatre owner and the distributors of the films the theatre showed. She also was in charge of ordering for the snack counter and supplies, and solving any other problems that arose running the theatre—at least during the day.

"It ended when I had my heart attack," Selma says. "Instead of giving me any help, they just let me go. And while I was recuperating from the heart attack, I had a stroke. Then my brother had a stroke, and we lost our little house to the bank. This place was all we could afford. We get a little social security, and between the two of us we've been able to scrape by."

Selma runs her fingers over the photos of herself dressed up in better times. "I don't know what I'm going to do now."

She begins to cry again, it seems to Anna as much for the loss of her former life as from the loss of her brother.

"If I didn't have these pictures," she gets out through a twisted face, "who would believe my life?"

Anna spends as much time with Selma as she can. She's glad to be able to help Selma deal with the grief she feels, and she's fascinated by Selma's backstory. But Anna doesn't want this to become her own life for the rest of the time she lives in this building.

Mostly, Anna doesn't want her life to turn into Selma's . . . alone at the end, penniless, dependent on the kindness of strangers for almost everything.

Sitting watching the older woman, Anna can too easily imagine herself in Selma's position, even down to the boxes and boxes of her photographs. Except they won't be photographs of her and her family and her growing-up (none of them exist, and she wouldn't want them anyway), they will be photographs Anna took of the other people and places she turned to in order to escape from the distress of her own life.

Anna repacks the box with Selma's photos and places it on the coffee table in front of the couch.

"Leaving already?" Selma says.

"Yeah. Sorry. I'm going out tonight, but I'll be back later."

"Promise?"

"Promise."

Upstairs in her attic room, Anna changes out of the clothes she wore at work at the Kaczmarek house that day. She doesn't have many good clothes, but she puts on a white cotton blouse and a pair of slate gray slacks. She doesn't wear makeup as a rule, but tonight she wears eyeliner. She sees herself in the mirror and thinks, *who are you trying to kid?* when there's a knock on the door.

Without waiting for her to open it, the door swings open and

Marianne Walker enters. Behind her is a slight woman in a camel-hued sweater and tartan skirt. She looks to be in her thirties, around the same age as Marianne and Anna.

"Hey, honey," Marianne says. "What's shaking?"

She gives Anna a kiss on the cheek, folds her in a hug. "Meet my friend Edie. This is Anna. The one I was telling you about."

Edie raises a hand in greeting.

"Almost ready?"

"Just about."

Anna collects her purse while Edie walks around looking at the drying photos clothes-pinned to strings along the walls.

Just make yourself at home, Anna thinks. She has a frisson of annoyance at someone looking at her photos without asking permission.

"Did you take these?" Edie asks.

"I did," says Anna.

"Cool stuff."

"Thanks."

Edie takes her time with each photo. They are Anna's shots of the homes around Riopelle. She had also walked up Conant and taken some shots of the stores—DeCamillo's Bakery, the Rexall Drugstore, and dry cleaners—and a few of the pedestrians she passed.

She has a lot of photos of Chester, too. Not handsome, exactly, but he has an interesting face . . . it's slightly lopsided from his condition, which throws the symmetry of his features off, like a cubist portrait.

"Wow," Edie says, "I love these. I love the houses, but I especially love these faces. Where did you take them?"

"I take care of this guy," she says, pointing to Chester. "The rest are photos from his neighborhood."

Edie looks closely at Chester's photos. "What's the matter with him?"

"He's slow. He's a great guy."

"I believe it. I love his face." She turns to appraise Anna. "You really captured his personality."

Anna feels herself blushing. "Thanks. Are you an artist?"

Edie and Marianne exchange a smirking glance, as though they know something Anna doesn't.

"Not really. I know a lot of artists, though." Edie looks away with a wistful smile.

Anna doesn't get the significance of this, but Edie likes her photographs and that's all that matters. Anna doesn't show them to anyone, so she gets no reactions to them, let alone the appreciation this woman seems to have.

"Get your coat," Marianne says with a wink. "Tonight, we're going to have a 'rendezvous with destiny.'"

Edie gets in the back seat with Anna in the front. Marianne drives her pre-war Chevy sedan fast and carelessly; Anna wishes she were in the back seat with Edie; she has to close her eyes as Marianne runs stop signs and red lights and weaves crazily around the traffic on the downtown streets until she gets to Jefferson Avenue, where she heads east.

Just after Jefferson turns into Lake Shore Road in Grosse Pointe, Marianne takes a left and drives a few blocks down.

She pulls up in front of a large faux-chateau with turrets and three levels. "Who lives here?" Anna asks.

"My friend Margaret," Edie says. "Her father's the radio announcer for the Tigers."

Standing by the front door, like a sentry, a young man in a black French beret holds onto a pair of sconces on the wall. He seems to be trying to steer them, like the helm of a ship. "Hard about!" he calls.

The front hall leads onto a massive sunken living room packed with people. They're a mixture of all sorts: men in suits and women in tight-fitting cocktail dresses; people who could be college or even high school students, standing or sitting on the floor in their blue jeans; men and women in white shirts and khaki pants and saddle shoes. Whites and Negroes mix in conversation and laughter.

At the far end of the living room, a woman with long white hair plays classical music at a grand piano. The music vies with people in a corner sitting around a young man playing a different song on bongo drums, and another group in another corner singing a folk song about the Erie Canal while a young woman strums a guitar.

A young woman comes up and asks Edie if she's heard from Jack.

Anna leaned close to Marianne. "Who's Jack?" she asks.

Marianne says, "You never heard of Jack Kerouac?"

"Is he famous or something?"

"Not yet. He will be. He's a writer. He's been trying to get his books published, but he hasn't had much success so far."

"How does she know him?"

"They were married. Haven't you ever heard of the Beats? You know, Allen Ginsberg and them?"

"Yeah, I've heard of them."

"Well, Jack is one of the original Beats. He lived in Detroit for a while with Edie when they were married."

"Are you from Detroit?" Anna asks Edie.

"Yup. I grew up not far from here. Until I moved away."

"Then where did you go?"

"New York City. I moved there when I was a teenager. I wanted to live a great, free life as an artist in New York. I fell in with an artistic crowd up at Columbia. That's where I met Jack. Eventually it all fell to me to earn a living, so . . . there went my dreams of being an artist."

"Sorry to hear it," Anna says.

"Don't be. The life I wound up living was exciting enough."

"Why did you come back?"

"I came back when Jack and I separated. We weren't married long. At the time, I didn't think we had any kind of future together. Excuse me."

Edie turns away from this topic and fades into the crowd. "How do you know her?" Anna asks Marianne.

"When Jack lived in Detroit, he worked for Fruehauf Trailer Company. My ex-husband used to work there. We met them and spent some time with them until Jack took off. I stay in touch with Edie. I like her."

Anna and Marianne are old friends, too. They met in classes they took together at the Society of Arts and Crafts. They have become close—or as close as they could be given Anna's isolation. Marianne continually tries to get Anna out of the house. Occasionally Anna says yes, like she did tonight, but most often she refuses; she doesn't like to appear in public spaces without her camera to hide behind.

Now Marianne, too, melts into the crowd, leaving Anna alone.

Someone hands her a bottle of Stroh's. She wanders through the downstairs. The rooms go on and on—a dining room with a table as large as her entire attic apartment; a library lined floor to ceiling with books; an enclosed back porch in dark shadows where couples (men and women, men and men, women and women) are draped across each piece of furniture and smooching madly, and a sitting room where a poet holds forth to a half-dozen listeners, reciting a poem from memory in a slow, dream-like chant.

She recognizes the Negro artists she saw at the Sarkisian exhibit at Arts and Crafts. They don't see her; everyone in the house talks, it seems, and no one listens.

In a music room with another overly-large grand piano, a man and a woman—actors, she would guess—are shouting lines back and forth at each other as fast as possible. It sounds Shakespearean, but Anna doesn't know which play.

Everyone has a glass of amber liquid or a beer bottle in hand, and everyone is smoking cigarettes or pipes or cigars; some are smoking skunky-smelling marijuana cigarettes they share with those standing around them.

Anna floats, tapping into clusters of people here and there, trying to listen to what they are saying but generally feeling invisible, with no one acknowledging her, and no one including her in their conversations, which, in any event, are about people she doesn't know and topics she doesn't recognize.

She stands listening to two men with beards argue about a book she has never heard of when she feels a presence gather beside her.

Edie. She leans close to Anna's ear. "Having fun?"

Anna doesn't want to admit she isn't, but she can't say she is. She hates parties; they only underscore her separateness. She shrugs instead of answering.

Edie guides her to the kitchen and into a butler's pantry stocked with boxes and cans and jars of food. She closes a sliding door. The sounds of the party retreat.

"These things can be a little overwhelming," she says.

"I'm not used to them."

"We had a lot of these kinds of parties in New York, Jack and me. Except the people were even more exotic. Broadway actors and dancers, poets and professors. Musicians. I was the one who brought them all together. All the Beats. Jack and Allen Ginsberg and Bill

Burroughs and Neal Cassidy . . . my friend Joan and I introduced them all to each other and we spent wonderful evenings at the West End Bar up near Columbia."

She looks at Anna and smiles in remembrance. "It was a wonderful time. We'd meet our friends at the West End, take the subway all over the city, from the upper west side down to the Village, then over to Brooklyn. We had no money in those days, but you could live in New York on practically nothing.

"Or on our salaries, I should say. Joan's and mine. Which was one of the reasons I left. I got tired of being the one who made the meals and survived on mayonnaise sandwiches while they lived out their dreams of becoming great writers. I had a dream, too, of becoming an artist. It's why I moved there."

Edie turns to face Anna. "When I look at you, Anna, I can sense a feeling of being bottled up. I saw your work, and you have a wonderful talent. Don't let it dry up. You need to nurture it. Be where people can see it and appreciate it."

"But how?"

"Be open to life. Don't waste away in your attic."

"It's funny you should say that, because I'd been thinking about moving to New York, like you did."

"What's stopping you?"

Anna doesn't even know how to answer . . . how can she afford it, how can she muster the courage for it, where would she live, how would she manage in *New York City* when she can barely cope in Detroit . . .

As though she already knows the questions, Edie says, "I know people in New York who could help you, if you decide to go. Think about it, okay?"

Edie opens the sliding door from the pantry to the kitchen. The noises from the other rooms return. "Don't sacrifice your dreams to other people," Edie says. "Don't look back years from now and wish you had done different things."

She disappears into the party again.

Anna wanders through the endless house with its multiple sitting rooms, dining rooms, family rooms, music rooms, libraries, porches, and studies. How odd, Anna has her fantasies of moving to New York, and here's someone who did it.

Yeah, but be careful, she warns herself: Edie did it, but she came back . . .

She moves wraith-like among the party-goers, listening to snatches of their talk, and wants only to go back to her attic refuge. These are not her people, and whatever plans and dreams they have don't include her.

Edie Kerouac may be sensitive enough to pick up on Anna's feelings of confinement and dissatisfaction, but this doesn't break down the reserve keeping her separate from all the people here, as though she moves through these rooms in a bubble. It doesn't give her the steel she'd need to break away.

At a certain point, she's had enough of this party. She goes looking for Marianne or Edie, but can't find either one.

She doesn't have any money, so she can't call a cab. She's depending on Marianne.

She checks the time. A little after ten.

She makes one more circuit around the ground floor, and when she still doesn't see Edie or Marianne, she goes up to the second level. She sees neither one.

She finds a relatively quiet library up there. She decides to wait until they come looking for her.

One other man also uses the library as a refuge. A Negro man sits reading a book in a wing-back chair.

He looks up when she enters. She nods a greeting, which he returns.

"Sorry to disturb you," she says.

"No problem," the man says. "I thought I was the only one trying to escape. Have a seat if you want."

She takes a wing-back chair across from him.

"I'm Malone Coleman," he says.

"Anna Miller."

They shake hands.

"Nothing worse than being trapped at a party you don't want to be at," he says.

"No."

She takes a close look at him. It's hard to tell in the dim light, but she thinks she knows him. "You look familiar," she says. "Have we met?"

He stares at her and nods. "We have. We met at the Sarkisian exhibit at the Society of Arts and Crafts."

"That's right—I remember."

"I remember you, too."

Her face feels warm. She hopes she's not blushing. Or if she is, the dim light in here won't show it. "You were with some other artists."

"I came with them tonight. I think they ditched me."

She pushes up her glasses with the back of a knuckle.

Malone smiles at the gesture.

"Yeah, me, too," she says. "I can't find my friend anywhere. I can't imagine she'd leave without me, but . . ."

"I'm going to have to leave for work soon, too."

"Work at this time of night?"

"I'm a custodian at Harper Hospital. The night shift. What do you do?"

"I have a few jobs. My main one is, I'm a caretaker for a man who's retarded."

"Sounds hard."

"He's actually pretty self-sufficient. He's a grown man and he can take care of all his own needs. Mostly I'm a companion for him. I make sure he eats right and stays out of trouble."

"You must be very patient."

"I like him a lot. It's only part-time. I also waitress, and clean offices. I also take photographs."

It feels weirdly boastful to say it. But Edie's praise earlier gives her the confidence to try out telling others.

Malone asks, "What of?"

"Scenes of city life. My favorite photographers are women . . . Dorothea Lange, Helen Levitt. Have you heard of them?"

"I've seen their work."

"You have?"

"Sure. Where do you find scenes of city life?"

"All around. Downtown, back and forth from my caretaker job. People on the bus, on the street, around the house where I watch

Chester. That's the guy I take care of. He lives on Riopelle, on the northeast side. You know where the Courville Elementary School is?"

"I certainly do."

"It's nearby."

"Near where the Sojourner Truth riot was."

"Yeah. There's trouble brewing over there again."

"In the housing project?"

"No, on Riopelle. A Negro family wants to move into one of the homes on the street."

"You don't read about it in the papers, but it's happening all around the city. White folks just don't want to live near colored."

"The whites are pretty unhappy on that street," she agrees.

"Has it gotten violent?

"Not yet. But I'm afraid it's just a matter of time."

Malone's handsome face turns sorrowful.

She picks right up on it. "Sorry. I didn't mean to upset you."

He shakes his head. "No, no. So disappointing. This never ends."

"I know."

Marianne appears in the doorway. "There you are! We've been looking all over for you. Ready to go?"

"I'm ready," Anna says. Marianne looks at the man she's talking with. "This is Malone Coleman. My friend Marianne."

They each raise a hand of greeting.

"Can we give you a ride to work?" Anna asks. She looks to Marianne. "Malone works at Harper Hospital. It's not far from my place."

Marianne says, "Sure."

"Would that be all right?" Anna asks him.

"If it doesn't put you out."

"No problem at all," Marianne says.

Anna goes into one of the bedrooms upstairs to find her coat in the pile on the bed. She hears a slight cry and realizes two people are on the floor on the other side of the bed.

She hurries out of the room and down the stairs. Marianne, Edie, and Malone stand by the front door.

"So nice of you," he says, "thanks."

"Happy to do it," Marianne says.

They drop Malone off first at Harper Hospital on John R.

"Thanks for the lift," he tells Marianne. "Good to see you again," Malone tells Anna. She gives him a smile and a wave.

In her building, she tiptoes up the steps, hoping Selma is asleep. Anna doesn't feel like any other human interaction tonight.

She makes it up to her attic apartment. It feels good to sit on her own sofa without having to talk to anyone.

She rests her elbows on her knees. She feels as if Selma's grief has been infecting her, too, tainting her with thoughts of death, of loss, of time irretrievably passing.

Not that Anna needs any help in that regard.

The party tonight was a bust, except for meeting Malone. It's nice to know other people are as socially awkward as she is.

Their paths have already crossed twice, she thinks. Maybe they will again?

The thought of seeing him again, while pleasant from a certain perspective, makes her uncomfortable.

She read a book once where the main character said he thought the world should be at a sort of moral attention forever . . . it's how she felt, too. After what happened to her when she was growing up, she never wanted a man to lay a finger on her. Never wanted to let anybody get close. Never allowed anyone to get intimate with her, physically or emotionally.

Whenever she has felt herself attracted to a man, she remembered she was tarnished goods and never pursued the feeling.

So . . . was she attracted to this man Malone?

She has to admit she is. It was his manner. She always liked humble men, and he seemed like he was. Maybe he was a raging prick, but he came across as modest and thoughtful.

Malone Coleman.

A Negro.

It would serve her parents well—her mother the Nazi Countess Frieda von Schoburg-Glauchau, and her father Prentiss Mueller the fascist apologist with a basement full of Nazi and antisemitic and racist literature, papers, and filmstrips.

It would serve them right if she wound up with a Negro after what they did to support Hitler before and during the war.

Whoa, girl, she cautions herself.

You're not going to "wind up" with anyone, let alone a guy you only talked with once.

No, she tells herself; you're not only not going to wind up with him, you're probably not going to see him again.

You had a nice talk with a nice man, and now it's time to get back to your life as an isolate.

And it will be just as well, because you don't want even the possibility of closeness with anyone ever again. After years of abuse, after all you've been through and seen, you want to be standing there, stiff-backed and apart.

She sits at the bridge table near the window and looks out onto the lights of the buildings of downtown. The world going on without her.

She imagines New York City outside her window instead of a bleak alley in Detroit. Would that make a difference in the small thing that is her life? Would she be jumping on subways rumbling down to Greenwich Village and hobnobbing at parties with poets and actors and musicians?

Probably not.

She's not doing it here, why would she be doing it there?

The world could go on without you in New York as well as it can in Detroit, she cautions herself.

And it probably will.

19

JAKE LIEBERMAN

Nancy Whiskey is a bar near Jake's flat in Corktown. A combo on the small stage blasts loud bebop.

The place is jumping. All the tables are full. Music and voices bounce off the tin ceiling. Cigarette smoke drifts in strands in the air and Jake smells the skunky odor of marijuana.

Ronny Barit says, "Hey, look who's here!'

He leads Jake and Anthony Morris to one of the back booths, where a half-dozen men and women sit around a large table. In the middle of the group sits a young-looking man with a long, animated face and close-cropped dark hair.

Ronny says, "Soupster!"

The guy looks up. He brightens. "Hey!" He stands and opens his arms for a hug.

Ronny reaches across the table to embrace the man. He knocks over an empty bottle of Pabst.

He calls Anthony and Jake over. "Guys—I want you to meet Soupy Sales."

Jake knows of him. He's a television personality; he hosts a lunch-with-Soupy show for kids at noon with puppets and comedy sketches.

"I heard you might be here," Ronny says. To Jake and Anthony, he says, "Not many people know Soupy's a jazz fan. He's got a late-night show on Channel 7 where musicians who come through

Detroit jazz clubs give live performances."

"Hey," Soupy says, "you know these two guys?"

He indicates the two Negro men on either side of him. "Clifford Brown," Soupy says, pointing at one. "Max Roach," he says, pointing to the other guy. They raise their hands in greeting.

Soupy's a high-energy guy even when he's not on camera. "Pull up some chairs," he tells Ronny and his friends. He waves his hand to get the waitress's attention.

Jake and Anthony find three chairs and push them up to the table.

"What's going on, man?" Ronny says.

"These cats are on my show tonight," Soupy says. "Clifford plays trumpet, Max drums. They had a gig tonight at the Blue Bird. We just stopped here to catch this band and get properly lubricated before my show. Afterwards, they're going to do a late set at the club. You should catch it!"

A waitress comes over to take their order. Jake orders an iced tea; he's working tonight so he has to stay sober.

Unfortunately, Ronny and Anthony have no such limits, even though Ronny's driving. Before long they're both in their cups, and Jake knows they won't be able to take him to work.

Nor do they seem like they're going to want to leave anytime soon. They're yukking it up with Soupy and the two musicians and their retinue.

Jake falls into his usual mode: offering appropriate facial expressions but mostly sitting and observing. He hates small talk. He's not good at it, so he doesn't do it.

At one point, he glances around the room.

And sees Detroit Police Sgt. Bridget McManus of the Women's Division sitting at the bar.

For a second, Jake wonders if she's been following him.

No, can't be, he guesses when he sees her chatting with two other people at the bar. He remembers she said her sister lives in Corktown; the sister might be the woman beside her, and the man next to her the sister's husband. The women look like they could share the same gene pool—similar bone structure, each with fine, high cheeks and a prominent forehead, though Bridget's sister has a larger frame than Bridget.

While he's watching her, she glances his way.

Oops.

She does an exaggerated double-take. He looks appropriately surprised and salutes her with his glass of ice tea.

She returns the gesture with whatever she's drinking in her highball glass and gives him a nod.

At ten, Soupy says he and his two guests are going to head out for Soupy's studio for his show. "Why don't you guys come along?" he says to Ronny and Antony and Jake.

"Great idea," Anthony says drunkenly, but Ronny reminds him they have to drive Jake to work, and the factory isn't near the Maccabees Building where Soupy tapes his show.

"No," Jake says, "you two guys go. I'll catch a bus."

"Are you sure?" Ronny asks.

"Yeah. Not a problem. Go ahead."

"Oh, man, sorry! This was supposed to be a fun night for you!"

"Forget it."

They all get up and make for the door. Anthony comes back and says, "Meant to tell you—I talked to James Aronson today."

"Who's that?"

"He runs the *National Guardian*."

Jake knows it. A progressive weekly newspaper published out of New York City. The paper was opposed to the Korean War and opposed the executions of Ethel and Julius Rosenberg.

"I told him about you," Anthony says. "He said they've been considering hiring a Detroit correspondent to write about labor and racial issues here. I told him you were his man. I'd have you get in touch with him."

"Thanks, man."

They shake hands and Anthony goes to catch up with Soupy and the musicians.

Jake looks back at the bar; Bridget McManus is gone, along with the couple she was with.

He steps outside. The air hangs heavy with impending rain but feels a relief after the suffocating bar. He plans to take the Michigan Avenue bus to Campus Martius, and from there walk down Woodward and pick up the Jefferson Avenue coach to the plant.

He starts down Harrison Street toward Michigan. It's only a few blocks and even though he can smell the rain in the air, he thinks he'll make it before the storm starts.

He hears a car following behind him. He glances at it. He can't see the driver for the glare from the streetlights on the windshield. He doesn't recognize the Buick.

Just before he gets to Michigan, he stops at a light and the car pulls up to the curb next to him. The passenger window rolls down.

The driver leaning over is Bridget McManus.

"Hey," she says. "Thought that was you. Where are you going?" It's a simple question, but she makes it sound like a grilling.

Force of habit, no doubt.

"Down to the plant."

"Hop in, I'll give you a lift."

"Seriously?"

"It's going to rain in a minute. Get in."

As though this cues the weather gods, big fat splashy drops start pelting the sidewalk.

The sky opens and rain drums down on the roof of the car.

"Don't have to ask me twice," Jake says. He jumps into the passenger seat.

The traffic light changes and she cuts over on the side streets to Jefferson.

"Made it just in time," she says over the clatter of rain.

"So does this mean I'm not a suspect anymore?"

"This ride?"

"I was a suspect, you wouldn't be fraternizing with me, right?"

She scoffs. "We're not fraternizing, Jake. I'm giving you a ride in a rainstorm. Besides, you never were a suspect. My talking to you didn't make you a suspect."

"Like you said, just routine."

"Although, for future reference: if you were a suspect, this would be entirely appropriate. I'd be building up trust with a suspected child killer."

"So it could be a cop move after all."

"You got it."

They drive in silence for a block. She says, "Your shift starts at eleven?"

"Right."

"How long have you been a night watchman?"

"Please. I'm an automotive industrial loss-limitation specialist."

This wrings a smile out of her. "My mistake. Sorry."

"Apology accepted. Just a few weeks."

"Do you have a security background?"

"Not at all. My main asset is, I'm a warm body who doesn't fall asleep standing up. Before this, I sold men's suits at Hughes & Hatcher at Northland. Before that I did the same thing at their downtown store."

"Quite a change, from suit salesman to night watchman—oh, sorry, automotive industrial whatever you said."

He grins. Jesus, he thinks, when was the last time I actually smiled? Or had a normal talk with a woman?

"I went from peddling the meretricious wares of capitalism to protecting them," he says.

She looks sideways at him, as though reappraising him. "You don't sound like a suit salesman. Or an automotive whatever."

"I used to be in the newspaper business."

"Oh, right, you said you were a photographer in the war. What did you do before the war?"

"I was an artist for the *Detroit News*. Pasting up ads, doing illustrations, things like that."

"Why did you stop? Can't imagine selling suits would be more interesting."

"It isn't. I got fired."

"For what?"

"Aren't you the curious one?"

"Occupational hazard. I'm asking questions all day long. Hard to turn it off. If you don't want to tell me . . ."

He waves it away. "I was called as a witness at the House Un-American Activities Committee hearings here in '52. I'd belonged to a few radical groups back in the day, and one of the other witnesses named me to the committee."

"You were fired because of that?"

"Soon as the paper heard I was subpoenaed by HUAC, they decided they didn't want a Commie working for them."

"Right. McCarthyism."

"What about you?"

"What about me?"

"Do you have a law enforcement background?"

"No. I was a social worker at Children's Hospital."

"What made you decide to be a cop?"

"We're called *policewomen*," she corrects with a wry grin.

"*My* mistake."

"I needed the dough. My husband Joe never made it back from the war in Europe. All of a sudden, I was a widow with two kids. I wasn't making much as a social worker, and I didn't want to live on the generosity of my parents forever.

"My sister's a social worker for the city. She told me the police department's Women's Division was looking for women with college degrees in social work or teaching. They respond to crimes against women and children, answer neglect complaints, and so on. That was mostly what I did as a social worker anyway."

"Sorry about your husband."

"Yeah, thanks. Me too."

"You like being in the police?"

"I do. More than I thought I would. Women make up my division. I suppose if I was assigned someplace else in the department and had to work with the men all the time, things would be different. Where were you in the service?"

"Europe."

"You must have seen some pretty awful things."

"I was with Eisenhower and the troops when they liberated the first concentration camps."

"Oh my. What was that like?"

"Horrible beyond belief."

She pulls up on Connor Street outside the gates of the factory. "Are you Jewish?"

"I am."

He hopes it doesn't come out as defiantly as it sounds. He waits to see what will come, how much bigotry she carries around.

She surprises him. "I still can't imagine it, the deliberate slaughter of people just because they're Jewish."

"It was horrific."

He can't help it . . . he needs to find out. "Do you know many Jews?"

"Not when I was growing up. I went to parochial schools all the way through high school. I didn't meet any Jews at all until I started Wayne."

"Were you surprised we didn't have horns?"

"To be perfectly honest, some of the nuns used to say terrible things about you. Well, not you personally."

"Nothing says Christian love like old-world antisemitism."

"I met a lot of Jews in grad school, and again as a social worker. Everyone I met made me rethink what the nuns taught me. There's so much hate in the world, isn't there? Sometimes it's overwhelming. And sometimes it comes from the people you least expect it from."

"I'm trying to come up with some artistic way of dealing with all the hate that keeps me up at night."

"You're an artist, too? Or should I say, what, a creative visual arts engineer?"

That gets an actual laugh from him.

When was the last time I actually *laughed,* he thinks.

I'm surprised I still know how.

A tall, heavy-set Negro man, his collar up and hat down against the rain, walks by them on his way into the gate. He nods at Jake and gives Bridget the once-over.

"That's the other guard I talked to?" she asks.

"Yeah. Sam. He's a good guy."

He glances at his wristwatch. He has to get inside. He says, "Gotta go. Thanks for the ride."

"Not a problem."

"Nice talking to you."

"Likewise," she says after the briefest of pauses.

He gets out of the car and trots through the rain toward the plant gate.

He looks back at her. She watches him. He raises a hand.

She raises a hand in response and drives off.

Another uneventful night at the plant.

Until the end of the shift.

Doing his rounds gives him plenty of time to think about Bridget McManus. He replays their talk in his mind, the way it seemed like she was interrogating him. And that pause before "Likewise"—what was that about?

"That the police lady drop you off out there?" Samuel says.

"Yeah."

"Getting some after hours?" Samuel says with a leer.

"I ran into her in a Corktown bar."

"That what you white folks calling it nowadays?"

"Very funny."

On their rounds, Samuel and Jake stop to jiggle doorknobs to check for locked rooms and key in at their checkpoints.

"What did she want before?" Samuel says. He never asked until now.

"They found the body of a little girl near the plant. She wanted to see if I knew anything about it."

"Why'd she come to you?"

"Pretty sure Dixon fingered me."

"What you going to do?"

"Nothing. Dixon wants to waste the police's time, it's no skin off my nose."

"You want, I can have a talk with him." Samuel gives Jake a nod to let him know it won't involve much talking.

"No. Thanks, but it's not worth it."

"You change your mind, let me know."

At the end of their shift, as they change out of their uniforms in the locker room, Dixon appears around the corner of a locker.

Whatever he's going to say, Jake gets ready to have it roll off his back.

"Hey, Jewboy. Cops talk to you the other night?"

Jake ignores him.

"Yeah, I told them you were a suspicious character. I know what you people do to Christian babies."

Jake ignores him.

"Tell you something else," Dixon says to Samuel sitting beside Jake on the bench, as if he and Sam are friends. "Hitler should have finished the job."

Jake says, "What did you say?"

"It speaks!"

"What did you say?"

"I said Hitler should have finished what he started. World'd be a lot better off without Jews in it. They ruin everything."

This is finally too much.

Jake stands. Dixon gives him a smarmy smile—*what are you going to do about it?*—and before he can react Jake punches him in the face.

It bounces Dixon's head against the locker with a metallic clang. Dixon slides down on his ass. His nose gushes blood.

Jake leans down and grabs him by his shirt front. "Any other opinions you want to share?"

Dixon scrambles to get his feet under him, but Jake holds him down.

"No? No more deep thoughts?"

Dixon says nothing, just snuffles from the blood stuffing up his nose.

"Didn't think so," Jake says. He lets Dixon fall backwards.

Jake steps over Dixon and grabs a towel from the washroom. He tosses it to Dixon so he can sop up the blood. Jake leaves him lying, still stunned on the floor.

Well, this was fun while it lasted, Jake tells himself.

He's not going back to the guard office and tell the night commander what he just did. He expects Dixon will soon enough.

Thus yet another job endeth for Jake Lieberman.

He hates what he just did.

Hates it because Dixon brought him down to his own level, and because he just may have broken his hand.

Still, Jake seethes inside. He deliberately kept away from Dixon, not because he didn't want to give him the satisfaction of knowing he got Jake's goat by siccing the policewoman on him, but because Jake couldn't trust himself not to go off on the slimy guy when he saw him.

And yet he did anyway.

By the time he takes the bus back to his Corktown flat, he just wants to put the night behind him. He makes himself a bowl of corn flakes and eats it with his left hand; his right hand has swollen to the size of a softball.

He wraps ice from his freezer in a towel and holds it against his knuckles. It doesn't do much for the swelling or the pain.

He pops three aspirin and puts Miles Davis's "Cool Boppin'" on the phonograph. He skips over the first few cuts and drops the needle on "Moondreams." Its hypnotic lyricism is exactly what he's in the mood for.

He collapses on his sofa in the living area and waits for the aspirin to kick in.

20

BRIDGET MCMANUS

Her phone rings just before noon on Sunday. The kids are playing outside, laughing maniacally.

She stares at the device, as if to scold it into silence.

It keeps ringing.

Hauser doesn't usually call during the day. She has to pick it up.

"Bridget?" A woman's voice. "It's Roz."

"Hey."

Roslyn Klein.

"Listen," Roz says, "I have a sort of emergency on my hands today and I'm wondering if you'd be able to help."

"I will if I can."

"One of my volunteers in Services for the Aged is supposed to make a home visit to a client later this afternoon. My volunteer's husband had a heart attack and she can't make the visit. I'd do it except I have a board meeting tonight, and we're terribly short-handed. Is there any way you can do the visit?"

Bridget considers it. There goes my dinner with my kids, she thinks.

"Before you answer," Roz says, "he's a Holocaust survivor. He's not elderly, but his experiences in the camps left him in very bad shape. He needs somebody to bring him his weekly kosher groceries, and help him put them away. And maybe just spend a little bit of time with him. He's been giving the aides a hard time. He's not very communicative, so . . . I thought maybe you could get through to him. I know it's a big ask, but . . ."

"No problem. Can I bring my kids?"

"His name is Chaim Lerner," Bridget tells Lydia and Timmy on the way to the man's home. She parks in front of a two-family flat on Tuxedo Street between Dexter Avenue and Linwood Streets. Roz said Chaim lives in the lower flat.

"He's a refugee from Europe after the war."

She has talked to them about the camps, and hopes this doesn't open up a whole discussion about the Holocaust right at this moment.

It doesn't. Lydia sits in the backseat and looks at the brick home thoughtfully. Timmy plays with his miniature Howdy Doody puppet, oblivious.

She stopped by the Jewish Welfare Federation to pick up a box of food for Chaim. Now she hefts it and walks with the two kids up the front walk.

This is supposed to be a temporary placement until Resettlement Services can find him a spot at the Jewish Home for the Aged. He's not an old man but he has trouble getting up the front steps here, Roz told her, and he had a rough go of it in the camps.

She rings the lower bell and waits.

No response.

She rings it again and hears a door opening inside the vestibule. The inside front door swings open and a small man stares out at her. His hair is sparse and white and his face is deeply lined. He wears an old-fashioned suit with a tattered white shirt buttoned at the neck.

He has the saddest eyes Bridget has ever seen.

For a moment, she imagines everything those eyes have seen and her heart breaks.

"Mr. Lerner?" she says.

"Who's asking?" he says in heavily accented English.

"My name is Bridget McManus. Your usual volunteer isn't going to be able to be here tonight, so they sent me with your food."

He looks at the two children. "Who are they?"

"My children. Lydia and Timothy."

They stand uncertainly on the step below her on the porch. Bridget thought this might be a good experience for them, but now she's not so sure.

"Can we come in, Mr. Lerner? These groceries are heavy."

He looks from her to the box she carries.

"Where's Esther?"

"She couldn't come tonight. She had a family emergency. I'm taking her place."

He looks from her to the children, and back to her.

"You're not Esther," he says.

"I'm not. But I have your kosher food for the week, Mr. Lerner."

He looks at the box, and back at her.

"Esther usually brings it."

"If you'll open the door, Mr. Lerner, I'll bring it in for you and help you put it all away."

She can't keep holding it, so she puts the box of food down. She puts one of her business cards on top of a jar of gefilte fish.

"Don't want it," he says.

He closes the inner door and turns to go. She sees him shuffling back to his flat. He limps, like her mother.

Lydia and Timmy look at her.

"Let's leave the food here," she says. "Maybe he'll come get it after we leave."

She takes them to Alinosi's Sweet Shop on 7 Mile Road for ice cream. They sit at the counter, the kids swiveling on their stools as they eat their hot fudge sundaes. Bridget has a chocolate malt.

"Who was that guy?" Lydia asks.

"Do you remember my friend Roz Klein? You met her when I worked at Children's Hospital."

Lydia remembers Roz. Timmy doesn't.

"Roz asked me if I would do her a favor tonight," Bridget says, "and bring that box of food to that man. She also asked me if we could spend a little time with him, but I guess he didn't want that."

"Why would we spend time with him?" Timmy asks.

"He's lonely. He lives by himself. His home in Europe was

destroyed, and all his family members are gone."

"Is he for-jen?" Lydia asks.

Lydia the reader. "For-jen" is her way of pronouncing "foreign." She's only seen the word in print.

"*Foreign*," Bridget says. "I was hoping we could get to know him a little. I thought he'd be interesting for you two to know because he's from another country."

"I guess he didn't want to get to know us," Lydia says.

"I guess you're right."

They leave the ice cream parlor. Bridget drives by Chaim's flat. The box of food remains on his porch. She stops and tries to get him to come to the door again, but he won't answer the bell.

Back home, the kids take their baths. Bridget lets them watch *The Ed Sullivan Show*, and then gets them both in bed in their rooms. She tucks each child in and gives each one a hug and kiss. "Sleep tight," she tells them. "Don't let the bedbugs bite."

When they're settled, she calls Roz Klein.

"He wouldn't take the food," she tells Roz. "He wouldn't let us in his house, but I left the food for him. I figured he'd take it after we left. I swung by an hour later and the box was still there."

"That's what I was afraid of," Roz says. "He's been getting worse and worse. Now he won't even open the door when somebody comes to drop off his food."

"Poor man. What are you going to do?"

"Let me see what I can arrange. If he doesn't open up soon, we're going to have to get the police to break in. That's going to cause a whole other set of problems."

"Oh boy."

"Any other ideas?"

"I might. I just might."

"Great. Let me know what they are. Meantime, let's plan to get together soon."

Bridget promises to keep in touch and settles down in front of *Goodyear Television Playhouse*.

But her thoughts are elsewhere.

She remembers Jake Lieberman—because he's the other idea she had when Roz asked her—talking about what he saw during the war when the army liberated the concentration camps. This man standing before her tonight, Chaim Lerner, was there, was one of the prisoners in the camp who not only saw what happened but underwent the tortures and deprivations Jake saw. His limp probably came from that time.

Her mother has a limp, too, but not from human tortures. When Bridget was fifteen, her mother came down with a mysterious illness that paralyzed the entire lower half of her body. At first, the doctors thought she had a stroke, but they ruled that out. And they ruled out polio. They never did decide what happened to her, but they prescribed physical therapy for her and ultimately the paralysis disappeared, except for leaving her dragging her right foot.

During the worst of it, her mother couldn't take care of Bridget and her sister, couldn't maintain the house, couldn't walk. Her father was useless; he couldn't deal with his wife's sickness, so he concentrated on earning his living as a sign painter.

It fell to Bridget as the oldest child to step in for her mother. Bridget took a year off school to care for her sister Siobhan and brother Darren, for her father, and for the house, washing the clothes and cooking the meals.

She also had to care for her mother. Bridget bathed her, she changed her diapers when Marian couldn't control her bowels, she learned to drive so she could take her mother to her doctor's appointments and physical therapy sessions . . .

Bridget thinks of that year and a half as the year she grew up. The year she realized what it meant to be an adult, including not only shouldering the responsibilities of an adult, but also expanding her understanding of the weaknesses of being human—not only her mother's physical weaknesses (which her mother fought against constantly) but also her father's inability to deal with his wife's condition.

At first Bridget was furious with him—it put all the onus for the family on her, at a time when she should be out having fun and doing well in school—but as she grew into her role as caretaker, Bridget also grew in her sympathies for what people had to struggle with, both physically and emotionally.

That's when she decided upon social work as a career for herself.

It's also when she realized the rigid behaviors and beliefs people tried to foist on her—how a woman should be, how a wife should be, how a Catholic should be, how a white American should be— were not so fixed after all. People did the best they could; sometimes it was enough, and sometimes it wasn't.

She closes her eyes.

She wakes up sometime during the night to the monotonous whine of the test pattern. She turns the television off and takes herself to bed.

21

MALONE COLEMAN

Malone does his weekly walking inspection of the Barlow building, noting where lights are burned out in the basement and hallways, where trash needs to be swept up and bagged, and anything else he needs to do.

He replaces the burned-out lights, saving the bad ones to exchange at the Detroit Edison store, and cleans the garbage up the best he can. He will have to wash these floors soon; the people who live here are dirtier than anybody he has ever known. He supposes it's because this is just a stop on their way down, and they don't care about much anymore, least of all this building.

The secretary of the National Negro Labor Council remembers Malone. She gives him a smile when she sees him come through the door to the office.

She even remembers his name. "Hello, Mr. Coleman."

"You remembered."

"Easy name to remember when you work for Coleman Young."

Unfortunately, Malone has forgotten her name until he sees the nameplate on her desk. Nadine Baker. "Hello, Miss Baker."

"Good to see you again. How can I help you today?"

"I'm here to see Mr. Young."

"Did you have an appointment?" she asks, suddenly concerned

and checking Young's appointment book open on her desk.

"No. I was just hoping to catch him in."

"He's not here. If you really need him, you might catch him at the airport. He's supposed to jump on a flight for Chicago in"—she glances at her wristwatch—"Well, in about forty-five minutes."

"Which airport?"

"City Airport. Do you have a car? You might just make it. Otherwise, he'll be back next week."

Malone races to the airport in Clarence's borrowed car. The air field is a small facility on the east side of Detroit, so he suspects he won't have trouble finding Coleman Young.

He stops at the information desk and the clerk there points him down a hallway.

When he gets down to the gates, Coleman Young stands talking with another man. Young catches sight of Malone and tells the other man he'll meet him on the plane.

He comes over to where Malone stands, panting, trying to catch his breath.

"You're here to see me?" Young asks.

Malone nods, too out of breath to get the words out.

"Cutting it close, young man. Two more minutes and I'd have been on that plane. Are you just going to stand there like a dumb motherfucker trying to catch your breath, or are you going to tell me why you felt the need to chase me down?"

"Nadine told me I'd find you here," Malone gets out.

"It's what she's supposed to do. Still doesn't explain why you're here."

"I went to see Willy Hodges, like you suggested."

"Bet he didn't have too many good things to say about me."

"He didn't."

"Didn't think so. Did he say anything helpful?"

"He said I should ask you about somebody named Frank Carmody."

Young barks out a shout of laughter. "Man, I haven't heard that name in ages."

"Was he in the National Negro Labor Council?"

"The hell he was. I'll tell you who Frank Carmody is. He's the rotten motherfucker who sank the Fair Employment Practices legislation."

"How?"

"Mr. Young?" A woman from the gate calls. "We can't hold the plane much longer."

"Be right there." Young tells Malone, "They're not going to leave without me."

"Who was he?"

"You remember the FEP never made it to the ballot because the Common Council disallowed eleven thousand signatures at the last minute?"

"I remember."

"Frank Carmody was a staff member of the Detroit Elections Commission at the time. And he's the motherfucker who disallowed those signatures. And because he did it as a favor for Mayor Cobo, Cobo appointed him to the Commission of Community Relations, a job he has no fucking qualifications for whatsoever."

"Didn't it used to be the Mayor's Interracial Committee?"

"It did. Until Albert Cobo came in and watered it down so much, now it might as well be called the Commission for Fucking Over the Colored People of Detroit."

"So why did Hodges say I should ask you about Carmody?"

"You'll have to get the answer from Carmody himself. If you see him, tell him I hope he rots in hell."

The woman's voice again. "Mr. Young?"

"I'm coming."

He looks around, gives Malone a wink. "You know, someday they're going to name this airport after me."

Dream on, Malone thinks.

The new City Hall they're putting up will be ready later in the year, but for now the Common Council and the other city departments met in the old City Hall, a dilapidated building from the previous century on Campus Martius on Woodward Avenue downtown. The cop on duty at the front doors tells Malone where he can find the Commission of Community Relations, but when he gets up to the floor, the clerk at the counter tells him Mr. Carmody is out.

"He's home sick today," the clerk says. "Got a bad cold."

Malone leaves his name and Clarence Brown's phone number, but Malone has no expectation Carmody will get in touch with him. He will have to track the man down himself.

In the lobby of City Hall stands a bank of telephone booths. Attached to the phones are phone books on chains, but most of the pages are torn out, including the page for Frank Carmody.

Malone calls information. The operator gives him the number for Francis Carmody, and tells Malone the man's address.

It turns out to be the Book Cadillac Hotel downtown.

At the hotel, Malone goes up to the fifth floor and knocks on Carmody's door. There's no answer, so Malone knocks again.

The door next to Carmody's opens and an angry white man's face juts into the hall.

"Are you deaf, boy?" the man shouts. "He ain't in!"

Malone writes out a message on a piece of paper from his wallet, and leaves Clarence's phone number. He slips it under the door to Carmody's room.

He returns the car to Clarence and Bessie's. Bessie stands at the stove in the kitchen, much to Clarence's dismay. The big man sits at the table in their kitchen, watching her leaning on her crutch and stirring a pot on the stove. He shakes his head.

Malone gives Bessie a peck on the cheek and sits down next to Clarence.

"Maybe you can talk some sense into her," Clarence says. "She sure don't listen to me."

"What's the problem?" Malone asks.

"She standing on her one good foot when she should be sitting down."

"Hush," Bessie says. "You acting like I'm made of sugar."

"You mean you isn't? You sweet as."

Bessie's look sends her husband into a spasm of tittering laughter. Clarence was diagnosed with diabetes, as his wife was. Where it took her leg, it seems to be paring down the big man mercilessly. When he was on the police force, he was a huge, daunting figure, made even larger by the metal shields he wore front and back under his suitcoat as a kind of homemade armor. Now each time Malone sees him, Clarence seems to have shrunk a little more, with less meat on his bones.

"Staying for dinner?" Bessie asks Malone.

"Wouldn't mind."

"Set the table, then."

When he comes to the Browns', Malone falls back into the routines and warmth of the couple who took him in and saved his life when he was younger. He showed up one day in their basement, where Clarence would hold parties for all the neighborhood kids, and he basically never left.

Tonight, after dinner—Bessie's chili over cornbread—she retreats with Clarence into their living room while Malone cleans up. Bessie wants to clean up herself, too, but Clarence convinces her Malone really wants to do it. And he does—he'll do anything for these two.

Malone joins them in the living room, and he has a flashback to so many nights like this, when Clarence would be sitting in his chair in their old place in Black Bottom, working on his baseball league schedules, and Bessie would be stretched out on the sofa reading the *Detroit Tribune*, both relaxing in their refuges from the world—Clarence from his days and nights on the streets of Detroit as one of the few Negro detectives in the Detroit Police, and Bessie from the stresses of her job cleaning patient rooms at Harper Hospital . . . rooms she wouldn't even be allowed to use as a patient.

There are differences now, of course: Clarence finally quit organizing his baseball league last year when Bessie had her operation. The *Detroit Tribune* was taken over by a Jehovah's Witness who turned it into a sanitized mouthpiece for his religion, so Bessie now reads the *Michigan Chronicle*. And a small television set replaced the substantial radio standing in their old living room in Black Bottom. Clarence's record player remains, along with his collection of Duke Ellington and Ella Fitzgerald records. Malone tried to get him to listen to some of the newer artists like Miles Davis, but Clarence isn't interested.

Malone sits in the third chair in the living room, reminded again of the papa, mama, and baby chairs in the Goldilocks story.

They settle in.

The doorbell rings.

Clarence is up in an instant. When he was on the police force, he carried two pearl-handled revolvers at his waist; in the house in Black Bottom, he kept them on a peg by the door so he could get to them quickly in case he needed them. He kept the habit, except now he keeps them on a coat tree near the front door.

He pulls one of the guns and peers through the glass in the door.

He turns to Bessie. "Just Ella," he says.

He holsters the weapon and unlocks the door. Ella Turner, one of their neighbors from Black Bottom who moved out here when their neighborhood was demolished for "urban renewal," which the residents who lost their homes thought of as more like "Negro removal."

Ella enters and Clarence gives her a hug. Malone stands (as Clarence always taught him to do when a woman enters the room) and she hugs Malone, too. Malone knows her from the old neighborhood; years ago, Clarence investigated the death of her son Darius; it was a complicated and terribly sad series of events.

Bessie pops up on her one leg. "Oh, now you sit right back down!" Ella cries.

"Let's have some tea," Bessie says.

"You sit right back down like she told you to, and I'll get the tea," Clarence says.

He waits until Bessie grudgingly sits down. Ella sits beside her.

"How you doing, Miss Bessie?" she says.

"I'd be better if all y'all'd let me do things. What's going on?"

"My cousin trying to move into a house on the west side," Ella says. "White folks in the neighborhood ain't happy."

"White folks never happy," Clarence offers from the kitchen.

Clarence comes back and takes his seat. "Kettle on," he says. "This thing there? Not going to end good."

Ella agrees. "The neighborhood improvement association already going to war against the family."

"Not good," Bessie sighs.

"No," Ella says.

Malone recalls the talk at the Mayflower Church with Lucille and her father. They talked about dozens of instances of white violence against Negro families trying to move out of the city center. It was exactly what Clarence and Bessie had done, except they moved into an already integrated neighborhood.

"What you thinking about, honey?" Bessie asks him.

"Nothing."

"No, you thinking about something."

"I'm just sick of hearing how many times this happens."

"Colored people just want a nice place to live and it always end in fighting," Clarence says.

"That's the way it is," Ella agrees.

The bus rumbles down 8 Mile Road toward Woodward Avenue. Even at this late hour, Negro men are still gathered at the sides of the road with their bags of tools, hoping to be chosen by contractors and construction workers who drive by looking for day laborers.

Malone pulls the cord signaling a stop at Livernois. I've been putting this off long enough, he tells himself.

He transfers to the Livernois coach and rides up to 6 Mile Road, past the shopping center known as the Avenue of Fashion. He gets off at 6 Mile and hikes down toward Marygrove College, at Wyoming.

Across the street from the park-like campus of Marygrove stands a nondescript building, a garage, really, in a row of insurance offices and a music store. Malone goes around the back and bangs on the door. The guy who comes to open it, one of the artists he met at the Sarkis exhibit at Arts and Crafts, Charles McGee, is the man Malone has come to see.

"Malone," Charles says.

"Hey, Charles. I took a chance on you being here tonight."

"Well, I'm here most nights, so it wasn't long odds. Come in."

Malone enters Charles's studio. It's an open space but it's crammed with art books, welding equipment (Charles works as a welder during the day)—and people, working on their art.

"I'm just finishing a class," Charles says. "But come on in."

Malone enters. Off to the side, Lucille Reid raises a hand in greeting.

The students are packing up their materials. Charles stops by one student's worktable, peruses the painting quickly, and takes the student's brush and begins to draw on the canvas.

Malone goes to the corner sink, where Lucille washes brushes.

"What brings you here?" she asks. She turns the faucet off. "I know you're not following me."

"Well, you caught me. I am."

She laughs.

"Actually," he says, "I was hoping to catch Charles and talk with him for a few minutes. I didn't realize he had a class."

"Charles always has a class. If I can, I help him with it. What did you want to talk to him about?"

"I was just hoping to get some advice from him."

"About your art? I hope this means you started painting again."

"More like life advice. But it can wait."

Students begin leaving. Charles starts turning out the lights.

Malone hears a horn honk outside.

"There's Melvin," Lucille says. "He picks me up the nights I work with Charles. Can we drop you somewhere?"

"I'm going to stick around. I want to catch Charles."

"Okay. Good night. Good night, Charles!"

She runs out the front door.

Malone watches her go.

He clocks Charles watching him watching her. Outside, he hears the car roar away.

"You can't compete with Melvin, Malone. Don't even try."

"That's not what I'm thinking about."

"What then?"

"Just wondering how a guy like that gets so lucky. Beautiful girlfriend, nice car . . . got the world by the short hairs."

Charles pats him on the back. "Not going to give you any stuff about how we make our own luck. We both know that's bullshit. Luck's just what it sounds like: something we don't have any control over. All we can do is respond in the right way. But we were going to talk, you and me."

"Yeah. I still have some time before I have to get to work."

"You work this time of night?"

"Eleven-to-seven down at Harper Hospital."

"Come on, I'll give you a ride downtown. We can talk on the way."

Charles drives down 6 Mile to Woodward Avenue, where they turn south, toward downtown.

"So," Charles says, "talk to me. Why'd you stop painting?"

Malone starts with all the reasons he's told himself: no fire for it anymore, discouraged by his lack of success, no longer able to find the inspiration . . .

"That's all bullshit," Charles cuts him off, "you know that, don't you?"

Malone, stung, doesn't want to argue so he stops trying to explain.

"Inspiration comes from the work," Charles says. "You sit around waiting on inspiration, you'll never get anything done. You'll be right where you are now, wishing you were painting. Know who waits for inspiration? Amateurs. Sunday painters. The rest of us just show up and get to work."

Malone doesn't know how to respond, except by saying maybe he just isn't a professional—which he knows will come off as whining, and which he knows will just make Charles jump on him again.

Still, Charles's dismissive attitude grates.

"Okay, why do *you* think I stopped?"

"I know exactly why you stopped. Despite what Clarence and Bessie did for you, you got less, not more confident as you got older. Once you left Arts and Crafts, all your self-doubts returned, and there was no one—no teachers, no fellow students—to counter them. Except for the Browns, and even their voices, kind as they were, couldn't outshout your belief you'd never be good enough. Whoever planted that in you, planted it deep."

Malone hears his mother's voice. You no good. You can't do nothing right.

You just a dummy.

After driving a while in silence, Charles says, "It takes courage to be an artist. It takes a special kind of fearlessness to be a Negro artist in this country."

"Maybe I don't have that. Maybe I'm just too afraid."

"Maybe. You're the only one can say. I know one thing, though. You keep telling yourself you're afraid, you will be. You tell yourself you're not good enough, you won't be."

"Maybe I'm not!"

Charles backs off, says, "Listen. I talked to LeRoy about you."

LeRoy Foster, Malone's former teacher and mentor at the Society for Arts and Crafts.

"He told me you were the most gifted painting student he ever had at Arts and Crafts. Sarkis said the same thing."

Sarkis Sarkisian, the head of the school.

Charles turns off Woodward and stops in front of the hospital's entrance on John R.

"What do you think about that?"

Malone can't speak; he's too emotional from Charles's words.

Finally, he gets out, "I wish they would have told me back then."

Charles lays a hand on Malone's shoulder, a large, strong hand, roughened by Charles's welding day work.

"I'm telling you now," he says. "Now's when you need to hear it. You don't have to prove anything to anybody, Malone. I can't make you start painting again. You got to do that for yourself. But you got the chops, son. If you don't know that, I'm telling you. And I'm not alone. You owe it to your talent to let it express itself through you. Just don't quit. Do whatever you have to do to get yourself together, but don't ever quit. Now go on, get inside. Don't want to be late for work."

Malone nods his thanks. He hopes he can get out of the car before he starts to cry.

He doesn't quite make it.

22

ANNA MILLER

After cleaning her trio of offices in the morning, Anna taps lightly on Selma's door.

Selma looks out, her face a mask of tragedy.

"Selma," Anna says, "what's the matter?"

Selma can't respond. Her face dissolves in tears.

Anna guides the older woman to her sofa inside the apartment. The bones of her back and shoulders are fragile, like a bird's.

Stricken with sadness and grief, Selma can't say anything.

"I know," Anna says. "I know."

She sits with Selma for another half hour. The photos they were looking at earlier are still splayed on the coffee table. It's likely Selma went through them again, which might be what's prompted this.

In time the older woman seems cried out enough to allow Anna to make a cup of tea in the kitchen. Anna adds a shot of schnapps and brings it to her and helps her get it to her mouth with shaking hands.

Selma accepts the help without a word. She seems beyond language, beyond the ability to verbalize how badly she feels and how lonely she must be. Anna is glad to be there for her to provide the touch and presence of another person, which Selma seems to need right now.

Because Selma's sadness now comes in waves of grief; for two minutes she'll be solid enough to sip her tea, the next minute she'll be overtaken by wracking sobs.

In another hour Selma has exhausted herself. Anna, exhausted in her own way, takes the empty teacup out of the woman's hand and lets her fall back on the sofa. Selma is half-asleep, as if drugged from the after-effects of expressing her heartache.

After a few moments, Selma's eyes pop open. She sits up. She looks dazed. Her eyes are rolling in her head.

"Selma? What's the matter?"

"Oh my. I'm so sweaty all of a sudden."

"What's wrong? Did you have anything to eat today?"

"No time. I'm too sweaty from playing basketball."

"What?"

"And I have a splitting headache," Selma says. "How am I supposed to play basketball when my head hurts this much?"

Anna drives Selma to Harper Hospital, the same place she took Selma's brother Fred. By the time Anna rushes them up to the Emergency entrance, Selma has passed out.

They sweep her right in to an examination cubicle. A doctor who looks younger than Anna checks Selma's vital signs—blood pressure, heart rate. He pinches the skin on the back of Selma's hands.

He snaps the stethoscope out of his ears and drapes the tubing over his shoulder in the efficient way they learn.

"We'll get some blood drawn," he says, "and an x-ray to rule out stroke. I'm guessing she's dehydrated. When older folks get dehydrated, they can get a little loopy. We'll set her up on an IV drip and your mother should be right as rain."

"She's not my mother."

"Sorry. What's your relation?"

"She lives in the apartment downstairs from me."

"You're a good neighbor. Not many would do this for a stranger."

There's no indication of stroke, but the doctor says he wants to keep Selma overnight for observation.

It's the early morning before Selma gets settled in a room. Anna stays with her the whole time. As soon as Selma gets to her bed, Anna races out of the hospital and drives back to her apartment so she can shower and change clothes in time for her shift as a waitress at Nick's.

23

JAKE LIEBERMAN

When he goes into work for the next few days, Jake expects the Cap to call him into his office about punching out Dixon, but nothing happens. The only unusual thing is, on Tuesday Cap tells him he's ready to start patrolling by himself.

Cap gives Jake the supply area route and transfers Samuel Jones to another location despite Jake's protest that he, not Samuel, should be sent somewhere else since the supply room has been Samuel's patch. Samuel takes it with his customary resignation.

Even though it's the middle of the night, the supply room is bustling. A shift of men prep boxes of automotive parts and supplies, securing equipment and filling trucks to carry their loads across Michigan and into Wisconsin, Illinois, Ohio, and other states as Hudson gets sold off.

The workers lift and tote steadily, though around three or four in the morning they start to get slap-happy. The Cap told Jake to keep an eye on things so nothing goes missing. He tells Jake how items go missing the first time you turn your back; he calls it falling off the back of the truck.

Jake makes sure the men notice him rocking on his heels on the margins of the supply room floor while they pack huge machines, a seemingly endless line of bumpers and sheet metal, and tools of every kind, hand tools to hydraulic tools. The drivers are private haulers under contract with American Motors and keep to themselves, drinking from their thermoses and smoking until it's time to sign for their loads and jump into their rigs and pull out.

At one point during the early morning hours, Lee Dixon wanders by with a few of the other guards. They point at Jake and whisper among themselves, as though plotting their revenge. Apparently, the plan is to intimidate him, but Jake takes out his notebook and pretends to make notes about them. He's actually sketching cartoons of Dixon's minions wearing Nazi uniforms with swastikas and sieg-heiling Dixon dressed as der fuhrer.

Soon they drift away, though not before sending some antisemitic remarks his way.

Jake has not been in many fights in his life, but the army was filled with Jew-haters who tried to take him on repeatedly. He's not usually a violent man but he is a tall man and can always give as good as he gets. He assumes Dixon will try another kind of revenge besides fingering him for the child murder, so he's waiting for it.

Samuel Jones thinks so, too, and makes a point of walking out with Jake in the morning when their shifts end so Jake doesn't have to be alone in case Dixon and his buddies ambush him. Usually, Samuel wants to get home to his family, but sometimes he'll stick around to have coffee or breakfast with Jake from one of the food trucks clustering around the plant at mealtimes. The others call them roach coaches, but the food is cheap and hot and the coffee's strong and Jake doesn't ask for more.

This morning, Samuel wants to head home right away after his shift. So Jake gets his coffee and scrambled egg sandwich from the roach coach solo and finishes the food in his car.

At home in his shed, he finishes work he's behind on. At the top of his list is laying out the next issue of *Correspondence*. In addition to the usual features, this edition includes a cartoon Jake drew, a satiric portrait of Walter Reuther as a literal fat cat sitting at a table with other fat cats of industry, gorging themselves while the starving mice-workers scramble for scraps at the next table.

When he wraps up *Correspondence*, he turns to a pamphlet from James and Grace Boggs describing how Mayor Albert Cobo dismantled Detroit's public housing plans in favor of private developers. The pamphlet details the problems that has caused for Detroit's Negro residents, who already have a hard time finding housing because of widespread racial segregation across neighborhoods.

When the mechanicals for those two jobs are finished, Jake turns to his concentration camp project.

He's trying not to duplicate "Guernica," but that's his model. It's going to be a massive painting; the focal point will be a column of stocky figures who rise from the crematoria with disembodied arms and legs and torsos and heads screaming in torment.

A knock at his shed door interrupts his sketching.

Bridget McManus.

"Hello," he says. "This is a surprise."

"Am I interrupting?"

"Not at all. How'd you find me?"

"Your landlady said you'd be out here. I don't have time to stop, but I wanted to ask you a favor."

"Ask away."

"I came across a man the other day, a Jewish man who was in the concentration camps during the war. He's in a resettlement program at the Jewish Welfare Federation and the aides are having a hard time with him. He's not letting them in the house, and he's not taking in the kosher food he needs."

Jake sees where she's headed.

"I wondered," she continues, "since you know exactly what he's gone through, if you have the time, would you mind looking in on him? Maybe because you're a man he'd accept help from you. All his other aides are women."

"Not a problem. Give me his address."

"You're sure?"

"Positive."

"Wonderful. You're a good man, Jake Lieberman."

"Don't tell anybody."

The house is on Tuxedo Street in a predominantly Jewish neighborhood, though gradually the Jews are moving further out into northwest Detroit, just as they moved out from Black Bottom.

Good thing Judaism is portable, Jake thinks.

The boxy brick American foursquare duplex has two porches, lower and upper, and a dormer on the third level.

The outside door is locked. Bridget McManus told him Chaim Lerner lives in the downstairs flat. He rings the lower bell on the doorframe and knocks on the door.

He crosses onto the porch to look through the window into the living room, but the shades are drawn. He raps on the window, but gets no reply.

He rings the upper doorbell. In another minute he hears steps coming down from the second floor. An old woman's orthopedic shoes, heavy ankles, and floral dress come into view on the stairs.

"Yah?" she calls through the glass of the locked door.

"I'm looking for Chaim Lerner."

"Who's asking?"

"I'm Jake Lieberman. I'm a friend of a friend."

She unlocks the outside door and steps aside so Jake can come in. "He lives there," she says, pointing to the apartment door on the first floor. "But I haven't seen him in days."

"Have you heard him moving around?"

"No. But I'm hard of hearing, so I wouldn't."

"Would you mind if I went in and checked on him? His caretakers haven't been able to get in to see him."

She shrugs in reply.

Jake goes over to Chaim's door and pounds on it. "Chaim?"

No response.

"Chaim, are you in there?"

Again, no response.

"Are you sure he's home?" Jake asks.

"Where else would he be?"

"That's what I'm asking you."

He pounds on the door again.

Again no response.

Jake puts his ear to the door. Nothing. He doesn't smell the telltale odor of human putrefaction, so that's one good thing.

"Do you own the building?" Jake asks.

"No. I'm a renter."

"I'm going to have to break through the door."

Another shrug.

He knocks again and when there is no answer again, he puts his shoulder to the door. It's a sturdy wooden door and doesn't budge.

He rears back and crashes against the door two more times. The second time the door separates from the doorframe with a crack.

Inside he smells no putrefaction, just the pungent reek of rotten food and human excrement. Newspapers in Yiddish are scattered over the floor of the living room. Empty boxes of cereal and empty cans litter the kitchen counter and floor. Stinking dirty dishes fill the sink.

Jake follows the odor of shit into the rear of the apartment. In the bathroom, he finds Chaim Lerner collapsed between the toilet and the bathtub.

"*Oy gevalt,*" the woman cries outside the bathroom. Oh, violence!

Jake kneels down. A faint pulse throbs in Chaim's grizzled neck.

"Chaim?" Jake says. "Can you hear me?"

Chaim's mouth gapes open. He tries to say something, but it comes out as a croak.

"We need to call an ambulance," Jake says. He brushes by the old woman and looks for a telephone. There isn't one in the apartment.

"Do you have a telephone?" he asks her.

She is too upset to answer. All she can say is, "*Oy gevalt!*"

He runs out of Chaim's flat and up the stairs to her apartment. The door is unlocked. He bursts in and spots a telephone on a table in the hall of her flat.

Jake gives the ambulance driver as much information about Chaim Lerner as he knows. "The Jewish Welfare Federation can tell you more."

"He's a Jew?"

"Yes."

"Sinai's the only hospital around here that'll take him," the driver says. "He'll have to go there."

Sinai Hospital, in northwest Detroit. Built two years ago so Jewish doctors would have a place to practice and Jewish patients can come free from the discrimination they ran into at other area hospitals. Jake waits beside Chaim's gurney in Emergency.

"You survived the war," Jake tells the unconscious man. "I hope you can survive the peace."

The nurses have stripped him and bathed him, and now he rests in a clean hospital gown on his gurney. An IV bag hangs from a hook on the wall and an oxygen mask covers his mouth and nose.

He's more with it than he was, but that just means he's more agitated. Jake sits beside him with a hand on the numbers tattooed on his arm, but Chaim waves his other arm and mumbles into his mask.

Who knows what's going on in his head, Jake thinks—what shattering glass, what wailing sirens, what angry shouts, what brutal fists are banging on his door or on him in his mind.

The nurses give Chaim an injection to calm him down, and when he drifts off into unconsciousness, Jake goes out to find a payphone. He calls Bridget McManus, but the administrator of her division tells him she's out in the field.

Next, he finds the phone number for the Jewish Welfare Federation and calls them. He doesn't know who to ask for, but he tells the woman who answers the phone that Chaim Lerner, one of their clients, is in a bad way at Sinai.

The secretary says she will pass on the information to those who need to know.

24

BRIDGET MCMANUS

The week before, a young man, nineteen, proposed to an older woman he professed to be in love with. She turned him down and told him she was marrying someone else. In a drunken rage, he killed her.

A woman who lived in his apartment building turned him in to the police. He confessed immediately.

Now Bridget McManus stands at the corner of Euclid Street and Woodward, in front of the Euclid Bar. It's a typical neighborhood joint, a bar with creaking wooden floors where the local sots pass their days. The young man told investigators he got drunk here.

Bridget's charges in the Woman's Division include making sure young people aren't illegally served alcohol at city bars; the legal drinking age in Michigan is twenty-one.

She goes inside and asks to see the owner. After a brief and angry exchange, she writes him up for serving under-age drinkers.

It's the fourth citation she has written today for this, although the others didn't result in murders (that she knew of yet, anyway).

When she gets back to her office at 1300 Beaubien, she finishes the report of her day's activities and gets ready to head for home. She promised her children she would be there for dinner tonight after so many late nights.

Until her phone rings.

Another dead child has been found.

A girl. This one near Kalamazoo.

So much for promises.

It takes her four hours to get to the Checker Cab test track south of Mosel Street between Pitcher and Harrison Streets in Kalamazoo. When she arrives, the Kalamazoo police are scouring the site for evidence. The detective in charge, Captain Fritz Richmond, fills Bridget in on the details. He tells her the coroner's van has taken away the body already.

When she gets to the Kalamazoo County morgue, the attendant tells her the child has already been transferred to the State Police lab in Lansing for the post-mortem.

Bridget knows the state pathologist there, Dr. Edmund Black. She gets through to him on the phone; the pathologist tells her the post-mortem will take place later tonight. He can only tell her an eight-year-old girl, Jeannie McCormick, has been found in a copse of scrub pine near the Checker Cab track. Signs of a beating and sexual molestation. He says he'll let Bridget know what his findings are as soon as he has them.

Home.

A wasted trip. Eight hours of her precious time on Earth she'll never get back.

Everybody's asleep, even Timmy.

Darren's in his basement, all's right with the world.

Yeah, right.

She kisses the kids without waking them. Apologizes silently for missing dinner—again.

She crawls into her own bed.

An hour later she lies awake with her head jumbled with thoughts. She will not be getting to sleep anytime soon. She slips out of bed and pads into the kitchen.

She makes a pot of coffee and takes the telephone off the hook. (No unwanted midnight callers tonight.)

She retrieves a photo of Jeannie McCormick from her briefcase. The Kalamazoo cops gave it to her. The photo shows an impish, dark-haired, dark-eyed young girl with a sunhat and a Peter Pan collar.

She finds her folders on Barbara Nicholson and Joey Gallagher, the other two murdered children. She reads through their reports again.

With the Gallagher boy, two witnesses saw a car at a gas station at Groesbeck Road and 10 Mile Road the morning Joey disappeared. They described the driver as a 40-45-year-old man, slender, dark haired, weighing around 150 pounds. The attendant pumping gas said the car was an older model brown Chevy Bel Air. He described a boy matching Joey Gallagher's description sitting in the car; the attendant said the boy looked frightened.

The sighting was followed up, but without any more detailed description of the car or the boy, nothing came of it. It might not have even been Joey.

Bridget goes back to Barbara Nicholson's file, but there's no mention of a similar car.

She starts again from the beginning of Barbara's report and reads through to the end.

Two little girls, one little boy, similar age, all beaten, sexually molested, killed. Disappeared between home and school, both the object of wide searches, all discovered at least ten miles away from their homes.

They must be connected, Bridget thinks.

But how?

And what will Jeannie McCormick add to their knowledge?

25

MALONE COLEMAN

Malone stands before the counter at the Commission on Community Relations at City Hall. The clerk attends to paperwork at his desk behind the counter and pretends to ignore him. From back in the offices, Malone hears a sneeze.

"Excuse me," he finally says.

The clerk looks up like he just realized someone was standing there.

"I'm here to see Frank Carmody."

"Do you have an appointment?"

"No. I came to see him the other day and you told me he was out sick with a cold."

Another sneeze comes from an office behind a frosted glass wall of cubicles. Both Malone and the clerk can't help but hear it.

"Sounds like he's back."

Malone looks the clerk square in the eye, as if daring him to say Carmody is still out when they both know he's there.

"What's your business with him?" the clerk asks.

"I need to talk to him about the Fair Employment Practices Ordinance from a few years ago."

"What about it?"

"I'd rather take it up with him."

The clerk looks like he's considering disputing it with Malone, but says, "I'll see if he's free."

In a few minutes he returns. He lifts the horizontal hatch in the counter and motions Malone inside.

Malone follows him to the office where the sneezes come from.

The clerk knocks on the door and opens it. He steps aside so Malone can enter.

It's cramped with wooden file cabinets and stacks of folders on every horizontal surface. The man behind the desk gets to his feet; he stands a foot taller than Malone with flaming red hair combed back from his forehead. Blue eyes in a round, red face like boiled beef.

He holds out a hand and Malone shakes it. Carmody's grip is like iron; the bones in Malone's hand crack. Malone has learned when white men want to intimidate you, they shake your hand and squeeze the life out of it, as this guy's doing.

"Frank Carmody," the man says.

"Malone Coleman."

"Have a seat. Just move a pile to the floor."

Malone removes a pile of folders from the guest chair and sets it carefully on the floor. He sits in the empty chair across the desk from Carmody.

Carmody is about to say something but he wrinkles up his face. He whips a handkerchief out of the breast pocket of his suitcoat and gives a mighty sneeze into it. He wipes his nose and stuffs the handkerchief back in the pocket.

Carmody snorts up a snootful of snot, says, "What can I do for you?"

"Coleman Young said I should talk to you. He told me what you did about the FEP ordinance."

Carmody folds his hands across his belly and sits back in his chair. He regards Malone with a polite smile. "Matter of record."

"I worked on that project, when I was with the National Negro Labor Council."

Carmody says nothing.

"I was working for the VA. Somebody must have told them about it," Malone says. "Nobody there knew I tried to help get the ordinance passed. Somebody must have told them and I got fired from my job there because of it."

Carmody snorts up more snot. Pulls out his handkerchief and

blows his nose into it. Stuffs the handkerchief back in his pocket.

"What I want to know is," Malone says, "who told the VA about my history?"

"Fair question."

"Do you know anything about it?"

"I do. I told the VA."

The starkness of—and the pride behind—the confession sends Malone back in his chair. "You?"

Carmody nods. "I did it."

"What have I ever done to you? We've never even met."

Carmody gives a little smile. "True. Don't feel so special. I've done the same to a lot of your people."

"My people?"

Carmody nods.

"But why?"

Carmody stares at Malone. Leans forward. "Because we're at war, young man."

"No, we're not."

"Oh, not a shooting war. But it's a war, all right. A war for the soul of the American way of life."

Carmody sniffs, dabs at his nose with his handkerchief.

"The people who supported the FEP proposal in '51 were part of the larger movement to sacrifice white men to a leftist political conspiracy whose goal was to give colored people jobs they weren't qualified for and homes they couldn't afford. And along the way, taking away the property rights of white Americans and setting the stage for the Communist takeover of America. Which I, for one, will never allow to happen."

Malone stares at him in disbelief.

"It was part of the liberal government's efforts to break the strength of American patriotism that won the Second World War and made this country as great as it is."

"I just tried to get people a fair shake on the shop floor. What's that got to do with the Second World War? Or the VA?"

"You don't have the same kind of historical perspective people like me do."

"People like you. You mean white people?"

"I mean people with a stake in America that goes back to the

Pilgrims. The best defense against the Communist threat is Americans who share the bonds of Americanness. Of whiteness, if you will."

Carmody leans forward. "You're an interloper in our dream, son. And you and your kind have to be expelled."

Malone sits stunned.

"I'm sorry to be so blunt," Carmody says, "but you asked. And I respect you enough to give you the truth, hard as it may be to swallow."

"So you told my employer I'm too much of a security risk to clean shit out of toilets? To take away my job? To get me *expelled*? Like I'm in fucking school?"

Carmody raises a hand. "You misunderstand me. I didn't tell your employer directly."

"Who did you tell?"

"I'm not able to tell you that."

"Why not?"

Malone realizes he is shouting.

A knock comes on Carmody's door.

The counter clerk peeks his head inside. "Everything okay in here?"

Behind the clerk, Malone can see a handful of other white men lurking, trying to see what's going on and if Carmody needs help with the dangerous screaming Negro in his office.

"Everything's fine," Carmody says.

"But who did you talk to?" Malone says in a fast near-whisper.

"I can't tell you."

"You can't or you won't?"

"Look, you asked and I answered. If there's nothing else, I have work to do." Carmody stands to his full threatening height. "I'll ask you to leave now."

The counter clerk opens the door all the way, and the white men standing behind him move aside to create an aisle for the dangerous Negro to leave by.

Oh, now you see me, Malone thinks. Now I'm not so invisible.

He walks to Black Bottom. Or where Black Bottom used to be . . . a big section of it is already gone, leveled in the name of "urban renewal," which the city's white politicians used as the excuse to uproot the tens of thousands of Negro families who lived here. Once the place in the world where Malone felt the most comfortable, now it's a stretch of weedy empty lots awaiting redevelopment.

He wasn't completely comfortable, of course, but his comfort is only a matter of relative degrees anywhere in this city.

In this world.

He remembers the words of a spiritual at church where Bessie took him when he just moved in with them . . . *this world is not my home.*

Paradise Valley has still not been destroyed, so he walks north from Gratiot through that neighborhood. He doesn't know how long he's been walking. He's still reeling from the hatred in Carmody's words. Though of course Carmody himself wouldn't think they were hateful—he'd say he was just being frank with Malone.

Malone wanted him to be frank. He just didn't expect this level of white hatred blasting him in the face.

Or the ridiculous rationalizations—couching race hatred as patriotism, the necessity for America as a white nation to save itself by doing battle with interlopers with dark skin.

He passes the stores and businesses in the Negro commercial district that formed his world when he was little. Jessie Faithful's Restaurant. Busy Bee Cabs. The Wolverine Barber Shop. The Investment & Loan Bank. Chenault Realty and Accounting. The B & C Social Club. Club Elsino. The Urban League. Hat Clean and Block. St. Matthew's Church. Muriel's Drugstore. Pendennies Restaurant. The Turf Bar. The Lark Club. The *Michigan Chronicle* building.

Most run by Negroes for Negroes.

He walks as if dazed, as if the skin covering a face has been torn off and he looked into the horror of the pale skull beneath.

He winds up at the Blue Swan, a jazz bar on Hastings. It's early, a quiet evening. Not many patrons at the tables. Malone knows two or three, but doesn't feel like engaging with them. The bar manager Louie Fiammo leans on the bar, paging through the evening *Times*.

Malone slides onto a stool at the end of the bar. Grabs a handful of salted peanuts.

Fiammo saunters over. "What can I get you?"

"Stroh's."

"You got it."

Louie draws it and sets it with a perfect head in front of Malone.

He goes back to his newspaper.

Malone downs his brew. Orders another.

Maybe Malone would be better off forgetting about the VA. Concentrate on staying at Harper Hospital and move on from all this bullshit.

He turns the idea over in his head while he finishes his beer. He thinks back to the time when he worked on the campaign for the Fair Employment Practices Ordinance at the city level.

The push for a statewide FEP law had failed in the 1940s because the people working hardest for it tended to be Communists, who were the only ones interested in civil rights in the workplace at that time—and who were also being purged from the ranks of the unions and civil rights groups.

In 1951, the National Negro Labor Council, along with other left-leaning groups, began pushing hard for a city FEP law. They needed thirty thousand signatures in support of a city law, which would have forced the Detroit Common Council to put it on the citywide ballot in 1951.

The problem was, all the civil rights and labor groups in the city opposed the initiative put forth by the "radicals." When the Common Council invalidated eleven thousand signatures, the drive failed and it never made the ballot.

Coleman Young told him it was Carmody who invalidated those signatures, and now Carmody himself told him why.

He raises a hand to call for another beer from Louie when he notices the time. He has to get to the hospital.

Floors need to be mopped.

Toilets need to be unplugged.

He has time for one more beer, but he knows he shouldn't go to work smelling like he's drunk. Or worse, *being* drunk.

He drops some change on the bar and gets up to leave. He pauses to collect himself—I'm not drunk, he tells himself, I've only had one—no, two—beers, and it still isn't enough to dull the rage burning inside him that Carmody lit.

Outside on the street, he takes a few deep breaths, hoping the fresh air will not only help him sober up but also quench his anger. It's about a mile to Harper . . . he should be able to walk it off so when he punches in he'll be, if not calm, at least functional for the next eight hours.

Still, he can't get Carmody's smug grin out of his mind.

26

ANNA MILLER

Friday morning. Anna speeds through cleaning her three offices, picks up her car, and goes back to Harper Hospital to take Selma home.

A nurse wheels Selma out in a wheelchair and helps get her into Anna's car. Selma's still confused, but the nurse says Selma was just dehydrated.

Anna helps her sign the discharge forms and takes her back to her apartment.

Anna makes a pot of tea but the older woman wants only to crawl into bed. She seems disoriented; she keeps looking around her apartment as if she's never been here before.

'The nurses kept waking me up all night," Selma says. "I didn't get any rest."

Anna puts the tray with the teapot and cup on the nightstand beside Selma's bed. She feels as though Selma's dehydration might be her fault; they haven't been having their tea together as often, and Anna hasn't been making meals for her. Selma hasn't been taking care of herself, either. So she wound up dehydrated.

Before she had her episode yesterday, Selma had been looking at her photos from the cigar boxes she keeps them in. They are spread out on the coffee table.

Anna at first thinks she should collect them back in their boxes, but she decides to leave them. Selma will no doubt want to keep going through the evidence of her life—or lives, more accurately. Childhood on a farm, young adulthood in a factory, middle age working in a movie house, and old age missing from the photos entirely but spent on a downward spiral in a decaying neighborhood of Detroit.

So many secrets in our lives, Anna considers. How can you judge a woman's life by what you see when you pass her on the stairs and exchange the merest nod? Or even what's represented in her photographs? How can you ever get inside her heart, her mind, to know what she's thinking and where she's been?

Look at me, Anna thinks. Who would know what I've seen and done—and lost—just by looking at me, a mousy little recluse . . .

She tiptoes in to check on Selma. Sound asleep. Anna hopes she'll be fine by herself while she's gone today.

An accident on Woodward Avenue holds up traffic for almost forty-five minutes. By the time the northbound bus gets moving again and she makes her transfer to the 7 Mile bus, Anna gets to the Kaczmarek home an hour late.

Dottie will already have left for work. Chester can be alone for short periods of time, so Anna hopes he didn't get into any trouble.

Except Chester's not in his usual spot, smoking at the kitchen table over his second cup of coffee.

She calls out his name. No answer.

She goes through the first floor living room and dining room. Upstairs in Chester's bedroom, his bed is neatly made—it's always the first thing he does in the morning—but he's nowhere around. She checks the bathroom and the other rooms upstairs. She goes down to the basement. He's not there, either. Roger's gone, too.

She goes to the backdoor to see if Chester's in the backyard. Not there.

She checks around the alley behind the houses. Not there.

Further up on Riopelle, a crowd has gathered in front of the house where the man is selling to a Negro family. At the edge of the crowd of a dozen white men and women and baby carriages, she sees Chester.

Heart pounding, she stops and takes a deep breath.

Chester was fascinated by the leaflet about the Negroes moving in. But how did he know to come down here?

She comes up behind the crowd and susses out what's going on. Three white men, including Roger Kaczmarek, stand on the lawn, facing two men on the porch, one white, one Negro. Anna assumes the white man is Stanley Rudzewicz, the seller of the house. The Negro man is likely the buyer.

Someone speaks quietly at the front of the line. Alois Swoboda, the head of the neighborhood association, the one who spirited Roger away from his house a few weeks ago to plan strategy for the Negro "invasion."

Anna wishes she had her camera with her. She was so distraught about Chester, she ran out of the house without it.

"Look," Swoboda says to the Negro man in a perfectly pleasant tone, "we know this ain't your fault. This one"—he points to Rudzewicz—"he's the one steered you wrong."

Rudzewicz shouts back, "I ain't steered nobody wrong. I told him exactly what was what."

"Did you tell him he's gonna be the only colored in the neighborhood?" Swoboda demands.

"I did not," Rudzewicz says.

"There you have it," Swoboda says to the rest of the large group.

He turns back to the Negro. "This is a white neighborhood. It ain't for people like you. Rudzewicz knows this and wouldn't tell you."

"Do you want to be the only colored on the street if you buy this house?" a woman from the crowd demands.

"No ifs about it," the Negro man says.

"What's that mean?"

Rudzewicz says, "We already signed the papers, me and him. I'm moving out next week. And he's moving in."

This provokes an outburst from the whites at the curb.

Rudzewicz turns and grabs the Negro man by the arm and hustles him into the house.

Anna darts forward and takes hold of Chester's arm. He looks terrified by the commotion—the raised voices, the general air of menace.

"Anna!" he says. "Why is everyone so mad?"

"Come with me."

"This ain't over," Alois Swoboda shouts through all the cursing and name-calling. "I just moved here, spent my life savings on my house. We let these niggers in, our houses won't be worth diddly squat. Come on."

He waves the crowd down the street, toward his house.

Anna tells Chester, "We have to get home. It's too dangerous down here."

Roger Kaczmarek spots Chester and Anna. He makes his way through the crowd toward them.

He reaches out toward Chester. "Come with me."

"No," Chester says. He pulls back from Roger.

"Come on, you fucking moron. Are you going to stand up for your race and be part of this or not?"

Roger grabs Chester and pulls him toward Swoboda's house.

"Roger," Anna says, "let him alone. Can't you see he's frightened?"

As though this gives him permission to resist, Chester pulls his arm away.

Roger gives him a disgusted sneer—"Stay here, pussy"—and pushes him back to their house down the street. Chester stumbles, loses his footing, and falls on the muddy lawn.

Anna helps Chester up. Now he fumes because his clothes are all muddy. He is compulsive about keeping his clothes and himself spotless.

"Come on," she tells him. "Let's go home and get you cleaned up."

Mud soaked through his clothes so he insists on taking a bath. She doesn't want him to sit in muddy bath water so she has him shower before his bath. By the time he rinses the mud off, he says he's too cold and doesn't want a bath; he just wants to get dressed.

She goes out on the front porch while he gets dressed. Down the street, the crowd has dispersed from Stanley Rudzewicz's house, except for a trio of teenaged boys who lurk around the elm tree on the easement near the street. She tries to think what to say to Chester.

Maybe she should just not say anything in hopes he'll forget it and move on to the next thing that grabs his attention.

He dashes this hope as soon as he comes down the stairs.

"Anna, why was everybody so mad?"

"Because that's a mob down there. It wasn't just a group of friendly neighbors, Chester. It was a mob, and they were on the verge of doing bad things."

"How do you know?"

"I just know. And anyway, they're gone. You saw them leave, right? Listen—are you hungry? Are you ready for some lunch?"

She puts a gentle hand on his shoulder and steers him to the kitchen table. "Here—let's sit down and we can read the paper together. We'll see how the Red Wings did."

The Red Wings are in the Stanley Cup finals against Montreal.

"I already know. They won their game."

Chester knows the stats for every player on both teams.

After Anna makes Chester a ham sandwich for lunch, he spends the next hour pacing around the house. The violence in the air down the street has upset him and he doesn't know how to deal with it.

She tries to get him to calm down but he can't; he's too on edge.

Finally he gets tired and lies down for a nap in his bedroom. When he comes downstairs again in an hour, he seems to have forgotten about the house down the street—until Dottie gets home. When he sees her, he starts talking about what happened earlier and how Roger pushed him in the mud.

She lights a Winston. She kicks her shoes off and wiggles her toes. Sighs. Murmurs, "Jesus, my feet are killing me."

"You should have heard those people yelling at that poor colored man," Chester says. "He was scared to death."

"People got no sense," Dottie says. "They think they can stop this one thing and it'll be over? They're nuts. The coloreds are going to take over this city one day. You mark my words."

Dottie goes up to change out of her work clothes. Chester follows her. Anna hears them murmuring. Whatever she says to him must work, because Chester comes down the stairs and sits quietly with the *Evening Times*.

He still seems sulky, but this is her last day until Monday and she hopes the weekend brightens his mood.

And if something else happens down the street, she won't have to deal with it.

Anna says goodbye. She grabs her purse and flies out the door. She can't wait to get out of this neighborhood.

She gets her camera out of her bag. It's a compact Argus A-4. Her photography professor at SAC gave it to her years ago. It's from his collection, which he was thinning out as he got ready to retire. She loves it; it's made of aluminum and black Bakelite, and it's a stylish little thing.

She walks back up Riopelle toward the house the Negro man bought. She stops to snap some photos. Through her viewfinder, she sees one of the teenaged boys step out from behind the elm tree and throw a rock through the living room window.

She catches it on film. She also photographs the other three boys, now emboldened to step out and throw their own rocks at the house.

The door to the house opens and Stanley Rudzewicz steps out with a shotgun.

Everybody freezes, until Rudzewicz breaks the tableau by letting fly a blast. Anna stands her ground; she needs to get this on film.

Rudzewicz peppers the elm leaves with buckshot. The boys take the hint and scatter. Two come running straight at Anna standing there taking her photos. She turns and races away down the street.

She easily outruns the two boys and ducks into the Kaczmareks' backyard and hides behind the corner of the house until she hears the slapping of the boys' Keds fading away down the street.

She emerges from behind the house and goes back up to the Rudzewicz home. Drawn by the gunshot, more people have collected there again, this time women and young mothers and baby carriages but a few men, too. A Detroit police car arrives at the scene with two uniformed policemen inside. It rolls to a stop across from the Rudzewicz house. The police stay in their vehicle; they sit smoking, watching the commotion across the street with complete disinterest.

As Anna watches, a car backs quickly down the driveway. It's a Cadillac sedan driven by the Negro man who bought the house.

Three white men run toward the car and stand behind it so it can't back out. They bang on the trunk and side doors. Anna can hear them shouting, but can't make out what they're saying.

One of the white men grabs a rock and cracks the Caddie's rear windshield. The cops in their squad car across the street watch this but do nothing.

Anna shouts, "Hey! Stop it!"

The white men look back at where she stands, taking photos. The Negro man in the car takes the opportunity to zoom back out of the driveway. He just misses the cop car. He peels away toward 7 Mile with star cracks on his back window.

Anna glares at the white men who attacked the car. She takes a few more photos so they know she's recorded the whole scene, and hurries down Riopelle Street where she will circle around toward 7 Mile Road so she can take the bus home and shut herself away from this world.

Selma is up and around when Anna checks in on her. They have dinner together. Afterwards, Selma wants to get back to bed.

Later, in her darkroom, Anna develops the roll she shot during the rampage in front of the Negro's new house.

She hangs the prints on lines around her attic apartment. The shots tell the story of the afternoon's events, from the teenaged boys throwing rocks to the Caddie's frantic escape from the street. She enlarges the photos showing the terrified look on the face of the Negro man, and the cold hatred on the face of the white boys and men who attacked his car.

It's not lost on Anna that no one on the street drives, or could probably even afford, a Cadillac like the one the Negro man drives. No doubt it adds to the fury of the whites.

She studies the faces of the people in the photos. What would Edie say about these?

Anna compares them in her mind with the faces in the photos Dorothea Lange took of the migrants during the depression. Those faces were lined with grim desperation, eyes clouded by worry over where the next meal was coming from, or what horrors the world had in store for the children it had never known existed.

These photos from the afternoon, on the other hand, are filled not with concern but vitriol . . . and yes, fear, too—fear their little islands in a changing world are being invaded by outsiders who are only after what they themselves have enjoyed: a place to bring up their families, a place where they could feel like they belonged with people like themselves.

Something they refuse to allow for the Negroes.

She thinks again of Malone Coleman.

With things between the races as bad as they are, he would never be interested in a white woman, let alone her, she decides.

She tries to put him out of her mind.

She focuses on developing more rolls of film.

27

JAKE LIEBERMAN

Jake sleeps through most of the day. After dinner, he works in the shed until it's time to go to the plant.

He tries to move his project forward, but today he's blocked. Usually he can work through the blocks; he learned how in his time on the *Detroit News*; blocks don't exist in the newspaper business. You can't wait until you're inspired; things get done when they're needed.

Alas, not today.

Instead of the Holocaust, he draws cartoons: Negro families pushing wheelbarrows piled high with their belongings ahead of a bulldozer with teeth tearing down their houses; a Godzilla-like steam shovel, labeled "Urban Renewal," laying waste to whole sections of Detroit; Albert Cobo and his fat-cat cronies counting their money as Mexicans drive off in the city's streetcars, which are being sold to Mexico at who knows what kind of below-board profit to the political class . . .

Later, at the plant, he's alone in the locker room changing into his uniform when one of the other guards saunters in. He nods to Jake and glances around. They're alone.

Before Jake can react, the guard jumps behind him and immobilizes his arms. Jake struggles, but the man holds him in an iron-tight grip.

Lee Dixon slips in front of Jake and with a shit-eating grin smashes him twice in the face, left-right. He finishes with a one-two to the stomach that leaves Jake gasping for breath.

The guy behind him releases his arms and Jake falls to his hands and knees on the cement floor.

A kick to the side topples him onto his back.

He doesn't lose consciousness but he's dazed and helpless. He tastes blood.

The world spins.

He braces for another kick, but it doesn't come.

Instead, Jake feels himself being picked up and set on the bench in front of his locker. Samuel Jones makes sure he can stay upright and goes over to the shelf leading into the shower room and grabs a towel. Wets it. Brings it back to dab the blood off Jake's face.

The numb surprise of the punches fades and pain replaces it along both sides of his face and his mouth.

"You okay?" Samuel says.

Jake shakes his head. He feels like he's going to puke. He leans forward on the bench. Samuel thinks he's falling over and puts a big hand against Jake's chest.

Jake can't bring himself to say anything. Samuel reaches for a trash basket and sticks it under Jake's face.

Jake can't hold it . . . he vomits into the basket.

Samuel says, "Dixon?"

Jake nods. He doesn't want to say anything in case it brings up another load.

Jake wipes his mouth with the bloody towel. In a minute he feels okay to talk. "Him and somebody else. Grabbed me from behind."

"Real heroes. You can't work tonight, not in the shape you're in."

"I have to. I need the dough."

"Man, you a mess. Look in the mirror."

Samuel helps Jake over to the mirror above the sink beside the showers. It's true, Jake looks like he fell from a great height and landed on his face. Dixon's fists tore his bottom lip and knocked a tooth out. His nose is lopsided and his face is already swelling. He has a terrible pain in his side where the kick landed. Blood covers his uniform blouse, too.

Samuel says, "Go home, man. I'll tell the Cap you took sick."

"Don't tell him who did this."

"Why not? You going to plan some other revenge, so this thing just goes on and on?"

Jake shakes his head. (It hurts: move it gently, gently.) His thoughts are too scattered to figure out how to respond right now.

"You got your car with you?" Samuel asks. Jake nods. "You okay to drive?"

Jake nods.

"You got to get yourself to the hospital, man. What happened to your tooth?"

Jake starts to look around on the floor for the tooth, but an attack of nausea discourages him.

"Want me have a word with Dixon?" Samuel asks.

"Don't. Not till I figure out what to do."

"I'll tell you what to do. You got to get yourself to the hospital. You need attention, man."

The plant has a first-aid clinic, but Jake doesn't want to go there. It'll only create more problems since they'll want to know what happened. Instead, he strips off his bloodied uniform shirt and changes back into his sweatshirt and leaves the plant. Samuel will tell the Cap he took sick—there's a bucket of puke in the locker room to prove it—so Jake doesn't have to worry about staying around.

The nearest hospital is Bon Secours, on Cadieux Street down Jefferson in Grosse Pointe. He makes his way there—the car going BLAT BLAT BLAT the whole way—and stumbles into the emergency department. A nurse with a tiny golden cross on her white cap helps him onto a gurney. Another cross hangs on the wall with an incongruously ecstatic-looking Jesus nailed to the crossbeams.

The nurse cleans him up and an older doctor comes in and examines him. "What's the other fella look like?" the doctor asks.

"A lot better than me."

Jake doesn't feel like going into the entire attack, so he just gives the doc the highlights: two guys jumped him at his work.

The doctor grunts. He brings out a suture kit and puts a couple of stitches in Jake's lip as well as in a cut on his cheek Jake didn't even know he had.

"Did you save the tooth?" the doc asks.

"Couldn't find it."

"Well, lots of people get by without all their teeth." He palpates Jake's side, which makes Jake grimace. "Feels like a couple broken ribs. We used to tape broken ribs, but that makes it too hard to breathe. They'll heal in about six weeks."

The doc manipulates Jake's nose gently, but even his light touch makes Jake see stars.

"Slight fracture of your nose, as well," the doctor says. "You can get away without surgery. But there goes your Hollywood modeling career, I'm afraid."

Jake's face hurts too much to fake a smile.

The nurse gives him two aspirins for the pain and Jake drives himself home; from the hospital, it's a straight shot down Jefferson to Corktown. He gets up to his flat without waking his landlady.

He lies down on the sofa in his living room. Getting beaten up has its advantages, he muses: he has a free night.

Except now he has to figure out what to do about Dixon. Jake can't let this go unanswered.

He sees a long feud shaping up.

As it turns out, Dixon will no longer be his problem.

He dozes off and on through the night, applying a dish towel wrapped in ice to his face as often as he can stand the freezing cold.

In the morning he hears the door buzzer.

Samuel Jones, standing there in civilian clothes.

"Hey buddy. Come in," Jake says.

"How you doing?"

"I've been better."

"Can you eat?"

Jake touches his lip. "Haven't tried."

"Get your coat. We're going to breakfast."

"My treat, as thanks for what you did last night."

"My daddy taught me never turn away free food."

Samuel drives them to a coffee shop on Grand River. He is the only Negro in the place except for the man bussing tables, but he doesn't seem to be disturbed by it, nor by the glares of the diners.

He orders bacon and eggs and Jake gets a short stack of pancakes. Before their food comes, Samuel examines him across the table. "Face doesn't look too bad," he says. "Could be worse. I told the Cap you took sick and had to go home."

"How'd he take it?"

"Well, got some bad news for you."

"The doctor told me my Hollywood modeling career was over, so I don't know how much worse it could be."

"So's your security guard career. At least at Hudson Motors."

"He fired me?"

Samuel nods. "Told me to tell you. Said you're still on probation and don't get any benefits, including sick time, so he can fire you without any reason. Told me to tell you you're done there."

"Well, damn."

"Sorry."

"Yeah, not your fault. Did you see Dixon last night?"

"I ran across him this morning. He didn't say nothing."

"I'm sure he knows I'm done."

"Did you decide what to do?"

"About him?"

"Yeah."

"Not a goddamned thing. With any luck, I'll never have to see him again."

"That's smart. Though the important word is 'luck.'"

"Yeah," Jake agrees. "Something in short supply at the moment."

28

BRIDGET MCMANUS

Saturday morning breakfast:
Pancakes made from scratch.
Orange juice.
Milk for the kids.
Coffee for mom.
Aunt Jemima syrup.

Bridget tried sneaking in real maple syrup once, but her kids caught her out immediately and made her redo the pancakes without yukky maple syrup.

They're sitting at the round table in the breakfast nook having their traditional, unchangeable Saturday breakfast. Lydia gobbles down her pancakes before they get cold while she reads her ever-present book (this morning it's *Charlotte's Web*), while Timmy makes patterns in the syrup on the plate with the tines of his fork, deliberately waiting until his breakfast gets cold. Bridget has explained to him what happens when you play before you eat, but it doesn't matter; carving figures in his syrup on the plate with a fork is as much a part of Saturday breakfast as Aunt Jemima.

Timmy has just started digging into his pancakes when the front door swings open and Bridget's father bursts in carrying a box with jugs of wax stripper and floor cleaner and a large round steel wool pad the size of a bicycle wheel.

The kids scream, "Grandpa!"

Ernest Thomas sets the box down and goes over to give the two kids a hug. He goes out to get the rest of his supplies.

He returns backing in the front door with a large industrial floor stripper.

"Um, dad?" Bridget says. "What's all this?"

"I told you I was going to refinish the kitchen floor today. What's the matter, Bridie, you forget?"

Bridget vaguely recollects her father mentioning the need for stripping her floor during a phone call last week, but she's certain they made no specific plans.

"We're still eating breakfast."

"Finish. I got more stuff to bring in."

He goes out to get more supplies. Bridget's mother limps in carrying a box of rags and sponges with a mop under her arm.

"Ma," Bridget implores.

"I know, I know," her mother Marian says. "You know your father."

"We're still having breakfast. The kids are still in their PJs. He could have called."

"I'm thinking we should get everybody out of the house before he starts," Marian says.

"Won't he need help?"

"Does he ever?"

Fair point, Bridget thinks. Her father would never ask for help if he could do something himself. And he always thought he could do everything himself better than anyone. He was usually right.

She hurries the kids along—Lydia finishes eating, but slowpoke Timmy with his late start still works on his breakfast. He cuts his pancakes into ever smaller bits and examines each ice-cold piece on his fork before gobbling it down.

Such a strange kid, Bridget thinks again.

Her mother stays with Timmy while Bridget goes with Lydia to get dressed.

In a little while, her mother brings Timmy back to change out of his pajamas.

Bridget calls her friend, Roz Klein, and asks if she wants to go to the movies with their kids.

By the time Bridget shepherds them out of the house, her father has already started moving the table and chairs out of the breakfast nook in preparation for cleaning the floor. Her mother was right; she does know her father; he is single-minded in his approach to projects; he will work alone, steadily, joylessly, until he perfectly strips the floor and even more perfectly refinishes it. An Ernie Thomas job, they call it.

This may not be the best idea we ever had, Bridget thinks.

She's sitting in the Redford Theatre with her mother, her friend Roz, and the five kids, her two and Roz's three. They came for a double feature, *Fantasia* and *20,000 Leagues Under the Sea*. The adults thought the kids would love both movies. Unfortunately, *Fantasia* is on first, and every kid in the theatre (including their own) is squirrely, talking loud and squirming. Children are racing up and down the aisles to the candy counter and the bathroom.

At least her kids are not pinwheeling empty popcorn boxes around the auditorium, which some of the unaccompanied kids are doing.

Whoever thought this would be a good kids' movie?

Bridget sighs, leans back. She stares at the ceiling. It's decorated in blue plaster with faux white clouds and stars.

At the end of the row, Roz tries to corral one of her kids.

Roslyn Klein. Friends since they met at Wayne University when they were both in the Social Work program. Young mothers, in the same program, they took to each other quickly. They lost touch after graduation until Bridget met her again as part of her job at Children's Hospital. Roz was a social worker at the Jewish Welfare Federation, an organization providing services for Detroit's Jewish community.

Bridget thinks about the average happy life Roz has made for herself, with a big house and a happy husband and a satisfying job and three kids who aren't monsters or even as weird as Timmy is. (Sitting beside her, Timmy at least watches the movie, held rapt by the sight of Zeus throwing lightning bolts at fauns on the screen.)

Once Roz's life was Bridget's dream, too, and she almost had it until her husband Joe was shot to death in a muddy patch beside the Weser River in Lippoldsberg, Germany, on April 7, 1945. According to what the army told her when she accepted the posthumous Distinguished Service Cross for him (fat fucking lot of good it did now), Joe jumped out from cover while under heavy machine gun fire to help his lieutenant, who had been hit. Joe was shot and killed instantly.

Your husband died a hero, they told her.

I wish he would have been a little more cowardly, she thought at the time. I might still have him. He might have been around to see his kids grow up.

As it was, he left her pregnant with Timmy when he went off to war. Timmy never met his father.

Probably explains a lot.

She thinks about the three sets of parents who will never see their children grow up: Joey Gallagher's parents. Kathleen Macready's, the girl killed by the sixteen-year-old Floyd Edwards. Barbara Nicholson's.

Who knows how many others who haven't been found? Or who will be found, killed by the same maniac if we don't catch him?

Or the legions of murdered kids who have been found but whom Bridget doesn't know about?

What kind of monster kills children?

As a social worker, Bridget was trained to see the world from her clients' points of view. She can almost—almost—understand about people who are sexually attracted to children . . . it's horrifying to think about, but she can at least wrap her mind around it. Sex is rarely about love; mostly it's about power. Sex with a child is all about power and brutality.

The world we live in.

But to *kill* a child?

To end an innocent life in blood and violence?

The thought turns her stomach.

Of course, she would have a hard time imagining killing anyone—though she has thought about it, as most people have. If she could have found the soldier who shot her husband, she knows she would have killed him, no question.

But she can't think her way into the mind of a creature who could put a bullet in the back of a child's head. Or wrap hands around a child's neck and squeeze the life out of her. Or batter her with fists.

Let alone a culture that kills children on the mechanized, industrial scale of the Germans in the war. She thinks if she's disturbed by seeing these three children's bodies, she can't imagine what Chaim Lerner and the thousands of others went through who lived the horror of the concentration camps.

Or what Jake Lieberman is going through after photographing them.

No wonder Jake seemed at sixes and sevens when she talked to him the night she gave him a ride to work. Bridget doubts she'd be able to get out of bed at all in the morning if she'd seen what he's seen.

Men like to think they're made of different stuff than women . . . tougher, less "emotional," as they like to say. She knows it isn't true, but maybe men have to tell themselves that so they can keep functioning in the world they've created. A world of violence and betrayal, constant power struggles from the domestic arena all the way up to world affairs.

But some men are different. Her husband Joe, for one. He even lost his life trying to save another human.

But to do what he did, maybe he needed to adopt those values of strength and courage the army tries to inculcate. Isn't that what the army said when they gave her his DSC—he died "bravely"? What if by then he had adopted the male military worldview as his own, become comfortable in it—in a way Jake Lieberman never had.

I'm not trying to be disloyal, Joe, she quickly tells his spirit, wherever it might be. I'm just trying to figure out why some people can make accommodations with the way things are and some never can. Jake Lieberman didn't seem crazy, but he must be sensitive enough for the sights he saw to have upended his reality in a way he's never been able to put right.

She's thinking about Jake when Timmy tugs on her sleeve. "Mom!"

"What, honey?"

"I need to go to the bathroom," he whispers.

"I'll take you."

"No—I want to go by myself."

She wants to say no, but he looks so plaintive. He wants to be independent.

Wants to take that first step into a man's world. Into a world of bravery and control.

Still, she says, "Okay." She hates to surrender him to that world, but she knows she can't stop it.

She watches him walk up the aisle and disappear into the lobby.

She has a momentary frisson of fear she will never see him again.

Is this what all parents feel? Or just a parent who has looked into the eyes of mothers and fathers who thought they would see their children alive after school and never did again?

It's all she can do to keep herself in her seat until Timmy gets back. She wants to run up the aisle and burst into the men's room and grab him.

If a deviant wants to troll for young children, she thinks, what better place to find them than at a Disney matinee on Saturday?

She takes a long look around to see if she can spot any men who might be sitting by themselves. Once she was called to the Royal Theatre on 7 Mile by the manager, who caught a lone male exposing himself to children. He bawled like a baby when Bridget and a male patrolman took him in.

Timmy's taking too long.

She decides to go find him when, to her great relief, her son thunders down the aisle back to his seat. She asks, "Did you wash your hands?" If you're going to be a man, you have to be a clean man.

He holds them up. They are still wet.

She puts her arm around him and they settle back to watch a troupe of dancing elephants blowing bubbles in the movie.

Popcorn boxes sail through the air, showing up as pinwheeling shadows on the screen, accompanied by whistles and shouts and children's laughter.

29

MALONE COLEMAN

B oth Clarence and Bessie are out. Bessie left a note for Malone propped against the sugar bowl in the center of the kitchen table. It's in her flowing hand:

Malone Honey,

A lawyer call, Charles Cornish, say to call him when you get a chance.
> Love,
> Bessie

He sits down at the telephone niche in the dining room and tries the number Charles Cornish left.

He's steeling himself for a brush-off.

A white man's voice answers. "Charles Cornish."

Malone takes the 8 Mile bus toward Woodward. He gets off three blocks east of Livernois and walks down Piccadilly to Shrewsbury in the Sherwood Forest neighborhood.

He's looking for a large red brick Tudor with gables and a bay window in the front beside the entrance door. A wiry, thin-faced man whose black-framed glasses magnify alert and intelligent eyes opens the door. He has thinning white hair combed straight back.

"Malone?" the man says.

"Yes." He's staying guarded. Waiting for Cornish to reel him in and then push him away.

The man holds out his hand. "Charlie Cornish. Please come in."

Cornish leads him inside. They step down into a sunken living room. The walls are filled with abstract art, like windows into a universe where nothing makes sense.

Kind of like this one, Malone thinks.

"Can I get you anything? Coffee? A Coke? Tea?"

"Coke would be great," Malone says.

"Let's talk in the kitchen."

Cornish leads Malone through a dining room with a vast table into a kitchen roughly the size of Clarence and Bessie's entire home. There is a large table in here, too, a butcher block table on an island in the center of the room.

"Have a seat," Cornish says. Malone slips onto a stool. Cornish cracks the lever on an ice tray from the freezer, uses tongs to pop two cubes into a glass, and pours Malone's Coke.

"Sorry it's taken a little while to call," Cornish says. "My former partner told me you were looking for me but I've been out of town."

"No problem."

"So." Cornish pulls his stool up to the table and rests his arms on the butcher block. "Tell me what's going on."

Malone tells him about what happened to him at the VA hospital.

Cornish listens intently, nodding as Malone takes him through it.

"Would you help me out?" Malone asks.

"Of course. You should know," Cornish says, "your case is part of a larger pattern. It's the fourth case I've taken on involving a Negro man being let go from a job with nothing to do with national security. In none of the cases were there sufficient grounds for bringing charges and subjecting the parties to suspension, loss of wages, and humiliation—exactly what you've gone through."

"I understand."

"I've already written to Congressman Diggs and Senator McNamara, demanding an investigation of security risk dismissals of Negro men. I'll get in touch with them again and ask them to add your name to the list."

"Thank you."

"My goal here is to get you reinstated, just like I'm trying to do with the others."

"Do you know where they got my name? I've been trying to think of who could have turned me in like this."

"I know exactly where they got your name."

"You do?"

"Of course. All the men in these cases were denounced by the same person."

"Who was it?"

"A rogue FBI agent named Barry Atkins."

Malone turns the name over in his mind. He doesn't recognize it.

"He's a special agent with the anti-communist task force in the Detroit bureau." Cornish says. "Apparently, he's taken as his mission purging Negroes from any federal government position, including minor ones."

"You met him?"

"I did."

"I wonder if he was the one who came up to me outside the VA."

"He's white, slender, with horned-rim glasses and a blond crewcut. Usually wears a tan raincoat. His most distinguishing feature is he's wall-eyed. Sound like your guy?"

"That's the one."

"These federal agents are nothing but thugs, Malone. Their job is to snoop and pry and cause trouble for people they don't like."

"Can we get him to stop?"

"Well, there's the problem. It's the FBI. They can do whatever they want. Whatever we can't stop them from doing. The best we can settle for is getting you and the others reinstated and hope this cloud of fear passes quickly."

"We can't do anything about this guy?"

"I'm trying to get him censured—and maybe even fired—but it's hard. The whole legal community's keeping their heads down since the bombing at Judge Skillman's house."

"What bombing?"

"You didn't hear about it?"

Malone shakes his head.

"Somebody threw a dynamite bomb outside the home of

Recorders Court Judge McKay Skillman. Nobody was hurt, and the bomber hasn't been found yet. But the rumor is, it's over a court case in front of him involving the rights of homeowners to sell to whomever they want."

"Anybody hurt?"

"No. And no major damage was done. Just an attempt to intimidate him. But it got the attention of the other judges and all the attorneys in town, as it was no doubt meant to. But . . . first things first. We get you reinstated. Want a refill?"

"No, sir."

"Don't worry," Cornish says, "I'm on the case, and I'm not going to stop until we get your job back for you."

"Are the others getting their jobs?"

"Some have. It's still in the works. I'm confident Congressman Diggs and Senator McNamara will come through. We have to let the process work."

The Federal Building on Lafayette Boulevard, a massive square structure whose modest appearance belies the Art Deco décor. Malone checks the board in the lobby and takes an elevator with elaborate brass grillwork up to the floor of the Detroit office of the FBI. He is the only Negro in the elevator riding up with a group of white men in suits. They look at him as though he smells bad. He knows he doesn't, but he shrinks under their gaze.

Several of them get off at his floor, and he lags behind them as he looks for the right room.

Cornish told him to let the process work. Yet here he is, standing in front of the local FBI office.

He pauses to gather his courage before stepping inside.

The offices are smaller than he expected. He enters a hallway lined on the right with cubicles made of wood on the lower half and frosted glass on the upper half. On the wall to the left are photos of J. Edgar Hoover and white men he assumes are FBI agents. He doesn't see a photo of the man who Charles Cornish called Barry Atkins. He does see posters of wanted criminals, the famous ten most wanted.

Behind the cubicle walls he hears typewriters and men's voices.

He continues up the hallway and comes to a break in the cubicle wall. He peeks behind it; a woman sits at a desk talking on the telephone. She glances up at him and says, "Call you right back."

In the instant before she hangs up, Malone sweeps his eye across the desks he sees. At once he spots the wall-eyed man who spoke to him at the VA bus stop. Barry Atkins.

The woman behind the desk says, "What can I do for you?"

His question answered, Malone says, "Oh, sorry, I think I'm in the wrong place. Sorry," he repeats, and withdraws down the hall and out the door.

He takes the elevator back down to the first floor. In a bank of telephone booths near the entrance to the building, he installs himself to wait for Barry Atkins to leave.

He waits all day before Barry Atkins comes out of the elevator at five after five o'clock. Malone steps from the telephone booth where he's been hiding and fades into the crowd of people leaving the building at quitting time. He tails Barry Atkins down Washington Boulevard and around the corner at West Fort Street. Atkins raises a hand in greeting to the parking lot attendant and makes his way through the labyrinth of cars in the lot. He stops beside a Packard sedan. Gets in, fires it up, and pulls out of the lot and turns a corner.

He's gone.

Okay, Malone thinks. Now he knows who the man is and where he works, Malone can make some plans for what to do next even though Cornish tells him to do nothing.

He feels like he's making progress for the first time in a while.

At the hospital, Malone pushes a trash bin from floor to floor. He collects large bags of medical waste—mountains of blood-soaked gauze, used needles and syringes, IV bags, bandage wrappers, all the endless waste produced in the hospital and collected for incineration.

The night becomes a constant circuit from the patient floors to the basement where he leaves his bins for other custodians to feed into the incinerator, and picks up empty bins to repeat the process.

In the nurses' lounge on the OB floor, he enters to empty the wastepaper basket. Two nurses, one white, one Negro, sit chatting and laughing.

Their voices go quiet when Malone enters the room.

He picks up the trash container, takes it out to his waste bin, and empties the contents.

He returns the basket and the women's talk continues. Malone tries not to listen. The white nurse gives him a glance and turns away. She has dark hair. She pushes up her drooping glasses with the back of a knuckle. This reminds him of Anna Miller's similar gesture.

He remembers it from the first time he met her, at Sarkis Sarkisian's Society of Arts and Crafts show. And he remembers it from the second time, at the party LeRoy Foster dragged him to at the mansion in Grosse Pointe.

A waste of time, the party was, except he saw Anna again. And that gesture that charmed him.

He doesn't usually find white women attractive, but there was something about her . . . some vulnerability, maybe? She didn't walk into a room like she owned it—more like she was trying to blend into the walls.

Careful, he cautions himself. Don't go too far with these thoughts. A white woman and a colored man don't mix these days.

It could happen . . . he knows mixed couples, usually artists . . . but the odds are against it.

Thing is, he doesn't even know how *he* would feel about being with a white woman, the way things are.

To say nothing of what she might think of him.

Walking home to the Barlow Apartments after his shift, he thinks of an old blues song he heard once at Club 666 in Black Bottom. "Morning Blues," the song was. He can't recall who sang it, but he knows the chorus:

I got the morning blues
Oh so bad—
Honey, come and kiss me they're the worst I ever had.

That's me, Malone thinks. I got the morning blues.
And the afternoon blues.
And the evening blues, for that matter.
Not to mention the night blues.
Except there's no honey to come and kiss these blues away.

30

ANNA MILLER

Each time she comes to take care of Chester, more whites are gathered outside the home the Negroes bought.

So far the family have suffered no personal physical attacks; with the exception of verbal abuse, all the violence has been visited on their property.

That's what really matters to these people, Anna Miller thinks: their property. It's why they don't want a Negro family on the block—or, heaven help them all, a parade of Negro families moving in. Because it would mean the property values would take a nosedive, and all their investments in their homes—financial and psychological—would be lost.

Not that they're okay with Negro people living anywhere nearby—they aren't. Anna has heard too many times from Dottie and all the neighbors how "the coloreds" are lazy, dirty, shiftless, and so on. If they would just keep to their own kind, Dottie and her neighbors insist, all would be well.

Anna worries that Chester seems to be getting sucked in to it. Already he's starting to talk about the Negro family—Loomis, their name is—with the same disrespect as those around him, calling the family the worst names, ascribing faults to them even though he's never met them, and moreover has never met or even spoken with a Negro in his life.

Every morning, like this morning, when she arrives at the Kaczmarek home on Riopelle, her first order of business is tracking down Chester. She finds him either at Al Swoboda's further up the block or at the Loomis home in the middle of the block, standing at the crowd's edge, pacing, frightened by the growing levels of violence at the same time as he's drawn to them and the lure of the roiling crowd.

Again, this morning when she arrives, Chester isn't home. He has left his coffee and his half-empty cereal bowl with the spoon sticking out of it on the kitchen table. She knows she 'll find him down the block.

Anna doesn't wonder how these people could be so nasty. She knows first-hand the depths of people's nastiness and depravity. She does wonder how long she can continue to come down here and have it thrown in her face.

She likes Chester, and she needs the money Dottie pays her. Otherwise, she'd be gone. Every day she's here lately her stomach knots up as soon as the bus passes 6 Mile Road because she knows she's not far from Riopelle.

She walks up to the Loomis house. The usual troops are there— women pushing baby carriages, and older retired people walking around on the sidewalk carrying their signs:

My home is my castle. I will die defending it.
The Lord separated the races for a reason.
Keep our neighborhood safe from outsiders.

Picketing the home of a family who just wants to live in peace. What a disgrace.

Today she also sees a half-dozen white men kneeling on the ground. They are saying the rosary together. They pray aloud for their Jesus to deliver them from the godless Communistic menace of civil rights that threatens the American way.

She scans the crowd looking for Chester. She can't find him in this crowd, so she goes up another half a block to Swoboda's house. Dottie said Swoboda works all different hours driving trucks for a haulage company, and it's never certain when he's home.

No one comes to answer the front door at Swoboda's, so she goes around the back. She knocks on the side door, and again on the door at the rear of the house, off the patio. No answer at either place.

In the far corner of the back yard, she sees a trash can with a pile of clothes sticking out. At first, she thinks the clothes are wet because they have dark stains on them.

She looks around, sees nobody, and hurries deep into the yard. She looks into the can. The clothes lie atop ashes. She lifts a jacket out. She smells it.

It's blood, not water. The work shirt is stiff with it, dried and crusty. There's no mistaking the coppery smell or the rusty stains.

She backs out of the yard. She sees a figure looming in the window of the back door of the house.

The door opens. It's Swoboda himself, hulking and scowling.

"Whaddaya doing back here?" he growls.

"I'm looking for Chester."

"What makes you think he's back there?"

"He's missing. I need to find him. I thought he might be up here with you."

Swoboda glowers at her. He sweats with a desperate, wild-eyed look, as though he could snap in a second at the wrong word or glance.

He turns and shouts Chester's name down the basement stairs.

Soon Chester trudges up the steps. When he sees Anna, he stops, says, "No!"

"Go on," Swoboda rasps, "get up here."

Anna steps up. "Chester, come on. You can't stay here."

"I can!"

Swoboda says, "Go on, you gotta go back with her. Go on."

Grudgingly, Chester comes out the back door. Swoboda pats him on the back as he goes by, says, "Just remember what I told you."

Back at his house, Chester sits in his chair at the kitchen table and takes a sip of coffee. "It's cold."

"Of course it's cold."

Anna dumps it in the sink. She makes a new pot and refills his cup.

She sets it in front of him. "What were you doing at that house?"

"Having a meeting."

"About what?"

"Those people."

"Chester, it's not good, what they're talking about there. They're talking about maybe hurting people. Maybe kids."

Chester peers at her through his pop-bottle eyeglasses. He looks like he's trying to decide if she's telling him the truth.

"You wouldn't want any kids to get hurt, would you?" she says.

"No," he admits. He adds, "Some people must have got hurt."

"Why do you say that?"

"The blood I saw."

"What do you mean?"

"I got up early a couple days ago and I went down to Al's house. You know, to see if he was up and anything was going on."

"What made you think he would be up? What was it, six o'clock?"

"No, but I know sometimes he works at night and comes home in the morning. Sometimes he meets with people. It was still dark and he didn't see me, but I saw him come home from work and go into the back yard and take his clothes off. The clothes he was wearing were all bloody, so somebody must have got hurt."

The trash can of clothes Anna saw in the garage.

"Did you ask him about it?"

"No. I went home and went back to bed. I forgot to ask him about it the next time I saw him. I just remembered to ask him about it today. It's why I went up to his house."

"What did he say?"

"He told me it was none of my business. And not to say nothing to nobody about it."

"He didn't say who got hurt?"

"No."

The Klan did this, is her first thought. There must be a resurgence of the Klan around here and Swoboda is part of it. A night rider.

"Oh Chester, is this the kind of guy you want to be friends with? Who hurts people badly enough to get blood all over his clothes?"

Chester thinks about this. He knows enough to want to say no, but he's also caught up in this circus.

"He's my friend," Chester says weakly.

"I were you, I wouldn't want to be friends with somebody like him."

31

JAKE LIEBERMAN

"We're doing a petition drive today," Ronny Barit says. "Why don't you join us?"

"What are you petitioning for?" Jake asks.

"We're petitioning *against* continued U.S. involvement in Vietnam."

"Where's that?"

"It's a country in Indochina. My Church Peace Mission is joining with the Quakers to get the United States to withdraw its support in that part of the world."

"What makes you think petitions will make that happen?"

"We have to try. We just got out of one war over there. We don't think this country should stick its nose into another country's business."

"Yeah, I think I'll pass on that. But thanks for the offer. I appreciate your endless—and unwelcome—efforts to get me involved in the world."

"Suit yourself. I'm not going to stop asking, you know. Especially now, when you're out of work and you have time on your hands."

"Why can't you just let me be a recluse?"

"It's not good for you."

"And who are you to decide that?"

Ronny shakes his head. This will continue forever, Jake thinks.

"Suit yourself," Ronny tells him. "We're going to collect

signatures at Northland."

Well now, Jake thinks.

That puts a different face on it.

Going back to Northland might be droll.

He can renew his acquaintance with his monkey friend.

Ronny is delighted when Jake changes his mind.

A blonde woman drives them to Northland with one other member of the Mission, an earnest middle-aged man named Phil who rides beside Jake in the back seat and gives a running history of the French defeat in Vietnam at the climactic battle last year when the Communist revolutionary Viet Minh overwhelmed the French colonial forces at Điện Biên Phủ. Phil says the United States aided the French, and now that the war is over, his group wants to stop any aid in Indochina—no money, no troops, no training . . .

Jake stops listening.

This is exactly the kind of thing he would once have plunged into head first, he thinks—protesting the suppression of a nationalistic movement on the basis of a fear of Communism. Now it seems pointless, two faulty systems vying for power, both authoritarian in their own ways, an endless cycle of suppression and repression maintained through violence, world without end.

The three Church of Peace Missionaries set up at the Fountain Court at Northland, an outdoor fountain featuring a ten-foot-tall statue of Noah, of all people, near Hughes & Hatcher and Thom McAn shoes. They immediately begin accosting passers-by with their spiel about Indochina (which, Jake notes, hardly anyone has ever heard of) and their petitions on clipboards.

Jake, meanwhile, goes into Hughes & Hatcher.

He walks through the familiar smells of the perfume section to get to the stairway leading to the lower level and the monkey house. He notices a new face standing in Men's Suits, his old assignment. It's a tall, snooty-looking young man with a hank of hair sticking up rooster-like on top of his head.

Jake looks around but doesn't see his old nemesis Manning Willis. Maybe he was swept away, too, after Jake quit. Or more likely he was promoted to some higher job and fussily clicks his heels in an office somewhere.

Really, though, Jake came for the monkeys.

They are active right now, swinging from branch to branch and squabbling over food. Jake hears their muted shrieks through the heavy glass of their enclosure.

At the top, he sees what he has come for . . . his little friend from when he worked here, which now seems to have been in another life.

The little guy looks down at him.

Hey, buddy, Jake thinks. It's Jake. Remember me? Did you miss me?

Abruptly the monkey swings down to the ground and scampers right up to the glass enclosure nearest Jake. Now they are about a yard away, separated by the glass of the cage and a rope line that keeps people from coming right up to the enclosure.

The monkey looks at him so intently, and so plaintively, that Jake actually believes the little guy recognizes him and is just now realizing (if he hadn't known before) how much he missed the odd hairless monkey who now looks back at him.

For a moment, Jake is stunned by the force of the connection the monkey makes with him.

As if he's overwhelmed, too, the little guy breaks it off. He looks away, and swings up to a branch and disappears into the cluster of leaves.

He recognized me, Jake knows.

And the monkey is the only one in the store who does. Jake strolls around the lower level but sees no one he knows from when he worked here.

He feels bereft, abandoned of connection with anyone who cares for him . . . except a little capuchin monkey who probably just thought Jake looked like a big banana until he saw Jake close up.

He takes one last look at the monkey house and climbs up to the main level. He gets outside in time to see more monkey business: Ronny and his companions being shooed away by a Southfield policeman.

Ronny argues with him. Jake can hear him talking about their right of free speech.

The police officer tells him he's on private property. The right of free speech doesn't apply.

Ronny replies and while Jake watches the policeman turns his friend around, handcuffs him, and hauls him away.

Ronny's two companions stand there looking flummoxed.

"This has never happened before," Phil the historian says. "I'm not sure what to do."

"The first thing you need to do is, get Ronny out of jail," Jake tells them.

The Church Peace Mission needs to work on their protest chops, Jake thinks, if they're going to keep this up.

The woman drives them to the Southfield police station. Jake asks to talk with the officer who arrested Ronny. Both the policeman and Ronny have calmed down. It turns out the policeman was in the war and thinks they were demonstrating against the United States; when Jake tells him he's a veteran of the war, too, and explains they were trying to keep more American kids from having to go to war, the policeman relents and just tells Ronny never again to collect signatures on private property in Southfield.

On the way home, they laugh about it.

It becomes a story they will tell from now on—the time they got run out of Northland and Ronny almost got arrested.

Jake doesn't care. The bubble he left the store in still envelops him; his feeling of disconnection stings.

Man, are you ever a sad case.

Ronny and the others want to go out for a meal together. Jake lets them celebrate their own little community; he just wants to go home.

He's been out in public enough today, and he must still look pretty bad from his beating.

His solitary flat beckons.

32

BRIDGET MCMANUS

They meet at the State Police post in Flint. It's centrally located for the investigators of the crimes in Detroit, Kalamazoo, and Flint.

Seated around the table are Bridget McManus, Raymond Rausch from the Flint post of the Michigan State Police, Ed Hauser from the Detroit Police Department, and Fritz Richmond of the Kalamazoo Police Department.

They discuss the three child murders discovered in the past few months. They go through the facts of each case, presented by the policeman in charge of the jurisdiction where the child was found.

Ray Rausch walks them through the case of Joey Gallagher, twelve-year-old boy, found in a rural area near Flint after being missing for five weeks. Shot in the back of the head with a small-caliber gun. The coroner said he had been sexually abused, and most likely died the day he was reported missing.

Ed Hauser presents the case of Barbara Nicholson, seven-year-old girl, strangled, beaten, sexually abused. Disappeared while walking to her Catholic school. Found in Chandler Park in Detroit. Likely killed the day she went missing.

Fritz Richmond presents the case of Jeannie McCormick, eight-year-old girl, found in a scrub area in Kalamazoo, beaten about the head, clothes torn from the lower half of her body. The post-mortem revealed she had been sexually abused, like the other two children.

Also like the others, probably killed the day she went missing. She was last seen walking home from school, resting on the curb.

They sift through all the forensic evidence, including plaster casts of tire tracks from around the areas, witness sightings, interviews with volunteers who took part in the massive searches looking for the children, and everything else (miscellaneous trash, cigarette butts, and so on) picked up from the areas around where the kids were found.

They look for patterns, similarities in the obvious mayhem committed on their small bodies.

They talk about the possible suspects they picked up and grilled—the known sex perverts, pederasts, and animal torturers—and had to release for lack of evidence.

They go through the reports one more time and Ed Hauser says, "Bridget, there's a report here on an interview you did with this guy, Jacob Lieberman."

"Yeah," she says, "he works near where Barbara was found. Single guy, seems to be a loner."

"Any record?" Raymond Rausch asks.

"No. Seems like he was fingered by somebody with a grudge against him."

"Well," Hauser says, "he drives the same model vehicle a witness says he saw Joey Gallagher in. The vehicle fits the tire tracks around Barbara Nicholson's scene. He can't account for his specific whereabouts during the days when the kids went missing."

"I checked him out," Bridget says. "Said he doesn't own a gun but has access to a rifle in the security office of the auto plant where he works."

"A firearm's not hard to get ahold of," Rausch says. "Or get rid of. Or lie about."

"Does he fit the witness description of the guy in the car with the first kid?" Hauser asks.

"Just like a million other guys in the State of Michigan."

"I think we should take another look at him," Rausch says. The other men around the table nod in agreement.

Bridget says, "He doesn't strike me as being capable of doing all that to those kids."

Rausch says, "And you know this based on your vast experience with homicide cases?"

She lets that one go by. The other men snicker, including Hauser, the bastard.

Rausch says, "I think you should talk to Lieberman again."

"Fine."

Hauser thinks he's got the upper hand with her, but she has to admit to herself she's glad for a sanctioned chance to talk to Jake again.

Ed Hauser waits for her in front of the station. He's smoking a cigar, which she hates. And he knows she hates it.

"Sgt. McManus."

"Detective Hauser. Thanks for backing me up in there."

He laughs it off. "Where are you off to now?"

"Home. I want to see my kids before they forget they have a mother."

"Got time for a quick conference about the case?" He winks. "We can talk in my car."

"I don't think so."

"Just a quick one."

"I know what kind of 'conference' you have in mind, Ed. No."

He steers her to his car in the station lot.

"Seriously?" she says. She disentangles her arm from his grip. "In your duty vehicle in broad daylight in front of a State Police post?"

"We'll fog up the windows quick enough."

"What part of 'no' do you not understand?"

"I figure you're just playing hard to get."

"I'm not playing, Ed. I *am* hard to get."

"Since when? You didn't used to be."

She holds up her hands as though to establish a physical boundary. "I can't do this."

"Maybe later tonight?"

"No, Ed. Never again."

"You say that every time."

"This time I mean it."

"Yeah, well. We'll see."

33

MALONE COLEMAN

Malone stations himself on the far side of the newsstand on the ground floor. Coming in are the bureaucrats who work in the building, men with their white faces and short hair and off-the-rack suits. The women bunch together. The few Negroes he sees are the custodians, mopping the marble floors or polishing the brass fittings on the elevators and the stairs.

So far he has not seen Barry Atkins. He's hoping he can catch him before the agent gets up to the Bureau offices.

He's in luck. Malone spots his man walking in beside two white men who are practically indistinguishable from him except for the outward cast of his right eye.

As he passes, Malone steps away from the newsstand into Atkins's line of sight. (Or lines of sight, Malone thinks, depending where his wayward eye looks.)

Atkins sees him, tells his two companions he'll catch up with them upstairs. He sidles over to where Malone stands. "Didn't think I'd see you again," he says.

"Got a couple minutes to talk?"

"Sure. Come up. We'll talk in my office."

Malone shakes his head. "Somewhere private."

"I know just the place. Follow me."

Atkins leads him outside the building and around the corner to a coffee shop on the ground floor of an office building. The tables are mostly empty at this time of the morning. Atkins leads him back to a table in a corner, away from the kitchen and the register.

They sit across the table from each other. Atkins leans in and before they can start talking, an older white woman comes over to their table with menus. She gives Malone the stink-eye. Atkins waves away the menus. "Just coffee."

"Two?" she asks, not looking at Malone now.

Atkins nods and she disappears. In another minute she comes back with the two coffees before returning behind the counter.

Atkins sips his drink. Malone pushes his away.

"How you been, Malone? Haven't seen you in a while."

Malone just glares at him. Atkins's eyes point in opposite directions; Malone doesn't know which one to look at.

He sits there, a mass of conflicting feelings—rage, anxiety, fear at confronting an FBI agent, the atavistic uncertainty about talking back to a white man with power—but they cohere into a cold anger at the man who has inflicted such damage on him, who doesn't even know him but feels privileged enough to be able to upset Malone's life from a distance.

Atkins says, "Been thinking about my offer?"

"I've been thinking about it, yeah."

Atkins raises the cup to his lips and blows across the mouth of it. Takes a sip. "So. Are we going to work together?"

Malone leans forward. He decides to concentrate on Atkins's left eye, the one looking straight ahead. "Why did you tell my boss at the VA about my background?"

Atkins plays dumb. "I'm not sure what you mean."

"I mean, why did you tell my boss about my background with the National Negro Labor Council?"

Atkins stares at Malone for another few moments. He takes another sip of his coffee.

"You found out about it from somebody named Frank Carmody," Malone says. "Don't bother denying it. I talked to Carmody."

Atkins puts down the coffee cup and folds his hands around it, as though warming his fingers. "You've been busy."

"Look, I know what you did. And I know you got your information from Carmody. Thing I want to know is, why would you do it? What did I ever do to you?"

Atkins doesn't answer right away.

The waitress comes over with a steaming pot of coffee. She tops up Atkins's, holds it up for Malone, who waves it away.

"You haven't done a thing to me. Not you personally, anyway. Your people, on the other hand?" Atkins shakes his head. "Where to begin."

"My *people*? What do you mean, my *people*?"

"The thing you don't realize is," Atkins says, "we're in the middle of a struggle between two categorically different political systems. On one side are the supporters of liberty, democracy, and freedom.

"On the other side are the Communists and socialists who are the sworn enemies of democracy and freedom. And under the control of those enemies of freedom are the government bureaucrats, liberal religious groups, and civil rights organizations and activists, who are their willing dupes. Who conspire, if you will, against the values we hold dear in this nation. It's a struggle to the death.

"And you, Malone, are part of it. You and your participation in Communist front organizations like the National Negro Labor Council, organizations that pretend to foster equality, but only spread the socialist lies that weaken the American family. And the American family is the bulwark against the Soviet threat."

His left eye keeps a steady aim on Malone, but his right eye jumps all over the place, like it's trying to escape Atkins's craziness.

Or, Malone thinks, it's trying to leap out of its restraints and go right for my throat.

"Among the biggest threats eating away at the basis of American exceptionalism is the rapacious sexuality and fundamental criminality of *your people*. So yes, I was the one who told your superiors at the VA hospital about your background, and I will continue to do what I can to rid the body politic of people like you— people who pretend to work for democratic ideals but who, in actuality, are doing everything they can to undermine them."

To Malone, this sounds distressingly like what Frank Carmody told him.

Atkins says, "Do I assume from the look on your face you're not going to join my crusade?"

"I'd rather fucking die."

Atkins shakes his head as though pitying Malone. "That's what I thought." He pulls his billfold from his pocket. He takes two dollars and drops the bills on the table. "We don't have anything else to talk about. This one's on me."

Atkins stands and walks away without looking back.

The waitress comes over to the table. She scoops up the two bucks and she, too, walks away.

Leaving Malone sitting by himself.

He sits for a minute, his thoughts scattered.

He gets up and sleepwalks out the door. He pauses on the street, still unable to harness his thoughts. Hard to sort through such blatant, unvarnished hatred.

Atkins said out loud what most of the white people Malone knows would never publicly admit: Negroes are un-American, don't have a stake in this country, and should be forever kept away from the real fruits of membership in its society.

He starts walking.

He gets down to the corner of Mack and Woodward Avenues. He stops. People rush by him without looking at him save for inscribing the silent arc away from where he stands, seemingly without noticing the human being there. He feels like a ghost, transparent except for the aura of trouble people sense from him as a Negro in a white city.

The thought reminds him of what Bessie's friend said about the Negro man who was trying to move into a white neighborhood except the whites didn't want him there. It was exactly the kind of resistance Barry Atkins exemplified.

Atkins was right. It is a war. Except it's not between Communism and democracy, but between us and whites who don't want us to share in their American dream.

Anna Miller also talked about a Negro family trying to move into a white neighborhood, and the resistance they were facing.

Where did she say the house was?

On a street called Riopelle, near the Sojourner Truth housing project, the site of a white riot in February 1942 when Negro defense workers tried to move into the public housing built for them. Hundreds of whites kept the Negro residents from moving in until April, after the Michigan governor and the state police got involved.

And of course, who got arrested at the time?

Negroes.

Malone had wanted to go down to the Sojourner Truth project and help, put his body on the line for people who just wanted to live in a decent place. But Clarence and Bessie talked him out of it. Gonna be bad down there, Clarence said. You don't want to be anywhere near it.

And Malone listened. And it was bad, Clarence was right.

And Malone listened when Clarence warned him not to go down to the 1943 riot that started on Belle Isle and spread across downtown Detroit. People were killed during that one. Whites pulled Negroes off of streetcars—such is the level of segregation in Detroit that street cars are among the few places where whites and Negroes routinely mixed—and beat them mercilessly.

Riopelle is on the northeast side of the city, far from where he stands. But what else does he have to do, this unwanted invisible ghost with no responsibilities and nothing to fill his time with until he has to go clean floors at Harper?

He wants to see where this house is, look in the eyes of those white bastards who want to keep a Negro from sharing a better life. He starts walking up Woodward, figuring he will cut over somewhere—maybe Boston Boulevard, where the rich folks (white and some Negro) live—and he'll keep walking north until he finds Riopelle.

He's not sure what he's going to do once he gets there. But he knows he's not going to sit this one out, whatever happens.

When he passes the swank Boston-Edison district on the left and the even swanker Arden Park neighborhood on the right, he decides to stick to Woodward, thinking it would be safer for him than walking through the neighborhoods.

He walks through Highland Park, passes the original Ford Motor factory where the first Model Ts were churned out. At 6 Mile Road, the border between Highland Park and Detroit, he cuts east, crossing railway lines. By the time he gets to Riopelle, dusk is already setting in.

He doesn't know which house he wants on this quiet street of small frame homes—until he crosses 6 Mile and gets four or five blocks up. From one end of Riopelle, he sees a bright glow down at the other end. He continues up the block.

And there it is. Someone had pounded a two-by-four wooden cross into a front lawn, doused it with gasoline, and set it ablaze. Malone takes a wild guess that is his destination.

Welcome to the neighborhood.

A ghoulish group of whites, men and women, stand in the street, their impassive faces lit by the flickering flames.

The door to the house bursts open and a Negro man stares in disbelief at what his neighbors have done.

"Do you have a water hose?" Malone shouts above the crackling fire.

"No," the man says. "I ain't unpacked nothing yet!"

Malone rushes around the side of the house and finds a garden hose left by the previous owner. It's connected to a spigot sticking out of the brick wall. He turns the water on and pulls the hose around to the front.

He douses the burning cross with water until only hissing charred wood is left.

Malone goes to turn the hose off and throws it down in disgust. The homeowner just stands there in disbelief at what people have done to him. Malone glares at the crowd. A voice sails out: "Get the hell out of here."

One by one, they drift away.

The Negro man takes Malone by the arm. He gently steers Malone inside the house.

"Thank you, my friend," the man says.

"I'm sorry." Malone shivers, near tears.

A burning cross, in Detroit in 1955.

"Nothing for you to be sorry about. I'm Henty Loomis."

"Malone Coleman." They shake hands.

A woman stands away from the living room, sheltering two frightened little girls. "My wife Dorothy," Henty says. "My daughters, Denise and Yvonne."

Malone nods. "Sorry you have to go through this."

Dorothy says, "Ain't your fault." She sweeps the little girls into the back of the house and Henty Loomis says, "How about some coffee?"

"Fine."

Henty leads Malone into the kitchen. He begins rummaging through boxes and comes up with a percolator.

"When did you move in?" Malone asks.

"This afternoon."

"So before you even get to sleep in your new house, you get a cross burned into your lawn."

"Dorothy and the girls were scared stiff."

"Welcome to the neighborhood."

A rock shatters one of the front windows, sending glass shards over the living room rug.

Like a shot Malone flies out the front door. The street is deserted. Whoever threw the rock has disappeared into the night.

"Fucking cowards," he yells into the darkness.

He comes back inside. "Any guns in the house?" he asks Henty.

"No. I wouldn't have one. I'd be too tempted to use it on somebody. Jesus said love thine enemies, it's the only weapon I need."

Dorothy Loomis says, "Come get your coffee, Malone."

They sit around the kitchen table. Malone takes a sip of coffee. "I'd stay with you, make sure the place makes it through the night. But I work a midnight shift."

"Appreciate it. But we'll make do. A couple of my brothers and cousins are on their way over."

Henty goes over to the broken window. He picks up the rock and puts it on the sideboard in the living room. "Souvenir."

Henty's relatives come to the house during the evening. One brother tells Henty the tires on his Cadillac in the driveway are all flat; they have been slashed.

Henty's brother Jerome comes over at eight. Henty asks Jerome to give Malone a ride to work.

Malone says he will be back in the morning.

Malone comes straight from his shift the next day. Dorothy gives him breakfast and after that he helps Henty drag the burnt cross off the lawn and dump it in the alley behind the house.

Jerome gives Henty a ride to work—Henty reads meters for the Ecorse water department. Another brother stays at the house with Henty's wife, along with Malone. Henty tells Malone he doesn't need to stay, but Malone doesn't want to leave; if something should happen here while he's away, he would feel terrible, like it would be his fault.

With Henty's brother here, Malone feels like he can get some sleep. The house is quiet, with the girls in school and Dorothy snoozing, too.

He lies down on the sofa in the living room with the intention of sleeping for an hour.

It's the middle of the afternoon by the time he wakes up.

More whites mill around outside. This must be the mothers' brigade, Malone thinks: women pushing their baby carriages up and down the sidewalk in front of the Loomis home.

Sure, because what is the biggest reason for a Negro incursion into a neighborhood if not to steal the flower of white womanhood?

He remembers reading in the newspaper when there was a huge community meeting at a local high school before the war to protest construction of the Sojourner Truth housing project for Negro defense workers. The local Catholic diocesan priest stood up and made an impassioned speech saying one of the worst effects of having a Negro housing project near a white neighborhood would be the danger to white girls and women that Negroes present.

Sure, Malone thinks, because in the white imagination, we're all rapists just waiting to deflower white girls. When we're not being thieves and dope peddlers and general lazy layabouts.

He goes out on the front stoop of the Loomis house, just to piss them off. They point and shout and call him nigger, but they don't actually threaten him.

Try it, his presence says.

Just try it.

After a while, he goes back inside and makes himself a ham sandwich and stands at the living room window, chewing thoughtfully while watching the women outside walk and chat.

There are several ragged holes in the window glass. Henty's cousin Alonzo Loomis said he will get the window covered with plywood.

This is a house under siege.

34

ANNA MILLER

As usual, Chester is gone when Anna arrives in the morning. Anna walks up to the Loomis house, but doesn't see him in the crowd. She walks around the perimeter of the home looking for him. Angry Negro faces inside the house look out at her through the few windows not boarded up. She understands their wrath; if the tables were turned, Anna would feel the same as they do. Indeed, it's a wonder to her they can restrain their anger; how do they keep from storming out of the house and beating these pathetic white people to a pulp?

One certain face follows her from inside. A man who looks familiar. A handsome man, with taut skin and almond-shaped brown eyes.

They exchange a look of recognition. The man motions for her to go around the side of the house.

She walks up the driveway until she gets to the fence gate closing off the back yard. A window on the first floor of the house opens and Malone Coleman looks out at her.

"Hey," he says. "What are you doing here?"

It's a question loaded with suspicion. . . here with these crazy bigots, he means.

"I'm looking for the guy I take care of. He lives down the block, but he keeps coming up here, with this crowd. What are *you* doing here?"

"Come through the gate, around the back."

She opens the gate and slips into the yard. He has come out the back door of the house. She feels an urge to hug him, but takes care not to act on it.

"I'm here because of you," he says.

"What do you mean?"

"You were the one who told me about what was going on here. At that party in Grosse Pointe?"

"I remember talking about it, yeah. Do you know these people?"

"Never met them before. I knew I couldn't stay away without helping them."

"That's so good of you." She peeks around the corner of the house at the crowd. "Do you believe this?"

"I sure can."

"I'm so sorry this is happening."

"Not your fault."

"Yeah, but I wish there was something I could do."

"Just keep your guy away from these nuts. It's going to get a lot worse. This is like a fever . . . it's going to have to burn itself out."

"You stay safe."

"Gonna try."

He raises a hand of farewell and ducks back into the house.

She finds Chester and takes him home. She makes them both tuna sandwiches for lunch.

Afterwards he wants to go back to the Loomis house.

"Why?" she asks.

"Because I have to."

"But why do you have to?"

"Because I *have* to! I want to be with my friends!"

She doesn't like it that he's getting so worked up.

"Chet, did you take your medicine this morning?"

"Yes!"

Defiant. Almost insolent.

Once, right after she started, Chester blew up because she cooked him an egg that was hard-boiled when he wanted it runny. He flew into a rage; she thought for a moment he was going to hit her. Luckily his sister Dottie was there and she calmed him right down.

Dottie said he forgot to take his meds.

What did Dottie do?

Anna remembers Dottie gave him an alternative ("You know what, Chester? Let's have some corn flakes instead.")

Now, she says, "Chester, I have an idea. Let's go shopping! Your sister left me a list of things to get at the store. Come on. Let's go."

"No."

"Come on. You'll see Mr. Tauber. Maybe he'll give you another 3 Musketeers?"

Chester weakens, calms down. "Okay." It's clear he doesn't have his heart in it. Anna doesn't care, she just wants to get him away from the insanity of this street, these crowds, these so-called "friends."

Rather than take their usual route, which would go past the Loomis house, Anna leads them in the opposite direction, south on Riopelle to Nevada and over to the next block, Orleans Street, and from there up to 7 Mile and their destination, Tauber's Market.

Chester sulks all the way to the market. But as soon as the grocer, Mr. Tauber, gives him his 3 Musketeers, Chester is happy as a clam.

On the way back home, Anna leads them on the same circuitous route. To get Chester thinking about what's going on down the street, she says, "Imagine how you would feel if someone hurt you. Do you think it's ever okay to make somebody else feel like that?"

"No."

"Why not?"

"Because it's never good to make somebody sad. Or cry."

"Right. Why do you suppose Mr. Swoboda hurt someone?"

"Because they want to move into the neighborhood."

"Why do you suppose they do?"

Chester thinks some more. "Because they want a nice place to live? But why do they have to invade *our* neighborhood?"

"They're not invading, Chester. The man who moved onto your street just wants a safe place for his family to live. Just like your father wanted for you, and your sister wants now. Who gives those people the right to say somebody can't move into this neighborhood? They don't own it."

Chester doesn't answer right away.

"And who gives them the right to throw rocks at the Negro

family's home, and terrorize the children and damage the house?"

"No one," Chester admits.

"And what about your friend Al Swoboda?"

"What about him?"

"Who gives him the right to hurt somebody, which he obviously did. I saw those same bloody clothes you saw, Chester. Whoever it was, judging by the state of the clothes, must have been badly hurt."

"Who was it?" Chester asks.

"I don't know. You have to ask him."

"Maybe I will," Chester murmurs, unwrapping his candy bar and taking a thoughtful bite.

35

JAKE LIEBERMAN

His landlady knocks on his door. "Phone call for you," Mrs. O'Neill says, standing there with her little teary-eyed dog Fifi in her arms. Fifi is her constant companion; Jake has never seen the woman without the pooch in her arms.

"Thank you."

In her elegant, parochial-school handwriting, she wrote, "Please call Sgt. Bridget McManus."

"I didn't know they were letting women in the police force these days," she sniffs, and turns to go back downstairs to her flat.

Mrs. O'Neill will take phone messages for him (increasingly grudgingly), but she draws the line at allowing him to use the phone in her flat. He heads down to the corner bar and uses the payphone in the back of the dark, beery-smelling joint. The phone hangs on the wall next to the men's room, which reeks of piss.

He calls the number the policewoman left. She's not in, but Jake leaves his name.

He's glad of the call.

Later, closing up the shed, he sees a Buick sedan pulling to the curb in front of the house.

The driver's door opens. Bridget McManus steps out. "Hey."

"Hey. Did you get my message? I tried you back."

"I did. Got a couple minutes?"

Upstairs he puts on the kettle to make instant coffee.

They sit at the kitchen table. Jake says, "What's up?"

"There was another little kid found dead."

"Oh no. Sorry to hear it."

"Yeah. Little girl."

"Where?"

"Near Kalamazoo. Same deal as the other ones—battered, signs of sexual violation."

She shows him a photo of an impish, dark-haired girl in a bucket hat. "Her name's Jeannie McCormick. Ever see her before?"

"Never."

"Ever been to Kalamazoo?"

"Never in my life."

"Know anybody who lives there?"

"Not offhand. Look, are you really still thinking I had something to do with these kids?"

"No. The detectives on the other kid murder cases asked me to talk with you again. This is mainly so I can say we talked."

She takes in his battered face. "What happened?"

"I got jumped at work."

"Who did it?"

"Remember the guy at work I told you I clocked?"

"Got his own back, huh?"

"In spades. One of his buddies held me while he went to town on me."

"Are you pressing charges?"

"Not worth it. I got fired."

"Why?"

"They said it was because I didn't report to work when I had to go to the hospital. I was still on probation, so they could fire me for any reason. Or no reason."

"I see they knocked a tooth out."

"Yeah. Busted my nose and a couple ribs, for good measure."

"Really worked you over."

"That they did."

She takes a cop-camera-look around the living room, her gaze lighting up the furniture, the lamps, especially the framed photos on the walls.

They are combat scenes—two medics tending to a third soldier on the ground, grimacing in pain; two more soldiers posing in a foxhole, tough customers with cigarettes hanging from their lips and their helmets jauntily askew; a group of nurses; soldiers pinned down, gun smoke like a ghost hanging over them. A photo of a quartet of officers looking both disgusted and disbelieving.

"You took those?" she asks.

He nods.

She gets up and takes a close look at the quartet of officers. She points to it. "This. You don't even have to show what they're looking at. Their faces tell the story."

"I was with them when they liberated the camp. I have lots of photos of what they were looking at, but I see them often enough in my nightmares. I thought if I showed them looking at the camp, it would tell the story without causing anybody else to have nightmares."

"Powerful."

The kettle on the stove whistles. He turns it off and searches through his cupboards. "Uh-oh."

"What?"

"No coffee."

"Tea would be fine."

"No tea, either."

"Fine way to treat a guest."

"I thought this was a police interrogation. Are you hungry?"

"Why? I suppose the cupboard's bare and you don't have any food, either."

"But I know where we can find some."

They walk to the Mercury Bar a few blocks from Jake's apartment. It's near the Michigan Central Railroad Station and Briggs Stadium, and so caters mostly to train travelers, Tiger baseball and Lions football fans, and Corktown locals.

They take a table in the back of the dim bar.

A young woman with orange hair comes over to take their order. Bridget orders a Coke. Jake orders coffee. They both order hamburgers.

"They fry their burgers in lard here, you know," Jake says. "Why they're so good."

"Healthy, too."

Their drinks come. They salute each other with their glass and cup.

"I'm not keeping you from fighting crime or anything, am I?" he asks.

"No. I'm supposed to be off-duty today, but I spent a couple hours at my desk, clearing reports. My kids are with my parents."

"I suppose there are some advantages to being unemployed. No schedules to keep."

"Where did you learn photography?"

"I spent a year at the Society for Arts and Crafts, and I took a photography course there, along with commercial art. I went to Wayne University for a few years, but I never graduated. Mostly I picked up my training in the army. As I think I told you, before that, I was a paste-up artist. I'd gone to a few Communist party meetings back in the forties. When the HUAC circus came to town, the interviewers subpoenaed me about it. As soon as my bosses found out about the subpoena, my job went out the window."

"And you haven't worked in newspapers since?"

"Nobody would hire me. I didn't want to move away, so . . . I've been picking up work here and there. And now I've gone and lost another job."

"You'll find something else. I think your talents were wasted being a security guard."

"I think that was fairly obvious."

"But things are looking up, aren't they?"

"They were. The city's turning a corner. Jobs are already starting to dry up. The factories are moving away—they're going south, or to the Midwest."

"Why?"

"The government's spreading out defense contracts so they're not so centralized. The car industry's moving out, too, partly to reduce the power of the unions, and partly because they're running out of room to expand inside Detroit. They also want lower taxes. So unemployment around here is starting to skyrocket."

"What will you do?"

Jake manages a small, pained smile. "I'll be fine. For a while, anyway. I don't need much."

"Why do you want to stay in Detroit? Why not move away, get a better job somewhere else?"

"When I was married, I stayed here because my wife's family was here. She became my ex-wife when the job became my ex-job, and she moved away to marry somebody else. I have a brother in town. Nothing, really, to keep me from leaving if I wanted to."

"So what keeps you here?

"Lethargy. Torpor. Ennui. Timidity. Take your pick."

"Oh, before I forget, I wanted to thank you for going over to Chaim Lerner's. You did good with him."

"Glad to help." He tells her about what happened with Chaim.

"Do you know if he's all right?" she asks.

"I haven't seen him since he was admitted to the hospital. He was in rough shape, but I think he's getting what he needs now. I'll check in on him again."

"You saved his life."

He brushes it away. I probably did, he thinks, but that was accidental. That same free-floating, random chance that brings calamity also might bring good fortune, again randomly, undeserved and unpredictable.

"If you do want to see him, my friend Roz said he's out of the hospital. They transferred him to the Jewish Home for the Aged. Do you know where that is?"

"I do."

They walk back to her car in front of Jake's.

She gets in and rolls down the driver's side window. "Thanks for the lunch," she says.

"Sure. Nice to see you again."

"Likewise."

"I'll let you know what happens with Chaim."

She starts her car.

"See you again, Sgt. McManus."

He gives her a wave and walks back to his flat entrance.

He thinks he hears her say, "Hope so," but the car engine muffles the word so he's not entirely certain.

But it's what he chooses to believe he heard.

36

BRIDGET MCMANUS

At her desk in the Women's Division after seeing Jake, Bridget sits with a cup of bad coffee and reviews her notes from the meeting of the principles in the murdered children's cases.

As she reads, she remembers something she thought about last night in bed, while thinking about Jake and his joke about being an "automotive industrial loss-limitation investigator." It's one thing they didn't talk about when the investigators discussed the case.

When they were talking about patterns, they overlooked one particular combination of events.

The three dead children were found in three different areas of the state. True, they were all dumped in overgrown, untended areas near population centers. But their discussions had been concentrating on where the kids were picked up, and yes, there wasn't anything constant about those; one kid disappeared hiking in the woods, another on her way to school, the third on her way home from a school in a different part of the state.

Their assumption was these were convenient locations for a sex deviant to pick up children.

What they didn't talk about was another shared feature of where the children were found.

All the locations are near automobile factories.

Joey Gallagher, the first victim, was found in an abandoned area in Flint, not far from the Chevrolet assembly plant.

Barbara Nicholson was found in a park in Detroit near the Hudson Motor Car Company factory.

Jeannie McCormick was found near the Checker Cab manufacturing facility and testing track in Kalamazoo.

There's a connection. But now what does it mean?

And how can it help find whoever committed these horrible acts?

She goes through all the police reports on the children again with this connection in mind.

And while she does, she keeps Jake Lieberman in the back of her mind. True, the automotive factory connection is another strand tying Jake to one of the deaths, Barbara Nicholson's. She doesn't want her developing personal relationship with him to blind her to a possible connection to the other children.

He might even be trying to encourage a relationship to throw her off the scent.

All the locations are close enough in Michigan for him to pick up the kids and still get back to the Hudson plant in time for his night shift.

Did he have a contact—maybe an accomplice—at the other locations?

Or maybe he was seconded to the security offices of the other plants. Bridget assumed each plant had its own security force; did Jake work for a company that sent security guards to the plants in Flint and Kalamazoo? Did he have any reason to visit those plants?

Okay, she cautions herself. Easy. Don't let his tangential connection to one death obscure other possibilities. And don't look for a reason to *not* get involved with him.

Sometimes, she tells herself, you can be too subtle about these things . . .

Let's step back from Jake and think about those other possibilities.

What would connect someone else to three different auto plants in three different locations around the state?

Are there jobs that send a guy from one plant to another, three different corporations, but with some commonality?

Maybe a jobber serviced all three plants. She would need to get a list of all the jobbers and support services for each one of the three plants, and coordinate the names. A huge undertaking, but possible.

A faster way to get there, she thinks, might be to get a list from the security offices at every plant of the jobbers who signed in with a delivery or a service around the times when the kids went missing. If one name showed up across all three locations, it would be a solid lead.

This was more doable, and it would yield more valuable information.

Again, here's a connection with the security departments of the plants, she thinks . . . should she be so certain Jake Lieberman has no involvement here? Or if he doesn't, somebody else in the security departments does?

Or does she *want* him to be involved?

Does she want him to have a connection as an excuse for not getting involved with him? A way of distancing herself, because she seems to be on a clear path to involvement with this guy.

She and Jake are getting along, there's no question. But she's fighting her desire to let her feelings for him develop.

She certainly doesn't have to worry about developing an emotional attachment to a boob like Ed Hauser.

She can see a future with Jake, on the other hand.

If she wants one.

She shakes her head to clear him from her thoughts, and makes a note of what she needs to get from each plant.

On Monday morning, she starts with the security office at the Hudson plant.

It's always best to talk to people in person, so she travels to the factory; it's not far from police headquarters downtown.

The process of getting the names of all jobbers who signed in to the plant's visitors logs on a certain date turns out to be more complicated than she thought it would be. The chief on duty doesn't believe he has the authority to release the records to Bridget; she has to wait while the request slow-walks all the way up to the vice president of administration.

She doesn't have enough evidence to apply for a warrant (which a male officer would have to apply for anyway, and she's doing this without a male officer, not by the book), so she has to wait as patiently as she can while the phone calls go higher and higher in the Hudson Motors management.

In the meantime, the security chief has no problem letting Bridget see the roster for the security unit. She copies down all their names and addresses. A harsh red line through Jake's name removes him from the security roster.

When she finally gets approval for the logs, the next problem is finding them for the date she wants.

By the time she gets the material and searches through it, recording visitors for the date she's looking for—the date of Barbara Nicholson's disappearance—it's already dinnertime.

She told her kids she would be home for dinner. She'll have to finish tomorrow.

The next morning, at the Flint Chevy assembly plant she goes through the same rigamarole as at the Hudson plant. Things move a bit faster, though, because unlike Hudson, which is in the process of shutting down, the Flint plant is thriving; the lines of administration are more robust.

Even so, the list of visitors to the plant stretches longer than she suspected. The U.S. mail, trucks carrying auto parts, janitorial supplies and services, temporary workers—everybody down to the guys who pick up the bad weather rugs in the building lobbies. Matching the lists will take some time.

Luckily, the security chief at the Flint plant is a former Flint police detective who sympathizes with her investigation. He has kids around the same age as the ones who were killed.

The Flint Chevy guy makes a call to the Kalamazoo security director and lets Bridget explain to him what she needs. The other man says he will work on getting the information right away. If Bridget doesn't make it to the Checker Cab facility by the end of the workday, he would leave it for her with the evening chief of service.

Sure enough, the information is waiting for her when she rolls into Kalamazoo in the afternoon.

She gets home in time to have dinner with her kids and brother. Twice in a row, the wiseacre kids point out to her . . . a new record.

She really does have to spend more time with them before they forget who she is entirely, she tells herself.

After she gets them to bed, she sits at the dining room table and spreads out the information she's collected. She starts with the security department rosters. There are no crossovers from one plant to the next; each employs its own security force.

She sets aside the lists of security officers.

Next, she lists the different kinds of visitors who entered each plant during the dates when the kids went missing and were found; according to the coroners' reports, all three children were killed on or about the dates they disappeared. She categorizes the lists by service, plant, and purpose of visit. Under each category she lists the individuals who signed in for each type of visit—employment, parts deliveries, inspections, mail and package delivery, gas, electric, telephone, and so on.

She winds up with a list of categories five pages long. And the listings of individuals add another twenty pages to each category. It's slow going, category by category, line by line. Bridget discovers several companies service all three plants, but with no common individual signatories.

Still she keeps at it, cross-listing, looking for a name in all the logs for all three auto factories at the right times.

Toward morning, with the day brightening outside and her kids starting to stir, she realizes this is going to take longer than she thought.

Two days later, during yet another late-night session, she finds what she has been looking for.

She sits back and rubs her eyes. She will have to go through this list again, when she isn't so exhausted. And the actual connections to the crimes will need to be proven.

But for the time being, she allows herself the indulgence of one beautiful word:

Gotcha.

At Police Headquarters at 1300 Beaubien in the morning, Bridget calls the security department at Hudson Motors. She speaks with the day supervisor, who nonchalantly gives her the information she asks for. Some of what he tells her sounds confidential, but she doesn't care; she pumps him for whatever she can get out of him.

Next she makes a few more phone calls, which lead down to Toledo, Ohio. On a hunch, she tries the Toledo Police Department.

Bridget identifies herself as a sergeant with the Women's Division of the Detroit Police Department, but the Toledo detective on the phone adamantly refuses to help. He tells her he doesn't even believe a Women's Division exists in the DPD.

Bridget asks to speak with his lieutenant, who, it turns out, knows Emily Richardson, the commander of the Women's Division in Detroit.

He says he will have one of his detectives give Bridget what she wants to know.

When Bridget finally hears back from him, she adds his information to her notes.

She calls Richard Rausch, Fritz Richmond, and Ed Hauser and tells them what she found. They're all away from their desks. She leaves them messages and the address where she wants them to meet her.

37

MALONE COLEMAN

"**I** wouldn't go out there," Jerome Loomis warns.

Henty Loomis's brother and Malone have spent the day guarding the house from whatever the crazy white mob might decide to do. Today the women have been walking around chanting with their baby carriages and the men have been kneeling and praying in front of the house.

Things are bad when you have to get down on your knees and ask Jesus to remove colored people from your sight.

Malone says, "I'm going to need to get to work."

"See them women out there? You go out there, they like to tear you to pieces. No, wait till Henty get home," Jerome continues. "Need to be at least two of us here all the time."

Now it's just Malone and Jerome, with Dorothy Loomis and her girls upstairs behind a locked door in Dorothy's bedroom. Dorothy kept them home from school so they wouldn't have to walk through the protesters and face children taunting them.

"What time does he get home?" Malone asks.

"After four. Sit back. Have another cup of coffee."

"I already had so much, my back teeth are floating."

"Sit tight. Won't be long now."

A rock knocks against the plywood over the living room window.

Malone feels trapped in this nightmare . . . a rapidly growing crowd of whites screaming for the blood of the Negroes who have the gall to move onto their street. And yet as much as he would like to leave, he feels compelled to stay. Their signs talk about Negroes invading their street, but who are really the invaders here?

"It's okay," he says. "I'll stay as long as you need me to."

"Time Henty come home, all the autoworkers in the neighborhood be home, too. This party gonna grow."

Malone walks through the back of the house. Thinks: If you feel trapped, imagine how Dorothy and her little girls feel. They must be terrified.

Two more rocks clatter against the front of the house.

Later that afternoon, Jerome calls to him from the living room.

"Look like they fixing to attack the house," Jerome says. He peers out the slit in the plywood over the living room windows.

Jerome moves over so Malone can see. The entire street roils with angry, shouting white men, women, and children, moving toward the house.

Jerome says, "Fuck this."

From the front hall closet, he grabs the shotgun he brought with him. He throws open the front door and steps out onto the porch.

Malone says, "Jerome!"

Jerome ignores him. "Get back!" he cries to the crowd outside.

Standing behind him in the front hall, Malone sees Jerome pump the shotgun and bring it to his shoulder. "Get back or I'll shoot every fucking one of you."

"He's got a gun!" someone in the crowd yells.

"So do I!" several men in the crowd say in unison, and produce their own pistols. "We'll see who gets blown away first," a man shouts.

Jerome fires a shot into the air.

For a long moment, that stills the crowd. Then they step back.

Malone goes through to the back of the house to make sure nobody tries to sneak in that way. The backyard, at least, is clear of people.

He goes out onto the patio. The gate is closed. Henty Loomis's Cadillac sits in the driveway. All the tires have been slashed and all the windows are broken out. There are long scratches down the sides of the body. With his car out of commission, Henty has been driving to and from work with his cousin, Alonzo.

Malone peeks around the side of the house.

The sight of the street takes his breath away.

There must be five hundred people milling around the front of the Loomises' small bungalow.

Jesus Christ, Malone thinks. Where did they all come from? Are they bussing them in?

Malone goes back inside. Locks the back door.

The windows in the back of the house are still intact, so the fading daylight gets through. The other windows in the front of the house have all been broken by rocks and boarded up from the inside with plywood.

Jerome is still out on the front porch, holding back the crowd with his shotgun. Malone goes up to the second floor and taps on the door where Dorothy and her daughters are holed up.

"Dorothy? You all okay in there?"

"We fine," Dorothy says on the other side of the door.

"Need anything?"

"I need this damn nightmare to end."

"Yeah, I hear you. Henty's going to be home soon, right?"

"I hope so."

"All right. Hang on until he does, okay?"

"Got no choice."

As it turns out, Henty isn't coming home anytime soon.

The phone rings. Jerome answers.

"Where are you?" Jerome says.

He listens. Grunts his annoyance. Says, "I'll tell her. Watch yourself, man," and hangs up.

Malone says, "What's going on?"

"That was Henty. He can't get down the street. People blocked his car. He had to go back with Alonzo. He'll try again later. But he don't know if he can make it home tonight."

Looks like Malone's going to get a night off from work.

He calls the hospital and explains his situation to the evening supervisor. He hopes for some consideration from the white supervisor but prepares himself in case he tells Malone not to bother coming in any more.

The supervisor surprises him.

He says he's sorry to hear it. He hopes Malone stays safe and can make it into work tomorrow.

"Planning on it," Malone says. "Thank you."

38

ANNA MILLER

It's her day at Nick's Grille, but when she gets there after cleaning her offices, she discovers the joint is shut.

A sign on the door reads:

THIS RESTAURANT IS CLOSED BY ORDER OF THE DETROIT DEPARTMENT OF HEALTH.

About time, she thinks.

Instead of going back to her apartment, she decides to go out to Chester's to check on him.

Neither Chester nor Dottie are home when she gets there.

"Chester?"

She looks around the downstairs, in his room upstairs, and the basement. Chester is not in the house.

She looks outside in the backyard. No Chester.

She looks in the garage. No Chester.

His half-eaten bowl of Rice Krispies and his coffee are still at his seat at the kitchen table. The other dishes have been washed up and placed in the dish drainer on the sink.

She goes out to the front yard. Up the street, a large crowd of several hundred has gathered in front of the Loomis home.

Has Chester reconsidered again and joined the screaming crowd pelting the Loomis home with rocks and bricks and anything else they can find?

The atmosphere hangs thick with the threat of violence; people are pushing each other and screaming in front of the Loomis house.

She calls Chester's name, but it's lost in the fury of the moment.

She spies Alois Swoboda at the head of the crowd, egging them on with exhortations about keeping the neighborhood white. She looks at the men standing around Swoboda, but doesn't see Chester.

The temper of the crowd begins to change. The voices get more strident. The faces twist in anger. The crowd surges toward the Loomis house, as if to get close enough to topple it over.

Anna tries to push through to get to Swoboda's house to see if Chester has gone there. She can't get through; people in the crowd push back at her.

A Negro man comes out of the Loomis's front door. He cradles a shotgun. For a sick moment she thinks it's Malone. It isn't. This man is taller and thinner.

"Get back!" he shouts.

The surge of the crowd abates, but they do not retreat.

The Negro pumps the shotgun and brings it to his shoulder. "Get back or I'll shoot every fucking one of you."

Some men in the crowd produce their own handguns.

Suddenly panicked at her charge's disappearance among the confusion of the crowd, Anna doesn't know what to do.

The Negro discharges his gun in the air and the crowd, like a tide, begins to recede from the front of the house.

Across the street, a pair of policemen lounge in a squad car. They watch this unfolding with seeming disinterest.

She runs to them.

She stands beside the driver's side window. He pretends not to notice her until she raps on the glass.

Lazily he rolls the window down.

She says, "Can you help me? I take care of a retarded man and I can't find him in this crowd. I'm worried something's going to happen to him if things get out of hand."

The cops look at each other. "Lotsa luck," the driver says with a smirk. He rolls the window back up and continues smoking his cigarette.

She runs back to the Kaczmarek home to call Dottie's work to see if she might have gone in today.

They tell her Dottie isn't working.

She leaves a message asking Dottie to come home immediately if they see her.

She can't avoid it: she needs to call the police dispatcher and beg for their help.

Of course, the cops don't come, despite her phone plea to them. The only police presence is the one squad car whose occupants seem to have no intention of leaving the safety of their cruiser.

She makes her way through to the other side of the Loomis house and continues up the street toward Swoboda's house.

She goes up and knocks on the front door. Rings the doorbell. Knocks again.

No response.

She walks around to the back of the house. The trash container with the bloody shirt has disappeared from its spot in the far corner. She peeks through the window in the garage door. The trash container sits in the far corner. She can't tell if the bloody clothes are still there.

She knocks on the back door of the house.

No response.

She goes over to a back window. Steps up onto an overturned copper washtub and tries to peek inside the house but the shade covers the window.

She returns to the back door. Knocks again.

She hears a muffled voice from inside the house. She can't make out words, and she can't tell whose voice it is, just that it's a man's.

She hears another voice, one she does recognize. She knows from the high pitch it's Chester.

"Chester!" she calls.

"Anna! Anna, I'm in here!"

She tries the back door.

Locked.

She pounds harder. "Let me in! Al! Let me in!"

She hears Chester, calling her name again.

She grabs the copper tub she stood on and carries it to the back door. Shielding her eyes with her forearm, she smashes the tub through the upper glass window of the door.

She reaches in and fumbles with the lock. It's a keyed deadbolt with no possibility of opening it.

She is about to try scrambling over the shards of glass and through the opening she's just made when she sees Alois Swoboda stomping up the stairs from the basement. He's not happy.

In fact, he's furious. He looks like he's snarling.

On the landing, he takes a set of keys from his pocket and unlocks the back door. The door swings open and he grabs Anna's arm and pulls her inside. Slams the door behind her.

"Where's Ches—" she gets out before he pushes her ahead of him down the basement stairs.

She tumbles down and knocks her elbow on the concrete basement floor. Swoboda tramps down the steps and pulls her across the floor to a door against one wall of the basement.

"Stop! Let me go!"

Swoboda unlatches the door and pushes her inside.

She's in a cedar closet, she realizes from the deep cloying smell. Wider than deep, it's stuffed with clothes hanging from a rod.

The door behind her slams, leaving her in total darkness. She hears a latch being thrown.

Chester stands in there with her. She smells his sour body odor and his voice threatens to skitter completely out of control. "Who's there? Who's there!"

His arms reach out wildly through the hanging clothes in the dark of the cedar closet. In his flailing panic, he slaps her face.

She fights down her own panic at being locked in this room. There's no doorknob on the inside. She pushes against the door, but it doesn't move.

Chester begins to cry.

"It's Anna. Calm down, Chester. Calm down!"

At the sound of her voice, Chester does indeed grow quiet, though his breathing remains raspy.

"Oh, Anna," he says. "Oh Anna. Oh Anna." He reaches out in the darkness and pulls her close to him through the hanging clothes.

"Chester," Anna says, "what happened? What are you doing here? Relax, Chester, okay?"

"I came over to tell Al I wouldn't say anything about those bloody clothes but I wanted to know if he hurt somebody and he hit me in the face and knocked me down. He broke my glasses! Then he pulled me down here and said he was going to make sure I didn't tell nobody, especially you."

"Oh, Chester, I'm so sorry. Are you hurt?"

They are still holding onto each other, still reaching around hanging clothes. She reaches a hand up to touch his face.

"Ow!"

"Sorry!"

"That's my cheek where he hit me."

"I'm sorry."

"I don't like this place. It smells."

"It's a cedar closet. It's where you store clothes you don't want the moths to get at."

"I want to get out of here."

"I do, too."

"How?"

"I don't know." She disentangles herself from him and throws her shoulder against the door in the cramped dark. She doesn't have any room and it doesn't budge and it makes her elbow throb.

They both hear a pounding. It sounds like it comes from upstairs. Could someone be at the door?

"Wait," she says. "I think I hear something. Listen."

She hears pounding again. It sounds like the front door.

"Come on," she tells Chester, "let's try to break the door down."

"He'll hear us."

"We have to try."

As much as the cramped closet will allow, she rears back and puts her shoulder against the door. It still doesn't move.

"Come on, Chester. Help me!"

Chester tries it on his own, but he does not have the bulk or the power by himself. She matches her movements to his and the two of them crash into the door again and again.

At their fourth try, the doorframe cracks. They hit it one more time and the cedar closet door swings open and Anna and Chester tumble out into the basement.

Anna helps Chester to his feet and they scramble up the steps to the first floor.

The door to the back hall is locked.

And too solid to break though.

They go back to the lower level. Set at eye-level on the basement wall is a glass-block window. She looks around for something to use to break the glass.

Nothing.

They stand at the window and yell for help.

39

JAKE LIEBERMAN

Bridget McManus told him Chaim Lerner was out of the hospital and in the Jewish Home for the Aged. He's a little young to be allowed a room, but because he's a survivor and not in good health they're making an exception.

It's a wide two-story brick building from the thirties with curved art deco architecture, on Petoskey Avenue west of Dexter, in the heart of the predominantly Jewish section. Jake visited a few times before the war, when his aunt and uncle were here before they died.

Behind the reception desk hangs a large multi-colored mosaic menorah. He asks at the desk for Chaim Lerner. The receptionist directs him to the second floor.

He passes a central nurses' station in the wing he's looking for and a nurse walks him down to Chaim's room. Jake passes a lounge where a half-dozen old men and women sit staring at a television set, the women in print dresses and the men wearing ties and suspenders, their canes propped against their chairs within easy reach. Two old men with yarmulkes sit away from the others, playing cards and murmuring together in Yiddish.

The door to Chaim's room is open. It's a small room, furnished Spartanly, with a bed, a dresser, a chair, and a nightstand; a tiny bathroom is attached.

Chaim lies in bed, on top of the covers. Jake knocks lightly on the doorframe and Chaim opens his eyes and raises his head to see who's here.

"It's Jake Lieberman."

"I dunno you. Go away."

"Can I come in?"

"Go away."

"I just want to see how you're doing."

Now Chaim takes a closer look at Jake. "I know you?"

"I'm the guy who found you and called the ambulance."

Chaim motions him closer. "Let me look at you."

Jake steps closer. Chaim peers at him as though through a fog. Jake stands at his bedside.

"You I don't know," Chaim says.

"No, we've never met."

"So what is it your business, what happens to me?"

"You needed help. I couldn't just leave you."

"What were you doing in my house?"

"A friend asked me to check on you."

"What friend?"

"Her name is Bridget McManus."

"McManus? A *shiksa*?" A gentile woman. "Her I don't know, either."

"She's a friend of one of your aides. Can I sit down?"

Chaim gives a shrug in reply.

Jake drags the chair over beside the bed and sits.

Chaim is slender, but he has a great, leonine head with thinning white hair, protuberant ears, and a bushy gray mustache. He's in regular clothes, a long-sleeved open-necked shirt and light woolen pants.

"You're the one who found me," Chaim says, like he's trying to get that straight.

"I am."

"I don't see so good. What's your name?"

"Jake Lieberman."

"A *landsman*."

"A *landsman*," Jake agrees. One of the tribe.

"Where are your people from?"

"Vilna."

"Ah, a Litvak. Me too. Maybe we're related."

"Maybe so."

"But your *zaydeh* was smart. He left when he could. Mine stayed. Now nobody's left but me. The whole *mischpacha*. All gone. I'm the last."

Jake doesn't mention that his *zaydeh*, his grandfather, had fled Europe for America with part of his *mischpacha*, his family, earlier in the century.

Jake studies his face: the curves, the shadows, the depth of the brown eyes, forehead like the prow of a ship, misshapen nose—probably broken many times—furrowed forehead and deep, deep circles under his eyes.

Chaim notices Jake examining him. "What are you looking?"

"I'm just wondering what your story is."

"My story?" He pushes it away with his hand. "You don't want to know my story."

"I do."

Chaim closes his eye and says nothing for a long time. Jake thinks he might have fallen asleep, but Chaim stirs and, still with his eyes closed, says, "I'll tell you my story. The Germans came to Vilna in 1941. They killed nine thousand Jews right off the bat, in the Ponary forest, including my father and brothers. Can you imagine? Nine thousand people, off the face of the earth.

"The rest of us they put in two ghettos. One was a work camp. The other was a killing camp, for those who couldn't work. That's where my mother and sister died. They destroyed that ghetto in 1941 and killed all the people. The work camp they destroyed in 1943. I was deported to the Kaiserwald camp in Latvia and after to the Sutthof camp in Poland. They forced me to work building ships. In 1945 they took us on a march to try and cover up their crimes until we were liberated by the Soviet army."

Chaim opens his eyes and stares at Jake. "They killed us like we were bugs, Lieberman. Because that's what they called us, you see. Vermin. To be squashed out of existence. They tried. And they all helped, all the Germans and the Poles and the Latvians, all of them. They were glad to see us go. Don't believe what you read: they all loved Hitler. They all loved what he was doing."

Jake puts a hand on Chaim's arm.

Chaim pulls it away. "Whatever you got to say, I don't want to hear."

"I want to ask you a question."

Chaim looks at him. "Ask."

"I'm an artist," Jake says. "Can I paint you?"

Chaim examines Jake's face for signs of mockery, but there are none: Jake is completely serious.

"Why?"

"I saw the camps in Europe. I photographed them. I talked to prisoners. I've been thinking for a long time about a project about the Holocaust. I think you're my way in."

"For this you saved my life?"

"You just have to lie there. I'll do the rest."

"*A ritch in kop,*" Chaim says in Yiddish.

Crazy in the head.

But when he doesn't object, Jake pulls out his notebook and makes a dozen quick sketches of the older man.

Who, meanwhile, closes his eyes again.

Before long, Chaim dozes.

Jake goes out and calls Bridget at her office. He wants to report on Chaim's condition.

She's not in; the Division assistant tells him she's out in the field.

He goes back to Chaim's room.

Chaim still sleeps. Jake makes more sketches of the lines etched in pain, worry, and horror in his beautiful, tormented face.

40

BRIDGET MCMANUS

B ridget finds a mob scene on Riopelle.

Hundreds of whites stand in front of 18075, shouting and heaving rocks at the house.

She nudges her car through the crowd, whose members part when they see it's a white woman behind the wheel. She parks down the block, not wanting to leave it in front of the house. For once she's glad she doesn't drive a marked police cruiser; who knows what these people would have done to it?

She pushes her way through the surly crowd to the front door. Two young Negro men answer her knock. She holds her badge up.

"About damn time," one of them says.

"What's going on here?" Bridget says.

"White folks trying to push us out," the tall man says. "How about you get all those people to go home?"

"I'll get more officers here," Bridget promises, and goes back to her car. She has to push through the crowd again, and when she gets inside the vehicle some in the crowd pound on the hood and roof.

She sees a Detroit Police car parked up the block. Bridget starts her car and radios in to her dispatcher, requesting help.

She inches the car through the crowd of people again.

She stops beside the Detroit PD squad car. Rolls down her window.

The two white cops inside the car make a show of gazing at her with complete disinterest. Only when she holds up her badge and motions for the driver to roll down the window does the cop behind the wheel deign to move.

"McManus, Women's Division. You fellahs planning on doing anything about all this?"

The two cops in the car exchange a glance. "What did you have in mind?" the driver asks.

"Dispersing this crowd, for one thing, before somebody gets hurt."

"Ain't nobody going to get hurt," the other cop says. "We got our eye on things."

"Yeah," Bridget says, "I can see it's completely under control."

The driver spits out the window, missing her and her car. "Bitch," the cop says, and rolls his window back up.

Bridget drives on. There isn't much she can do here by herself. Other cruisers should arrive, following her request for help.

She's not looking for 18075 Riopelle anyway.

No, the address Bridget wants is further up the block. The sunny yellow house at 18199 Riopelle.

The home of Alois Swoboda.

She parks in front of the tidy frame home slightly larger than the one under siege down the block. No one loiters in front.

She radios again for backup. She wants another officer here for herself, and she wants more officers for the mob scene down the block.

It's twenty minutes before a single officer in a squad car arrives.

Still no sign of Rausch, Richmond, or Hauser.

Thanks, guys, she thinks.

She explains the situation to the cop who just came, and together they walk up to the front entrance of 18199.

She bangs on the door.

When she gets no response, she bangs again. She thinks she hears muffled shouts coming from somewhere inside. It's hard to tell against the background of the clamor down the street.

She tries the front door. Locked.

She tells the uniform, "Wait here," and walks up the driveway beside the house.

Glass blocks form the window to the basement. She can't see

through them, but she hears a man and a woman calling for help.

Using the butt of her service weapon, Bridget tries to break the glass blocks, but it's no use; the windows hold together.

"How many are down there?" she shouts through the glass.

"Two of us," a woman's voice says. "We're locked in!"

"Hang on," Bridget tells them.

"Please hurry!"

She goes around to the back door. The top window in the door is shattered but the door is locked. The door opens directly on a hallway with an interior door. It's closed. Bridget guesses the door leads down to the basement. She would further guess it's locked to keep the hostages down there.

She reaches in to feel for a key to unlock the back door. She sees through into the kitchen where a man hurries towards her. He's carrying a shotgun.

He stops, raises the weapon to his shoulder.

Bridget throws herself to the ground.

The man lets off a blast. The pellets splinter the back door and wall.

She runs around to the front of the house. Through the picture window she sees Swoboda inside running through to the front. He throws the entry door open and fires two shots out the door.

The patrolman dives off the porch and hotfoots it around the other side of the house.

Bridget runs to take cover behind her car.

A few people from the demonstration down the block begin filtering up here to see what's going on.

Bridget waves them back. "Don't come any closer!"

They ignore her and spill forward.

"Get back!"

They continue to approach.

Sirens fill the air and a half-dozen Detroit Police cruisers skid to a stop in front of Swoboda's. Police pour out of the cruisers and Swoboda shoots at them from inside the house and they take cover behind their cars and return fire with their small arms and shotguns.

A big bear of a man in plainclothes gets out of one of the cruisers. Ignoring the shooting around him, he strides over to Bridget. "Senior Inspector Emanuel Wycoff. Situation commander. Who are you?"

"Sgt. Bridget McManus, Detroit Police Women's Division."

"Are you the one who radioed for backup?"

"Yes sir."

"What in the holy name of Christ is going on here?"

"You might want to get down."

A shot ricochets off the roof of Bridget's car and Wycoff ducks behind it.

Bridget fills him in. She points to the looky-loos. "We have to get these idiots out of the line of fire."

Wycoff turns and orders a pair of the police who are taking cover behind their cars to set up a cordon on each side of Swoboda's house.

"He has two hostages inside," Bridget says. "In the basement. I couldn't get to them."

The shooting from inside the house continues with different weapons and different ammunition.

"There's just one guy in there?" Wycoff asks.

"Far as I know. His name is Alois Swoboda."

"And what's your business here?"

"I came to talk to him as a suspect in three child murders."

More shots come from inside the house. "Don't seem like he plans to come quietly," Wycoff says.

More police arrive and deploy around the house, racing and diving like infantrymen under fire.

Bridget thinks of her husband under these same circumstances, bullets whizzing around. She's terrified, but he was brave enough to run out in to the fusillade to try and save another man's life.

The standoff enters its second hour. A fire engine arrives and shines spotlights on the house.

"We can't get near enough to the house to retrieve those two in the basement," Inspector Wycoff says. "We have to drive him out. I'm sending in tear gas."

"Are you going to try and negotiate with him?" Bridget asks.

"Negotiate?" Wycoff looks at her as though she asked if there was a Martian on the way. "You think this guy'll *negotiate?* Only way he's coming out is feet first."

As if in reply to Wycoff's statement, Swoboda sends another

volley of rifle fire into the street.

When the shooting stops, Wycoff makes a whirling gesture with his hand. A cop with a tear gas launcher hustles up. He sends a cannister toward the house. It smashes through the attic window. The gas fills the attic and drifts out into the street.

The cop fires another cannister straight through the living room window downstairs.

Wycoff says something to one of the other policemen, who disappears behind a car. He and another cop reappear wearing gas masks; he's also carrying a shotgun. The other cop carries a small battering ram.

The police send up a stream of gunfire while the two cops race across the street and up Swoboda's driveway.

She can see Swoboda's shadow darting around the downstairs amid the billowing tear gas. The two policemen pause at the basement window. One pounds at the glass blocks with the battering ram while the other stands guard.

The battering ram breaks through.

Before either cop can do anything, a handgun sticks out of a side window of the house and shoots them both pointblank.

They go down.

"Jesus Christmas!" Wycoff says.

Swoboda appears at the front door. He has a machine gun now. The police take cover behind their cars. It's a miracle none of the people watching are injured.

"Get that sonuvabitch right now!" Wycoff screams.

More tear gas goes into the house, along with a salvo of bullets. There must be two hundred cops here now, Bridget thinks, all directing their fire into the house.

They wait. The shooting from inside the house stops.

Wycoff says, "Cease fire!"

After a quiet minute, Wycoff says, "Get me a mask."

He and two other police arm themselves with bullet-proof vests and tear gas masks and trot across the street. They barge through the front door.

All is quiet for five minutes—until the bang-bang-bang-bang of an exchange of gunfire rings out.

The two policemen come running out the front door of the house supporting Wycoff. He stumbles and holds his hand, a mass of blood.

"Ambulance," Bridget shouts.

With more shots coming from inside the house, the three cops dive behind a scout car.

"What happened?" Bridget says.

Wycoff is in shock; he's ashen, can't say anything. One of the other cops says, "We found the guy upstairs in a bedroom closet. Must have been trying to get away from the tear gas. As soon as he saw us, he opened fire with a Tommy gun. Manny nearly had his hand blown off and the bastard drove us out."

An ambulance technician leads Wycoff to the ambulance. His clothes are soaked with his own blood.

"More tear gas," the second-in-command says. Another round of tear gas sails into the attic.

Bridget sees flames breaking out up there.

Immediately the firemen who have been waiting behind their fire truck jump into action, but gunfire from the house drives them back.

They pull the truck up close to the house to block the gunshots and extend a ladder from the truck. Firemen clamber up the ladder. Those guys have guts, Bridget thinks.

A voice from the back of the house cries, "He's coming out!"

The gunman bursts out the side door of the house firing a shotgun. He runs down the driveway spraying pellets.

Shotguns from ten cops in the backyard and dozens more out front perforate him.

"He's down!" someone cries.

"Go go go!" the second-in-command beside Bridget calls.

A dozen police fly up the driveway and surround Swoboda lying on the ground. Another dozen race into the house. Ambulance attendants race up the driveway to where the two shot cops lie.

Bridget, too, runs up the driveway. She peers into the basement through the broken glass blocks. The two hostages are lying on the floor in the far corner.

She takes the downed cop's rifle and clears glass shards from the broken window's frame and slips through the opening. She drops to the floor and crosses to the hostages. They're alive. The young woman is short and slender; Bridget throws her over her shoulder and carries her up the stairs as the cops kick through the door to the basement.

Bridget slips out—"There's one more down there," she tells them—and takes the woman outside.

A patrolman stands among the confusion of police. He holds out his arms and Bridget transfers the woman to him.

Bridget goes back inside the house and searches through each room to make sure there aren't any other prisoners or gunmen.

She comes back outside, where one of the other cops carries the male hostage slung over his shoulder.

The cop lays the man on the driveway. Bridget waves for another ambulance attendant to come over for him.

A pair of ambulance attendants have lifted the two shot police officers onto gurneys. Another pair lift Swoboda onto a stretcher.

From the extent of his injuries, Bridget guesses Swoboda is a goner.

41

MALONE COLEMAN

Pounding at the front door shakes the house.

Malone throws the door open and sees a white kid on the porch with a shit-eating grin. Malone sticks the shotgun right into the kid's face.

The teenager is too surprised to do anything other than move his lips even though no words come out.

Before Malone opened the door, the kid was standing there hollering about how nobody in this neighborhood wanted niggers living next door.

He started banging on the door.

Now with a long gun pointed at his face, the kid isn't so talkative.

Malone says, "Run out of things to say?"

In a few moments, the kid recovers his nerve. Malone sees it in the kid's eyes: they harden and he fixes a mocking smirk on his face.

The kid says, "You won't shoot me."

Oh, but Malone wants to.

Malone aches to shoot this motherfucker's head off.

It's what would happen if he pulled the trigger now: he'd separate this shit-eating smile from the rest of his body.

How he wants to do it more than anything in the world right now.

Wants to summon all the times he's been called a nigger, all the times he's been rejected—from the army, from schools, from the VA, from a thousand incidental run-ins with whites—because of his race, and send all his anger and frustration boiling up into his finger on the trigger and wipe this white motherfucker off the face of the earth.

And who would really miss him? One more cracker gone, thousands more—millions—wait in line to take his place.

Now Malone smiles. Pumps the shotgun. Sights down the barrel. "In three seconds, I'm going to blow you to kingdom come."

He lets the moment stretch out and the kid's eyes go funny and Malone can see he's losing his nerve.

"One."

The kid's jaw starts to tremble.

"Two."

The kid steps back off the porch, never letting his eyes stray from Malone's.

When he reaches the ground, the kid turns away. He's absorbed back into the group of teenagers, who slap him on the back and make shooting noises with their mouth as if the kid had stepped up to Malone and shot him instead of backing down.

Another kid throws a rock at Malone. It misses him and hits the side of the front door.

Malone turns his back on them in a sign of total disrespect and goes back into the house.

Inside, Jerome says, "I thought you were going to do it."

"I wasn't going to." He starts to tremble from the rush of adrenaline. "I just wanted him to think I could."

"Why didn't you?"

"I would have turned into just one more violent nigger in their eyes. I wouldn't give them the satisfaction. Plus the others would have shot me dead."

"You a better man than me," Jerome says. "I'd have shot the motherfucker right in the face."

42

ANNA MILLER

She has a cut on her forehead and a purple bruise on her cheek. She sits inside the ambulance. The ambulance attendant cleans the cut and bandages it. Her eyes are streaming with tears from the tear gas; the attendant gently rinses her eyes with water.

"It's called tear gas," the attendant says, "but it isn't a gas at all. It's a powdered mist that can drift anywhere."

After a few minutes of rinsing her eyes, Anna says, "I thought I was going to die."

"You're safe now," the ambulance attendant says.

"What happened to the man who was in the basement with me?"

"He's being taken care of."

"Alois Swoboda? What about him?"

"Who's that? The guy who was doing all the shooting?"

"Yeah."

The attendant shakes his head.

"He's dead?"

The attendant nods.

He finishes rinsing off Anna's eyes. "Better, miss?"

"Much. Thank you."

"Let's look at your elbow."

The attendant bends it. She grimaces but she has full range of motion.

"I'm just gonna fix you up with a temporary sling for your arm. Don't use the arm for a few days and you should be fine. Do you want to go to the hospital and get checked out?"

"I think I'm okay."

"You've been through an ordeal."

"Is the man I was with someplace around here?"

"I'll find out," the ambulance attendant says.

He goes over to talk to other attendants. He comes back and says, "After they checked him out, they took him back home."

She walks down to the Kaczmarek house. Dottie Kaczmarek opens the door and hugs her. "My god, Anna, are you all right?"

"I'm fine. I'm more worried about Chester."

"He's upstairs."

"Can I go up to see him? I won't disturb him—I just want to see how he's doing. He was pretty frightened in that basement."

Dottie hesitates, but nods okay.

Upstairs, Chester lies on his bed, facing the wall. He rocks back-and-forth. The bedsprings squeak in rhythm. He's trying to calm himself.

"Hey Chet," she says. She goes over to him. "This has been a terrible day, hasn't it?"

Chester doesn't answer.

Anna sits on the edge of the bed. "I just wanted to make sure you were all right. I was proud of you today. You did really well."

No reply.

She gets up from the bed. At the door she turns to see him still rocking.

Downstairs, Dottie asks Anna, "How are you going to get home?"

"Bus, I guess."

"After all this, it's too late to take the bus. Why don't you stay here? The sofa opens into a bed. You look a wreck."

"Sure you wouldn't mind?" Anna asks. "I can see how Chester feels in the morning."

"By all means," Dottie says. "I'll make up the sofa for you."

43

JAKE LIEBERMAN

After filling his notebook with more sketches of sleeping Chaim, Jake tries Bridget again at the pay phone.

Again the administrative assistant tells him that she's out in the field, but this time adds, "At the disturbance on Riopelle."

"What disturbance?"

"There's a standoff on Riopelle Street between a gunman and police."

"And she's there?"

"Yes," the assistant says. But she won't tell him anything more.

He goes back to the nurses' station. A radio plays WWJ.

He hears the news.

According to the reporter, one man, a gun collector, has held a couple of hundred police at bay in an armed standoff at a home on Riopelle on the near east side.

The reporter continues, "Police believe two hostages, a woman and a man, are being held in the house under siege."

That's good enough for Jake.

He goes in to say goodbye to Chaim, who, finally, thanks him for what Jake did for him.

Jake trots out to the parking lot. In a minute he speeds toward the Riopelle address he heard on the radio.

A half-dozen police cars are scattered in front of a home that's pock-marked with bullet holes. Bridget McManus's Buick is in front of the house. She is here.

Jake parks behind her car and goes up the front walk. A uniformed Detroit policeman stops him. "No entry."

"I'm looking for Sgt. Bridget McManus."

"You can't go in."

"I don't want to go in. I want to talk to Sgt. McManus."

"Move along."

Bridget appears in the doorway. "I thought I heard you." She comes out onto the front stoop. "You can't come in."

"I'm starting to get that idea."

She sidesteps the officer and leads Jake to the sidewalk.

"What happened here?" he asks.

"Alois Swoboda was inside."

"Who's he?"

"He killed the three children."

"How do you know that?"

"I'll explain later. I came to pick him up and it turned into an armed standoff."

A woman comes out onto the porch. Like Bridget, she wears civilian clothes, a plain dress, but she carries herself with authority.

"Hang on," Bridget says to Jake. She goes up to confer with the woman on the stoop.

Bridget comes back down to where Jake is. "That's my boss, Lieutenant Richardson. The lab guys are inside, combing through the house. She said she'll oversee the rest of the evidence collection. I can go home."

"Do you want to stop for coffee? You can explain all this to me."

"I'd love to."

She stops in front of her Buick. "Oh shit," she says.

Both side panels of the Buick are riddled with bullet holes from the hours-long gunfight. Both side windows are shot out; the windshield is cracked but intact.

"At least you'll have lots of ventilation in the summer," Jake says.

"Everybody's a comedian."

The car starts right up.

"A miracle," she says.

An even bigger miracle: all four tires are intact.

She tells him about a twenty-four-hour Clock Restaurant on Woodward south of 7 Mile Road. She said she lives off 7 Mile, so the diner's on her way home.

"And you live in Corktown," she says, "so Woodward works for you, too."

They drive separately. She's at a table by the time he gets there.

He slips into the seat across from her.

A waitress comes by. Young, in her early twenties. "What'll you have, honey?"

"Just Sanka for me," Bridget says.

"Ditto."

The waitress leaves and he says, "Sure you don't want something to eat?"

"My stomach is doing flip-flops."

The waitress brings their decafs.

"So," he says. "What happened?"

"Like I said, I came to pick up Alois Swoboda for the murder of those three children."

"How did you know it was him?"

"I realized one thing we hadn't talked about in the task force for the murders was how all the kids were found near automobile plants. I looked at everyone who visited plants near the three murder dump sites and correlated the information with the dates of the kids' deaths.

"Swoboda's name cut across all three locations. He's a truck driver for a cartage company with a contract with American Motors, which took over Hudson. He hauls supplies and equipment from that plant to other car plants that bought the equipment. I discovered his trips to the three plants coincided with dates the children went missing, which was around the same time they were murdered. When I called his employer, I found out he moved up here from Toledo. On a hunch, I called the police down there. They told me he had arrests for indecent exposure to children, and they looked at him when two kids were kidnapped and turned up dead."

"Why'd they let him go?"

"They couldn't make it stick. But I put it all together. I came out here today to talk with him, and it turned into the siege. The evidence team will find enough in his house to make certain he's the one."

"You broke the case."

"More importantly, this will give the parents some justice. It won't bring their children back, but it's what we can do."

"Why did he do it?"

"We probably won't ever know. He was killed in the gun fight. For the kids, I'm guessing it was just bad luck. He was there, they were convenient. Sometimes that's how it works."

Free-floating, random mischance, he thinks. It lands on its victims and grinds them to death with no justice or justification. The same thing killed all the millions overseas.

"What kinds of urges must a man have to rape and murder children," he says.

"Some people don't believe in evil. I do. This is why."

"I believe in evil. It's good I'm not so sure about."

They drink their coffee in silence.

She yawns. "Oh, sorry," she says. "I've been up for a while."

"Don't worry about it."

"I think I need to get home."

They walk together out to their cars.

"Want me to follow you, make sure you get home okay?" he asks.

"You're such a boy scout. But thanks, no. It made it here, it'll get me the rest of the way."

She yawns again.

"If you stay awake," he says.

They smile at each other.

"Go home," he says.

They hug. Instead of a quick clinch, which he expects, she wraps her arms around him in a sensual languid embrace.

They separate, but still hold onto each other as though neither wants to let go. "Sure you're okay to drive?" he asks.

"I'm fine. It's not far."

They stare into each other's eyes, their faces inches apart. They move together and kiss. Her lips are warm, soft, pillowy.

They hug again. She sighs.

"I didn't ask you what you were doing here," she says.

"I heard on the radio there was trouble. Your secretary told me you were here. I wanted to make sure you were okay."

She sighs. "Such a boy scout."

She's either enjoying this or she's going to fall asleep on her feet, he thinks.

"Thank you," she murmurs.

"Get yourself home in one piece," he says.

They separate and she gets in the car. He kneels down so their faces are on the same level. "If for some strange reason, you should be in the market for a new car, my brother has a used car lot."

"I'll keep it in mind."

"Good work today, Sgt. McManus."

"Thanks, ex-automotive industrial loss-leader blah blah blah."

He stands and steps away. She starts up, blows him a kiss, backs out, and drives away.

One of her taillights is out. He watches the other light disappear up Woodward.

Before he goes home, he stops at the Jewish Home for the Aged. He goes up to Chaim Lerner's floor.

The night nurses won't let him go back to see Chaim—it's way past visiting hours—but he says he wants to know how he's doing.

"He's resting comfortably," the charge nurse tells him.

That's all he can get out of her.

Back at his apartment, he turns on the phonograph. Lester Young with the Oscar Peterson Trio. Keeps it low so it doesn't disturb Mrs. O'Neill downstairs. The crazy sax of "Ad Lib Blues" eases his soul.

Making it up as we go along, indeed.

44

BRIDGET MCMANUS

No pleasing aromas of Darren's dinner greet Bridget when she gets home.

Also, her mother is here, which is unusual.

"What happened?" Bridget asks.

"I've been trying to get ahold of you all day."

"Yeah. We had a situation."

"I heard. Are you okay?"

Bridget shrugs. She doesn't feel like reliving her day for her mother right this second.

"Darren called me this afternoon," her mother says. "He asked me to come over."

"For what?"

"He said he was leaving."

"I don't understand."

"Neither do I. He called me up and just said, 'I gotta go, ma, can you come over and watch the kids when they come home from school.' I told him I could come over in a couple of hours. He told me he couldn't wait, he had to go right then and there."

"Did he sound like he was on something?"

"You know your brother. He always sounds like he's on something."

Bridget goes down to the basement. He made his bed (one good habit he picked up in the army), but his personal things are gone—

he never had many clothes but they're gone; he never had much in the way of personal hygiene products but whatever he did have—razor, soap, brush—is gone.

"Oh Darren," Bridget says to the empty basement. "What have you done now?"

"He's gone, all right," she says to her mother back in the kitchen.

"He didn't leave a note or anything?"

"No."

"He'll be back."

"Maybe. When he runs out of money."

Until he does, she and her mother will have to work out a schedule for watching the kids when they get home from school.

"How are the kids?" she asks.

In the back, Timmy shrieks under Lydia's relentless teasing.

"Do they know Darren's gone?" Bridget asks.

"I told them. I'm not sure they understand."

"Yeah," Bridget sighs, "I'm not sure I do, either."

Bridget tells her mother she isn't hungry, but her mother makes her a cold chicken sandwich anyway. She sits at the kitchen table staring at the food, trying to muster some appetite.

When she went back and kissed her children hello and goodnight, Timmy said, "Where's Uncle Darren?"

"We don't exactly know, honey," she told him, truthfully.

Now her mother reads the two kids a story.

Bridget has never been shot at before. She knows some of the policemen were in the war, and they handled the siege better than she did, running and jumping around as the gunfire poured out of the Swoboda house. It must have been what her husband went through in the final minutes of his life.

She kept it together pretty well, all things considered. And she walked away from it, which puts her ahead of her husband Joe.

Jake was there, too, after all the excitement ended.

He said he came out to see if she was okay.

Not that there was anything he could do if she wasn't, she thinks. She was going to mention that while they were standing in the parking lot, but didn't think the timing was right.

There's something about that man, she thinks.

And there's something off about him, too. As though he's present and not-present at the same time. Almost like he's translucent, like a ghostly manifestation of a man.

Almost, but not quite as bad as her brother Darren.

She supposes that's a result of what Jake saw in Europe. She has no idea how she would have reacted to the horrors, just like she had no idea how she would react to what Joe went through. She suspects it would be similar to what's happening with Jake.

Jake and Joe, she thinks.

Double Js.

There's a coincidence.

The question is, does she want to get something started with a ghost?

Even though you're a bit of a ghost yourself, she tells herself. Alive but not alive. There but not there since the war.

So *can* she get involved with him? Can *he* with her? Is it even a possibility for him?

He's obviously interested in her—as much as he can be, and there's the rub. How much of him is left for her? She doesn't want it all—doesn't want to possess him body and soul—but she does want some significant part of him, and if he can't give her even that . . .

Her mother Marian sits at the table with her.

"They asleep?" Bridget asks.

"Lydia's almost there. I think Timmy will be up for a while."

"He's like the mayor of Westmoreland Road. Keeping an eye on things."

"How are you?" her mother says. "You had yourself a day."

"That I did. I hope you weren't worried about me."

"Of course I was. But after the fact. I didn't even know it was going on. Your brother had me going in circles."

"As usual."

"I wish he could just find a way to calm down."

"It's not that easy."

"I suppose not. You're not going to eat that sandwich?"

"I don't think so, mom."

"I'll wrap it up. Take it for lunch tomorrow."

"Thanks."

Marian gets up and stows the chicken in the fridge. "I better go. See what your father's been up to."

"Thanks for coming over."

"Want me here when they get home from school tomorrow?"

"If you can make it. Until we figure out something else."

"Big smooch," her mother says, and plants one on the side of Bridget's face.

The phone rings at two in the morning.

Instead of running to snatch it off the cradle as she usually would, Bridget stays where she is, comfy in bed. She doesn't have to worry about waking up Darren, Timmy is probably still up, and Lydia sleeps like the dead.

It's only going to be Ed Hauser anyway, she thinks, and I don't want to talk to that bastard. He never even came to the scene, even after she called him and even after the whole city knew what was going on. At least Rausch and Richmond showed eventually, after it was all over. Hauser couldn't be bothered to get there.

She lets the phone ring.

She's too anxious to put this day behind her, and answering is just going to prolong it.

45

MALONE COLEMAN

T he crowd outside faded away during all the trouble down the street, but now, going on eleven o'clock, some of them are back. Mostly teenagers. The others have gone home for the night. Malone had gone out on the porch to watch the shootout down the street, but when the bullets started flying he went back in. He had more important things to worry about.

Like somebody setting this house on fire and killing all the people inside, which he has no doubt they would love to do.

At eleven-thirty, Henty Loomis finally makes it home. His cousin Alonzo parks in the driveway and walks him to the front door. The white kids pace on the front sidewalk like predators. Alonzo goes into the backyard to open the gate and gets back in his car and drives it up into the yard behind Henry's damaged Cadillac. He closes the gate and goes into the house.

Inside Dorothy comes up and hugs her husband. They hold each other like a couple trying to keep each other from drowning.

Henty hugs his brother Jerome. He shakes hands with Malone. "Thank you for standing by me," Henty tells him.

"As long as you need me, I'll be here," Malone says.

"You eat?" Dorothy asks her husband.

"I had something with Alonzo and Ramona."

"Want anything now?"

"Cup of tea, baby, you don't mind."

"Coming up."

Dorothy, Henty, Jerome, Alonzo, and Malone sit at the kitchen table. Jerome tells them about what happened down the block—or as much as he knows.

"Maybe this'll be the end," Jerome says. "Maybe things'll start to quiet down with that motherfucker gone."

Malone demurs. He thinks it's going to be worse than ever; violence breeds violence, and the shitstorm down the street will only make these white people worse, not better. More likely to resort to violence to drive out the "invaders."

"You don't think so?" Henty asks Malone.

"Maybe someday," Malone says. "But these people out here, they're going to put up a hell of a fight till then."

"That's right. You can't give in to them," Alonzo says.

Henty sits sipping his tea and nodding his head.

"I come to this city on July 4, 1923," he says. "When I left Alabama, I knew life up here wasn't going to be no picnic. Didn't think it would be this bad. Thought we was leaving all this behind."

He looks at Dorothy. "I didn't know the kind of danger I was going to put my family in."

Dorothy looks at him like she knows what he's going to say.

"I don't want to stay here," Henty says. "I don't want to stay someplace where the whole neighborhood hates us and don't want us here."

Dorothy's eyes fill with tears, and she nods in agreement.

"You a pioneer," Alonzo says. "Pioneers always got it rough. After, things calm down."

"I don't have that long to wait. Ain't worth my family going through all this."

Later the four men sit in the living room while Dorothy puts the girls to bed upstairs.

"Appreciate what you've done," Henty tells Malone. "'Specially for a total stranger."

"No, man, I had to do it. Otherwise, I couldn't live with myself."

"Tomorrow I'll talk to the real estate man, get this place on the market. What's left of it, anyway. Shape it's in now, won't get back anywhere near what I paid it for. Malone, you don't need to stay. We can take over from here."

"I'll spend one more night, if it's okay with you."

"You're welcome to."

"Malone," Alonzo says, "I never asked you—how you get so much time off work?"

"I work nights," Malone says. "When I thought Henty wasn't coming home tonight, I told them at work I was taking the night off."

"And they give it to you?"

"Yeah."

"Where you work at?"

"Harper Hospital. I had a job at the VA hospital, but they fired me."

"Why they do that?"

"They called me a 'security risk.'"

"What's that mean?"

"Means I'm colored."

Jerome scoffs. "I hear that."

"What you do there, the VA?" Alonzo asks.

"I was an orderly. I did everything from pushing wheelchairs to swabbing toilets."

"So you not looking for work now?"

"I'm trying to get my job back at the VA. I got a lawyer on the case. I hope Harper's only temporary."

"What's your background?" Alonzo asks.

He's about to say, "I'm an artist," but doesn't, knowing in his heart he might not be an artist anymore.

Still, he gives Alonzo a quick summary of his past: art school at the Society of Arts and Crafts, turned down by the army, a union job at the Ford Rouge plant, joining with the National Negro Labor Council, work on the Fair Employment Practice ordinance in the early fifties, fired from Ford in a cutback, scrounging for a job until the VA opened up for him. Now waiting for the VA again.

Alonzo nods. "Ever hear of James Boggs?"

"I know of him. Don't know him personally."

"Union man, like you were. Works at Chrysler. I met him there, that's where I work, too. Smart? You got no idea. Brilliant, even. I think you'd like him. Surprised you never ran into him before."

"Like I say, I've seen him here and there. We never actually met."

Malone remembers the nod of recognition they shared at the Mayflower Church meeting Lucille Reid took him to.

"He's somebody you should know," Alonzo says. "He is one of the people who make a difference. James and his wife are at the head of the colored struggle for liberation in this town."

"What are you filling this man's head with, Alonzo?" Henty asks.

"Just telling him the truth."

Henty says, "Alonzo's assistant pastor for Rev. Albert Cleage. Know who he is?"

Malone does. He's the activist pastor of the Central Congregational Church in Detroit.

The men sit in silence. For the first time in days no one outside hurls rocks against the side of the house.

Or praying to wipe out the existence of the people who live here.

Alonzo says, "Quiet out there for a change."

The others agree.

"Won't last," he says. "Like Malone says. This a temporary truce. Won't see the end of this war for a while. If ever."

"That's why I'm going to get my family away from here."

"You might think you just one man trying to live a better life," Alonzo says, "but you part of something bigger."

"Well," Henty sighs, "I guess it just ain't my time yet."

"Maybe not," Alonzo says. "But it will be."

46

ANNA MILLER

Voices wake her.

At first she doesn't know where she is—the morning light in the room is different, oddly diffused through curtains. The furniture is different. The smells are different; no harsh smell from the chemicals in her little darkroom, no burnt toast wafting up from Selma downstairs.

Most of all, the sounds are different. Water splashes in a sink, a metal pot clunks on a stove, voices murmur.

Gradually she remembers where she is. And why.

She straightens her clothes and runs her fingers through her hair. In the kitchen, Chester sits at the table, drinking a cup of coffee and spooning from a bowl of Rice Krispies.

"You're up," Dottie says. "Hope we didn't wake you. Coffee?"

"Yes, please."

Anna sits at the table. "How are you doing, Chet?"

Chester has a purple bruise on the side of his face from where Swoboda hit him, but otherwise seems fine. "I'm good," he says. "What are we going to do today?"

"I'm staying home today," Dottie says. "Anna isn't going to be here."

"Oh." Chester looks at Anna. Disappointment clouds his eyes.

And confusion: but she's already here, he seems to be thinking.

"I'm taking today off, anyway," Anna says. "But I stayed last night because I was worried about you."

"That's sweet," Dottie says. "Isn't that sweet, Chester?"

"Sweet," Chester agrees.

"What would you like for breakfast?" Dottie asks her.

"Oh, thanks, but nothing for me. I have to get going."

She won't be able to clean her offices this morning; she'll have to do it later in the day, or tonight. She needs to get home and shower before going in to Nick's (assuming the Health Department lets it open).

And before that she wants to make a stop up the street.

The windows in the Loomis home are boarded-up. The wooden siding is pock-marked from a barrage of rocks, the grass in the front yard trampled to mud.

The morning finds two women walking back and forth in front of the house, pushing their baby carriages and carrying signs about keeping the neighborhood white.

They shake their heads at Anna, who walks up to the front porch. "Race traitor," one of the women hisses.

The bell doesn't work—it's been pulled out of the doorframe, its wires snipped in an act of vandalism. She knocks.

The door swings open and a tall Negro man glares at her. He holds a shotgun across his arms and says nothing, as though daring her to make the first move, toss the first insult.

"Good morning," Anna says. "Is Malone still here?"

"Who want him?"

"Anna Miller."

"He know you?"

"We're friends."

She hopes they still are after all that's happened.

After a moment's reflection, the man says, "Ain't here."

He shuts the door in her face.

In another minute, the door opens again and Malone stands there. He looks at her in surprise.

"Hi," she says. "I just wanted to see how you're doing."

Before Malone can answer, a Negro woman comes up behind him. "There a problem?" she asks roughly.

"No," Malone says. "This is a friend of mine."

The woman gives Anna a hard look. "I don't think so," she says, and turns away. "Shut the door."

"This isn't a good time," Malone says to Anna.

"I guess not."

Anna doesn't know what to say to him . . . how to apologize for the behavior of the people in this neighborhood. How to explain that not all whites feel the way these people do.

But she can't say that, knowing how many actually do feel like that.

And yet she wants to tell him she's not one of them. She understands. She's suffered, too.

He's looking at me, she thinks, waiting for me to say something.

She's tiptoeing up to the line where she never goes. Usually, she retreats when she gets near the line. Will she cross it for him? Open up about her background? Where she comes from, what she's been through?

He looks at her and manages a weak smile. Does he know what she's thinking?

Is he waiting for her to leave so he can rid the house of this white woman?

Tell him.

No.

Not the time. Not after all they've been through in this house. Because it would still feel like a contest to him. The suffering sweepstakes.

She'll tell him another time. If she still feels the need to tell him at all. If there ever will be another time.

"Well," she says, "I just wanted to make sure you were okay."

"Thanks. I appreciate that."

She raises a hand in farewell and turns and goes down the walk. She feels his eyes on her until, in a few moments, she hears the front door close behind her.

47

JAKE LIEBERMAN

Jake's landlady has been giving him grief about taking too many phone messages for him. So when he hears the knock at his door in the morning, he knows she will be standing there with Fifi in her arms and a scowl on her face.

And so she is.

Without a word, she hands him the message slip.

"Last time, Mrs. O'Neill," he says. "Promise."

"Hmph," she says, and turns away.

Fifi looks back at him wistfully, with her ears at a sympathetic angle.

The message comes from his pal Anthony Morris. It's two words, "Call him," with the home phone number of James Aronson, who runs the *National Guardian* newspaper out of New York City. Anthony said he would talk to Aronson about Jake.

He goes down to the phone booth at the corner bar to make the call.

It turns out Anthony has some complicated family connection with Aronson, who gave Jake the okay to call him. Aronson says Anthony told him all about Jake. Aronson says he's been considering hiring somebody in Detroit to report on labor issues, racial problems, the effects of automation on the automobile industry, and so on, all from a progressive point-of-view.

Jake says, "I'm your man." He gives Aronson a quick summary

of his background, from his time in the Party in the thirties up to his current work on *Correspondence*, which Aronson has heard of.

And just like that, it's settled. Jake will start the following week.

Jake calls Anthony at his legal office to thank him but he's not in.

He calls Ronny's office at the Wayne University Theatre Department to give him the news, but the secretary says Ronny's in class.

He calls his brother Saul at the car lot to tell him, but the secretary says he's out on a test drive with a customer.

He calls Saul's wife Pauline at their home, but there's no answer at the house.

Jake wishes he had somebody to call to share this news with.

There must be someone on earth who would be happy for him. Mustn't there?

He takes Bridget McManus's business card from his wallet. He tries her at her office in the Women's Division.

She's not there, either.

He walks back to Mrs. O'Neill's.

It starts to rain.

Because of course it does.

Jake can't work on his project; too antsy to concentrate. Instead, he takes the latest folder of articles for the next *Correspondence* out of the envelope that James Boggs delivered to him, and goes down to his shed. He plugs in the waxer to warm up and sifts through the pages.

In the middle of the afternoon, Mrs. McNeill and Fifi knock on the door to the shed with another phone message for him.

"Getting tired of this, Mr. Lieberman," Mrs. McNeill says. Even Fifi gives him a disapproving weepy-eyed look.

The message is from Bridget, returning his call. With a suggestion for someplace to meet.

48

BRIDGET MCMANUS

"Didn't think we'd see you today," Lieutenant Emily Richardson says when Bridget gets to her desk after morning roll call in the Women's Division.

"I have to get started on the report. It's going to be a bear."

"When you're ready, come talk to me and I'll tell you what the forensics team turned up at the house."

"Thanks."

"Did you get the notice?"

"Of what?"

"The press conference. They scheduled it for noon. They're going to announce they caught the child killer."

"*They* caught him?"

"Right."

"And they're deliberately leaving me out of it?"

Bastards.

"I think you should show up and muscle in on their glory," Emily says.

"They want it so bad, they can have it."

"I want you to know—I'm putting you up for a departmental commendation."

"For what?"

"For the bravery you showed on Friday, and for cracking the case when all those *men* were stymied."

She says *men* as if the word were something distasteful.

"Thank you," Bridget says.

When she gets settled at her desk, Bridget discovers a message propped on her telephone. It's from the night sergeant on the desk at the Wyandotte Police Department downriver from Detroit.

It turns out the call that woke her up the other night wasn't from Ed Hauser after all.

She shows her badge to the Wyandotte day watch desk sergeant, but he still doesn't believe she is police. He has never heard of the Women's Division, and doesn't think women should be police officers.

She asks to see his commanding officer.

Who, fortunately, knows about the Women's Division.

Captain Wilson takes her back to the holding cells. Behind the bars in one of the cells she sees her brother Darren lying on a bench. He appears to be asleep.

"He's been like this since we picked him up," Wilson says.

"What happened?"

"We got him in a stolen vehicle."

"Who reported it stolen?"

"The Livonia Police. Apparently, he stole it from the collision shop where he works."

She watches her brother sleeping in his holding cell. Like he doesn't have a care in the world, she thinks. Happy like he's in his right mind, their father used to say about him.

"I appreciate the call," Bridget says. "Sorry I didn't pick it up."

"I heard you had some fun up there on Friday."

"I hope I never have that much fun again. Has he been processed?"

"He has. He was arraigned first thing this morning."

"It's his first arrest. I'm hoping—"

"Sgt. McManus, there's more."

"Oh dear."

"He also had in his possession a significant amount of money."

"How much?"

"Five hundred bucks."

"Do I want to ask how he got that?"

"He claims he found it in the glove compartment of the car he stole. A car belonging to Ray Malvino."

"Ray Malvino the gangster?"

"That would be the Ray Malvino to which I refer. Allegedly, Mr. Malvino had that money stashed in the glove compartment of a car he left to get a dent bumped out. Your brother worked on the car."

"And discovered the money, and stole it, and stole the car for his getaway."

"'Fraid so."

"So you're also holding him for theft from an auto?"

"Correct. If it was just the stolen car, we could talk, but stealing the car and the money . . ." Wilson shakes his head.

"No way you can release him?"

"Not at this point. He's already in the system. If you know a good lawyer, now would be the time to call him."

Back at her office in the Women's Division after lunch, she finds another phone message, this one from Jake Lieberman.

She knows she won't be able to speak with him directly because he has no phone, so in her return message she suggests meeting at the Flaming Embers, a restaurant on Woodward around the corner from the Madison Theatre, near police headquarters. She doesn't know if he'll get the message, or will be at the restaurant if he does.

First she makes calls to lawyers she knows. None of them are in, so she leaves messages for them.

Jake sits at a table at the front of the restaurant. When he sees her, he stands and opens his arms.

They hug. It feels like they've been separated for a long time.

"Thanks for your call," she says.

"Are you okay? You look kind of anxious."

"I was in Wyandotte this morning. Visiting my brother in the lockup down there."

"What happened?"

She tells him about Darren stealing the money in the glove

compartment at the collision shop and stealing the car.

"He stole money from a gangster?" Jake says.

"Genius move, right?"

"What's going to happen to him?"

"I tried to get him out, but the police chief down there said he can't let him go."

"Right—sure."

"Considering who he stole the money from, he's probably safer in jail than he would be out in the world."

"What possessed him to do this?"

"No idea. Since he got back from the war, he's never been the same."

"No, it changed everybody, that's for sure."

She thinks of the demons Jake struggles with, which he has only mentioned obliquely.

"So what did you want to talk to me about?" she asks.

"I wanted to tell you about my new job." He explains about it and how he got it.

"Wonderful!" she says. "So glad to hear it."

A waiter with a white apron tied around his waist comes over to them with menus. They both order just coffee.

"Are you excited?" she asks.

"'Excited' is perhaps a bit overstated."

"Yeah, sorry, I forgot who I was talking to for a second."

"I'm glad of it. I'm glad to be back in journalism."

"Told you you weren't cut out for security work."

"You were right."

He's giving me all his attention, Bridget marvels. She feels it like a spotlight shining on her.

"Also, I wanted to see you again," he says.

The direct statement catches her off guard. She debates with herself whether to say she feels the same—or whether she shouldn't appear too anxious.

Oh, the games we play, she thinks . . .

Screw it.

"I'm glad," she says. "I wanted to see you, too."

"Even though we're on opposite sides, you being a policewoman and me being a known radical?"

"And now back in the newspaper business."

"Another strike against me."

"Natural enemies," she agrees. "Like a cobra and mongoose."

"Who's the cobra and who's the mongoose here?"

"I suppose we'll have to sort that out."

"The mongoose usually wins, you know. They can withstand cobra bites, and they're fast little buggers."

"I'll keep that in mind. If this continues," she says, moving her hands back and forth, indicating them both, "you're going to have to spring for a telephone."

"That's for sure. My landlady and her little dog are both tired of being the go-betweens."

"She made that very clear to me when I called."

"I hope this does continue."

"Ditto. I have some good news myself. My boss is putting me in for a departmental commendation."

"For the shootout?"

"And for breaking the case."

"That's terrific, Policewoman McManus. Congratulations."

"Thank you, automotive—oh wait, you're not an automotive industrial loss-limitation specialist anymore."

"See, you knew what the title was all along."

"Picked right up on that, did you? Ever thought about going into police work?"

The waiter brings their coffees. "Would you like anything else?" he asks.

I think I'm looking at what else I want, Bridget tells herself, basking in the warmth of Jake's regard.

Judging by the intensity of his gaze, Jake could be thinking the same thing.

49

MALONE COLEMAN

Alonzo and Henty Loomis give Malone a lift to Clarence and Bessie's. Henty's brother Jerome stays in the house with Dorothy in case anything else happens during the day.

Alonzo pulls to the curb at the Browns' house and Malone gets out. "Remember what I said about James Boggs," Alonzo reminds him.

"I will."

Henty gets out, too, and wraps Malone in a hug. "Thanks again, Brother Malone."

Inside, Bessie tells Malone she took a message for him under the phone in the dining room. First, he showers and changes into an old shirt and pair of pants he left here. He tells Clarence and Bessie about his last forty-eight hours. He leaves out Anna Miller; he doesn't know how they will react to him getting close to a white woman.

Malone himself doesn't know how *he* feels about it. He doesn't even know how to think about it.

Clarence has finally persuaded Bessie to relax, and now he's making the lunch: chicken stew with string beans and corn. The smells of the meal and the familiar smells of Clarence and Bessie's home are comforting.

After the meal, Malone settles himself in the dining room chair beside the phone niche. He dials the number Bessie left for him on the message.

A woman answers on the second ring.

"Hello," Malone says, "I'm returning Mr. Cornish's call."

"Who's calling, please?"

"Malone Coleman."

"One moment."

A minute later, a man's voice says, "Charles Cornish."

"Mr. Cornish, it's Malone Coleman. I got a message you called me?"

"I did, Malone. How are you doing?"

"Fine."

"Well, I wish I had better news for you. So far, I haven't been successful at getting you your job back at the VA."

Malone doesn't know how he feels about this. It's not good, but also, in its way, not terrible.

Finally, he musters, "What happened?"

"I've been trying to get in touch with Representative Diggs and Senator McNamara. I haven't been able to reach either one so far."

"Okay."

"I haven't given up hope, and you shouldn't, either. I'm still trying. I just wanted to keep you posted."

"Thank you, Mr. Cornish."

"I'll be in touch as soon as I hear something."

"Good news or bad news?" Clarence asks when Malone hangs up.

Malone thinks about the question. It's not so easy to answer.

Finally, he says, "The lawyer hasn't been able to get me my job back."

Clarence chews on that. "But it's not final yet."

"No. He's still working."

Malone can't stop thinking about the ferocity of both Barry Atkins and Frank Carmody's racial hatred, and guesses that outweighs whatever influence the politicians might have.

The problem is, Malone thinks, he doesn't want the job anymore. The interchange with Alonzo Loomis got him thinking: what *do* I want to do?

The answer has always been, I'll take anything if it will let me keep painting. But I haven't been painting . . . so what do I want?

Two voices echo in his head:

Alonzo's admonition: *Remember what I said about James Boggs.*

And what Charles McGee told him: *you owe it to your talent to let it express itself through you.*

Grace Boggs answers the door. A small woman with a wide smile, she welcomes Malone inside and takes him into the kitchen, where James Boggs sits at the table paging through the *Detroit Free Press.*

"I read the *New York Times* every day," Grace says. "Jimmy won't touch it but he practically memorizes the *Free Press.*"

James Boggs smiles at his wife's jibe and stands to shake hands with Malone. "Good to meet you, finally," he says. "Can we get you anything? Coffee? A beer?"

He is a medium-tall, lean, handsome man with a sharp, high-pitched voice full of his Alabama roots. Malone expected an intense firebrand; in fact, he is as warm and welcoming as anyone Malone has met.

"I'm good, thanks," Malone says.

James sits back down. "Have a seat."

Grace takes the chair next to James, and Malone sits across the table.

"Alonzo Loomis called me about you. He had good things to say," James says. "You stepped right in like you were part of the family."

Malone doesn't know what to say to this famous man. Tongue-tied, he can only dip his head at the compliment.

"Alonzo told me a bit about your situation," James says. "Tell me more."

Finding his voice, Malone gives him the in-depth story, including his meetings with both Frank Carmody and Barry Atkins.

"They said that?" James asks. "The National Negro Labor Council weakens the white American family?"

"They did."

James scoffs. "Proves what I've said time and again. The American system is rotten. It needs to be torn down and rebuilt from the ground up."

James pages through some more of the *Free Press* on the table in front of him.

"The auto industry's going great guns right now," he says, "but the working man won't see any of that. We're going to go through the same cycle of boom and bust we go through every year, and as usual it'll be the working man who suffers. People like to call this the 'golden age' of the American worker thanks to the unions. But they don't understand the revolution will never come from the unions, or from groups like the NAACP. Walter Reuther and Walter White both owe their jobs to the continuation of the conditions they're supposed to be fighting against."

Reuther, president of the United Auto Workers, and Walter White, the executive secretary of the National Association for the Advancement of Colored People.

"If the workers' problems were solved," James says, "Walter Reuther wouldn't have anything to do. Same thing for Walter White. If the fight for Negro rights was settled, White'd be out of a job. Neither thing's going to happen anytime soon."

A knock comes at the door. Grace goes to answer it.

"Them and people like them?" James continues. "Their whole reason for being is *not* reaching the goals they claim they want to reach."

Grace returns to the dining room followed by a white man holding a large folder.

James says, "Jake."

The man says, "James. Good to see you." The two shake hands.

"Hey," James says, "you know Malone Coleman? Malone, Jake Lieberman."

The two men nod at each other.

James says, "That the new *Correspondence*?"

"It is."

Jake hands him the portfolio. James opens it and delicately takes out the set of boards pasted up with strips of articles and letters.

"Grace told you this might be the last one for a while?" James says.

"I did," Grace says.

"Ever seen *Correspondence*?" James asks Malone.

"Few times."

James opens the boards so Malone can see the paste-up.

"Tells the workers' point of view on colored people, women,

youth—everybody whose voice isn't heard," James says.

"We're going through a reorganization right now," Grace Boggs says, "and we're getting ready to stop the paper for a bit. Even though we specifically say we don't encourage action and activism—we encourage dialogue—the FBI and the government are all over us, trying to suppress what we do. They put us on the subversive list and the Post Office took away our mailing rights. We told them we're anti-Communist, but they're constantly harassing us."

"We're going to start publishing again when we figure out what the paper's going to do," James says. "I'm looking for people to write pieces based on their own experience of struggling for justice. We also transcribe pieces other people dictate. Want to be part of it?"

"Absolutely," Malone says.

"Good. Here's your first assignment. I want you to write me an article about your entire ordeal, from losing your job to trying to find out who named you. We'll publish it in the first revised issue of *Correspondence* in the fall.

"After that, we can talk about getting you on the editorial advisory board from the new paper when it's ready. Meantime, I'll work on getting you a job with me at Chrysler so you can get back to your union roots. How's that sound?"

Malone says it sounds just fine.

50

ANNA MILLER

Anna walks with Edie Kerouac outside the house Edie shares with her mother in Grosse Pointe Park. It's a large home, but the grounds are spectacular—beautifully landscaped with trees and shrubs Anna doesn't know the names for. Walking the grounds with Edie, Anna says she has never seen such lovely gardens.

"Thanks," Edie says. "When I came back from New York, I got a master's degree in horticulture up at Michigan State College."

"You did this all yourself?"

"I did. Did you ever hear Dorothy Parker's joke: someone challenged her to come up with a rhyme for 'horticulture' and she came up with, 'you can lead a horse to water but you can't make it drink; you can lead a whore to culture, but you can't make her think.'"

She laughs at her own joke. Anna smiles politely; Edie called her and asked her to come to her house, so she's waiting to hear the reason.

"Are you still thinking about New York City?" Edie asks.

"I don't know . . ."

"Having second thoughts?"

"I just don't know if I'm ready to take it on."

"It's a big step," Edie agrees. "I left Michigan for New York when I was seventeen. But I had relatives there. I stayed with my grandmother in Morningside Heights. That's in upper Manhattan. I started art school at Columbia but once I met Jack and the rest . . . well, school didn't seem so important."

They stop in front of an enormous oak tree. Edie pats it, like a trusty horse.

"The thing is," Anna says, "I don't know if I'm hesitating because I'm frightened or if it really isn't a good move right now."

"Only you can answer that. A little fear gives you an edge. A lot of fear holds you back. On the other hand, don't do it just because you're afraid to do it. It takes a special wisdom to know what to do and when to do it. Sometimes we don't develop that until long after we need it."

Anna nods. She's not used to another woman giving her motherly advice. Her own mother never bothered, so Anna always figured that wasn't a mother's job, and she didn't need it anyway.

But now, with Edie's good words . . . Anna starts to get how much she's missed in her life.

If only she'd had someone like Edie for a mother instead of the Nazi ice queen . . . things would have been different.

Edie says, "You have to remember one thing, though. Wherever you go, you're going to meet yourself there."

It's true, Anna thinks. You can miss out on life as much in New York City as you've missed it here. The problem isn't where you are; the problem is *you*.

"If you decide you want to go, I know people in New York," Edie says. "They live in Greenwich Village. Bernard teaches English at New York University. He's a poet. I met him at a party with Allen Ginsberg and some of the others. Bernard's wife Sophie works in Admissions at NYU. I'm sure they'll let you stay with them while you get yourself settled."

They start back toward Edie's house.

"I have some more news for you," Edie says, "which is really why I wanted to see you. It might have an impact on your decision. I was talking with a friend who owns a bar downtown. She likes to have local artists show their work at her place. I was raving to her about your photographs, and I got her intrigued. She wondered if you'd be interested in having a show there in the fall. I told her I'd talk to you about it."

"A show? Of *my* photographs?"

"This could be the beginning for you. Should I tell her you're interested?"

"I'm definitely interested."

Edie's message: wherever you go, there you are.

You can't outrun yourself. You're always waiting for yourself, around a corner.

And an exhibition of her photos?

Which scares her more, the thought of moving to New York without knowing anyone, or showing people her work? Even though her subjects are not especially personal, it would be like baring her soul for strangers.

A little fear gives you an edge. A lot of fear holds you back.

Maybe she should start by baring her soul to someone who isn't a stranger. Meet those fears halfway.

She waits for Malone Coleman by the timeclock in the basement of Harper Hospital. Already employees are lined up to punch out and punch in.

She spots him at the end of the line.

She takes a deep breath—"Screw your courage to the sticking place," she tells herself—and walks up to him.

"Hi," she says.

She watches him closely, looking for anything resembling a smile indicating he's happy to see her. She thinks she sees it—it's brief, but it's there, beneath his look of surprise.

As the line starts moving forward, she says, "Can I talk to you?"

"Sure."

"I have something to tell you."

"I have to clock in right now. I don't have the time to listen. But I want to hear it."

"When do you get off?"

"Not till seven in the morning."

"Can I meet you then?"

She gets up extra-early to clean her offices and make Selma some breakfast. Anna is waiting for Malone outside the main entrance to the hospital when he comes out, blinking in the morning sunshine.

"Maybe we could go to the hospital cafeteria," he suggests.

"That's fine."

They go through the cafeteria line. He gets only coffee, so she does, too.

They find themselves a table that straddles the Negro section and the white section. She looks around and notices a few integrated tables where nurses sit.

"Before you start what you want to talk about," he says, "I need to say something. I didn't mean to insult you at the Loomises yesterday. And if Dorothy insulted you, I apologize for that, too."

"Who's Dorothy?"

"The woman who asked if there was a problem. She and her husband and their daughters stay in the house, and they're pretty bad-tempered from the last few days."

"I get that. My white face was probably the last thing they wanted to see on their doorstep."

"It was a friendly white face. But yeah, they didn't know that."

"But you do, I hope?"

"I do."

She wells up with tears at what she is about to do. He notices, and his face softens. "Hey," he says. "It's okay. Whatever you're going to say, it's okay."

"I want to tell you something," she says. "I'm not sure why. I think I want you to know I understand, in some small way, what you've been going through."

He gives her a nod to continue.

"I was abused," she says. "By my brother. When I was fourteen, he started getting in bed with me at night. We'd cuddle, and honestly for a while it was nice. Our parents weren't affectionate toward us at all, and that was the only warmth I remember getting. And I thought, if you can't get it from your brother . . .

"But after a while the cuddling turned into touching and then kissing. I told him I didn't want to do it anymore, but he ignored me. On the night of my fifteenth birthday, he came into my room and had sex with me."

Malone says nothing, watching her with kind eyes.

"I told my mother about it, but she didn't believe me. My brother denied it, of course. My mother told my father I was making up horrible lies about my brother. My father called in a doctor, who decided I was having episodes of hysterical fantasies. He started giving me medicine that made me so dopey I couldn't function.

"In the meantime, my brother kept on coming into my room at night, and I couldn't fight him off because I was too out of it. Finally, when I was sixteen, he got me pregnant."

"Is that when they finally believed you?"

"That's when my father put a lock on my door so my brother couldn't get in. Except he put it on the outside of my door, so I couldn't get out, either."

"You were a prisoner."

"The baby was born and died right away. A beautiful little boy. This guy took him away and left him in an apartment building in Black Bottom and tried to make it look like a couple of Negro men kidnapped him. He wanted to start a race war. But it didn't work."

She watches him and sees sympathy in his eyes.

"So it might not compare to what you've gone through," she continues, "and I don't want it to seem like a contest, because it isn't. But I've seen enough to know how the world works. How it can be so ugly and sad."

He looks like he's trying to sort through the thousand possible things to say, without finding one.

Finally he says, "I appreciate you telling me."

"You're the first man I ever told about it. No," she corrects herself, "actually the second one. There was a policeman at the time who helped me. He was the first man outside the family I ever told."

She's remembering Denny Rankin, who helped her separate from her parents for good, and got her into the Society of Arts and Crafts.

"I can live with being the second," he says.

She sits back in her chair. She closes her eyes. It's done.

"So now you probably think I'm damaged goods," she says.

"Not at all."

She doesn't want to open her eyes—afraid she'll look at him and he'll be repulsed, despite what he says.

She's afraid he'll be repulsed, because she finds herself repulsive. She opens her eyes.

He does not seem repelled. He looks at her with something she hasn't seen for a while: understanding.

"I don't know how you get over something like that," he says. "All this racism—yeah, it stinks, but we know we all go through it together. We give each other strength. But you? To go through this by yourself? The strength you must have."

"I don't. It ruined me."

He leans forward. He sits across the table from her, and they are in public—otherwise she thinks he might put his arms around her.

"I don't think you're ruined at all," he says. "I'm so sorry."

"I guess we've both seen the worst of people."

"And we're both still standing."

"More or less."

After a moment, he asks, "How did you get here today?"

"I have a car."

"Do you have time to take a ride? There's somebody I want you to meet."

He directs her north on Woodward. At 8 Mile Road they go west to Wyoming and pull up in front of a ranch house on Wisconsin Street in the neighborhood, down the block from the Higginbottom Elementary School.

"Where are we?" Anna asks.

"You'll see."

Malone rings the bell. Anna hears a presence gather behind the door, which opens on a large Negro man in his sixties. He starts to say, "Why you not using your—" and sees Anna.

"Somebody you need to meet," Malone says.

A woman's voice comes from the back of the house. "Malone, that you, baby?"

A Negro woman comes out, hobbling on a single crutch. Her left leg ends at the knee, wrapped in gauze. "Well," she says. "What we got here?"

"This is a friend of mine," Malone tells them. "Anna Miller. Anna, I'd like to introduce to you my parents, Clarence and Bessie Brown."

The older couple are clearly shocked by this visitor, but Bessie says, "Come in, come in," and Malone ushers Anna into the tiny living room.

Bessie closes the door behind them and Anna notices a gun belt hanging on a coat tree near the door. Two pearl-handled revolvers in holsters hang on the belt.

"Can we get you something?" Bessie asks Anna. "Are you hungry?"

Anna realizes she is, but she doesn't want to impose on them, so she shakes her head.

"Malone?" Bessie asks.

"No, mamma."

"Well, let's sit down," Clarence says. He holds out a hand inviting Anna to sit on the sofa.

She sits. Clarence and Bessie sit in what Anna suspects are their usual chairs. Malone remains standing.

"I wanted Anna to meet you both," he says.

Anna can tell by the looks on their faces that Clarence and Bessie Brown do NOT want to hear Malone say he wants to marry this white girl he has just brought into their home.

"Clarence," Malone says, "remember the little white baby you found in Black Bottom just before Pearl Harbor?"

"I'll never forget him."

"Clarence is the policeman who found your son," Malone explains to Anna, "and even though everybody told him to drop the case, he didn't stop until he found out who that baby was, and what happened to him."

"Everybody told me to give it up," Clarence says. "I couldn't."

"He found out the child was being used in a scheme to start trouble between whites and Negroes in the city," Malone says. "Sound familiar?

Anna can't speak for the emotion welling up in her chest.

"Tell her what you did with the child," Malone says.

"Took me a while to find him. But I did. Poor child had been abandoned, alone in the world. Didn't matter what color he was. When I found him, I took him to an undertaker I knew, somebody who would bury him with the dignity he didn't get in life."

"That was Anna's baby," Malone says.

Clarence and Bessie exchange a look. It's more than a look of surprise—it's a look of wonderment in the face of what life brings.

"Praise Jesus," Bessie murmurs.

Anna buries her face in her hands and weeps. Finally—finally she knows the end her baby came to. And it was a better end than she ever could have hoped for.

Bessie says, "Oh child," and hobbles over to Anna on the sofa. The older woman sits beside her and folds her in a hug. Anna sobs against her shoulder. "Oh, you poor child."

Anna makes herself stop crying. She picks her head up, wipes her eyes with the heels of her hands.

"I don't know how to thank you," she gets out.

"No thanks necessary," Clarence says. "If I hadn't done it, I wouldn't be able to live with myself."

Anna fills in the other half of the story, her half—the abuse, the aftermath for her, her failed attempt at starting a new life, the other policeman's efforts to find her work and then pay for art school for her, what she's been doing since then.

And how she and Malone came to connect. What happened to her on Riopelle Street.

All the while Bessie sits with her arm around Anna's shoulders, rocking her gently.

The Browns make Anna and Malone lunch. They send her off with hugs and an invitation to come back anytime.

She drives Malone downtown to his room at the Barlow. They don't speak on the journey, but when they exchange glances, an entire silent conversation seems to transpire in the space between them.

He directs her to his building. Before he gets out of the car, she says, "This means so much to me, I don't even know what to say."

"Don't need to say anything. I'm glad to do it."

"Bessie and Clarence are amazing."

"I agree."

They are both silent for a few moments. Then Malone says, "Can I see you again?"

"I would like that. Bu—I'm white and you're Negro. Aren't you sick of white people? Don't you hate us? I would if I were you."

"When I was at the Loomises', this white kid pounded on the front door and called us every name you can think of. I opened it and stuck a shotgun in his face and I came this close to giving him both barrels."

"Why didn't you? I probably would have."

"One thing Clarence and Bessie taught me, hate is corrosive. Plus I would have wound up in prison for the rest of my life and that little shit wasn't worth it. You'll get more grief for being with me than I will for you."

"That's probably true."

"So you're not worried about that?"

"Not at all. I guess that's one of the advantages of being a recluse. You start out not caring what people think."

"I have a feeling your recluse days are over."

She leans across the bench seat and puts her arms around him. She feels him lean into the hug and return it.

In the middle of the afternoon, she falls asleep on the sofa in her apartment.

Instead of her usual dreams—nightmares, rather—of her family, she dreams of being lost inside a huge building—a hospital, maybe, or a hotel, something with closed doors. She couldn't open the doors, and couldn't find her way back to any exits through endless hallways.

What would Dr. Freud say?

She splashes water on her face from the sink and looks at her own photographs, still clothes-pinned to the lines around the room. These are still the ones she developed from the near-riot on Riopelle.

As always, she looks at them with the most critical eye, finding the smallest mistakes.

Even so, she has to admit these are not terrible. Edie Kerouac wasn't lying when she praised them to her friend who owned a bar.

She opens the flat drawers in the cabinet outside her makeshift dark room. She has more photographs here, and more photos and negatives in a file cabinet. Her photos fill her little home.

She's always been covetous of them, never wanting to show them to anyone lest someone make a critical comment about them to her.

But now someone Edie talked to wants to give her a show of her own.

Edie also said she knows someone in New York City who would give Anna a place to land should she decide to go there.

The overwhelming question: should she go to New York, or should she stay here and have an exhibit and who knows what might come after that?

Of course, she doesn't have to do one or the other . . . she could have her show and go to New York after. If she still wanted to.

Suddenly she sees lots of advantages in staying.

If she stayed, she could continue helping Selma in her grief. She's grown fond of the older woman. And if she's going to start having health scares like her most recent one, she might need Anna all the more. Selma doesn't have anybody else.

Anna could also continue to help Chester, who will need someone he can rely on to help him get through the aftermath of what has just happened to them both.

And of course, she could have her show . . . and who knows what that might lead to in the art community of Detroit and beyond.

And there's Malone. . . She told herself that she wanted to let him know that she understood suffering because she had suffered, but she knows in her heart it was more than that. She needed to open up to him in a way she never had before to anyone. It was her invitation to him: come inside my bubble and *see* me. And he had responded in the best way possible.

And he took her to meet Clarence Brown, the man who wouldn't stop until he found her son and helped him come to a decent end. A kind man. A good man.

And Malone was the same way.

But would the Browns have conflicted feelings about Malone seeing a white woman?

She didn't think so. Didn't they invite her back?

And didn't they pick up on that silent conversation that went on between her and Malone?

What was that saying? The heart wants what it wants . . .

She wants Malone's heart. She thinks—hopes—he would want hers.

So all of that weighs on one side. On the other: taking a flying leap into the lonely mystery of New York City.

She's not good at making decisions. Never has been.

She learned a long time ago that people whose lives have always been controlled by other people have trouble making decisions. They haven't had practice.

This explains so much about her.

The afternoon turns to evening. She sits at her window and looks out across the city; lights come on in buildings and on the streets.

She knows now, in the clarity of the coming night, she is having so much trouble making this decision because she has already made it; she just hasn't realized it. She has been trying to talk herself *out* of the decision she knew she had made: that's where all the trouble lay.

She will stay.

Does this come from wisdom or fear? Is it a life-expression arising from maturity, or an obstacle thrown up by timidity?

Whatever the answer, she hopes she will look back at this time in her life years from now and know she did the right thing.

September 1955

Epilogue

The Bronx Bar, Second and Prentis. It's small and dark but Anna's photos are displayed on all the walls, and to showcase them, the bar owner has set up spotlights trained on them.

The photos are in simple black frames. There are black and white shots of Detroit homes—bungalows and small frame houses from the neighborhoods as well as mansions from the Grosse Pointes and Palmer Woods—and color shots of downtown architectural gems like the Aztec elements of the Guardian Building and the soaring art deco Fisher Building.

There are also portraits of ordinary Detroiters going about their lives—shopping, sprucing up their homes, having parties in their postage-stamp-sized city yards, living their turbulent mid-century lives, whites, Negroes, Chinese, Hispanics, and Indians, all with the tough, take-no-shit airs of people for whom existence in Detroit means wringing moments of joy out of daily struggles.

The bar is packed. Anna doesn't even know this many people. Most must be friends of students and teachers from the Society of Arts and Crafts rounded up by Sarkis Sarkisian.

Among the crowd are Jake Lieberman with a woman, the policewoman who carried Anna out of the Swoboda home.

Malone Coleman is also here, along with the group of Negro artists who were at Sarkis's exhibition earlier in the year: LeRoy

Foster, Ernest Hardman, Harold Neal, Charles McGee, and Harold Montgomery.

Also here are Chester Glowaki and his sister Dottie, Anna's friend Marianne Walker, and even Anna's neighbor Selma sitting at the bar, watching the gathering with a wistful look.

Her old boss, Eva Perlman, and her photographer husband Hal were in earlier, along with Denny Rankin and his wife Elizabeth Rankin, who both helped Anna so much.

They all congratulate her, and tell her they love her show.

Her show.

Anna's head spins . . . she can't remember ever being this happy.

She hasn't seen Edie Kerouac yet, but now Anna spies her coming in with a slender man whose most prominent feature is a high forehead with a hairline already starting to recede even though he appears to be only in his early thirties.

He goes straight for the photographs hung on the walls.

Edie makes her way across the crowded bar to Anna.

"You made it," Anna says as they hug.

"Sorry I'm late. I had to pick up Robert." She points to the man looking at her photos.

"Who's that?"

"Robert Frank."

The photographer who came through the city earlier this year.

"He has a Guggenheim to take photographs all across America. It's going to be part of a book he's going to write called *The Americans*. When he's finished, I'm going to suggest he meets Jack."

Jack Kerouac, Edie's ex-husband.

"I think they'd have a lot in common," Edie says.

"He certainly seems interested in my work."

"With good reason."

Frank stands up close to the series of photos of Chester Glowaki. He examines Chester's expressions.

"Come on," Edie says. "I'll introduce you."

She takes Anna by the hand and walks her over to Robert Frank. "These are extraordinary," he says to Edie.

"I want you to meet the photographer," Edie says. "Robert Frank, Anna Miller."

Frank extends his hand to Anna. "I'm honored," she says.

"The honor is mine. Wonderful work." He has a slight European accent, somewhere between German and French.

"Thank you."

One of the premiere photographers in the world is telling Anna she does wonderful work.

"I love your portraits," he says. "The candid shots especially. Outstanding."

Anna gets out, "Thank you."

"Where else have you shown?"

"This is my first exhibition."

"Well, it won't be your last. Have you met Lloyd Goodrich or Russell Cowles?"

"No."

"They're jurors for this year's Michigan artists exhibition at the Art Institute. I met them this summer. I'm going to ask them to come by and see your work. I think you'll be a shoo-in for the show. It's in November. Will you be around?"

Edie says, "Anna was thinking about moving to New York."

"New York! Why?"

"I was considering getting away to a bigger city," Anna says. "But I'm going to stay here."

"Of course," he says. "Detroit gives you everything you need. New York will have you spending all your time scrambling for a living. Do you want to do fashion photography? Or commercial photography? Because that's what you'll be doing, if you don't wind up washing dishes in some diner. No, if I were you, I'd stay. You have the eye and the vision and the opportunities all right here. You want to travel, take a trip across the country. But move to New York?"

He mock-shudders. "I did it, but I wouldn't recommend it now."

He turns to Edie. "Thank you for introducing me to this talented young lady."

"I thought you'd like her work," Edie says.

"I do. I love your black-and-white photography," he tells Anna. "Those are the colors of photography, black and white. They symbolize the alternatives of hope and despair, you know. The extremes we're always subjected to."

He returns to Anna's street photography. "The hatred on the

faces of these people," he murmurs in front of her photos of the Riopelle disturbances. "Chilling."

Edie reaches out to squeeze Anna's arm. "I'm glad you're staying," Edie says.

She drifts away, following Robert Frank.

Suzie Callahan, the owner of the Bronx Bar, comes over to Anna. Suzie puts an arm around her. "How's it going, kiddo?"

"Couldn't be better."

"Did you see a couple of the pictures over there with red dots on them?" Suzie asks. "That means they're sold. Already! I convinced the buyers to leave them up till the end of the show."

Anna finds it hard to admit any of this is happening. But it's especially hard for her to admit she has earned this.

"I don't know what to say."

"Don't say nothing, honey," Suzie says. "Just enjoy the moment."

Malone leaves the reception early, but not before he arranges for Anna to stop by his apartment at the end of the night, after she's taken Selma home.

He stands before three canvases in his basement room. They are the largest pieces he has ever done. So big, he has to prop them against three different walls to work on them; there's no one wall big enough to bunch them together.

It's still early in the process, and still rough. Yet he already knows what he's going to do.

It will be a triptych, a series of three canvases. One will be from the point of view of somebody standing behind the unruly crowd outside of the Loomis home on Riopelle; the focus will be the modest home and the backs of the heads of the dozens of whites gathered around it watching the burning cross they have left on the front lawn. That's the one he's working on now.

He has sketches for the others. The second painting will be from the perspective of those inside the house looking out through the slit in the plywood boards that cover the front window. He will show the throngs of people outside the house, their white faces distorted by hatred.

The third painting will be of the people inside the house—Loomis and his wife and his relatives and children, along with Malone himself.

He felt called to start these works—as a witness to what had happened during the weeks of the siege of Henty Loomis's house. That was his working title: "The Siege of the Loomis Home, Detroit."

He paints in the morning before he goes to his job at Chrysler. James Boggs came through for him. He paints after work at night.

Henty's cousin Alonzo was right; James Boggs is an amazing man. Malone loves talking to him and hearing him expound on everything from why they should not refer to themselves as "Negroes" (it's a name given to them, not one they should use themselves) to how a society reconstituted around equality and respect would look.

James Boggs predicted the red-hot auto industry would begin shutting down at some point toward the end of the year, the whole reason for the push in production earlier being so the companies would have a backlog when the inevitable fall slump begins.

And he's right; that's just what's happening. But he got Malone hired in before it started to slow.

Now Malone examines what he's done with his new work.

He's given the Loomis house an air of danger despite its happy yellow color. It'll all be there—the burning cross, the menace radiating from the crowd, the pock marks on the exterior walls of the house, even the suggestion of people, Negro faces, looking out of the attic window, taking in the sea of hatred below them.

He's been covering the canvas whenever Anna Miller comes over because he doesn't feel like it's ready to share yet. And she hasn't pushed him.

But as he stands looking at it, he knows he will show it to her tonight. Not just for her opinion—it's not even half-way finished yet—but as his own way of validating that he's returned to what has given him so much pleasure in his life.

Only now it's not simply for the pleasure of artistic expression. It's in service to the goal of social revolution.

For Malone, this is just the beginning.

The lights are on, but otherwise her house is quiet when Bridget McManus gets home from the Bronx Bar.

Lydia is under a blanket in the living room, engrossed in her latest book, *The Lion, The Witch, and the Wardrobe*.

Timmy sits at the dining room table, his face three inches away from a sheet of paper where he draws a lurid hot rod with an exposed engine compartment and exaggerated exhaust pipes belching smoke.

Her mother Marian sits beside him, reading the *Detroit News*. Her father Ernest snoozes in a chair in front of the television set, which is thankfully off.

Darren is not here, of course, but she takes some small comfort knowing that he's not at large.

She kisses Lydia on the top of her head, Timmy on the side of his head (both children fragrant from their baths), and her mother on her papery cheek.

"Well," Marian says, "how was it?"

"Very nice," Bridget says. "This young photographer does pretty good work."

"And how's your gentleman friend?"

"Fine."

She does not mention that her gentleman friend Jake will be her gentleman caller later tonight, after he finishes up work he wants to do at his place. Best not mention this to her mother, who will tell her father, and she's not ready for the uproar that will result. They'll be gone by the time he gets here anyway.

She sits at the table with her mother and son. "You've had yourself a week," her mother says.

"That I have."

And it's true, she's exhausted from racing around lower Michigan, flouting most of the rules of the Women's Division, best of all breaking open the case of the sex-slayings of three children . . . not a bad result.

"Bet you'll be ready for bed tonight," her mother says.

I bet I will, too, Bridget thinks. But not the way her mother means.

She told Jake she would leave the front door unlocked for him.

Don't bother knocking, she said; just come in.

"Well," her mother says, as if reading her mind, "now you're home, I guess we'll get going."

His large canvas, eight feet by ten feet, primed, stands against a side wall of the shed. Jake Lieberman sets it aside for now, before he even really starts it. He might come back to it, but he has a different idea.

He remembered something Bridget McManus said when she saw his photographs, especially the photos of the soldiers reacting to the sights and smells of the concentration camp. You don't even have to see what they're looking at to know, she said.

That's what he's going to do here. Rather than portray the scenes of the camp, as he initially planned to do, he will focus on individuals in whose faces the entirety of the horror will be etched.

The first subject is Chaim Lerner.

Now, with his sketches of Chaim spread out on the counter beside him, sitting at an easel before a three-by-four-foot gessoed canvas, Jake takes a piece of charcoal and sketches the general shape of Chaim's skull, oval but with a broad high formidable forehead and a thicket of curls at the sides of his head. Chaim is jowly, so Jake adds some flesh to the man's jaw.

The look in his eye will be the hardest, and most important part of the painting—its focal point. Like Sarkis Sarkisian's faces, his portrait of Chaim will stare out at the viewer with frank accusations.

He has the color palette figured out already. It's going to be on the dark side, of course—in the background will be the horror in the man's eyes: the browns of the wood of the sleeping quarters, the pale colors of flesh in different stages of putrefaction and starvation of the prisoners, the faded black and white stripes of tattered uniforms, and over everything the dark, dark cloud of human bestiality that made this possible.

And which makes it not only possible to happen again, but likely.

He squeezes the colors out of oil tubes onto his palette, and with a brush mixes the tones. He will work for two hours and go to Bridget's. She said she'd leave the door open for him.

He leans into the canvas and begins.

EXTRAS

Cast of Characters

Author's Note

About the Author

Also by Donald Levin

CAST OF CHARACTERS

BARRY ATKINS, a rogue FBI special agent.

RONNY BARIT, Jake Lieberman's friend, an actor.

GRACE BOGGS, the real-life Detroit activist and wife of James Boggs.

JAMES BOGGS, the real-life visionary thinker and husband of Grace.

FRANK CARMODY, a member of the City of Detroit Commission of Community Relations.

MALONE COLEMAN, an artist.

CHARLES C. CORNISH, an attorney.

LEROY FOSTER, the real-life Detroit artist.

ROBERT FRANK, the real-life photographer.

JOEY GALLAGHER, one of the murdered children.

CHESTER GLOWAKI, Anna Miller's charge.

WILLY HODGES, a Communist turncoat.

SAMUEL JONES, Jake's coworker at the former Hudson Motors plant.

DOTTIE KACZMAREK, the sister of Chester Glowaki.

ROGER KACZMAREK, the husband of Dottie Kaczmarek.

MELVIN KENNEDY, Lucille Reid's boyfriend.

KENNETH KENYON, Charles Cornish's law partner.

EDITH KEROUAC, the real-life ex-wife of Jack Kerouac.

ROSLYN KLEIN, a social worker.

CHAIM LERNER, a Holocaust survivor.

JAKE LIEBERMAN, a former newspaper artist.

ALONZO LOOMIS, a cousin of Henty Loomis.

DOROTHY LOOMIS, Henty Loomis's wife.

HENTY LOOMIS, Dorothy Loomis's husband.

JEROME LOOMIS, a brother of Henty Loomis.

KATHLEEN MACREADY, one of the murdered children.

JEANNIE MCCORMICK, one of the murdered children.

CHARLES MCGEE, the real-life Detroit artist.

BRIDGET MCMANUS, a sergeant in the Detroit Police Department's Women's Division.

ANNA MILLER, a photographer.

ANTHONY MORRIS, a poet, friend of Jake Lieberman.

DARREN MURPHY, Bridget McManus's brother.

HAROLD NOLAN, the real-life Detroit artist.

NICK PAPAGEORGIOU, the owner of Nick's Grille.

REV. ARLIE C. PORTER, the real-life local fair-housing advocate.

LUCILLE REID, a young artist.

STANLEY RUDZEWICZ, a white man selling his house in Detroit.

SOUPY SALES, the real-life Detroit television personality.

SELMA STENHAGEN, Anna's downstairs neighbor, Fred's sister.

FRED STENHAGEN, Anna's downstairs neighbor, Selma's brother.

ALOIS SWOBODA, the leader of the white resistance to Henty Loomis.

FRANK TANNER, the real-life legal counsel for the House Un-American Activities Committee hearings.

MARIANNE WALKER, a friend of Anna Miller.

JOHN STEPHENS WOOD, the real-life chairman of the House Un-American Activities Committee hearing in Detroit.

EMANUEL WYCOFF, an inspector with the Detroit Police Department.

COLEMAN YOUNG, the real-life labor activist and future Detroit mayor.

Author's Note

Maryanne Moore called poetry "real toads in imaginary gardens." I think of this novel similarly. Though the characters and their interactions are fictional, "real toads" hop throughout these pages, including the following actual events:

There actually was a trio of unsolved child sex killings that shocked Michigan in 1955. The names and locations are changed in the novel.

The kind of sickening violence depicted in these pages directed by whites against Black families who tried to move into certain neighborhoods around Detroit has been documented, including cases of crosses burned on their lawns and other sorts of mob terrorism as described here.

Then-mayor Albert Cobo did dismantle public housing plans in favor of private developers during those years, creating even more housing pressure for Black Detroiters.

Several Black men actually were dismissed from their jobs around that time for "security concerns"; they got their jobs back thanks to the work of an attorney, Charles C. Lockwood, and two politicians, Congressman Charles Diggs and Senator Patrick McNamara.

A shootout and hours-long standoff in a Detroit neighborhood did take place in the summer of 1955 involving more than two hundred policemen and a lone gunman. It was not connected with the child killings.

The House Un-American Activities Committee met in Detroit in 1952 in its anti-communist fervor, leaving shattered lives in its wake here, as across the country.

The deindustrialization of Detroit was a historical fact, as the auto industry deserted Detroit for the suburbs or other states across the country, leading to the systematic breakdown of city economic and social functioning.

As I have incorporated these and other "real toads" into my story, I have changed names, locations, and circumstances to serve my narrative purposes.

In my efforts to portray as accurately as possible the real-life events and tenor of the times, I am grateful for information retrieved from the following sources:

Steve Babson, *Working Detroit*.
Grace Lee Boggs, *Living for Change: An Autobiography*.
Daniel J. Clark, *Disruption in Detroit: Automakers and the Elusive Postwar Boom*.
Colleen Doody, *Detroit's Cold War: The Origins of Postwar Conservatism*.
Martin Halpern, "'I'm Fighting for Freedom': Coleman Young, HUAC, and the Detroit African American Community."
Thomas Klug, "The Deindustrialization of Detroit."
David Maraniss, *A Good American Family*.
Ryan S. Pettengill, *Communists and Community: Activism in Detroit's Labor Movement 1941-1956*.
Smithsonian, "Oral History Interview with Sarkis Sarkarian, 1973."
Thomas Sugrue, *The Origins of the Urban Crisis*.
Stephen M. Ward, ed., *Pages from a Black Radical's Notebook: A James Boggs Reader*.
Coleman Young, *Hard Stuff: The Autobiography of Mayor Coleman Young*.

In addition, I consulted the following newspaper archives: *The Detroit Evening Times*, the *Detroit Free Press*, the *Detroit News*, the *Detroit Jewish News*, the *Detroit Tribune*, and the *Michigan Chronicle*.

I am indebted to historian Thomas Klug, Ph.D., for his help with Detroit history, and for reading an early draft of this book. All errors are my own.

Warm thanks to Joan H. Young for her keen editorial expertise, and to Lisa J. Allen for reading an earlier version.

I also wish to thank the following individuals for their suggestions, interest, support, and encouragement: Paul Burns, Bruce Harkness, Jerry van Rossum, and Peter Werbe.

My great thanks to Joe Montgomery for his design of the cover.

As always, my deepest appreciation goes to my wife, Suzanne Allen, my first and best reader, whose love and support continue to sustain me.

ABOUT THE AUTHOR

Donald Levin is an award-winning fiction writer and poet. He is the author of *Savage City*, a historical novel set in 1932 Detroit, and *The Arsenal of Deceit*, a historical novel set in 1941, the two precursors to *The Ghosts of Detroit*; seven Martin Preuss mystery novels; and *The House of Grins* (Sewickley Press, 1992), a novel; three books of poetry, *Are You Listening* (West Vine Press, 2024), *In Praise of Old Photographs* (Little Poem Press, 2005), and *New Year's Tangerine* (Pudding House Press, 2007); *The Exile* (Poison Toe Press, 2020), a dystopian novella; and co-author of *Postcards from the Future: A Triptych on Humanity's End* (Whistlebox Press and Quitt and Quinn Publishers, 2019). He lives in Ferndale, Michigan.

To learn more about Donald and his works, visit his website, www.donaldlevin.com, and follow him on Instagram at donald_levin_author.

If you enjoyed this book, please post a review on Goodreads, Amazon, or your favorite book review site.

ALSO BY DONALD LEVIN

The first two books in the Detroit Series

Detroit, 1932. The fates of four people converge during a violent week of labor unrest in the bleakest year of the Great Depression. Against the backdrop of the bloody Ford Hunger March, events hurl these four into the center of a political storm that will change them—and their city—forever.

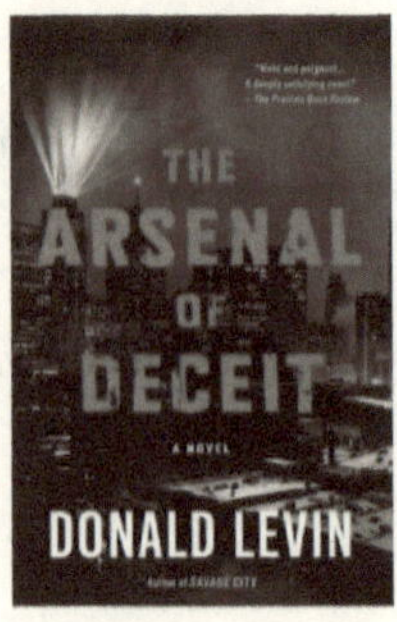

Detroit, 1941. With the nation on the brink of war, four people unite against the subversive forces that threaten Detroit, America's "arsenal of democracy." *The Arsenal of Deceit* recreates a rich historical period with chilling parallels to our own time.

The Martin Preuss Mystery Series

One cold November night, police detective Martin Preuss joins a frantic search for a seven-year-old girl with epilepsy who has disappeared from the streets of his suburban Detroit community. Probing deep into the anguished lives of all those who came into contact with the missing girl, Preuss must summon all his skills and resources to solve the many crimes of love he uncovers.

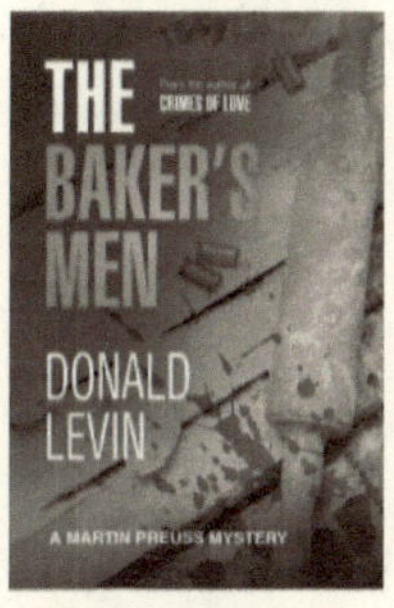

Easter, 2009. Ferndale Police detective Martin Preuss is spending a quiet evening with his son Toby when he's called out to investigate an after-hours shooting at a bakery in his suburban Detroit community. Struggling with the dizzying uncertainties of the case and hindered by the treachery of his own colleagues who scheme against him, Preuss is drawn into a whirlwind of greed, violence, and revenge spanning generations.

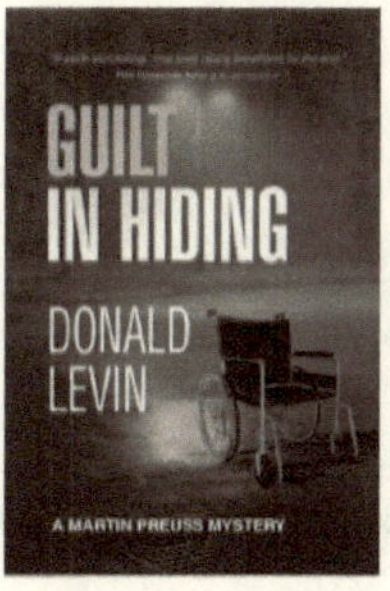

Preuss is called out to search for a van that has disappeared along with the woman who was driving and her passenger, a handicapped young man. Working through layer upon layer of secrets, Preuss exposes a multitude of contemporary crimes with roots in the twentieth century's darkest period.

When a friend asks newly retired detective Martin Preuss to look for a boy who disappeared forty years ago, the former investigator gradually becomes consumed with finding the forgotten child. Preuss revisits the countercultural fervor of Detroit in the 1970s—and plunges into hidden worlds of guilty secrets and dark crimes that won't stay buried.

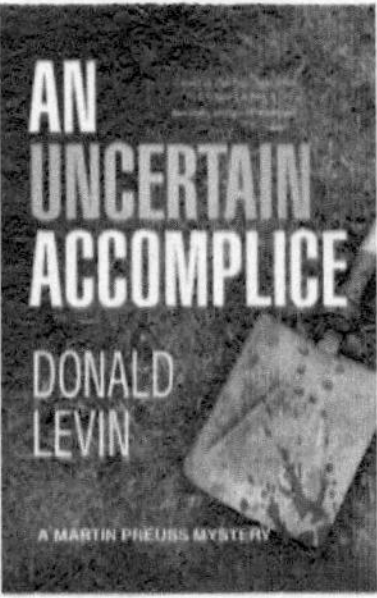

Twenty years have passed since Raymond Douglas went to prison for the kidnapping and murder of a local businessman's wife. Now Douglas's daughter has hired private investigator Martin Preuss to track down a previously-unknown accomplice to the crime—who may or may not even exist.

A young man takes a walk on the wild side and ends up clinging to life in a suburban Detroit motel. When private investigator Martin Preuss searches for the reason, he plunges into the young man's dark world of secrets and lies.

When the police investigation into the murder of a retired professor stalls, friends of the dead man plead with PI Martin Preuss to learn what happened. The twisting tale leads him across Detroit into a treacherous world of long-buried family secrets . . . where the painful relations between parents and children meet the deadly gathering storm of domestic terrorism.